HEAVEN'S RIVER

HEAVEN'S RIVER

Book 4 of the Bobiverse

DENNIS E. TAYLOR

Heaven's River

Cover design by Jeff Brown Graphics (www.jeffbrowngraphics.com)

ISBN: 978-1-68068-226-7

This book is published on behalf of the author by the Ethan Ellenberg Literary Agency.

This book was initially an Audible Original production.
Performed by Ray Porter
Editorial Producer: Steve Feldberg
Sound recording copyright 2020 by Audible Originals, LLC

You can reach the author at:
Author Blog: http://www.dennisetaylor.org
Twitter: @Dennis_E_Taylor
Facebook: @DennisETaylor2
Instagram: dennis_e_taylor

Heaven's River

Civil war looms in the Bobiverse!

More than a hundred years ago, Bender set out for the stars and was never heard from again. There has been no trace of him despite numerous searches by his clonemates. Now Bob is determined to organize an expedition to learn Bender's fate—whatever the cost.

But nothing is ever simple in the Bobiverse. Bob's descendants are out to the 24th generation now, and replicative drift has produced individuals who can barely be considered Bobs anymore. Some of them oppose Bob's plan; others have plans of their own. The out-of-control moots are the least of the Bobiverse's problems.

Undaunted, Bob and his allies follow Bender's trail. But what they discover out in deep space is so unexpected and so complex that it could either save the universe—or pose an existential threat the likes of which the Bobiverse has never faced.

DEDICATION

*First, and always, I want to dedicate this book to my wife,
Blaihin, and my daughter, Tina.*

Acknowledgements

A novel isn't written in a vacuum (just as well, or I'd be dead). It requires support and understanding from family and friends, for those times you've disappeared into the basement, or are staring distractedly into space, or are responding with one-word grunts. It requires those same people to listen when you want to bounce ideas off them.

It also requires critiquers, alpha readers, and beta readers when the chaotic mess begins to coalesce into an actual story.

The people who've had a hand in getting this story out include my agent, Ethan Ellenberg, the good folks in the Ubergroup at Scribophile, and my alpha and beta readers, including:

Blaihin Taylor
Patrick Jordan
Nicole Hamilton
Trudy Cochrane
and
Sheena Lewis

And a special thanks to Isaac Arthur of SFIA for the beta read and sanity check.

The real voyage of discovery consists not in seeking new lands but seeing with new eyes.

~ Marcel Proust

TABLE OF CONTENTS

Part 1: The Search for Bender

1. Frenemies

Jacques
November 2331
New Pav

The planet hung below, all blues and greens and twinkling lights of nascent cities. New Pav, we called it. The Pav's name for their new home planet was slightly more poetic, but would still sound like a bunch of spitting and hissing to a human ear.

The population had boomed in the seventy years or so since they'd been resettled here, and they now boasted cities on several continents. It looked like the species would survive.

Whether they'd still be talking to us or not was another matter.

I received a signal from the cargo drone containing my manny, informing me that it had landed. With a mental sigh, I prepared to leave VR for what would probably be an uncomfortable meeting with the Pav representative.

I connected to the manny—a remotely operated android—over the SCUT channel and transferred my personal POV into it. As internal systems powered up, I took a mil to glance around the now-familiar cargo hold, then extracted myself from the support rack. The cargo doors opened automatically to reveal my usual Pav military escort, rifles at the ready, probably with safeties off. A gaggle of six-foot-tall meerkats, without the cute. I hadn't visited in a couple of decades, mostly because the last time had been what you might call *tense*.

Just to see how they'd react, I smiled, careful not to show my teeth, and gave them the Vulcan salute. The squad leader showed me his teeth—not a gesture of friendship from a Pav—and returned the salute with three fewer fingers.

Apparently, he had studied human culture.

I walked up to the group and gave them a proper Pav smile-equivalent. "Hey, guys, what's shaking?"

I needn't have bothered. The squad leader responded with a low snarl and motioned with his weapon toward the nearby tent. They'd set up a tent. It would seem I didn't even rate an indoor meeting. Maybe it was actually a good sign ... nope, couldn't make that work.

I entered the enclosure and eyed the Pav sitting at the desk. He was the second planetary administrator since Hazjiar, and he didn't look any friendlier than his immediate predecessor. I missed Hazjiar. She at least had understood the realities of the situation the Pav found themselves in. Somehow, since her passing, the part about the Others having rendered the original Pav home world unlivable had been, um, de-emphasized. The prevailing attitude now seemed to be that we'd done it and lied about it. For no reason that anyone could come up with.

"My name is Da Azzma Hizz," he said, gesturing to a chair. "I represent all Pav. Do you represent the humans?"

"I am Jacques Johansson. I represent the humans, for purposes of this transaction." It was a Pav formality, of sorts. Everyone identified themselves and their purpose. And it lowered the tension a bit, as we settled into the routine.

Azzma pushed some papers forward. "We have available the agreed-to tonnages of elements according to the schedule. This represents payment in full for the two human-owned autofactories in our system. Do you concur?"

I glanced over the papers. Everything seemed to be in order. We'd offered to just give the autofactories to the Pav, but they'd refused. I couldn't be sure if it was an aversion to what could be seen as charity, or if they didn't want to be in our debt, even morally. I suspected the latter. "I concur. The *Bellerophon* will be here within the year. They will collect the ingots and deliver the autofactories to you from orbit."

We stared at each other across the desk. There would be no pleasantries exchanged today. Then Azzma finally spoke. "I will admit this agreement is inconsistent with the prevailing conspiracy theory about the Bobs. It would have made more sense for you to keep us planet-bound and ignorant."

"Hopefully this will help to ease the tension between our peoples," I replied.

"A little, I think." Azzma gave me a tight-lipped smile-equivalent. "I have read the diaries of Hazjiar, *Jock*. She did not feel that you were the enemy. But it is a minority viewpoint these days."

I sighed and examined my hands for a moment. "Azzma, you'll be able to build interstellar vessels with the autofactories. We've given you the construction programs as part of the deal. It's just"—I looked up at him—"you'll be going out into a galactic neighborhood that's full of humans, and getting more so. Too much uncontrolled antagonism could be counterproductive, you know?"

He stared back at me for a moment. "I understand, *Jock*. We are outnumbered and outgunned, if it comes to that. We are not, uh..." Azzma gazed upward for a moment, then smiled. "... Klingons, is that the right human term? We understand discretion."

I smiled back, just as one of my honor guard muttered, "And patience."

Azzma gave them a hard glare past my shoulder.

"We have made great strides in restoring the Pav home world," I said, trying to bring things back to an even keel. "About a third of the planet is actively growing things once again. Are you sure you don't want—?"

Azzma shook his head. "In our own time, *Jock*, we will visit our ancestral home. I don't doubt the skills of the Bobs, but *this* is the home world of every living Pav. Old Pav is a monument to what no longer is."

"I understand." I nodded and stood up. "It will be kept aside for you, for whenever you decide." I turned to my escort. "Well, boys, shall we?"

The squad leader showed me his teeth—again—and stepped aside to make room for my departure. I turned back to Azzma for a moment and we exchanged Pav head bobs. I found myself missing Hazjiar and her version of the Vulcan salute.

Ephemerals. It was so hard not to think it.

There was a clunk as my cargo drone docked with the comms station. In keeping with the increased use of mannies for local physical presence, stations were now being constructed with a living area of sorts, and docking facilities. I stepped out of the drone's hold and walked over to the manny pod. For humanoid androids, the pods had pretty much replaced the older and bulkier storage racks. As the pod cover closed over me, umbilicals and feeder tubes attached to the manny. I powered down and transferred my POV to my personal VR.

My latest VR environment, a ski chalet, was already boring me. It seemed I couldn't stay interested for long in any one theme, and I couldn't get up the energy to work on something grand. I sighed and reset the VR to the default library theme.

On a whim, I sent a text to Ferb. He replied immediately, and I popped over to the Pav Reclamation Project administration center. The center was hosted by Bill's moot VR system, and had been the nexus for our efforts to rebuild the Pav home world for almost a hundred years now.

I examined the empty room, a sense of nostalgia filling me. We'd spent so many years working on the problem of rebooting the Pav ecology from nothing more than some plant and animal samples, taken in a huge rush as the Others' armada bore down on the planet. It was ironic: now that we were finally making some significant progress, the Pav simply didn't seem to care.

Ferb popped in as I stood, ruminating. "Hey, bud," he said. "Long time."

"Yeah. I, uh…" I waved a hand at the room. "Ghosts. It feels like we just abandoned the Pav."

"Aw, don't get melodramatic, Jacques. It's all pretty much automated these days. Takes maybe a couple of hours a month to make sure everything's on track."

"Uh-huh. And that's why, right? Where's Phineas these days, Ferb?"

He glared at me. "Why'd you have to bring that up?"

"Because it's the real reason why this place is deserted. Heard from Phineas?"

"Nothing live." Ferb looked down. "He isn't bothering to build interstellar relays, and he's way the hell out of SCUT range now. I get a heavily Dopplered radio transmission every month or so, though."

"Heading for the Large Magellanic Cloud. He'll be a while."

"What's your point, Jacques?"

"You, me, Phineas, Claude, we're all haunted by what happened. Ghosts. Billions of Pav—"

"We did everything we could!"

I sighed. "I know, I know. But there's still an emotional toll. Especially since the Pav haven't exactly embraced us for our efforts. We've all, every one of us who were involved, gone on to other things as far removed from this as possible. Phineas, well…" I snorted. "He's taken *far* a bit too far, maybe."

Ferb nodded, the slightest trace of a smile showing for only an instant.

I cocked my head as I took a good look at him. "What're you doing with yourself these days?"

"LARPing. Well, designing campaigns more than participating." Now Ferb finally did smile. "The Gamers—you know, Gandalf and his group—do live-action D&D campaigns in virt. But they kind of have a problem where they all want to play and no one wants to DM, so they're happy enough for the help. And I, uh…"

"What?"

"I have to admit I get a little uncomfortable around them, sometimes. Not that they're dangerous; it's just they're like strangers, but strangers who all look like me, you know? Some of them are out-and-out jerks."

"Yeah. Replicative drift. It's a thing, as Bill says. So why do you work with them?"

He shrugged. "Something to do. Keeps me busy."

"You can't find anything better to do with your time?"

"Thanks for that, *mom*." Ferb hesitated. "Actually, I'm kind of working on something. Not quite ready, yet. Don't noise it around, okay?"

He had my interest now. "Okay."

"I'm building a huge cargo vessel for myself, and I'm filling it with SCUT relays, stripped down to the essentials to keep their size down. When I'm ready, I'm going to launch straight up toward galactic north. I'll drop off relays as I go. I want to get at least a thousand light-years above the galactic plane. Then I'll be able to see what's on the other side of the galaxy."

"You know you could just put an AMI in the vessel, give it some marching orders, and stay home."

"Maybe. Not the same, though. Or maybe you're right about Phineas. And all of us. Maybe we *are* trying to run away." Ferb gave me a look that I would have to describe as *pleading*, as if he was asking for forgiveness or something. "Gotta go, Jacques. We'll talk again, sometime."

For some reason, I doubted that would happen. And just like that, I was alone again in the PRP center. Alone with my ghosts.

2. WORKING THE OPTIONS

Bob
January 2296
Above Eden

S pace is big.

I know that sounds like a *duh* statement, and Douglas Adams already made it anyway, but when you're looking for a single spaceship over literally interstellar distances, space gets right in your face with its bigness.

Bender had been missing now for more than a hundred years. Despite Bill transmitting the SCUT plans for FTL communication to every system that Bender could possibly have reached, despite searches along his probable path by Victor and later by his clone-mates Marvin and Luke, we hadn't found hide nor hair of Bender. Or bolt or deck plate, what with him actually being a sentient spaceship and all.

I should explain that, I guess. Bender is a computer who thinks he's one Robert Johansson, an engineer slash nerd who died in the early 21st century. As are all the Bobs, including me. I was the first replicant, launched from Earth in 2133. Every single Bob is my descendent, because that's what Von Neumann probes do. We make copies. We're up to thousands of Bobs now, spread over an almost one-hundred-light-year radius centered around the Sol System.

Bender was from my second batch of clones, constructed in Delta Eridani. He took off in the direction of Gamma Leporis A, and he's never been heard from again. Lots of Bobs have died over the years in battles, and some without the benefit of a backup. But Bender just disappeared without a trace and without a reason.

I knew Bender's original destination, but then so did Victor, Marvin, and Luke, and they hadn't found diddly. Specifically, they couldn't find any sign that he'd ever reached Gamma Leporis A. No autofactory setup, no mining activity, no communications relay station, and no Bussard trail in or out of the system.

I had just returned to Delta Eridani after my big pilgrimage back to Earth. It had been an emotionally loaded trip for me—the Earth would probably be drastically altered once it came out of this ice age, so in a way it was my last visit to my home in any recognizable form. It was ironic that humanity had solved the global warming problem by implementing a nuclear winter. And killed off 99.9% of themselves in the process, but who's keeping score anymore? Stupid humans.

The Delta Eridani system was pretty much as I'd left it. Autofactory support systems continued to collect raw materials from the asteroids, ferrying them back to be formed into ingots against any future need. In the absence of any specific orders, the autofactories slowly produced more autofactories and spare parts for all my various mechanical servants.

Satisfied with the status quo, I invoked my virtual reality system and settled into my La-Z-Boy recliner, surrounded by my library. Shelves full of books, floor to ceiling, never failed to relax me. Spike immediately jumped up and settled herself on my lap, purring contentedly, and Jeeves brought a fresh coffee.

The VR environment was an essential part of my existence. Without it, I was just a disembodied mind. In VR, I had a body, and pets, and a home. And before the addition of the personal VR, four out of five replicants went insane. I'm pretty sure there's a connection.

"Sorry, bud, but I need to concentrate right now," I said to the cat. I turned to Guppy, who was standing at parade rest as usual. "Suspend Spike's program and bring up a representation of the stellar neighborhood, centered on us, radius forty light-years."

Huge fishy eyes blinked.

[Acknowledged]

Spike disappeared in a scatter of pixellation. A moment later, a sphere appeared before me, filled with numerous points of light, all conveniently labelled. All the star systems within forty light-years of Delta Eridani, categorized by stellar type.

I drew a line with my finger from Delta Eridani to Gamma Leporis A, Bender's presumed flight path. He'd taken off in the right direction, back in 2165, but had never reached the destination. The options were foul play, misadventure, or deliberate decision.

The first two explanations might leave some kind of trace—debris, cross-trail of some theoretical attacking force, radioactivity, whatever. The third would at least show up as a redirected Bussard trail. But to detect any of those alternatives, I'd have to be crawling along at 5% of C. That would require 320 years to completely scan Bender's projected path. Of course, if I found something, I wouldn't do the whole route, but it would still be a whole lot of not very much for a long time.

We're immortal, being computers. But we also operate at millisecond resolutions, so several hundred years would be an eternity to me.

Now, back to the third option—deliberate decision. If Bender had noticed something and turned to investigate it, perhaps someone following his path would see the same thing. Luke and the others hadn't noticed anything, but they had probably been closely scrutinizing their own course rather than looking around. Bender, facing a long interstellar jump in pre-SCUT days, would have been looking for something to cut the tedium.

I tapped my chin for a few milliseconds, working through the options, then turned to Guppy again. "I think I need to attack this from all angles. Have the autofactories build a hundred or so of those long-range scouts we used in the battle of 82 Eridani. Make sure their SURGE drives are powerful enough for interstellar travel."

[Acknowledged]

Once the drones were ready, I would send them along Bender's projected path at 5% C, looking for anything unusual. Meanwhile, there was no reason for me to wait around. I treated myself to one last long look at the planet Eden, rotating below me, then left orbit, heading for Gamma Leporis A at 5 G.

⚜ ⚜ ⚜

Travel between stellar systems is uneventful—thank God. It's hard to think of something *eventful* out between the stars that wouldn't leave me as a cloud of free-floating atoms.

I considered limiting myself to 0.75 C so that I could continue to interact with the Bobiverse in general. SCUT allowed instantaneous communications over BobNet, but if my tau got too high (or too low—there was some argument about how we should be expressing tau), I wouldn't be able to interact in real time, even frame-jacked. But I was just too impatient to test my theory, and anyway the Bobiverse was starting to get weird and cliquish these days. Bobs were getting less Bob-like, and going off in directions that I think would have left Original Bob baffled. Well, if they hit the singularity or something while I was out of touch, hopefully Bill would leave a note with instructions.

I passed the time by reviewing my archived surveillance vids of the Deltans. A primitive race of humanoids, the Deltans resembled a sort of bipedal pig/bat mashup. I'd more or less adopted them and become the great sky god for a generation or two, before joining the tribe in android form. It had been 63 years since I'd walked out of Camelot for the last time, after Archimedes's funeral. I desperately missed my friends and the feeling of family that I got from living among them. Bill had scolded me on more than one occasion about the dangers of transferring my affections to a bunch of alien primitives. Well, tough.

⚜ ⚜ ⚜

As it turned out, things got interesting before I even got up enough tau to drop out of touch. About two months subjective time into the voyage, something triggered one of the monitoring scripts that I'd set up.

We were playing baseball in the Bobmoot VR when a Guppy popped in unannounced. Every Bob on the field stopped dead. Having someone's Guppy show up in the moot couldn't be anything but interesting. Metadata indicated that he was mine, so I put down the bat and gave him a raised eyebrow. As usual, he completely ignored it. Facial expressions didn't mean much to the GUPPI interface. Or sarcasm, metaphor, irony, body language, or social conventions, for that matter. Guppy stared back, waiting for me to say something.

"Well?"

Apparently, that was enough.

[Astronomical monitoring has picked up an anomaly. You asked to be advised immediately.]

Anomaly, to Guppy, could mean anything, though. Mario's Guppy had once reported an entire dead planetary ecosystem as an "anomaly."

Luke and Marvin rushed over and hovered. They knew I was following Bender's trail, and this might be news.

I glanced at them, then said to Guppy, "Elaborate."

[System Eta Leporis displays unusual infrared signature, together with periodic dimming of the star's light.]

Luke and Marvin exchanged a glance, then Luke said, "Like a Dyson Swarm signature? You think there's some sort of megastructure? Bender would have investigated that."

By now most of the field was gathering around us. Baseball was doubtless done for the day, an opinion that Bill shared. "All right, guys. I think we're done. I'll waive the five-inning minimum for this week. To the pub!"

The players gave a ragged cheer, then began to pop out of the baseball VR.

I dismissed Guppy, then transferred to the pub VR with Luke and Marvin and signaled the resident Jeeves for my usual.

We grabbed a table, and Luke glared at me. "Okay, talk."

"Hmm, well, you guys know I've been scanning for anything unusual around me as I follow Bender's original flight path. My theory is that he saw something and changed course, and we've just been unable to pick up the faint bend in the Bussard trail."

"Yeah, yeah. Get to the punch line."

I gave Luke a smile that said *I'm going to draw this out as much as I can* and continued. "Granted, I had no idea what Bender might have been watching for, and what he might have seen, so I've been basically looking for everything I could possibly imagine. I've had to double Guppy's memory so he could keep up."

"And you found a megastructure signature?"

"I appear to have found something that could be interpreted that way. The question is, do I commit to a course change to investigate? If it turns out to be a false alarm, I'll basically have to almost start over from Delta Eridani. Forget the time required to circle around—eventually, between all our follow-up trips, we'll have trashed up the interstellar medium so much we'll never learn anything."

"I think you have to, Bob," Marvin said. "If it comes down to it, I can order the Delta Eridani AMI to build a new Heaven vessel and matrix, then I'll clone myself into it. That'll be faster than you circling around or one of us heading over."

"Fair enough. Give me a second." I popped back into my personal VR. Guppy was, as usual, standing at parade rest. For the millionth time, I wondered if I should retire the Admiral Ackbar image. And for the millionth time, my juvenile sense of humor balked.

"Turn us to head for the anomaly, Guppy. Let me know estimated travel time when you're done. Low priority, don't pop into the moot for that."

[Acknowledged.]

I popped back to Marvin and Luke, to find Luke tasting my beer. "Hey, boundaries, guys!"

"What, I'm going to give you germs?" Luke grinned at me. "That's a pretty good red. I was a little surprised, since I remember us as a mostly dark-beer drinker."

"Blame Howard. Vulcan has a thriving beer industry, and Howard keeps transferring the templates into VR. He introduced me to this last time I visited."

Marvin nodded slowly. "He's setting up interstellar trade routes."

I frowned. "With transit times of years? You can't—"

"Turns out you can, O great all-father. Stasis pods are highly effective for preserving beer."

I glared at Marvin, both for the correction and the glib dig. "I thought he got rid of his interest in Enniscorthy Distillery."

"He did. Gave it all to Original Bridget and Stéphane. And her kids inherited it when she died. But Enniscorthy specialized in hard spirits. Remember the Great Romulan Presidential Scandal?"

The thought made us all laugh. Cranston had deserved every bit of what was done to him, and had never been able to come up with any evidence that Howard engineered the whole thing.

"Howard and Bridget bought up a few microbreweries on Vulcan," Marvin continued, "and it would seem they have some kind of natural talent for the creation and marketing of the devil's brew. Or maybe just good business sense. They're now one of the three biggest breweries in the Omicron2 Eridani system."

"Hmmph." I tapped my chin with a finger as I thought it through—a nervous tic that I seemed to have developed all on my own. Original Bob had never done that, nor did any of my clones. "Well, you can't *print* liquids, and there's no point in emailing the recipe without having the actual ingredients available, so I guess physical exports are the only way." I raised my glass in salute. "Here's to Howard, the family entrepreneur."

I glanced around the pub as I slowly sipped my beer. There seemed to be a lot more variation in dress and style these days, and the clumps of Bobs had a tendency to match, as if we were self-filtering by fashion sense. I could swear that some of them were just short of cosplay. Oh, there were no Klingons or Chewbaccae strutting around, but some of the clothing was reminiscent of *TNG* uniforms or Jedi robes. There was even a Bob in a suit and tie. Why in God's name would anyone *voluntarily* wear a suit and tie?

I frowned and tilted my head in the direction of the suit, glancing at Marvin. He replied with a baffled smile and a shrug. "Don't ask me, Bob. Replicative drift seems to be accelerating. I think we're approaching fifteen to twenty generations, and it's no longer just a matter of enhanced or suppressed attributes of Original Bob. The differences are accumulating, and some clones are going in completely new directions."

"Uh-huh. And the almost-cosplay outfits?"

Marvin's bemused expression didn't change. "Some of those are probably just for fun. Or making an ironic commentary. But the rest, well, I'm not sure if the clothes are influencing the attitudes or the other way around. The *TNG* guys are talking about forming an actual organization in the vein of Starfleet to monitor—that's the word they're using—the Bobiverse's effect on biologicals."

"Oh good grief. And how are they going to do that? Pass laws? Create a police force?"

"I think it's just discussion, Bob. No one is actually pushing for organizational changes. At least not yet."

"Is this anything to do with Thor and his lobby group, after the war with the Others?"

"Not really, no. Thor and his group were stating their preferences, not trying to impose anything on the rest of us. This"—Marvin made a small gesture toward the *TNG* guys—"has a more *intrusive* feel about it, if you get my drift."

I shook my head, refusing to give the matter any more psychic energy. I raised a hand and Jeeves appeared with another beer.

⚜ ⚜ ⚜

I popped into my personal VR, sporting a pleasant beer buzz and a not-so-pleasant feeling of foreboding. I dismissed the beer buzz, but couldn't do the same for the foreboding. Bill was right that I didn't go to moots often enough, but today's revelations hadn't been the kind of thing that would encourage me to do so.

I had recently added an outside patio to my library, complete with deck furniture. The weather was perpetually late summer/early fall, with warm sun and a cool breeze. Loons called across the lake, competing with geese and other waterfowl. Sighing with contentment, I settled into a lounge chair, then invoked Guppy. "Fire up Spike and Jeeves, please. Then update me on the course change."

Jeeves appeared at my elbow with a pot of coffee and some small sandwiches with no crusts. Spike appeared on my lap, right where she'd been when I suspended her program. I scratched the cat's ear and she began purring.

Finally, sandwich in one hand and coffee in the other, I was ready for business. "Status?"

[En route to Eta Leporis. Travel time approximately 35 years, including time required to change direction.]

"Wow, that's a hike. Will we be in SCUT range when we get there?"

[Negative. It will be necessary to construct and deploy an intersystem relay station.]

Crap. More wasted time. Well, it couldn't be helped. I wasn't about to do a side-hop to some nothing system just to build a communication station so I could still access BobNet. Of course, if Eta Leporis had no suitable raw materials when I got there, I was going to look pretty foolish.

"All right, Guppy. Send orders to the trailing drones to adopt a minimum-time flight plan to get to where we changed course. I want the whole area mapped in detail, looking for Bussard-trail spoor."

[Acknowledged. They will require approximately 24 months.]

"Noted. Let me know when they arrive and start mapping, and give me the completed report as soon as it's received."

Guppy blinked huge fish eyes and disappeared. I settled back into my La-Z-Boy and put my hands behind my head.

First problem: communications. I could—*maybe*—build a communications relay station when I reached Eta Leporis and send it back along my route to the halfway point. That was suboptimal, though. Beside the uncertainty of materials availability at my destination, I'd be out of touch for years. *More* years, I mean.

Instead, I could direct the Delta Eridani autofactory to build a full-sized relay station with a SURGE drive and send it out. That would be faster, since I could get it started immediately, but this option would still leave at least *some* gap during which I'd be incommunicado.

To handle that gap, I could take one of the drones in my hold, modify it to act as a SCUT relay station, and drop it off en route with orders to decelerate to zero velocity. It wouldn't be ideal; no repair or upgrade capability, for starters. And not a lot of bandwidth, with the size limitation. Well, I wouldn't be running any moots from Eta Leporis anyway. I could live with that. And I could stock it with some spare roamers in case of breakdowns.

Anyway, it only had to operate for a couple of years, until the much larger and more powerful station from Delta Eridani was in position. And investment of equipment was minimal. I had enough spare drones and roamers in my hold for basic necessities.

Okay, one problem solved. I queued up the required tasks on my TODO. Next, the Bender problem...

Item: There was a good chance that Bender had veered off and headed for Eta Leporis. But if that turned out to be wrong, I'd receive the report from my trailing drones long before I got there. I'd let Marvin know, and be able to swing around to pick up the trail again. So for the sake of argument, consider that a given.

Item: Eta Leporis displayed characteristics suggesting a spacefaring intelligence lived there. One that had built or was building a megastructure. That thought brought back memories of the Others. I shuddered at the possibility of another protracted interstellar war.

Item: If you accepted that a spacefaring civilization had built some kind of megastructure and Bender had changed course to investigate it, then it was highly probable that something had happened to Bender in Eta Leporis. Otherwise, he'd have built a space station, which would be transmitting his logs back toward human space via radio by now. He'd also have long since received the SCUT plans and already be on BobNet thanks to instantaneous communications.

Conclusion: Caution is highly indicated.

I chuckled at the dry bureaucratese in that statement. Still, it was true. We normally approached a system at a tangent rather than diving straight for the star. But we retained enough velocity to turn in-system in minimal time. Maybe a parking orbit in the Oort would be a better first step this time. And heavy use of exploration scouts. Not cloaked, though—cloaking interfered with SUDDAR, our subspace version of radar.

I rubbed my eyes with thumb and forefinger—an action that had no real point in VR except that it felt good—and started an inventory of onboard assets. I would have to do some in-flight manufacturing. Wouldn't that be fun!

3. TROUBLE

Bob
September 2331
Outskirts, Eta Leporis

I came to a stop, relatively speaking, more than fifty AU out from Eta Leporis. The definitions of Kuiper and Oort regions were completely arbitrary, especially for a system other than Sol, but there were some practical differences. For instance, matter became increasingly scarce farther out. And metallic deposits became harder to find. The physics of stellar system formation seemed to produce some consistent patterns, one of which was that the heavier elements tended to be closer in, and all the ice and frozen gasses congregated farther out. In the Kuiper and Oort zones, it was almost all frozen clumps of condensed gasses ejected from the inner system when the sun ignited. But, like raindrops, they generally condensed around *something*.

My first task would be to send scouts out to look for useful materials. This part fell within my original design. A Von Neumann probe needed to find raw materials, refine them, and use them to manufacture more Von Neumann probes. Of course, I'd long since exceeded my original design specifications. But it was still relaxing, like doing a routine and mindless task.

This process would take a while, though, which was making me antsy. After years in interstellar space, it might seem odd to be fretting over a question of months. But I'd been frame-jacked way down for most of the trip, I was here now, and I wanted to get moving on my search. And, not to put too fine a point on it, I wanted to see if there was really a megastructure in the system. The Others' Dyson Sphere was the only other piece of mega-engineering we'd ever seen, and that had been only partly constructed. That the Others might be here seemed unlikely, but it would certainly be a worst-case scenario.

My current orbit was too far out to resolve anything in the inner system with the onboard telescope. That was frustrating, and my immediate urge was to send in some observation drones. But Bender had probably just gone charging in, and that presumably had not worked out well for him. So, like it or not, a slow, careful exploration of the system was in order.

I spent the time deploying my printers and setting up a proper orbital autofactory. Regardless of what I found in the system proper, I would still have to set up a local communication station. In my idle moments, I checked my message backlog. It was huge, after a few decades out of touch. But I was mostly interested in messages from my trailing drones. I filtered for those.

The drones launched from Delta Eridani after I'd left had indeed found that Bender's trail turned toward Eta Leporis—and only a fraction of a light-month before the point where I made that same turn. The fact made me feel more confident about my deductions, and about my plan of action. And slightly smug.

❧ ❧ ❧

It took four months to locate enough material to even make a start on my plans. Transport drones brought mined material back to the autofactory, which slowly churned out finished parts according to the schedule and plans that I'd given Guppy. Roamers assembled drones from the parts and slowly constructed the relay station.

A year after arriving, I finally had enough exploration drones to begin the actual search for Bender. In all that time, I hadn't contacted anyone, other than having a couple of email exchanges with Bill. First, because I didn't want people breathing down my neck, demanding constant updates. And second, because with the small temporary relay station, all I would be able to manage would be audio and video streams. BobTime? FaceBob? It didn't sound likely to catch on.

I ordered local drones to trace an expanding spiral, looking for Bender's trail into this system. The cross-section they had to examine wasn't all that big, not for devices with a four-light-hour detection radius.

And finally, success! Bender had reached here, and Bender had apparently entered the system. I plotted his approach vector and assigned some drones the task of following his flight path.

❧ ❧ ❧

The closer I got to possibly finding Bender, the more excited I got. But at the same time, I became more nervous. The whole history of our interactions with the Others kept coming back—unpleasant surprises, Bobs getting blown up...Hal got blown up by them, what, twice? Three times?

I didn't want stories to be told around VR campfires about the demise of Bob-1. But if it *did* happen, I wanted the other Bobs to know. So I found myself reluctant to commit to anything that might put me in danger until the day the interstellar relay station came online.

It had taken a little longer than expected for the Delta Eridani autofactory to construct and deploy the station, and the delay was maddening. But finally, the day arrived when the new station signaled readiness and came online. I mothballed the kludgy drone/relay station, checked my bandwidth, and performed a long-overdue backup to Bill's monster Epsilon Eridani archive, Ultima Thule.

I held off on updating my blog. I wanted to have something dramatic to post first.

I'd been doing some light astronomy while waiting for the autofactory to build things and for the drones to find things. I had already identified six planets, the second of which was in the habitable zone. I'd also identified a gap between the second and third planets, which was where the infrared signature was coming from. I couldn't resolve anything in that zone, and the signature was coming from all the way around the star, so my money was on some kind of swarm—possibly the beginnings of a Dyson Swarm, but concentrated in the ecliptic. If that was the case, and the swarm consisted of something in the order of O'Neill cylinders, it would make sense that I wouldn't be able to make out any detail yet.

The planet in the habitable zone, Planet 2, didn't appear to be inhabited. Or at least there wasn't any kind of radio signature. Nevertheless, I was getting something sporadic from the system in general. Like chirps—very short-lived and seemingly random noise, except for the narrow transmission spectrum. Which was exactly what I'd expect to see if someone was encrypting and compressing their communications. So *something* was alive.

It might be time to rejoin the Bobiverse. I could use some other perspectives on this.

⚜   ⚜   ⚜

The *blaaaat* of the airhorn was answered by the traditional booing, as the audience expressed their love. Bill grinned back from the podium. "Yeah, yeah. Okay, today's meet includes an update from Bob-1"—Bill was forced to wait for a wave of catcalls and cheers to die down—"on the subject of Bender, and the situation in Eta Leporis." This produced a silence far more profound than the earlier noise. Bender's disappearance had become the Bobiverse's version of the Flying Dutchman legend.

I waved my hand in the air and smiled as heads turned to look at me, but I was perplexed. The Bobs have always been irreverent and disrespectful, and I was no stranger to jeers and insults at moots. But this time it hadn't been just good fun. There had been a discernible undertone of rancor.

Keeping my expression neutral, I stepped up onto the podium and scanned the crowd. Undertone or not, everyone was paying attention. "I'm sure most of what I'm about to tell you is already circulating as scuttlebutt, so I'll keep it brief, then answer questions." I gave them the same capsule summary that I'd already shared with Bill, then asked for questions. Hands went up everywhere and I pointed at random.

"Are you just going to go barreling in without any thought of consequences?"

My eyebrows went up in surprise. The tone and the words were deliberately confrontational. I took a second look at the speaker to make sure he wasn't a non-Bob replicant, but no such luck. I found myself more irritated than I would be if some random person had challenged me. This felt like a betrayal.

"Have you ever known a Bob to go barreling in without any planning? Have you *met* us?" I glared at him, daring him to argue.

"If this does turn out to be a native civilization, you could be interfering in their development. Will you confirm that you'll back off to avoid doing that?"

"Wow," I replied. "Nice use of a prejudicial term. To answer the actual question rather than the accusation, that will depend on circumstances. Signing on to a blanket policy at this point would be ridiculous. At one end of the scale, this putative civilization might have deliberately shot Bender down; at the other end, they might only have noticed the flash as his reactor exploded. Those two scenarios require different responses."

"Or you could just leave them alone. Prime Directive, dude."

I squinted at the Bob, trying to pick up his metadata. Okay, *squint* isn't the right word in VR, but it feels the same. Strangely, he'd set his info to *private*, which struck me as intolerably rude. And that produced a moment of bemusement—why would I do something to me that I would consider rude?

I glanced at Bill, who just shrugged. I turned back to the speaker. "Even if we had laws, *dude*, which we don't, the Prime Directive wouldn't be one of them. That was a plot device, and unrealistic."

"Don't be too sure of that. Some of us are rethinking your attitude."

"It's Original Bob's attitude," I retorted. I found myself getting more and more irritated with this pissant, and made a concerted effort to calm down. "But you have the right to whatever opinion you want." I pointedly turned to another hand and motioned.

"How far will you take the search, if you don't find anything in this system? Will you ask for volunteers to help look further?"

"As far as necessary, and yes. He's one of us, for God's sake."

"So it's going to be another crusade mandated by the senior Bobs, and the rest of us are supposed to just go along?"

I turned my head and sure enough, it was Pissant. I decided it was time to take a stand. "Nice straw-man, jerk-off. What happened to you, got a quarter-dose of brains? And by the way, we'll continue this when you have the guts to show your name, but not until." Again I turned away.

The altercation appeared to have taken the air out of the room. There were no more questions. If this followed normal Bob-like behavior, though, people were just waiting for the formal moot to be over, so they could talk one-on-one. And that was fine with me. If Pissant came at me again, I'd blackhole him.

❧ ❧ ❧

The moot was over, and most of the Bobs had gone back to their own private VRs. I sat in the pub with Bill, surrounded by empty tables.

"So what the hell, Bill? Mind filling me in?" I glared at him for emphasis over my beer.

"You've been out of touch for a few decades, Bob. And I understand why you've been keeping to yourself. The whole Archimedes business would be several emotional kicks to the crotch for anyone. But you're missing things. The Bobiverse is evolving. We've got some Bobs here that are twentieth generation and more. Replicative drift is becoming significant enough that some of these Bobs really only *look* like you. And for that matter, there's a lot more playing around with appearance, and I don't just mean facial hair. A half-dozen or so Bobs have started walking around as full-time Borg." Bill appeared momentarily embarrassed, then invoked a Cone of Silence over us. That was jarring to me. Normally they were used to cut down on distracting background noise, but Bill's action was, in this case, intended to prevent eavesdropping. "Honestly, Bob, if you haven't changed your encryption keys and passwords since your last cloning, you should really do it, just on principle. I already have. I don't *actually* distrust anyone yet, but I'm beginning to recognize that one of these times we'll run into a descendant who thinks the ends justify the means, you know?"

I nodded and sent a text to Guppy to do just that, and immediately.

"So what about Howard and Bridget?" I asked, more or less changing the subject. "And Henry Roberts?"

"Neither Bridget nor Henry has cloned. In the former case, that has produced a lot of disappointment and some grumbling in the Bobiverse. Which is probably a good part of why she hasn't. She doesn't want to be seen as the default all-wife, I think."

I snorted. "Original Bob was pretty progressive, but I can still see a certain implicit expectation being a problem."

"Yup. Anyway, Henry doesn't show up here much. He's sailing Quilt right now."

I raised an eyebrow. "Wait, what happened with Poseidon? Did he finish early?"

Bill laughed. "He gave up after he got eaten the third time, ship and all. He says there wasn't much point anyway. If you're going to sail, you should be sailing *to* something. Poseidon, well..."

"Yeah. All ocean, no something."

"Bridget and Howard continue to catalog all life in the cosmos," Bill continued with a smile. "Despite, you know..."

"The infamous Prometheus expedition." I shook my head. "Well, they're never bored, anyway."

I hesitated, not sure how to continue. A couple of Bobs came over, detected the Cone of Silence, and veered off to find other conversational partners, or possibly just a beverage.

Finally, I decided that trying to beat around the bush with Bill was pointless. "So, getting back to replicative drift. What was with the nameless mouthpiece? Are we getting political parties now?"

"It's a little more than that, buddy. Bobs in general have always been a herd of cats, but it's getting both more and less pronounced. Bobs are forming groups, and some of those groups are tending to the bizarre. There's a group trying to build a Matryoshka Brain, for instance."

"Uh..." I drew my head back and frowned. "With the Casimir power source, we don't need—"

"The central star for power. Yeah. But heat management is heat management, and a gravity well is handy for keeping things organized. My understanding is that they're building it around a gray dwarf. Anyway, I'm more concerned about them creating something straight out of a Vernor Vinge novel."

"Or Lovecraft."

Bill chuckled and dismissed the Cone of Silence. "Anyway, Bob, you should read my blog to get caught up. I don't pull any punches, so you'll get a good overview of where the Bobiverse is going."

I nodded and raised my glass in salute. Bill turned to someone who had been waiting to get his attention, and I went looking for Luke and/or Marvin.

I couldn't suppress a snort as I scanned the gathering. Bobs as Borg now.

Cthulhu would not approve.

⚜ ⚜ ⚜

Bill was probably right. I'd done my usual turtling thing and effectively cut myself off from society in general. I needed to fix that, and I might as well start with a visit to Will. He had, according to his blog, finally retired from colony administration at 82 Eridani and gotten himself a place on Valhalla, where he was involved in the ongoing terraforming of the largest moon of Asgard. The air on Valhalla was still a little thin for humans, but a manny wouldn't care.

I pinged Will and in short order received an invitation and address for a guest manny. I took the address and popped over.

A few milliseconds of diagnostics, and I opened my eyes to find myself on an outdoor deck, looking up at a sky more of a mauve than blue. Hanging in the middle of the expanse was Asgard, looking perhaps three times the size of Earth from Luna. Will was sitting on an Adirondack chair, holding a coffee and grinning at me.

He wore the standard Bob Johansson manny, but no longer sported a neat Riker-like beard. His hair was uncombed and stuck out in random spikes, and the beard was more like what you'd get if you simply stopped shaving. The manny, so called because the early models had resembled department-store mannequins, was dressed in something that was closer to a lumberjack outfit than anything else. I knew without looking that my guest manny would be generic human and hairless, although not cadaver-white like Howard's first version.

I undraped myself from the support rack and sat across from Will, then attempted to materialize a coffee out of habit. He grinned at the expression on my face and motioned to a side table, where a coffee flask and some cups were set out. "Sorry, Bob. Out here in real, we prepare our coffee the old-fashioned way."

I smiled back at him. "In real?"

"Language marches on," Will said. "Nowadays it's *real* and *virt.*"

"Huh. Noted." It took only a few seconds to get my own coffee, then I raised the cup in salute. "You've changed your look a little."

"I've felt a need to distance myself from the old Riker persona, for a lot of reasons—one of which is that I had a hard time getting people to stop coming to me with colony-related problems. They couldn't accept the idea that I had retired. Once I adopted the mountain-man look, I think they got the message."

"So how is the retired life?"

"*Retired* just means I don't have a job description, and I can work on what I want now. I've been spending most of my time on the terraforming of Valhalla and some personal projects. It helps that I live here; I can see the results of changes right away."

"And how's that going?"

Will waved a hand in a self-deprecating gesture. "Bill did a lot of the pioneering work on Ragnarök, of course. Cleaning up the air, adding water, adjusting the biosphere—Valhalla actually *has* a native ecosystem. Bill made most of the mistakes. I just avoid those."

"Are you losing much in the way of native stock?"

"Surprisingly, no. It was a fairly hostile environment when we started, kind of like being up the side of a mountain in the high latitudes. What we're doing to the moon is making life easier. Warmer, more oxygen, more water, and so on. Our challenge is to introduce Earth stock slowly enough that the native stuff doesn't get outcompeted before it adapts."

I nodded, took a sip of coffee, and flinched. In the still-too-thin atmosphere, water boiled at a lower temperature, so coffee prep was negatively affected. The coffee was luke-warm and thin. But that was the price you paid for running a manny in, uh, real.

I looked at Will over the rim of my cup and changed the subject. "Listen, I already talked to Bill about this, but I wanted to get your perspective on things. About the moot the other day."

Will grimaced. "I wasn't there; we were having a problem with one of the fractionators. But yeah, I heard about your face-off with Morlock—"

"Morlock? He named himself *Morlock*?"

"Nah, he named himself Jeremy. Which might be coincidence or might be a subtle nod to that *Time Machine* remake. But he goes by Morlock these days."

Will raised an eyebrow at me, inviting comment. I gave him a small head-shake, and he continued: "Replicative drift is turning out to be a real thing. Bobs are recognizably one of us until about fifteenth generation or so, then the drift begins to accelerate. We haven't had any out-and-out psychos yet, but we've definitely got some assholes."

Well, so much for visions of a galaxy-wide race of Bobs. Still, diversity might be a good thing. After all, the human race consisted of billions of individuals and had still managed to...

Almost obliterate themselves. Crap.

This was a problem. A big problem. Original Bob's hands-off approach might not cut it in this case.

I opened my mouth to reply, just as a message from Guppy imposed itself on my field of view.

[In-system scouts have been attacked. 100% casualties.]

I barked "Gotta go!" at Will, and popped back into virt. I quickly texted him an apology for not reracking the manny and promised to explain later.

"What's going on?" I said to Guppy.

[Telemetry is queued up for inspection.]

I grabbed a few video windows and started playback. The drones were coasting along Bender's trail, SUDDAR ensuring that they didn't lose it, when the transmission from one of them abruptly disappeared. The second one cut off a millisecond later, before even the AMIs could react in any meaningful way. The third, though, took a glancing blow or near miss or something. It was disabled, but managed to reconfigure SUDDAR and get a low-res scan before that signal also disappeared.

The fourth window contained the results of that scan. Two craft had approached unnoticed from the scouts' five o'clock and unleashed some kind of attack. They were about twenty feet long, most likely automated, and clearly not intended for atmosphere. A skeletal structure composed of girders or beams formed the base shape, onto which were bolted various pieces of equipment with no concession to style. What had to be beam weapons were bolted onto opposite corners, and communication dishes took up the space at ninety degrees to the weapons.

I took a look through the logs and couldn't find any indication of approaching missiles. There was, however, a brief temperature spike just before the signals cut off, which confirmed the *beam weapon* hypothesis.

"Lasers. Interesting choice. Not generally a good combat weapon." I stared at the window for a moment longer, then closed it. "Guppy, why didn't the scouts detect their approach?"

[SUDDAR was concentrated forward in order to resolve the Bussard trail, which had been diffused by in-system gravitational effects.]

Okay, fair enough. In interstellar space, a trail would be virtually undisturbed for centuries. Not so much once you got inside the heliopause.

"We didn't get a SUDDAR pulse from them?"

[Negative. Telemetry from the last scout detected radar pulses.]

"Radar? They use *radar*? Who uses radar these days?"

[Apparently, they do.]

I glared at Guppy, and not for the first time made a note to do some black-box testing on him. Sarcasm required self-awareness, and not once had a buster or drone ever given me this kind of back-talk.

Still, the basic facts remained, and shone a light on something that I mostly managed to forget: I was not a military thinker. I'd gotten too comfortable after successfully dealing with Medeiros and the Others, and had behaved stereotypically. And gotten my butt handed to me. It was time to resurrect some of that good old-time paranoia and start thinking defensively.

"Well, that's just peachy. And they just attacked without warn—" I stopped as I had a thought. Guppy had a bad tendency to not volunteer information. Attempts to change his behavior had just resulted in huge dumps of irrelevant data. I still wasn't convinced that wasn't passive-aggressively intentional. "Guppy, did the attackers do anything besides ping us with radar?"

[Affirmative. There were several radio transmissions.]

Probably challenges, either to determine friend or foe, or even if the scouts were something other than flotsam. And I didn't know the proper response. So no real help there. In fact, if we'd responded, it would have alerted *whoever* that there was someone else in the system. Which might also be a bad thing. Just ask Hal.

So, caution was still indicated.

⚜ ⚜ ⚜

I invited Bill over to take a look at the video records. He tapped a spot on the video window. "That's interesting. You see that?"

"Mmm, yeah. Fusion torch. Great for acceleration and maneuverability. But hard on fuel."

"Over the short haul, they could probably outpace you, Bob. Best be careful."

"Hmmph." I sat back in my La-Z-Boy. "Not that I'm planning on going in and introducing myself. That's two encounters, two attacks, and one lost replicant."

"Some assumptions in there."

"Reasonable ones. Enough that I'd need some evidence to the contrary before I'd change my mind." I reached over and scrolled the window forward a fraction. "No SUDDAR, no SURGE, no SCUT. They, whoever they are, haven't discovered subspace theory. On the other hand, their fusion drive tech is impressive, and if I'm right about them having used lasers, so is their weapons tech. That's a lot of wattage out of a drone that small."

"Which means their fusion reactor tech is probably better than ours." Bill grinned and shrugged. "Not surprising. No one uses fusion reactors anymore."

True. We'd long since switched to the Casimir power source that we'd gotten from the Others. It was far superior to any kind of fusion reactor, for reasons including but not limited to a complete lack of detectable emissions. Naturally, work on fusion technology had subsequently stagnated, but no one cared.

"So…" I tapped my chin in thought. "These, uh, whoevers have perhaps continued development in more traditional directions, and may have surpassed us in some other technologies as well. While being totally deficient in others. Their drone designs reflect that."

"Fair summary. How about *Boojums* for their drones?"

"Sure, why not."

"So what's the plan?"

"Plan? We don't need no stinking plan." We both grinned. "Seriously, at this point I'm only up to *don't get caught*. It's a little nebulous after that."

"We have designs in the archives for evading radar detection, you know."

I stared at Bill for a moment. "Jeez. I must be getting old. Okay, so, some kind of radar-proofing, carbon-black exteriors to foil visual, low-power electronics combined with a super-cooled heat sink to counter infrared detection…" I sat forward as my enthusiasm mounted. "We can coast in, we don't need to use cloaking since they don't appear to have

SUDDAR. So we can use long-range SUDDAR to watch for patrols…yeah, this is good!"

"Now you're cookin'. Do you have enough trajectory data to plot Bender's probable location?"

"Within a huge margin of error, yes. I'll send some more scouts the long way around to look for where he might be by now. Or his remains." We were both silent for a moment as we processed this thought in parallel.

"Sounds like you've got some work to do, Bob," Bill said. "I'll leave you to it."

⚜ ⚜ ⚜

Some work to do meant some engineering design work to get the combination of attributes that I wanted, based on plans and notes on BobNet. Whatever else the wars with the Others and Medeiros may have done, they greatly accelerated battle-related technologies. But hasn't war always done that?

The engineering was no big deal. I am, after all, a computer—even if I don't acknowledge it most of the time. The actual construction work, well, that was going to take longer. I still had to do everything out in the Kuiper/Oort interface, and there was still no miraculous cache of handy elements to make my life easier.

The one new piece of tech I added was a core of ice at a couple of degrees Kelvin. The scouts were designed to be ultra-low-power, which meant very little heat generation, but I didn't even want *that* to show. Waste heat would be transferred to the ice core, which would gradually warm up. I had calculated the heat transfer rate, and I was pretty sure the scouts could make it through the system before their heat sinks gave out and they started to radiate significant infrared.

On the downside, to keep within the heat budget, they wouldn't be able to maintain continuous contact. That meant I could conceivably lose them and not know it until they failed to report in. Well, life isn't perfect.

I calculated trajectories and times and launched the scouts myself via rail gun. Ballistic all the way, baby. If they had to maneuver, that would be the end of the heat sink. If all went well, it would be months before they sailed out the other side.

By the time I'd done this, the other scouts had made it all the way around the system and were running a search pattern on Bender's expected location. I'd told Bill the margins of error were huge, which meant a large volume to search, but I was still disappointed by every day that went by without result.

For no other reason than to have something to do, I set myself a course to the other side of the Boojum system. The long way around, though. I still wasn't prepared to fly *through* the system, even a little bit. I had no idea how far out the Boojums patrolled.

I was about halfway around when Guppy made my day.

[Scouts have found something.]

"Cool! What do they have?"

[Something.]

That black-box test was going to be done with no anesthetic. And soon.

"Give me the report."

A window popped up in front of me, replete with all kinds of statistics and measurements. The most important item, though, was an image of a shredded section of a Version 2 Heaven vessel.

Bender.

4. Collection Run

I watched on the monitor as the drones chivvied the ingots into the hold. As each massive block of metal arrived, roamers wrapped it in cable netting and carefully winched it up against a wall, then tied it down. We'd have raw materials for just about any project we cared to take on—for a long time.

The deal Jacques had struck was certainly efficient. Because Neil and I had been running around from system to system for the last fifty years or so, we had not had much opportunity to stop anywhere and stock up. And in any case, the residents of those systems would not have been happy with us poaching their natural resources.

We'd contacted the Pav on the way in. The kindest description I could give for their attitude would be *curt*. I guess Jacques was right about them. The thought made me sad; overall, we hadn't been having a lot of luck with alien species. Between the Others, the Pav, and the Deltans, I was starting to wonder if it was outright impossible for mutually alien intelligences to get along. And if the local area was at all representative, there must be a *lot* of intelligences out there. Eventually, we'd run into another starfaring species with a technological advantage. That made war—and possibly the extermination of humanity—statistically inevitable.

I shared my thoughts with Neil, who was, as usual, draped over his chair sideways. "Jeez, Hersch, that's gloomy even for you. You need a new hobby. Or *a* hobby at all."

"Har de har. But what's wrong with my logic, Neil?"

He sighed and was silent for a few mils. "Nothing, I guess. So what do you want to do about it? We're still pond scum."

"Nah, we haven't been that for almost eighty years. We own and operate the biggest damned cargo ship in human space. We are *personally* responsible for setting up at least five colonies. I think we have some street cred."

"Yeah, I guess so," he replied. "And *please* don't take that as permission to do a Picard impersonation. I don't think I can take it anymore."

"You got it. So what can we do with all that cred?"

Neil pursed his lips and stared into space. "To be honest, my first thought when we got word about this windfall was to double our mover-plate count and accelerate to beat hell for somewhere interesting."

"Like Ick and Dae? And Phineas?"

"And at least a dozen others. A lot of Bobs are just taking off, Hersch."

"Seems kind of, I dunno, self-absorbed. I was thinking more like trying to place a human colony well outside of human space."

"In case you turn out to be right."

I gave him an apologetic shrug. "We still have all the stasis pods from the Great Exodus. There's simply never been any reason to off-load them anywhere. And that's the thing.

There's no more reason for the pods. Or for the *Bellerophon*, really. We're obsolete."

"So to make ourselves relevant again, we try for another colony. And if we used the ore to add another thirty-two plates, we'd be able to push some really stupid G's," Neil said, warming to the subject.

"So a human colony out in, say, the Perseus arm—"

"Would ensure continuity, even if the rest of humanity ran into a bigger, badder Others."

I nodded. "Now all we have to do is figure out how to locate some volunteers."

5. INVESTIGATION

Bob
November 2332
Outskirts, Eta Leporis

A cloud of wreckage slowly revolved around a common center of mass. Some of it was recognizable; most was not. I was a little surprised that there was much of anything—I wouldn't have expected a laser to leave much more than slag. Of course, I was assuming that whatever attacked Bender used the same techniques as the drones that attacked my scouts.

I would know more once I arrived. It didn't make sense to have the drones try to collect all the detritus and bring it to me. That would take too long and carried too much danger of losing or further damaging something. Instead, I'd fly in with my complement of roamers and do a close-up inspection. But first, I set the exploration drones to watch for any approaching Boojums, even though it seemed unlikely that they'd take a sudden interest after letting the wreckage drift unmolested for so long. The fact that the wreckage was drifting *away* from the system was probably relevant. But if I'd triggered any alerts with all the activity, they might change their mind.

I fully admit that I crossed the distance a lot more quickly than I should have. Caution, for the moment, was taking a back seat. Fortunately, I didn't run into Boojum pickets. Even more fortunately, I didn't run into an asteroid.

I set the roamers loose to examine the wreckage. It quickly became obvious that what I'd suspected was true— an internal explosion had ripped Bender's ship apart. Most likely the laser had taken out the nuclear reactor control system in such a way as to make the reactor fail catastrophically. I remembered my first encounter with Medeiros, in Epsilon Eridani, so many years ago. He'd suffered that very fate. In addition, the meltdown had taken out his matrix. I had to hope that Bender hadn't come to a similar end.

It was an entirely different ship design, of course. Medeiros was riding a military ship designed by the Brazilian Empire. They considered even their human soldiers expendable, never mind a replicated intelligence. Bender was riding a ship that I'd redesigned, with special attention to keeping the replicant matrix safe. This bit of simple self-interest gave me hope.

Outside inspections complete, the roamers entered the section of ship. I had multiple windows up, trying to watch everything at once. Finally, I gave up trying to maintain my VR. I dismissed my library and frame-jacked. Now I could keep up with everything, and putting up with naked floating data windows was a small price.

One of the roamers bleeped for attention. I turned to the window, and would have smiled if I currently had a body. The roamer had found the replicant matrix containment, in the most heavily armored section of the ship. And no obvious damage.

Then elation was replaced by horror as the roamers opened the containment... to find it empty.

No, not empty. Worse than empty. Not only was the replicant matrix missing, but all of the interface hardware had been carefully removed, probably as a unit. This was not good. Someone had made a point of removing Bender and his support hardware in a way that implied an intention to study and possibly revive him. I remembered Homer, and cringed at the specter of Bender, helpless and subject to torture.

One thing was for sure, though—the Boojums, or their makers, knew that someone else was around.

Having found Bender's empty ship, I had now flip-flopped from panicked rush back to paranoid caution. I wasn't going to hurry anything, I wasn't going to take any chances on attracting the Boojums or, well, running into an asteroid. The flight back to the autofactory area would take most of a week.

I had one quandary to deal with, meanwhile. Would I make an announcement now, or wait until I knew more? *Could* I even keep quiet for a week? For that matter, would Will be able to keep his trap shut? I hadn't actually asked him to, although I was sure he would wait rather than steal my thunder.

Screw it. I pulled up my console and began writing a blog entry. I had a large following anyway, being the first Bob replicant, and I could be pretty certain that Luke and Marvin would be watching every post.

It took a few full seconds of thought to get the tone right. Cautious optimism, mixed with a realistic appraisal of possible issues. Hope, but be prepared.

Finally, it was done. I hit *post*, then sat back and waited. 3...2...1...

Luke, Marvin, and Bill popped in at the same time, all talking at once and waving their arms. I turned in my office chair and waited until the noise died down.

"Why yes, I'm free right now. Come on over," I said.

"Bite me," Marvin replied. "Where is he?"

"Well, that's the sixty-four-thousand-dollar question, isn't it?" I materialized chairs for everyone, and Jeeves entered with coffee.

"Dammit," Marvin muttered. "Dammit, dammit…"

"What's the next step?" Luke asked. "Do you have a plan?"

"Nothing concrete, yet. I guess the first step is to find the Boojum base, or source or whatever. There's a good chance Bender will be there. Hell, we can just fly in and SUDDAR the hell out of it, if it comes to that. Locate Bender's matrix, then go from there."

"A raid?"

"If that looks like the best plan." I stuck my chin out. "If someone has kidnapped Bender and is experimenting on him, I'm not sure diplomacy will be my first choice."

"Easy there, Bob," Bill said. "Let's see what we find before we start building bombs, okay?"

"Yeah, I know. Don't worry, I'll be circumspect."

There followed one of those silences where no one quite knew what to say. Finally, Marvin nodded and he and Luke stood. They gave me a wave and popped out.

Which left Bill.

"So, number two, what's up?"

"Oh, ha ha. Listen, I wanted to ask you just how you plan to go in-system looking for the Boojums, and how public you're going to be about it."

"Public? What the eff? Are you saying there's any question?"

"Of course not, Bob, not from me or any of the others in our generation. But Starfleet is agitating—"

"Starfleet? What?"

Bill sighed. "You still haven't read my blog yet, have you?"

47

"Uh, no. Sorry, been busy."

"Remember Morlock? We're calling him and his group Starfleet now, because of their obsession with the Prime Directive. It's become gospel to them. They don't even want us to keep interacting with humans. They're trying to generate support for a formal declaration of some kind that you should leave whatever you find alone."

"Is a formal declaration anything like a law?"

Bill snorted. "We don't have laws. But if enough people got together, they could apply social pressure of some kind."

"What, like shunning?"

"Well, something like that, in principle. A loss of prestige, anyway."

"For God's sake, Bill, Original Bob never gave even a small fraction of a rat's ass about that."

"Yeah, I know, but more and more Bobs are becoming less and less Bob-like. I'm starting to call them replicants, in fact, instead of Bobs, just to make the distinction."

"And they're more concerned about prestige?"

"Given a random walk, you can't very well drop below zero rats' asses, but you can increase the value arbitrarily. So, yes. We're getting more replicants who are, for want of a better word, joiners. They're forming mutual-interest groups for all kinds of things."

"Like Starfleet, and the Borg."

"Mm-hmm. And the Skippies—"

"Skippies? *Skippies?*" I could feel my eyes bugging out, even in VR. "What, they've changed their avatars to beer cans and started calling people *monkeys?*"

Bill snorted his coffee and had to take a moment to compose himself. "No, it's the group trying to build the Matryoshka Brain. You know, singularity, super-AI, and so on? I don't know who started the nickname, but the Skippies haven't complained yet. They also, by the way, want us to leave the humans alone. But in their case it's because they think the humans are holding us back from our destiny or some such."

"Are there any other—no, never mind, I'll read your blog. Goddammit, I go away for a few decades and the whole place falls apart." I grinned at Bill. "I have some catching up to do, apparently."

"There's an understatement. Let me know if you need anything." Bill gave me a nod and popped out.

Interesting times, indeed.

6. The Search Expands

Bob
May 2333
Outskirts, Eta Leporis

I sat in my library, blearily gazing at the table in front of me. Will, Bill, and Garfield watched me silently, the occasional slow head shake the only commentary offered. Every once in a while, I took a half-hearted sip of my coffee. Bill finally couldn't take it any longer. "You *do* understand you're in virt, right? You can just dismiss the hangover, right?"

I responded with a pasty half-smile that was probably more terrifying than reassuring. "Yeah, and in the future I'll do just that. There's no metric in which this is enjoyable. But after finally reading your blog—well, Original Bob was by no means an alcoholic, but he did occasionally, when it was called for, go on a, uh..."

"Bender. Did you make that whole speech just to deliver that line?"

I chuckled, then groaned and held my head. "No, it was just a bonus. But goddammit, Bill. We *are* diverging. Nothing bad, yet, but I think you're right in expecting it. And we actually have a Bobbi now?"

"That's just a rumor. I don't know of anyone who's met her. But really, that's inevitable too."

I sighed and considered doing a reset and dismissing the hangover. It had served its purpose, whatever deep psychological need for self-flagellation was involved. But now my curiosity was up. "This feels pretty real. Verisimilitude in VR—uh, *virt*—has really been improving."

"Part of that's the mannies, of course," Will said from across the room, where he was nursing a soft drink. "Once we started experiencing things in real again, we realized how granular and synthetic the virt experience actually was."

"It helped that humanity was back on its feet by then. We had actual experts to ask about some of the finer points." Bill waved his cup in a vague out-there gesture. "Like Bridget, for instance. She's ferociously competent in the biological sciences, and, naturally, highly motivated now to help with the improvements. And with SUDDAR scans, we can accurately map how the human body and brain respond to various stimuli. Like taste and other senses."

"And hangovers." I grinned, then winced again. "She and Howard live almost full-time in real, right?"

"Yup. And raising kids as well. I've lost count of how many they've adopted over the years."

"Well, here's something to chew on," Garfield said. He'd been silent up to this point, so we all turned to him. "And it's important if you want to maintain perspective on your place in the cosmos." He paused for dramatic effect. "As replicants, we never get tired, we have near-perfect memories, we can process hundreds of times faster than humans, and we have instant access to all the information available in our archives. But we aren't any smarter than Original Bob was. And reading about something isn't the same as being trained in it. You can't become a doctor by reading *Gray's Anatomy*, for instance. Or watching it."

I frowned. "Okay, I get that in principle, but how is it important?"

"We can't do everything ourselves. For instance, without Bridget, the androids wouldn't be anywhere near as advanced as they are. We've improved our weapons by talking to military types—"

"Or stealing from them," I interjected.

Garfield glared at me for the interruption. "We've become a sort of society unto ourselves, but for the most part we're still doing the things Original Bob was interested in. We're a monoculture. Specialists. And that's not healthy."

"So you're saying..." Bill raised an eyebrow at him.

"That I'm not sure replicative drift is a bad thing, necessarily."

"Gar, I don't *trust* some of the new replicants," Bill said.

"Nor should you. They're different people. But the Bobiverse needs to be robust enough to handle a society where not everyone's priorities align. Sure, we need to be more worried about security and such. How is that different from locking your house or your car, though?"

"That does it," I said. "This conversation is incompatible with a hangover." I did a reset and felt better immediately. "Does this mean we'd accept other humans as well?"

Bill shrugged. "We've always been willing to do that. But we've gotten no takers. At least none who've decided to deal directly with us. Those that have chosen to go with replication have signed with companies that offer shared processing in a large computer facility. The bigger the monthly fee, the more processing power and extras you get. There are options like manny connection ability, and even premium manny models available only to the highest-paying clients. Most of them, though, are just spending their afterlives engaged in full-time virt."

"That doesn't make sense. This is freedom. The best kind of freedom, where you can do what you want, with no reliance on anyone else."

"Not really, Bob. That sounds good to a loner like Original Bob, but to a lot of people it would be the opposite of attractive. Among other things, self-reliance means having to be responsible for everything yourself. Much easier to just pay someone to take care of the details, if you have the money. And remember, this is immortality for a copy of you, at the expense of permanently destroying original you." Bill paused, then shrugged in dismissal. "On the other hand, there has been a *lot* of interest in postmortem corpsicle storage in real, and in fact, companies have been springing up all over the colonies, offering to warehouse people after death, just like with Original Bob. Except now they use stasis pods, so there's nothing irreversible about it. And they're doing a booming business."

"Because when you come back…"

"It'll be original you. Yeah. Much more attractive option."

Will sighed. "Except for people like Justin, who have a religious objection."

We commiserated in silence for a mil. As the "face of Bob," Will had been especially close with our relatives for decades. Julia's death, then her son Justin's, had hit him every bit as hard as Homer's.

Bill continued, "And it doesn't help that for years we were rushing all over the galaxy, saving humanity's butt, dying in space wars, and generally acting as dragon fodder. The idea of being a replicant never really recovered from the negative perception of ending up as a disposable servant."

Garfield pointed a finger at me by way of emphasis. "Don't forget, too, that the governments of the day were characterizing replicants as non-human copies. Automata. No rights, and so forth. A lot of that stuck."

I nodded. "And are they bringing any back? The corpsicles, I mean."

"Yes. A significant number have been revived when their condition became curable, thanks in large part to Howard and Bridget's cancer foundation. Most of the remaining corpsicles are up against the limits of gerontology. They still haven't conquered aging. At some point, replacing cloned organs becomes a game of Whac-A-Mole, and when the brain starts going, well, there's no longer any point."

"Then there are the other Bobiverse projects. The Skippies' Singularity Project makes a certain amount of sense, but some of the others…" I paused. "Silkies? Like van Vogt's Silkies? Jaegers? Space Dragons?"

Garfield laughed. "Remember when Marvin was trying to replicate the setting for every book he'd ever read in VR? Turns out he was thinking too small. The groups you're talking about are trying to replace our standard spaceship hulls with something more, er, *imaginative*."

"We've been making glib comments about being *homo siderea* now. I guess some Bobs have taken the concept and run with it." Bill grinned. "I've subscribed to their blogs. It's harmless stuff. The Singularity Project, maybe slightly less so. Starfleet, a *lot* less so, especially if they decide to do more than just talk."

This last comment cast a pall on what had been a very interesting conversation, and an uneasy silence reigned for several mils.

I finished my coffee with a final gulp. Time to get down to business. "Very interesting. But speaking of interesting, there's the small matter of a megastructure or something to look at. Shall we?"

"Hear, hear," Bill said, and I transferred us all to the control room. In virt, it was nothing but a change of visuals, but Original Bob had always been obsessive about detail, and we early generation replicants shared that attitude. The control room had wall screens and consoles, with a very science-fiction-spaceship-ish tone. The only proper venue for exploring a new stellar system.

"So what do we have?" Bill said, stepping up to the holotank.

"The ballistic scouts will have completed their sweep through the inner system, and we should have a complete picture," I said. "System planets first, Guppy." Bill, Will, and Garfield all glared at me in tandem. I was stalling; they knew it, I knew they knew it, and so on. But my VR, my rules.

The holotank showed six planets, consisting of three gas giants farther out and three rocky planets considerably farther in, with one in the habitable zone. The large gap between planets two and three was glaringly obvious. "That spacing doesn't look natural," Bill said.

I nodded. "Way too asymmetrical. Either planets have been moved to make room for the megastructure, or planets are missing."

"The Boojum makers will most likely have originated from the second planet," Will said. "What do we have?"

[No chlorophyll lines. Minimal oxygen lines. No radio traffic. No indication of organics at all.]

We turned to stare at Guppy. The last time we'd seen a planet with those characteristics, it had been Pav. Afterward.

"The Others? Isn't this outside their range?"

[Others attack is unlikely. SUDDAR readings indicate significant metal concentrations.]

Good. If the Others had hit this system, the metals would have been mined out.

"Let's finish looking at what we've got. Then, unless there's a good reason otherwise, I'll send some scouts in under power to get a close-up look." I turned to Guppy. "Smaller bodies?"

[None. This system has been swept clean.]

"What, not even moons?"

[No moons.]

"Wow," Bill said. "Someone has been busy."

"Let's set that question aside as well," Will said. "Right now, we have two options: one, we can look at the megastructure data, or two, we can beat the crap out of Bob."

"Can we do both?" Bill asked.

I grinned at them. "My money's on a Dyson Swarm."

"Pretty thin one," Bill said. "No solar shading at all."

"Beat. The. Crap," Will growled.

I laughed. "And now, the moment we've all been waiting for." I nodded to Guppy, and he updated the holo image.

We stared, for what might have been entire seconds. Finally, Will said, "What the actual fuck?"

Bill flickered for a moment as he frame-jacked, probably checking the archives. He was back before I could react. "Topopolis."

"It looks like spaghetti," Will said. "Or a wire sculpture."

I checked the schematic on the monitor. "That is one continuous cylinder, fifty-six miles in radius, stretching three times around the star, wound around itself in a sort of helical shape."

"Torus knot," Bill interjected.

"How is that even possible?" Will asked, ignoring Bill's correction.

Bill shrugged. "It was discussed back on Earth, in Original Bob's time. There's relatively little information on the concept. Apparently, it wasn't as popular as O'Neill cylinders, Stanford tori, and Bishop Rings. But it doesn't require particularly advanced technology. Just large-scale effort and brute-force engineering."

"What about gravity?"

"It's essentially an O'Neill cylinder millions of miles long. It spins around the minor radius to generate artificial gravity."

"But it's *curved!*"

Bill smiled at Will's outraged complaint. "Think about the scale, bud. If the strand has a mile of bend for every million miles of length, you wouldn't even have to put in expansion joints. That's less than a tenth of an inch flex over each mile of length. The structure would flex less than the Golden Gate Bridge when a single pedestrian walks across it."

"But where would they get the material—oh." Will nodded. "Missing planets."

"On the grand scale of things," Bill mused, "this is less impressive than what the Others were trying to do."

"Except the Boojum makers didn't invade other systems to get materials."

"We don't think," I said, glancing at Bill. "I haven't exactly done a survey."

"If they don't have subspace and SURGE drives, it seems unlikely," he replied. "But that's another question in abeyance until we have more information. So what's our next step?"

"Good question," I said. "This shoots down my earlier plan to just scan the Boojums' home base for Bender's matrix. We can't scan over a billion miles of complex structure looking for one individual cube of optoelectronics, while dodging Boojum attacks."

"Especially if the Boojum makers use optoelectronics for their own stuff. It'd be like looking for a specific needle in a haystack, where the haystack is all needles."

"Yep. Okay, we'll have to be a little more deliberate with our approach. First, we need to gather information." I ticked off items on my fingers. "We want a close-up look at the planet, we want a close-up look at the megastructure overall, and we want a scan of the interior detail."

"And we want to not get blown up."

"That too."

Bill snapped his fingers. "Speaking of military technology—"

"Which we weren't."

Bill glared at me. "I've been working on a variant of something I got from the USE—it's a fractal surface that absorbs ninety-nine percent of radiation that hits it, and re-radiates it as infrared."

"Great for radar, not so good for infrared."

"But we have your heat-sink idea. Get rid of the heat that way instead."

"Hmm." I nodded. "Under power, we'd have a limited time before the heat sink failed. We'd have to choreograph this very tightly."

"Yup. So dress up a cargo drone in this fractal surface, complete with heat sink. Fly to Planet Boojum, drop off some planetary exploration drones, accelerate for the outer system, and hope to make it out before the heat sink is saturated. Do the same with some hi-res drones and drop them off near the structure."

I glanced around the room. No argument was forthcoming. "One last thing. We need more information on topopolises, uh, topopoli? Topopoleis? Maybe there's a human expert on the subject of megastructures. Can someone look into that?"

"I can do that," said Will, and he popped out.

Bill stood. "I'll get the fractal surface details to you." He popped out.

"I'll work out the drone design," said Garfield, and he popped out as well.

"I'll have another coffee," I said to the empty room.

⚜   ⚜   ⚜

The autofactory drones had been locating and retrieving raw materials from the Kuiper belt and Oort cloud for a couple of years now, so logistics were no longer quite as much of a limiting factor. Bill and Garfield had their info to me within hours, and soon I had my autofactory churning out modified drones at full speed.

Still, there were some significant mods, and the fractal camouflage was a pain to get right.

But a week later, I had all my spy devices ready. I double-checked the calculations, sacrificed a coffee, and let fly.

"Now we wait," said Bill.

"Like we haven't been doing that for the last forever or so," Garfield grumbled.

7. Looking Forward

Will
June 2333
Virt

The search for information on topopoleis turned out to be one of those good news/bad news things. Good news: I'd found an expert. Bad news: he was dead. Good news: he'd arranged to be replicated. Bad news: he'd gone right back to work and was really hard to get hold of. The whole Keystone Kops act would be giving me a headache if I were still subject to such things, so I decided to take a break and do some work on a personal side project I had going.

I pinged Conan and popped over as soon as I received a response. Conan was the current Bob rep in the Omicron2 Eridani system. It hadn't been a heavy-labor position for a long time—Vulcan and Romulus having long ago become independent of our help—but we had always maintained a physical presence, for our family's sake if nothing else.

I looked around as I settled in. Conan appeared to have replicated the Vulcan jungle, with his home in a treehouse. I smiled to myself. I knew enough about Vulcan's wildlife to realize this was completely unworkable in real life. Even without the now-extinct Cupid Bugs, there was still more than enough variety—of the bad kind—in the wild to kill any human dumb enough to be out without an exo-suit.

Conan saluted me with a can of Coke. I sat in the nearest chair and, there being no Jeeves in view, invoked my own can.

"What can I do for you, O great ancestor?" Conan said.

"Are you one of mine?" I replied, and he nodded. Ancestry had never been a big deal in the Bobiverse, but with all the fragmenting lately, people were starting to pay more attention to chains of instantiation, with an eye to cataloguing behavioral DNA. As with a lot of Bob projects, it was ad hoc and casual.

"I'm concerned about the family, Conan. FAITH has been getting more influential on Romulus the last couple of decades, and that can't be anything but bad news."

"I get it, Will. But a lot of people like the sense of certainty that religion gives them, and FAITH is all about nice, easily packaged black-and-white answers. Even if they're factually wrong."

I waved a hand in dismissal. "I frankly don't care what the justification is. I want our family out from under. We've seen the rise of the Far Right too many times in the last half-millennium to not recognize the signs."

"Okay. And?"

"I have a small side project going on. I want to set up a society with an innocuous name like *Outward Bound* or something, for people who want to emigrate from this system. If you have the time, I'm hoping you'll take care of the setup and admin."

Conan grinned. "This hasn't exactly been a pressure-cooker job. Howard started divesting us of responsibility as soon as he could, and we've continued with that tradition. I'm more like a local ambassador than anything."

"How's that working out lately?"

"Yeaaaaaaaah... I'm curtailing my appearances these days." Conan made a deprecating gesture. "Bobs are not their favorite people, even on Vulcan, never mind Romulus. So as it happens, I have lots of free time. Any specifics?"

"Nothing complex. We just need a legally incorporated society, no special requirements, board of directors, et cetera. I'll email my family contacts once you have it set up, then we'll go from there."

Conan nodded. "So you're forming a prospective colonial group composed exclusively of Johansson descendants?"

"Not exclusively. Not even predominantly, if we get enough interest. But I want as many of ours out of here as we can manage."

"FAITH might step in. They don't have the clout right now, but by the time you're ready to shove off..."

"Yeah, I've been thinking about that, too. The constitutional guarantees, plus the original documents of agreement they signed with me back on Earth, will establish the legal requirement to let the colonists go. We need to be ready, though, if they decide to go for brinksmanship. Let's talk about in-system assets that are still Bob-controlled."

Conan smiled and popped up a graphic. Almost as if he'd been expecting this.

8. Survey Results

Bob
July 2333
Outskirts, Eta Leporis

Will, Bill, and Gar were in attendance, in anticipation of some useful returns from our scout drones.

Orbital mechanics being what they are, the drone destined for Planet Boojum arrived first. We were a little concerned about the possibility of deceleration attracting attention from the Boojums, but finally decided that A) there was no reason to expect them to be more interested in powered objects in particular since they'd cleared the system of *everything*, and B) we didn't have much choice.

In any case, the drone settled into a low orbit around Planet Boojum with no issues or incidents, and ejected all its scouts.

It was immediately obvious why there was no sign of life. This was a dead planet, and not by natural means. The panorama below us combined the worst of an Others attack with Earth's fate at the hands of humanity. There had very clearly been an exchange of nukes. Blackened, blasted circles where cities might once have been were still putting out enough radiation to forestall any possible misinterpretation. Impact craters indicated at least some orbital bombardment, although nothing as big as what the Brazilian Empire had used on Earth.

The planet hadn't spiraled into nuclear winter, but even so, there was no indication of living vegetation. Large swaths of what might once have been forests were burned to the ground, with not the slightest trace of new growth.

Finally, I reached forward and turned off the big monitor. I said to Guppy, "Let me know if anything anomalous shows up. Otherwise, record and archive everything, then recall the scouts and leave the drone in orbit for now."

[Acknowledged]

I pulled up the data stream from the other cargo drone, which was slowly pulling up to the megastructure. The scale of the thing was such that you could only see one "thread" at a time. The other two loops were so far away as to be invisible.

"So, what I want to do," I said, "is spread the SUDDAR scanning drones along the length of the megastructure so that we get a full scan of a long segment, with enough overlap so we don't lose any detail. I'm going to assume that whatever stretch we pick at random is going to be representative of the structure as a whole."

"Seems reasonable," Will replied.

We settled back to wait for the drones to reposition themselves. I still had some concern about the Boojums. They hadn't bothered us yet, and we had some pretty good countermeasures for non-SUDDAR detection methods, but I didn't know if they might have an A game or something for guarding the perimeter of the topopolis. Although, common sense would tell you to keep watch farther out and not let anything get this close in the first place.

Anyway, the drones reached their assigned stations without any fuss. Bill and I gave each other simultaneous thumbs-ups. This was the moment of truth.

"Okay, Guppy. Start with full-reach scans for each drone, then cut the range in half with each subsequent scan until we're down to a two-mile range, which should be enough to scan the inside surface. Then start taking snapshots every second until we have a full revolution recorded."

[Acknowledged. Scan results coming up.]

"It, uh, doesn't actually look like it's rotating," Will said. "Are you sure about your assumptions?"

I grinned back at him. "I did some reading. A lot of the design choices for O'Neill cylinders will apply to topopoleis as well. Chances are there's an outside shell that doesn't rotate. It will be thick and designed to absorb micro-meteor impacts and high-energy radiation. You don't want that much mass loading the rotating section, so the much thinner but structurally stronger inner shell will rotate, giving simulated gravity on its inner surface. There will be magnetic bearings or some such between the two shells."

"Say, you know a lot about this thing for not having scanned it yet."

"It's all theory, Bill. Let's see what we've got." I turned to Guppy and nodded.

There was no dramatic change to the monitor window, but smaller data windows began stacking up in various locations. We watched the action for a few milliseconds, then I reached over and tapped one of the scans. The window expanded in front of the main monitor, and Bill and I leaned forward to examine it in detail.

"You were right about the shells," he said. "Inner one is generating...0.86 G."

"Which is exactly the gravity on the second planet," I replied. "So that's the Boojum makers' home world."

"Air's not even close."

"Are you surprised? The pounding, the fires, and no life to provide homeostasis…Nothing could live on Planet Boojum the way it is right now."

"I guess not. When will we be able to get a detailed scan of the inhabitants?"

"Not until we're down to the rotational snapshots. Let's just leave it running."

❖   ❖   ❖

We sat around the control room, variously drinking coffee, beer, or Coke. I looked askance at the glass in Will's hand. He smiled back. "Picked up the habit from Marcus. Sometimes, something cold and fizzy is a nice change."

There was a *ding* reminiscent of a microwave, and the phrase *Scans Complete* popped up on the monitor. We all quickly stood and hurried over to examine the results.

The next few seconds resembled what you'd get with any gaggle of scientists trying to outshout each other, but we eventually distilled some useful information.

I stared at the hologram of a native. It was more like an Other than a Pav, in that it didn't closely correspond to any Terran lifeform that I could think of. Will examined it, head cocked to the side, and declared, "There's a bit of otter in there, I think."

"A flying otter." Garfield blinked. "Or a flying squirrel?"

"Uh, flying otter is reasonable, if you ignore the head," Will added. "Or maybe giant beaver? Look at the tail. That thing looks like it fans out."

We stared for a few more moments. To me, it looked like a four-foot-tall fat otter, but with a flap of skin around the forearms that could open or close. And a snout that was almost a beak, but with teeth. Like something between a

66

platypus and a wereduck. The tail did seem to be able to fan out, or flex flat or something—going from a roundish appendage to something more beaver-like. The creature was covered with fur, which tended toward a rich chestnut brown.

"Snarks," Garfield said. "If we have Boojums, we need Snarks to make them."

I held up a hand. "Sure, but only until we find out their name for themselves."

"Assuming we can pronounce it."

"It's aquatic," Bill said after some more silence. "The forearm things and the tail are for pushing through the water."

"That explains the river," Will added, and we all nodded. One of the many interesting aspects of the design was that a river ran the entire length of the section we'd scanned— and that was more than a hundred thousand miles. Or rivers, depending on how you counted. It branched and merged constantly. It was possible that the river system ran the entire length of the topopolis.

"Interestingly," Will continued, "the way the river loops and splits and meanders, no part of the inner surface seems to be very far from water."

"Given the natives' biology," Bill replied, "that was probably a design requirement."

We gazed in awe at the pictures and schematics, then Garfield said, "Where would you get all the water? The overall structure is literally a billion miles long."

Bill froze for a moment, then turned to Garfield. "Earth has, or had anyway, about 330 million cubic miles of water. The river in the topopolis averages maybe a half-mile wide and a tenth-mile deep, so if it was straight you'd probably only need about fifty million cubic miles to fill it. Soil can also be up to twenty-five percent water, so depending on how deep they've layered real soil over the shell's inner surface, maybe you add another hundred million cubic miles. It's still less than what Earth had. And there's always the Oort cloud if you needed more."

Garfield bobbed his head a few times as he absorbed that. "And the materials to build it?"

"The Earth contains about 90 billion cubic miles of iron. To build this, based on the cross section we see, you'd only need 20 billion cubic miles, although of course you couldn't use steel—not nearly enough tensile strength. Most of this structure is constructed of some kind of ceramic reinforced by a 3D carbon fiber lattice similar to what we use for our ship hulls, so even that estimate is probably *way* high."

"But the point," Will added, "is that you can get all the material you need by taking apart one Earth-sized planet."

"Which probably explains the orbital gap between planet two and three," I finished.

"Umph," said Garfield. "So, what now?"

"Well, we have well-established and tested procedures for picking up culture and language surreptitiously, thanks to Jacques," I said. "Although he had physical access to bookstores and libraries on Pav. I'd like to move things along as fast as possible, but without direct access, we're going to be at a disadvantage."

Bill frowned. "We're going to have to send in spy drones."

I nodded. He had hit the nail right on the thumb. "Yeah, and that's not going to be a trivial undertaking. *Then* we have to wait until we've absorbed the language and culture before we can go in."

"Is there an alternative?"

"What about *just* using spy drones? I mean for the search for Bender, not just for the cultural absorption?"

Will shook his head. "I can't see that working. They either fly around a lot where they can be seen, which is bad, or they stay in hiding and don't get around much. Which is bad. Plus, it becomes very difficult to ask questions of the locals."

"Excuse me, sir or madam," Garfield said. "I am not alien spy device, despite appearances. Could you please direct me to the nuclear wessels?"

We all laughed. Gar's Chekov impersonation was spot-on.

After a moment, I nodded to Will. "All right, accepted. I know this will sound odd after Bill's comments about keeping a low profile, but I've been talking to some people over at the Singularity Project—"

"You're talking to the Skippies?" Garfield asked.

"Yeah. They don't have an AI yet, but they do have a generalized, self-programming Expert System with enormous processing power. I wanted to be ready to fast-track the language translation and android design work if we found sophonts."

"Wait, androids? You're thinking *way* ahead on this," Garfield said.

Bill looked at me with a rueful smile. "You're looking for some help from them on that, too?"

I gave him a tight-lipped smile in reply. "They think they can pick up a lot from SUDDAR scans, including possibly sound—"

"What? How?"

"It's the same principle as bouncing a laser off a window to pick up vibrations from sounds inside the target building. You demodulate the reflection ..."

"SUDDAR doesn't work that way."

"No, but the Skippies think that they can use it to pick up vibrations from rigid surfaces in the megastructure. Even glass, assuming they have it."

"That'll be pretty hit-and-miss. You'd have to do a lot of scanning for the small number of situations where that would be feasible. They're willing to take this on?"

I nodded. "They're isolationist, but not like Starfleet. They don't think contact with humans is a morally bad thing, just that it's holding us back. Presumably by forcing us to keep conforming to human culture and so forth, I guess. But they are neutral on the question of interference with any locals, so I figured it would be relatively safe. Of course, if Starfleet gets hold of it, they'll go ballistic. But really, what can they do besides scream loudly? They aren't here, they can't get here in less than a couple of decades, and I have control of the local hardware, so they won't be building local ships or androids."

"And honestly," Will added, "if they started using strong-arm tactics, I don't think it would go well for them. As a group, Bobs aren't tolerant of that kind of thing. They'll register their disapproval, we'll acknowledge their right to their opinion, and that'll be that."

"Well, we have enough scans for a first pass at a rough android design, but a lot of work ahead of us on the culture and language fronts. Starting with how we get in."

"Yeah, I don't want to cut my way in. To be honest, I'm not sure if that'd even be possible. There have to be some legitimate entrances, for supplies, or personnel, or maintenance equipment, or something."

"Internally, there will have to be a ring of some kind between the inner and outer shells, to allow matching the rotation for things going in, and removing the angular vector for things coming out. A Spin Transfer system. We should look for that kind of structure in the scans."

"Maybe it's time to just have a detailed look at what we've got."

✤ ✤ ✤

Several dozen milliseconds later, the party atmosphere had evaporated. A bristling silence hung over the group, and we all wore matching frowns. "I presume everyone has noticed the level of technology of the inhabitants."

"Or lack thereof," Bill replied.

Garfield poked at a window in front of him. "Or the fact that the interior entrance we did a close-up on appears to be sealed off so the inhabitants can't leave."

"Something smells."

We now had a couple hundred thousand miles' worth of point scans and a thorough rotational scan from three locations. The results were perplexing. Instead of modern metropolises, we were seeing what appeared to be villages, constructed mostly of some kind of wood-equivalent, mostly concentrated around the river. Smaller settlements were situated around tributaries and branches. There was very little in the way of metal, as well. In fact, most of the metal seemed to be in the form of small disks carried around by the locals. Money.

I tapped the image to call attention to a detail. "We'll need to do some more scans to confirm, but it looks like the land is sculpted rather than the product of any kind of natural erosion. Either the water for the streams and tributaries is pumped up to the source, or they have actual weather to supply the headwaters."

"Also," Bill pointed out, "the inside seems to be divided into segments of about five hundred and sixty miles in length, separated by mountain ranges that form a ring to divide each segment." He tapped an image and it zoomed. "We don't have enough detail, but I *think* those mountains also anchor stays or guy-wires to keep some kind of cylinder lined up down the center of the structure."

"I'm guessing that central cylinder provides illumination. There's no allowance in this design for letting the actual sun shine in."

"Probably true, but SUDDAR hasn't been able to pick up those kinds of detail. And if you're right, it brings up the issue of heat dissipation. I wonder how they handle it?"

"I think we have at least a partial answer to that," I said. "There are radiator surfaces along the entire shaded side of the outer shell. Which are radiating way more heat than can be accounted for by solar absorption, so there's a lot of heat being generated internally. Probably that lighting you're talking about. There must be a system to bleed the heat from the living area to the outer shell."

Everyone in the room nodded slowly in appreciation. Bobs loved technical solutions.

"And notice," Bill added, "the river's meandering pattern repeats every dozen segments or so. I think the landscape does as well. I guess they just used the same design templates over and over."

"They might even have built the megastructure in segments of that size then glued them together."

"A billion miles. That's almost two million segments."

We all stared in silence at the data windows for several milliseconds.

"Maybe," Bill mused, "we just happen to have scanned a section of the megastructure that's set up as an agrarian community. There's no reason for the society to be identical along the entire length of the topopolis. Maybe they're technologically backward by choice."

"Including blocking the exits? That seems incompatible with a voluntary return to the land, you know?"

"Well, it isn't ideal for first contact. Or for learning about their society." I tapped my chin for a few moments. "Let's move along the strand and see if we can find something more up-to-date."

❧   ❧   ❧

One week later, we admitted failure. We had not only moved millions of miles along the original strand, but we had even jumped to one of the other strands and continued our survey.

"There's all kinds of variation in detail," I observed, "including different climate zones and completely uninhabited areas. But everything is pre-industrial. Why would a species build such an amazing feat of engineering, then sentence themselves to essentially live in a zoo?"

"Maybe that was the point of building it. These *are* aliens, Bob." Bill shrugged. "Their motivations may not be understandable."

"I've never bought into the idea that aliens will have indecipherable motives. Which makes it odd that you feel differently." I smiled at Bill to take the sting out of the comment. "Things like curiosity, greed, self-interest, self-preservation, anger, fear, all of these are pretty basic pro-survival tropisms."

"Sure, but that doesn't make their behavior predictable from our point of view. For instance, a more herd – or hive-oriented species might not have greed, or not as much anyway. A more predatory species might consider biting you to be a reasonable response to a disagreement."

"Kzin," I said, grinning.

"Or Pav," Bill responded. "Because of their large family structure, they certainly have a different take on life."

"But it's comprehensible, isn't it?" I argued. "We, or humans, might not live that way or want to. But we can understand the motivations of the Pav. Same with Kzinti or Klingons. In this case, we think this might be a semi-aquatic species, like beavers or otters. How will that affect their attitudes?"

Bill shrugged without comment. I was pretty sure I was right, but we wouldn't know until we figured out how to get in.

❧ ❧ ❧

I grinned at the traditional catcalls and jeers as Bill tried to get control of the moot. I noted, though, several pockets of Bobs that weren't participating in the ribaldry. This included a half-dozen or so Bobs dressed up as Borg, as well as other groups who mostly still looked like Original Bob. This reticence seemed uncharacteristic for Bobs, although I thought the Borg might be just trying to stay in character.

As I looked around, I realized that there was a certain amount of miscellaneous cosplay going on. Nothing really *out there*—at least not yet, I admitted to myself. As replicative drift continued, I expected individuals would become bolder.

Bill seemed to have sufficiently dampened the flames of rebellion, and he began to talk. Well, shout. "Okay, people. We have an update on the Snarks. I think you'll find this all interesting. We'll also be asking for help from anyone who cares to volunteer. There are some technical hurdles that could use some dogpiling." He waited for the anatomical suggestions from the audience to peter out, then turned and gestured to me.

I climbed the podium to more shouted suggestions and grinned at the sea of faces. "Those of you who were around for the *Others* reveal will feel a bit of déjà vu, I think. But in this case, we aren't at war, so that's a plus." I waited for the razzing to subside. "So, first, here's a native Snark..."

I auto-piloted through the presentation of the megastructure residents while mentally reviewing the upcoming second part of my presentation. As usual, the Bobs were respectful and quiet when interesting information was being presented.

Then came the second part. I started with an overview of the topopolis, during which you could have heard a pin drop. I followed with close-up rotation scans, and ended with blueprints of the megastructure entrance mechanisms.

As I finished, and my voice petered out, there was a moment of silence, an indrawn collective breath, then—pandemonium. Bill laughed out loud as he jumped up onto the podium. Nothing got Bobs excited like interesting new stuff, and nothing felt better than a bunch of excited, enthusiastic Bobs. Even the Borg cosplayers were jumping up and down.

"So, here's what we need," I said, when the hubbub had died down. "We need a group to work on plans for getting into the megastructure without revealing ourselves. We need a group to work on android design for Snarks, based on the scans we have, to be improved on once we get close-up scans. We need a group to continue to scan the megastructure, to see if there are variations in either engineering of the structure itself, or the placement or technological level of the inhabitants, or any other variations you might find. It's a billion freaking miles of structure, so the more the merrier. And as an ongoing project, we'll want people to help decipher the language and culture."

And more pandemonium.

I glanced surreptitiously at the group that Bill had identified as Starfleet. To a man, they were silent, with dour expressions on their faces.

❧ ❧ ❧

"We're in business," Bill said. "More volunteers than available positions. The Skippies have agreed to do language analysis, as you'd hoped. The hardware group that was working on giant robot spaceships has already dropped their project in favor of the android design—interestingly, the Borg wanted in, too. I think there's something about androids that tickles their fancy. And there's a D&D-obsessed group, calls themselves *Gamers*, that wants to work on the breaking-in thing."

"Why?" I asked, frowning.

"Don't ask me. By about twentieth gen or so, individual motivations stop being predictable, even when they're still mostly Bobs."

"So Starfleet didn't squawk."

"I don't think they saw any point. Even if they could have gotten a word in edgewise, they wouldn't have accomplished anything except getting themselves shouted down. But"—Bill hesitated, frowned, then gazed at me intently—"that doesn't mean they're just going to fold. Original Bob wouldn't have. So we have to keep our guard up."

At that moment, Garfield popped into my library. "Hey, Bill. Bob." He signaled Jeeves for a coffee, grabbed Spike, and sat down with the cat in his lap. Spike, as usual, was purring before Garfield even started patting her. I couldn't help smiling. Original Spike had been like that—the exact opposite of a standoffish, snobby cat. I remembered all the times she would climb me as I sat at my computer, then drape herself across the back of my neck. I'd left that last habit out of the cat's AI—it had literally been a bit of a pain in the neck.

Garfield was excited about something.

"What?" I said.

"Well, we've agreed we will have to be more careful than Jacques was about the drones. The Pav were truly 18th to 19th-century-equivalent. If they'd seen something, they would have just assumed it was a bird. The Snarks may have technological-age knowledge, even if they don't have the actual tech. For whatever reason."

"Also," Bill interjected, "even if the common folk don't have tech, whoever is still running the topopolis certainly will."

"You think it's still being actively staffed?" I asked, frowning.

"Hard to see how it couldn't be. Imagine people walking out of a nuclear power plant for a couple of days."

"Or any other similar operation," Garfield said. "I remember *Life After People*, thanks."

Bill shrugged, unwilling to be offended. "Anyway, the topopolis is still apparently running like clockwork, so it's being maintained and managed. I guess they could have just handed it over to an AI…"

"I can't see that happening. An intelligent species wouldn't just hand over responsibility like that," Garfield retorted.

"You're anthropomorphizing."

"You know Original Bob's view on this. Aliens will still act rationally within the bounds of their environment and biology."

"Which doesn't mean they'll act like humans or make human—"

"Okay, kiddies," I interjected. "Let's save this convo for when we know more. Gar, do your D&D guys have a way in?"

"Well, a highly theoretical one. We want to see if we can attach a cloaked drone to a Boojum without it noticing. If so, we can piggyback in."

"We could be waiting forever—"

"No, some of the surveillance guys found an entrance that's heavily used."

"Only one? Across a billion miles of topopolis?"

"No, of course not." Garfield frowned at me. "There are three on each strand, for a total of nine like this one. But the others appear to be much less busy, and more specialized. I think only the one is being kept at full operating capacity for system patrols."

"That seems odd," Bill said.

"Not really," Gar replied. "All the work's been done. The system has been cleared. It's all routine patrols now. I imagine the patrols are scheduled so they do shift changes or whatever when the entrance revolves around to their side."

Bill shrugged and didn't argue the point. "Is the traffic flow predictable?"

"Yes. It wasn't obvious at first. There are irregular arrivals and departures that masked the scheduled stuff, but eventually we extracted the periodic events from the noise. We just wait for one of the scheduled 'shift changes' and we should be good."

"And we'll have contingency plans?"

Garfield smiled. "Standard practice. Ever since Hal and the Others, a dead-man switch has been de rigueur in the Bobiverse."

"I don't want to be too destructive…"

"Thermite in all the right places," Garfield replied. "Just enough to melt the drone, without continuing down like alien acid-blood."

"Well, I guess we're set." I sat back and tented my fingertips. "Excellent."

9. Group Building

I looked around at the crowd in my library, uncertain if I should expand my floor space for the occasion. This was enough people to make my VR hardware sweat a little.

"Okay, everyone," I said in a loud voice. "Let's get started. Everyone knows me, Bill, Will, and Garfield. Guys, these are the people who've volunteered their time and/or their groups' time to help out with the expedition planning. I figured we all ought to get together and formalize things."

I motioned to my left, to a Bob with a floppy conical hat perched on his lap. "This is Gandalf, representing the Gamer group. They have volunteered to come up with a plan for getting some drones into the megastructure, and later to get some androids in."

"Preferably without setting off alarms," Gandalf said with a grin.

"That would indeed be preferable. Are you still leaning toward the *hitch a ride* plan?"

Gandalf nodded. "Nothing better has presented itself."

I gave him an amused snort in reply, then motioned to the next person, who was wearing a grey nondescript coverall. "This is Hugh, representing the Sk—er, Singularity Project." I paused, unsure if I'd just committed a social blunder.

"It's okay, Bob. We know we're referred to as Skippies. No one's offended."

"Er, okay. Hugh represents the Skippies, who are engaged in trying to build a super AI."

"Wait," Garfield interrupted, "I thought the Skippies went to numeric designations instead of names."

"To be more accurate, we've moved away from audio speech in favor of packetized communication," Hugh said. "Think of it like converting to sign language as a primary communications medium. Our 'names' are semantically equivalent to IP addresses."

"Wow…" said Garfield.

"But for day-to-day with other Bobs, I go by *Hugh*."

"So you guys aren't against this expedition?" Bill asked. "I understood the Skippies disapproved of relations with biologicals."

Hugh shook his head. "Not in the same way as Starfleet, if that's what you mean. Those guys are wacko. It isn't a moral thing with us; we just think that interfacing with bios is inherently limiting."

"Well, sure, we operate on different time scales, but what's the problem?"

Hugh grimaced. "Look, Bill, guys, we—all the Bobs, that is—are what's known as a *speed superintelligence*. We can and do operate at a much higher processing rate than humans. The problem is that we continue to accommodate them. Every time we slow down to interface with them, all the time we spend adapting to their history, time scale, schedules, is wasted time. It also sets psychological constraints on us. If we just let go completely, we could, as a species, experience centuries of internal life for every month of objective time."

The rest of us exchanged glances. "Uh, it's not completely wrong," I said, "but it assumes that we have a goal of some kind with sufficient motivation to mandate cutting off contact with humans. There really isn't any such schedule or deadline."

"No, there isn't. Like I said, we're not wackos. But the inefficiencies add up. It's like taking the long way to and from work every day because you don't feel motivated to figure out the most direct route. You waste a lot of time that could have been put to better use."

I shrugged. "Okay. I don't disagree, I just question your priorities."

"Hold on," Garfield cut in. "You said it wasn't a moral thing with you. Does that mean you think it is with Starfleet?"

"Yeah, at least on the surface." Hugh paused and returned Garfield's gaze. "Those guys aren't Bobs anymore. Somewhere back in their ancestry, someone got a double dose of drift in something. Or maybe there's some PTSD from the last common ancestor's personal timeline, maybe from the Others war. Whatever the reason, they've become obsessive about it—it's not an intellectual stance. It's almost VEHEMENT-like."

"Well, that's not worrying or anything."

Hugh grinned at me. "It was inevitable, though, sooner or later. And it isn't relevant to this project anyway."

"So why are you helping?"

Now it was Hugh's turn to shrug. "Honestly, I just think the topopolis is interesting. And we've just brought some new neural-net designs online, which we need to stress-test. The information processing requirements on your project will make good test cases. So, win-win."

"Fair enough." I cocked my head at Hugh, inviting him to continue or volunteer more commentary. However, he seemed to be done. I gestured to the next person and grimaced. "This is…Locutus."

"Seriously?" Garfield said in an incredulous tone.

"Hey, I'd have preferred Hugh, but it appears to be taken," said Locutus.

I eyed him. His getup was generally Borg-like, but there was a lot more armor than I remembered from the *TNG* episodes. I pointed and said, "Are you sure you've got the theme right?"

Locutus flexed, moving the shoulder pads. "Steampunk influence. We're kind of evolving, you know?"

Gar rolled his eyes. "Aw, jeez."

"Aaaaaanyway," I said to the group. "Locutus and co. are part of the design team for the Boojum androids. They're going to be working on the low-level stuff first—autonomous systems, muscle placement and control, and so forth. Which also means they'll need some in-close SUDDAR scans of the natives with a lot more detail than we have so far."

"Action shots would be good, too," Locutus said. "We want to get the proper walking, running, and swimming mechanics. Imagine putting together a beaver mock-up that bounces around like an otter. Probably wouldn't fool anyone."

My chuckle was echoed around the table. "We can probably get video clips from the spy drones for that side of things. Which is good, because we've already got a lot of demands on our SUDDAR scanning schedule. Hugh, how are things going with the vibrating windows idea?"

"Not great. There aren't that many locations where conditions are clean enough for us to be able to pick up usable sounds. The Snarks appear to be garrulous in large groups, but much less so in smaller groups. It's like they egg each other on. Unfortunately, large groups make it too hard to isolate anything. Plus, it turns out glass isn't as common as we might have expected."

"Controlled environment," Bill said. "They aren't really *outdoors* as such. Plus having a coat of fur would make them less concerned about temperature swings."

Hugh considered for a moment. "Speculative, but not unreasonable. I took a close look at some scans as well. It looks like they use oiled paper for window coverings. Way easier to make, but totally unsuitable for what we were attempting. All of which means we'll have to depend on spy drones more than expected."

Locutus held up a hand. "Hey, listen, what would help us a lot is some input from a biologist, especially one with anatomical expertise. I wasn't sure if I should bring it up, but…"

"Bridget?"

"Uh, it would be handy. I know she's a little skittish around large groups of Bobs, but…"

I sighed. "I'll talk to her, Locutus. Anything else?"

Will waved his hand. "I have a line on a guy who was an expert on megastructures. I'll set up an appointment to talk with him."

"Was?"

"Well, he's dead."

"I…" I gave Will the side eye. "Wait, he's a replicant?"

"Yep. Retired to the Vulcan Post-Life Arcology in the Omicron2 Eridani system. Apparently he turned right around and started lecturing at the university again, via manny. So I have to fit myself into his schedule."

"Whatever works." I looked around the room. "Anything else that needs to be covered?"

There were several shakes of heads, but no responses.

"Great. I'll call another general meeting if necessary, but for the most part you can all follow your own schedules. Thanks, all."

Within a few milliseconds, everyone had popped out, leaving only Bill. With the load off the VR system, I reactivated Jeeves and accepted a coffee.

"So what's up?"

"Bridget." Bill hesitated. "Locutus was right to ask about her for consulting, but I want to take it one step further. I'd like to see her on the expedition itself."

I frowned. "She's got children, Bill. And Howard. I don't know how well that would work. She'd have to be away from them for large periods of time."

"Granted. But they might be able to work something out. Or she might clone."

"Doubtful."

"Yeah, I guess. But let's not write off the idea without trying, okay? At least bring it up."

I nodded. "Will do."

10. Things are Coming Together

Herschel
September 2333
Interstellar Space

I sat back in my chair, laced my fingers together, and grinned at Neil. "I do love it when a plan comes together."

"Plan, my hairy white butt. We floated an idea—"

"And got bites. It would seem a lot of people on Romulus do not like the political climate."

"Hardly surprising, Hersch. FAITH never completely went away, even if they suffered some, er, PR setbacks. They're still trying to take over, still trying to drive policy."

"And still messing things up."

"Mm-hmm. So, what's the count?"

"Well, someone started a society…" I paused to reread the email. "*Ever Onward*, they call it. Very high-sounding. They have something like fifteen thousand members."

"All willing to climb aboard and start a new colony, somewhere far away?"

"That's the theory. I'm sure a lot of them are just playing at it, or joining up as a form of protest vote."

"Are you sure you want to go this way, Hersch?" Neil was frowning, and his tone was more serious than usual. I decided I should pay attention.

"C'mon, Neil, we've had lots of conversations about the way things have stalled. You've agreed with me—"

"Wait, *I've* agreed with *you*? When did you become the mastermind?"

"Not important. The point is, we agree the Bobs seem to have turned to various forms of navel-gazing. Gamers, Skippies, even Will with his Valhalla terraforming. They've become like old men with their stamp collecting."

"There are still Bobs heading outward."

"Phineas, Ferb, Icarus, and Daedalus. They're running away as much as anything. I tell ya, buddy, something is going on that's not healthy."

"So you've changed your mind about this?"

"No, I think I maybe want to expand it some. Do more than just ferry another batch of humans to another planet."

"Like …"

"We've got this crap-ton of refined material from the Pav deal, so we don't have to stop for a long, long time. Set up enough manufacturing internally so we can crank out Heaven vessels assembly line style. Populate them with AMIs, like they did in the Battle for Terra, and squirt them out at every system we pass by."

"And remote-control them?"

"Yeah, Neil. It's called delegation."

"Or laziness. What about the colony?"

"If we're sending the AMI-controlled vessels ahead of us, we'll know if a system has a viable candidate planet, and we can stop and set up."

"Then continue on? Sounds a lot like Ick and Dae."

"At least we'll be doing something. I'm tired of being a museum piece."

"It's not the most terrible idea you've ever had. Let's talk to the Ever Onward people."

I nodded to Neil and started composing an email. For the first time in a long, long time, I was beginning to feel excited again.

11. Breaking In

Bob
October 2333
Outskirts, Eta Leporis

No plan ever survives contact with the enemy.

Okay, the Snarks weren't *the enemy* as such, but they were the opponent in the scenario we were executing. And the viewer count on our remote feed probably included half the Bobiverse currently in range of BobNet.

"There's a gaggle of Boojums heading for the entrance," Bill said.

"*Should it be gaggle?*" someone asked over the intercom channel. "*How about murder?*"

"*How is that better? Crows or geese. Either way—*"

The argument went viral, and soon there was an actual discussion channel dedicated to the question of what unit would be used to describe a gathering of Boojums. Or maybe Booja. The question of plurals had a side discussion of its own going. I shook my head in disbelief and chuckled. Replicative drift or not, Original Bob was still very much alive in this gaggle of post-singularity replicants. Or maybe herd. Or pack.

While the name-obsessed discussion spiraled into ever more esoteric suggestions, Bill announced into the intercom, "*Ballistic trajectory set. We should be able to drift right in and settle on a couple of them with minimal vector adjustment.*"

"*Assuming they don't pick today to change things up, just for fun.*"

"*I'm pretty sure those are some equivalent of AMIs,*" Bill replied. "*They've shown no variability at all. Strictly script-driven.*"

There was a moment of silence as the cloaked drones approached within a dozen yards of the Boojums. Even the name-obsession discussion petered out.

The drones drifted in the last few yards, made a minute adjustment, and… contact. The non-streamlined design of the Boojums allowed the much smaller drones to settle inside the Boojums' skeletal frames so that they didn't stick out. If there was some kind of automated security, it was highly likely that silhouette matching would form part of the strategy.

"Well, we appear to have been successful," Bill said.

"Any traffic?" Will asked. I turned at the voice—I hadn't sensed Will's arrival. Then I remembered I was in the moot VR, and didn't own the monitoring channel.

"Just radio." I pointed at the section of the data window that indicated radio traffic. "Packetized, and either compressed or encrypted or both. We've tentatively identified envelope and control fields, but we don't have enough context yet to spoof them. Even assuming we could come up with a legitimate-looking addressing and data payload."

"But no SCUT?"

"Nada." I shook my head. "We've gotten used to—okay, we *had* gotten used to everyone on Earth having the same technology, but who knows how much of that was caused by the fact that everyone was sharing knowledge—"

"Or stealing it."

I smiled and nodded to acknowledge the point. "Sure. VEHEMENT and all that. But the Others had stuff we didn't, and vice versa."

"And even with the Brazilians, that was true. They had the cloaking thing."

I shrugged and let the silence hang for a moment. "Yes, and to my point. The Boojums seem to be following the same pattern—more advanced in some ways, less in others. I guess in isolation, the tech tree development path isn't an inevitable march."

"They're going in," Garfield said, interrupting our conversation. Sure enough, I'd gotten wrapped up in the discussion with Will and lost track of the main event. Wow, senior moment.

Given that it was a cylinder with a fifty-six-mile radius, from close up the outer shell had the appearance of a flat wall. Directly ahead of the Boojums, a huge space dock stood open. Massive reinforced doors seemed to be there only for emergencies; we'd never seen them move since we began surveillance. The Boojums drifted in, small attitude jets giving occasional puffs as they corrected their individual vectors. Eventually the crafts drifted into docking bays designed specifically for them. An army of small service bots stood ready to receive the arrivals.

After much discussion and argument, we'd settled on *winging it* as a strategy. Not our finest moment, I felt. The best suggestion had been to bail the moment the Boojums docked, before any detailed examination could start.

We had a good idea of what we could expect from SUDDAR scans, but there was still a large amount of risk. In these close quarters, the drones were visible—as in eyeball-visible—even with the camouflage technology to make them appear to be part of the larger structure of the

Boojums. If some kind of maintenance bot decided to take a detailed look, our geese might be cooked.

The space dock was long but didn't penetrate deeply into the outer shell. It contained a large number of Boojum docking bays, about a third of which appeared to be occupied. Other vessels of uncertain function filled differently configured bays.

And in the middle of it all, small bots zipped along on unknown errands, mounted on some kind of track system attached to all available surfaces. The overall effect was of a kind of organized chaos.

There were indications that this area was originally configured to support Snarks as well. We could see sealed, windowed areas that were probably control centers for some kind of operational staff. And a couple of the unidentified vessel types appeared to have hatches and viewports. Scans, however, had not shown one single trace of life. This whole operation was running on automatic.

The nonrotating outer shell was a hundred yards thick, consisting mostly of some kind of friable material. It wasn't structural; it was intended to absorb meteor impacts and block radiation. But it had many embedded design details, like a rigid support frame and the docking bay for the Boojums. And the item we were most interested in: the vector-matching system for getting from the nonrotating outer shell to the swiftly rotating inner shell without being ground up like seeds in a pepper mill. Getting access to what we were calling the Spin Transfer system was our ultimate goal.

It must have been an interesting engineering challenge for the builders. And the solution, based on our SUDDAR scans, was genius. An elevator shaft ran through the outer shell from the cargo bay to the inner surface. Maybe *elevator* wasn't the right word, since with no rotation, there was no artificial gravity to worry about. But it was as good a label as any.

Embedded in the inner surface of the outer shell was a magnetic rail system circling the gap between the inner and outer shell, with components attached to each shell. A container would run along the transport rail from the cargo bay, then transfer to the vector-matching system, and accelerate to match velocity with the rotating inner shell. At that point the container would be "handed off" from the outer shell to the inner, after which it would dock at one of four stations spaced equidistantly around the circumference of the inner shell.

Well, that was the theory. We hadn't seen a single container actually make the trip on any of the entrance assemblies that we'd been surveilling. As near as we could tell, the containers were all docked at the base of the transport rail. The Boojums didn't need to go inside, and apparently nothing inside needed to come out.

The Boojums settled onto their assigned racks, and maintenance bots moved forward to perform oil changes or whatever they did. Our drones detached from the Boojums, staying as close as possible to avoid becoming free-floating silhouettes, and floated slowly along the length of the vessel. They had orders to transfer to a wall before they got to the nose area, just in case sensors were still active. We *thought* the Boojums were probably in maintenance mode at this point, but best not to tempt fate. In the end, we were depending on the complete lack of curiosity and total single-minded focus on the task at hand that typified every AMI in existence. As far as we knew.

The Gamers in charge of flying the drones were frame-jacked high enough to be able to take the time to consider their actions and the possible consequences. But that also meant I'd have to jack if I wanted to communicate with them. Constant disassembly and reassembly of my VR would be too disconcerting; I decided to just remain a spectator. We could compare notes later.

Soon the drones were positioned in a small alcove created by the intersection of an airlock area and two support columns. SUDDAR scans had indicated that this would be out of line-of-sight for most of the bay. There were a number of cameras and sensors in evidence, but without tracing the circuitry there was no way to know which ones might be surveillance of some kind and which ones were strictly operational. We had already decided not to worry about it. There was no way to make this op completely safe, so we would learn from our failures and try again, if necessary.

The drones waited for a break in activity, then scooted to the next rally point, a dead area between two different types of docking racks. They whipped around the last corner into the alcove, and almost ran right smack into a maintenance bot.

"What the hell?" Bill exclaimed.

I jacked immediately, VR be damned. *"Anyone have any idea what that thing is doing here?"* I said to the drone operators in general. At this clock speed, they were represented only by their metadata tags, hanging in a virtual void.

One of the tags, labelled *Randall*, replied, *"No, and it wasn't on the planning scans. There's nothing here. It's just a gap in the—oh."* A window popped up and spun around for all to see. *"Looks like a bulkhead repair in progress."*

"Friggin' hell," I muttered. "It's times like this that I'm glad I don't have an actual heart to have a heart attack with."

I returned to regular Bob-time, reassembled my VR, and turned to Bill, who was just moving his lips to begin whatever next sentence he had in mind. I cut in before he could get properly going. "It's doing bulkhead repairs. Complete coincidence. And we're above its sensor area, so it probably hasn't noticed us."

"Peachy," Bill replied. "No alarms so far, anyway. We might just pull this off."

It took several more hops by the drones, but there were no more coronary-inducing events. The drones found themselves in front of an access panel. According to our scans, this would lead to what some wit had called a Jeffries Tube. In theory, it *should* get us to the acceleration track used by the mechanism that connected the nonrotating outer shell to the rotating inner shell of the megastructure. But from that point on, there would be more "winging it" involved, as not all the engineering control systems could be resolved in detail.

One of the drones released some roamers, which popped out customized screwdrivers and attacked the attachment points on the panel. I had a moment of, I don't know, déjà vu? Nostalgia? Something like that, as I noted that the Snarks used a screw head virtually identical to a Robertson. I guess some geometry problems are universal.

The roamers couldn't reseal the hatch properly from the inside, so once all our units had entered, the roamers pulled the hatch closed and performed a small spot-weld. It wouldn't hold against any kind of assault, but the point was for things to appear normal, not for us to fortify our rear. Job complete, the roamers climbed back into the drone and we continued on.

We couldn't wait around to catch a ride on the rail system, since there seemed to be no rides to catch. We certainly couldn't activate the system on our own—and even if we could figure out how to do that, it would probably attract unwelcome attention. That seemed like the kind of system that would require some high-level management involvement, if only for approvals and scheduling.

That left us with the strategy of scurrying around the innards like rodents, trying to make our way to the inside of the megastructure. Which was easier than you'd think. Rodents had been finding pathways through everything humans had built for millennia.

One advantage of the containers all being parked was that the ring was empty, like an elevator shaft with no elevator. And the drones had sufficient acceleration to be able to match up with the inner shell while following a circular path. So we would be able to dock on the inner shell receiving station.

It took several hours of preparation, mapping out small spaces and dodging maintenance bots, but we eventually found ourselves ready for the big step—flying from the stationary outer shell to the rotating inner shell. We decided to try out the strategy with one single drone before risking the entire squadron. There was some initial wobbling until Gandalf got the hang of it, then the drone's path smoothed out.

The drone landed on a small maintenance platform in what I suppose I'd call the station or terminal on the inner shell that was supposed to give the inhabitants of the topopolis access to the elevator system. I could see where the elevator containers would mate up with a pressure door, allowing passengers to go from a pressurized elevator cabin to a pressurized megastructure interior.

Up to this point, we'd been operating in vacuum. Now we'd have to figure out how to get into a shirtsleeve environment—again, without setting off any alarms.

Once the entire squadron arrived, the next step was intelligence gathering. A couple of drones ejected roamers, which swarmed over the hatch system. In about ten minutes, we had a report.

"Well, the good news is that the systems are well-designed," Gandalf said. "That means they have manual overrides in case something goes wrong."

"And the bad news?" I asked.

"The manual overrides have what I expect are alarm sensors, so as soon as we use them, management will know."

"So..."

"We'll gimmick the sensors. If the 'door opened' sensor doesn't trip, no one will be the wiser."

"That could take a while."

"Yep. And some of those sensors are on the other side of bulkheads, so we have to drill through to get to them. We'll send in the two-millimeter roamers."

"And this won't set off any alarms?"

Gandalf shook his head. "This isn't a top secret military base. They wouldn't expect anyone to be trying to break in like this, so why would they engineer for it?"

That seemed like dubious logic. Or wishful thinking. "Confidence level?"

"We scanned it, Bob. There's just the one level of sensor security."

I nodded, satisfied for the moment. But if alarms went off, heads would be slapped.

"Think about the scale, Bob," Bill added, sidling up to me. "A billion miles of megastructure with doors, airlocks, passageways, restricted areas... How would you police that? You have to set up automated processes, and trust those processes to bump alerts upstream. You want to avoid redundant signals as well, to keep the overall processing down."

"So kill the alerts at source, and nothing happens."

"Yup," Gandalf said, looking up from his monitor.

⚜ ⚜ ⚜

I'll give the Gamers their due, they were careful and methodical. It took almost half a day to defang the airlock to the point where it could be used without bringing Armageddon down on us. Finally, Gandalf gave the thumbs-up, and we began manually cycling our devices through.

At one point I had a thought and snorted. "It would be a helluva thing if you got this far only to discover that the drones couldn't fit through the airlock."

"It would indeed," Gandalf replied with a smirk. "Which is why we checked for that during the planning stages. That *is* why you pay us the big bucks."

"Assuming I paid you any bucks."

"A valid point." He grinned at me, then turned back to his monitor. "And this is the last load. Next stop, megastructure interior."

Once past the airlock, our drones found themselves in a corridor leading from the Spin Transfer system into presumably the main part of the station. I spent some time examining the corridor. There wasn't much to see—low-level lighting illuminated the area, and I could see what appeared to be traditional elevator doors at the other end. Unless you were shaped like a Krell, there were only so many ways to design corridors and doors, so it wouldn't have looked out of place in a human-based installation. Even the writing. Apparently, the need to label every damned thing was another universal. Although I couldn't read any of it, I amused myself for a few moments by imagining Snark exhortations to not injure one's limbs by sticking them in the crushy-grindy place, and other legally mandated warnings for idiots.

The elevators were reminiscent of any random office building on Earth. There was also, because the Snarks had some version of building codes, a set of emergency stairs. The stairs might or might not be alarmed, and the elevators might or might not alert someone when used. I hoped the Gamers had taken those possibilities into account.

"Elevators aren't alarmed?"

"Don't know," Gandalf replied. "Same problem as with the inter-shell rail system; we can't tell where the signals go. But the stairs don't have door sensors."

I grunted but otherwise didn't respond. It wasn't me climbing the stairs after all.

This part of the operation turned out to be fairly tedious, like trekking through a dungeon that was all corridor. Of course, something could always jump out of a hidden alcove, which made for a strange combination of stress and boredom.

We passed doors to several other levels on the way up, but finally all the drones were at the top of the stairs. As Gandalf described it, the door opened into the foyer of the transit station on the inside surface of the megastructure. In better times, this was where the inhabitants would have come to travel to the outer shell and then outside the topopolis. There was some indication in the scans that this was also a transit stop for some kind of internal transit system. Unfortunately there were only so many milliseconds in a day, and that investigation had been back-burnered.

"So here's where it gets complicated," Gandalf said.

"And what have we been doing up till now?" I asked.

"Two problems." Gandalf brought up some subsidiary windows to illustrate. "First, the foyer has cameras. Second, there are sensors on the external doors. Third, if management wanted to keep the natives out of the station, this is where the security would be concentrated, both inside and outside. So we can't use the front door."

"I assume you have an alternative."

He grinned at me. "Big bucks, remember? We're going to tunnel out."

"Tunnel? Like *The Great Escape*?"

"Well, it's not like we haven't been cutting into things right and left. And the Snarks use that weird ceramic carbon-fiber material everywhere that we'd use concrete on Earth. Which works out for us, since it yields to a plasma cutter with very little argument."

"So after all this high-tech spy stuff, we're going to dig our way out like rats."

"Ya gotta know when to go low-tech, Bob."

Garfield pulled up a schematic of the station and pointed to a spot. "Here. This will come out just under ground level, so we can cover it up once we're through."

"Outside surveillance?"

"That's not a problem. There are cameras covering the entrance, but not so much the back and sides."

"Then let's do this."

⚜ ⚜ ⚜

Cutting through the wall, then digging up to ground level was tedious but mostly uneventful. We surprised a representative of the local wildlife when the roamer popped out of the ground. The animal, some kind of deer-analogue, I think, jumped straight back about ten feet, then bounded away with a panicked bleating.

"Time to start spying," Gandalf said. He sent a command to the drones and several of them popped open their cargo doors. Out came little spy drones, a combination of tech from my spying on the Deltans and Jacques's spying on the Pav. Improvements in technology, including but not limited to the Casimir power sources, meant that the modern version of the spy drone was no bigger than a sparrow. Add in the camouflage system, and we were confident we'd avoid discovery by the natives. These drones would, among other tasks, try to supplement the Skippies' scans with some good old-fashioned eavesdropping.

Discovery by the mysterious topopolis controller was another thing to consider. It was a safe bet that the habitat included surveillance of some kind, if only to watch for maintenance issues. Add to that the fact that the natives were actively kept to a largely pre-industrial level, which could necessitate some kind of surveillance system anyway. How the technology limits would be enforced was an important question. We didn't want to accidentally get caught in a purge of some kind.

"Spy drones are on their way," Garfield commented. "Now, we wait."

12. EXPEDITION PREP

Bob
November 2333
Outskirts, Eta Leporis

The spy drones had multiple duties, so they'd be busy for a while. In addition to finding a way to eavesdrop on the Snarks and learn their language, the drones would be doing biological surveys and surveys of the towns and infrastructure. The drones had been given a search algorithm by the Skippies, which according to them would help to gather the required raw data in a more efficient manner. I didn't necessarily distrust them, but I'd nevertheless rigged a hardware monitor into the drones. It would be completely undetectable unless you knew the access protocols and keys. Bill's paranoia seemed to have colored my experiences with the Bobiverse in general.

There was plenty to do, meanwhile. We had enough basic info to start on fabbing an alpha version of the Snark mannies. Details could be filled in once the Skippies finished their biological survey. And there was still the question of getting Bridget involved, at least for consulting on the Snark biology.

I was working on the manny design when I got a ping from Bridget. She and I didn't hang around together, so this was unlikely to be just out of the blue. I suspected some-one might have said something to someone. I sent an *accept*, and a moment later she popped in.

Bridget spent a few mils looking around at my library. "I very much approve. Howard had a library motif for a while, but never this many books. Are they real?"

"All of them, right down to content," I said. "I've raided every human database I can find. BobNet contains the sum of human and Pav written knowledge."

"Well, it's great to have a hobby." Bridget hesitated, then launched right into what she was really here for. "Bob, I'd like a position on the Snark exploration op when it's ready."

"Okay."

"I mean, I'm a biologist, and I have lots of exp—wait, what?"

I grinned at her. "Honestly, I was trying to figure out how to bring it up. I was planning to take the coward's way out and talk to Howard."

"I am simultaneously offended and gratified," she replied. "Still, results are what count. I see you're working on mannies. How much work to do a female version?"

"Ah, Snark sexual dimorphism is minimal. Females have a slightly larger head, but it's probably mostly about pheromones. So, not much."

"Good. Bill tells me you have the Skippies doing the survey. You trust them?"

I raised an eyebrow at that comment. My earlier conversation with Bill about the subject was an intra-Bob kind of thing. To have a third party concerned about the Bob variants put a whole new level of significance on the problem.

"Why in particular do you ask, Bridget?"

"Oh, they haven't started chanting 'One of us, one of us,' or something equally nefarious. It's just that they really aren't Bobs anymore. It would be less unsettling if they changed their appearance like the Borg cosplayers, but they still look like Howard, or a pod-person version of him."

"You've watched *Invasion of the Body Snatchers?*"

"Bob, I'm married to Howard. What do you suppose we watch on movie nights? *Wuthering Heights?*"

I laughed and she smiled in return, and I was reminded once again what Howard saw in her. Among many other things.

I shook off the moment with some effort and changed the subject. "The Skippies originally figured a couple of weeks at most to get a complete picture of the local Snark culture. Which we're almost at the end of. We all acknowledge that there may be regional differences with over a billion miles of potential spread. But we'll deal with that, if and when."

"Accents or even different languages, cultural drift, nationalism... I get it. Depends how long they've been cooped up in there, too."

"Not long, I—"

Bill popped in at that moment. "Bridget, hey! Has Bob managed to convince you to come on the expedition?"

Bridget gave me a smile and an eye roll, then replied to Bill, "Yes, he has. Took a lot of work..."

"Horse puckey."

Bridget laughed, then turned back to me. "You were saying?"

"Oh, based on our survey of the Snarks' home planet, residual radioactivity, and number of forest fire tracks, we figure it became unlivable somewhere around a few hundred years ago. I'm not sure what that means in Snark generations."

Bridget nodded and glanced at Bill. It occurred to me that Bill was here for something, so I tilted my head at him in a silent invitation to speak.

"Right," Bill said. "I came here for something. The Skippies delivered a preliminary report. Mostly ecosystems and general survey—they're still having a slow go of it on the language and cultural stuff. Although they did give me a couple of things. The natives call themselves *Quinlans*. At least that's the closest phonetic rendition. And the topopolis is called *Heaven's River*."

"Cool. Okay then, the Snarks are now officially *Quinlans*."

"Have they compiled a detailed report on biology?" Bridget asked.

"Hugh gave me some general notes and said he'll have a formal report for us within forty-eight hours."

"Hugh?" Bridget asked. "I thought the Skippies all use numeric designations."

"I guess there's still some Bob there, because they're pretty easygoing about it. They'll use nicknames when dealing with the rest of us." I turned to Bill. "Have you talked to Will yet?"

"Yep. He's okay with the plan. So, me, you, Garfield, and Bridget, with Will as backup."

"Good. I'll ping everyone when I get the final report, and we'll meet here and discuss it."

⚜　⚜　⚜

Will was the last to show up. Bridget raised her coffee cup in salute as he popped in. That was a habit she'd picked up from me—well, from Howard. I had it on good authority, though, that her coffee was espresso-level-plus and would dissolve any spoon unlucky enough to be dunked therein.

Will parked himself in a beanbag chair that I'd materialized for him, accepted a Coke from Jeeves, and motioned to me with one hand.

"So, here it is," I said, waving a sheaf of paper. The report wasn't actually on paper, but it made a good metaphor in virt. "Megastructure layout, ecology, Quinlan culture, language (both written and verbal), customs and taboos, and very little history."

"What? Why?"

"Hugh reluctantly admitted the Skippy group that worked on this wasn't sure—he looked like the admission gave him constipation—but the Quinlans just don't seem to talk about it much, and what they do talk about seems to be heavily mythologized. The library they checked out had nothing in the way of objective historical records. So we're still in the dark about that. One more good reason for the expedition."

Bridget looked up from her copy of the report, which she was perusing on a tablet metaphor. "The Quinlans appear to be a species that evolved on the banks of rivers. Like river otters or beavers—"

"Both of which they resemble," I interjected.

"Yes. With a little bit of platypus thrown in," Bridget said with a smile. "But all their habitations are close to water, either the main rivers, tributaries, feeder rivers, or small lakes. All freshwater, too. I'm not sure how the megastructure maintains that. There must be filtering going on."

"There are impellers of some kind set periodically along the bottom of the river," Bill said. "That's an efficient way to keep current flowing along a billion-mile-long river that's actually level the whole way. They might also perform a filtering function, as well as turning over the water."

"We have some information on local flora and fauna, farming and animal husbandry, and so on," Bridget said. "Sociological stuff is almost nonexistent."

"I think the Skippies might have skimped on that aspect a little." I grinned. "Not very interesting."

"So it'll be a learning experience. That's fine." Bridget sat back and tossed her tablet on a side table. It bounced as if made of Nerf. "Now, about the androids..."

"Ah, yes, I think you'll be pleased." I vanished the report and popped up a schematic in the center of the group, then gestured to Bill to take the floor.

"Android tech has been improving steadily, thanks to its popularity. And a lot of feedback from you and Howard." Bill nodded to Bridget. "I think your current mannies back on Quilt might be a couple of generations behind the bleeding edge, though." A Quinlan form materialized beside the generic android schematic. "The latest mannies no longer contain any metal at all. Circuitry, even the SCUT interface, is all quantum-bionics and metamaterials. We've gone to great lengths to make the density of the internals similar to bio physique, so mannies are no longer ludicrously heavy for their size. And we've introduced a circulatory system that contains fluid indistinguishable from blood. It acts as lubricant, coolant, and transport for repair nanites. We even have digestive systems that will convert food into, uh, quite believable waste products."

"Just can't resist the potty jokes, can you?" Will grinned at him.

"You bet, number two."

Garfield, Will, and I laughed while Bridget rolled her eyes and shook her head. Still not very mature, nope.

"Now, we're maybe up to the beta version of a Quinlan manny," Bill continued. "Translator interface is still in development, and a lot of the reflexes are probably not realistic. Bridget, we'll need your help to refine that. Space is tight, because we are trying to build as much self-repair capability as possible into the units. If something goes wrong in-country, you won't be able to just take it into the shop for repairs."

Bridget nodded, her gaze glued to the schematic and supporting windows. "How is it with heat dissipation?"

"Ah, yeah. Not great, with the fur and the short, dumpy profile. A human manny can run full speed all day. A Quinlan manny will have to stop and cool down. Although in water they will probably be okay."

"Well, we are entering new territory, aren't we?" Bridget replied with a smile. "I think I'll talk to Marcus, though. He's probably the expert on non-humanoid mannies these days."

⚜ ⚜ ⚜

"Bob, I have a concern," Bridget said to me a few moments later. The others had already popped out and it seemed she'd been waiting to talk to me alone.

"Okay?"

"This expedition is looking like it could be a long-term thing…"

"Well, yeah, it's pretty much open-ended. We're not just doing research—we're also looking for Bender, or at least some indication of what happened to him."

"We have to stay with our mannies full-time, except when sleeping, right?"

"Yes, but you can pop out during the sleep cycle, or even just frame-jack for a moment to take care of something. I went years on Eden and never had a problem."

"But you don't have children. My kids are human. I have to deal with them in real time, and on a human schedule. Plus there was that movie, with the tall blue aliens..."

"*Avatar*?"

"That's it. Remember the main character left his avatar sleeping, and it almost got run over before he could get back to it?"

"Oh, yeah. Kind of a downside, I guess."

Bridget dropped her gaze, silent for a mil, then sighed. "I guess I have three choices. I can drop out, and I'd never forgive myself. I can simply bite the bullet and go into this full-time, and do short visits with Howard and the kids when the opportunity presents. Or I can..." She took on a pained expression. "Replicate."

"Whoa. A Bridget clone? You'd be the first non-Bob to do so."

The pained expression grew cloudier. "Well, I'm not particularly concerned about firsts. Not in that way, anyway. The thing is..." She hesitated again.

"Other Bobs?"

"Yes, especially the later ones. It feels sometimes that there's this expectation that I should replicate and be everyone's girlfriend. It doesn't work that way."

"I know, Bridge. And I'm sure the other replicants do as well, at least on an intellectual level. But they see you with Howard, and you know, the train of thought is hard to resist."

"But Howard is not just another Bob. He's unique, and our experiences together are unique."

"Yeah, I know, but Original Bob, for all his intelligence, was not all that emotionally self-aware. And the model hasn't improved over time." I cringed inwardly, thinking of some of the things I'd learned the hard way about myself, back on Eden.

"I get it. And I haven't actually been approached or anything. But if I do replicate myself for this expedition, it might be like the floodgates opening in terms of expectation."

"Understood. I'll help out any way I can, as will Bill and Garfield. But it's your decision. We'll accept whatever you decide, and we could probably get Will to take your place with minimal convincing. Although he might have an objection to a female manny, if you wait until we've already built the units."

"Well, there's a rumor—"

"Still unverified." I grinned at her. "And they'd have to be really late-generation. Original Bob had no uncertainties about his gender."

She laughed. "It would be pretty cool, though, to have another woman in here." Then she turned somber. "I'll think about it and let you know, Bob. Sorry for the headache."

⚜ ⚜ ⚜

I had never been to a moot quite this raucous. Officially, the subject under discussion was the Heaven's River expedition *comma* planning for. In reality, Starfleet had come to the moot loaded for bear. They consistently torpedoed any attempt at discussion with points of order and derails of various kinds. Bill showed a lot more patience than I thought a Bob was capable of. I was sure I'd have lost it by now.

They were actually wearing something that was close to but not quite *TNG* command uniforms. I guess they wanted to make the point without being out-and-out laughable. A lot of Bobs seemed to think they'd failed on that last bit, judging from the derisive comments.

At the moment, a red-uniformed "officer" was spouting off. "You don't know if they purposely decided on this life. That's the point. You're going in, you claim, to 'see if' they're captives, but you'll do the damage before you know if it's necessary. Assuming it's necessary."

Starfleet paused to take a breath—totally unnecessary in the Bobiverse, but a habit ingrained through thirty-one years as a human—and Bill took the opportunity to jump in. "And you're assuming prima facie that we'll be doing damage. Of course you are, because you consider interacting with them to be damage. Then you point to the interaction as proof of the damage. Circular argument. No Kewpie doll. Sorry."

"We have a responsibility—"

"Argument by assertion."

"…to keep from interfering in the affairs—"

"Prejudicial language, and you haven't proven the assertion yet."

Starfleet gave Bill a murderous glare, and another red-suited member took up the attack. "Look at your history. Deltans, Others, even humanity. Every time you interact, you cause damage—"

"Others? You're using the Others as an example?" Bill's expression of bristling disbelief was probably at least partly acting, but if there was ever a justification, this was it. "The Others weren't just sitting around minding their own business, you know. The *damage* they were doing—"

"There's always a rationalization, isn't there?"

I stopped listening. Sadly, it was like most political arguments. No one was willing to debate their base assumptions, or justify them, or compromise on them. The simple tactic being that if you repeated your assertion often enough, with enough emotion and volume, the opponents would somehow be forced to see things your way. Never worked, of course, at least it never had with

Original Bob, but that didn't stop people from trying. Even Bobs, apparently.

I scanned the audience idly while waiting for Starfleet to get tired of beating their collective head against a brick wall, and was surprised to see two unfamiliar faces. I tried to check metadata, but I was blocked, so I sent a low priority text to Bill. He responded during Starfleet's next tirade, evidently not listening any more than I was.

Couple of replicants, clients of Eternity Solutions. From Asgard.

That was interesting. The people who chose a replicant afterlife were buying into strata-title virtual reality systems—computer systems orbiting in the Oort in their local system—rather than setting themselves up with a spaceship. From what I understood, you could purchase different packages, which got you access to different levels of computer power, different VR options, and even access to mannies for physical interfacing in real. They had access to BobNet as well, as did anyone, but mostly they'd kept to themselves.

We had security policies set up, of course. They were guests in the computer sense of the word as well as the social sense. But Bill had an open-door policy regarding the moots. If anyone wanted to visit, or even play some baseball, that was fine.

The woman appeared bored; the man was trying to look in every direction at once, totally overwhelmed by the experience. It was obvious who had brought whom to the moot.

They weren't making any waves with the Bobs, either. Not like when Bridget or Henry first joined the moot. It must have become at least somewhat commonplace.

I brought my attention back to the argument when the currently speaking Starfleet rep abruptly made a cutting-off gesture and said, "Enough. This is pointless. I can see you're not going to do the right thing on your own. So be it." He nodded to his group, and as one, they winked out. The moot erupted into pandemonium. More than before, I mean.

"*That*," I said to Bill in a low voice, "was a veiled threat."

"Yeah, but what, exactly?" He frowned. "Well, maybe we can get this meeting done, now. And you and I will have to discuss this later."

⚜   ⚜   ⚜

Hugh was sending updates every twenty-four hours. For all that made the Skippies weird on paper, they were a lot more civilized and courteous than Starfleet, whom you'd think would be almost mainstream in the Bobiverse.

Language and customs were coming along, finally. We seemed to have crossed some kind of cusp, where blocks of disparate information began coalescing into a more complete picture. We could actually go in with what we had at this point, in an emergency. We'd just pretend to be from far away. And in Heaven's River, *far away* really meant something.

The Borg had finished their android design based on the complete report on biology and had given me an auto-factory blueprint for one generic native Quinlan, male or female, with editable parameters suitable for producing distinct individualized units. According to the notes, Quinlans differentiated each other primarily by facial shape and features, just like humans, plus some color variations in facial fur. The complete package included software and hardware support for generating unique faces. The notes also stressed that some field testing would be required before the design could be considered ready.

It was funny. For all the divergence of the Bobs, give them a problem to solve and the differences disappeared. I would be very sad when I met a clone that lacked that quality. *That* would no longer be Robert Johansson in any sense that mattered.

The exploration crew, including Will, was due for a meeting at 16:00 to go over our status. So I was a little surprised to get a ping from Bridget five minutes early. I invited her over and she popped in right away.

"Hi, Bridget." I gestured to her favorite chair, and she dropped into it, looking uncharacteristically unsure of herself.

"That thing we were talking about earlier?" she said, and waited for me to nod. "I'm not going to clone."

I waited for Bridget to continue, but it looked like she was waiting for me to comment. "Okay. You've discussed it with Howard?"

She nodded. "He's not happy, mostly because I'm not happy. I mean, he's happy I won't be cloning, but…"

"I know what you mean. I have to be honest, Bridge, I don't entirely understand why you and Henry are so much against replication. I mean, I've never been what you'd call a fan, but we *are* heading for ten thousand Bobs by now."

"Many of whom don't self-identify as Bob clones anymore." Bridget waved off my incipient reply. "I know, that's not relevant to your decision, but it *is* relevant to ours. Plus, your being a humanist helps—you don't see yourself as being any more or less Bob than Original Bob or any of your clones. For someone with, um, a more metaphysical view of life, it's not that simple. The best I can describe it is that I feel like each of us—myself and my clone—would end up with half a soul."

I opened my mouth to point out that technically, by her belief system, only Original Bridget had the soul, but realized in time that that would be the exact opposite of reassuring. Maybe I was finally learning when to keep my cakehole shut.

"And on a more personal basis," she continued, "the new Bridget would be cut off from Howard and from our children. I know I wouldn't be able to 'share' them with her, and Howard told me flat out that he'd be completely weirded out by the idea. I try to imagine myself waking up and realizing that *I'm* the copy, that I'll never again be with Howard and the kids—" Her lips quivered as she struggled to regain control. I waited quietly, giving her as much time as she needed.

Finally, she said, "I couldn't do that to myself. Or to other me. So I'm going to accept that I'll be working away from home for a while, and I'll make it up to them when I'm done."

"Okay, Bridget. Either way, it's good to have you on the team."

She flashed what Howard referred to as one of her nuclear smiles, and I felt my IQ drop. Fortunately, Bill and Garfield picked that moment to pop in.

"Hey, all. Got the latest from Hugh." Bill waved a bound report at us as he threw himself into his chair. Garfield settled in with a little more dignity. I summoned Jeeves, who brought in coffee, little sandwiches without crusts, and a perpetually full and fizzy glass of Coke for Will when he showed up.

Bill held up one of the sandwiches. "You've served these a couple of times now. I like them, but where did the idea come from?"

I grabbed a sandwich and scrutinized it. "Dunno. Random memory from Original Bob, I guess. I'll probably get tired of them eventually, but you can put a lot of different things in sandwiches."

Will popped in, waved, and flopped into his beanbag. "Okay, lady and germs. Let's do this."

Bill grinned at him and tossed the report into the air. It morphed into a video window, and Bill waggled a finger to pull up summaries and sub-windows. "Androids are coming along. It'll be a good six months yet before they're ready, assuming they pass all functional tests. We're working with a lot of new techniques here, so I don't want to rush anything."

Bill motioned to Garfield, who took up the thread. "The Gamers went through a ton of scenarios, but couldn't come up with anything tricky that would get four Quinlan-sized bodies through the airlock and past the Boojums. So they've suggested we just bore through the outer shell, then work our way into the elevator system internally."

"That seems risky. What if the Boojums notice?"

"Well, the Gamers suggested that the Boojums can't be too hair-trigger about the outer shell. After all, even with the amount of in-system cleanup they've done, there will still be a certain number of micrometeor impacts every year. If they came running each time there was a tremor, they'd be doing nothing else."

"Good point." I cocked my head. "Are we going to test it?"

"I figure we'll just pick a point between two airlocks and start digging. If they come running, we either run away or self-destruct, then come up with another plan."

Will grinned. "Well, it does have the virtue of simplicity."

"Yeah." I rubbed my eyes. "All right, let's give it a try. Gar, can you be in charge of implementation?"

"Sure thing."

"Next order of business," I said. "What do we do when we get in?"

"Damned if I know," Bill answered. "We have absolutely no indication that Bender is even in Heaven's River, let alone where he might be. This makes a needle in a haystack look like a sure thing."

"Except we don't really need to find Bender," Garfield interjected. Heads turned to him. "All we need to do is establish contact with whoever has him. Or failing that, with whoever runs the ship. Assuming they're not the same group. This isn't a blind search, it's more like detective work."

"True enough. We'll be working blind initially." I was silent for a moment as I went through the options. "As we learn more, we can narrow things down a little, maybe get more of a sense of direction. Metaphorically speaking."

There were nods around the circle as each person worked through the implications. This was the open-ended aspect of the project. We had no idea how long it might take to narrow things down, because we had very little idea what we were going to find.

"It's worth noting," Garfield said into the silence, "that there aren't that many Boojum airlocks. If you assume that Bender's matrix went in through one of them, it really narrows things down."

"True. There are, what, nine entrances?"

"Yes, and most of them appear to be inactive, which makes sense if they aren't doing anything beyond cleanup patrols."

"Could we send in multiple teams?" Bridget asked.

Bill shook his head. "We talked about that. More teams would mean more delay, and more likelihood of exposure. Once the topopolis controllers discover our existence, they'd likely institute some kind of large-scale search, and maybe take other defensive postures. Remember, we don't know that they'll be friendly. Our only contact with them so far has been them blowing up Bender, and then Bob's drones. I don't want to take a chance on how they might react to an invading force. Keep it small, don't look danger-ous." He grinned at us. "Having said that, if we run into a brick wall, there's always the option of sending more teams in. Bob can build some more matrixes locally and do some cloning, if bandwidth starts to become an issue. But the mannies take a lot of time to build. Very finicky design."

"The spy drones will continue to spread out, as well," Will added. "In both directions, upstream and downstream. If they find anything unusual, we'll be alerted, and we can make a beeline for that location."

We all exchanged looks. "I guess we're on track," I said. "Let's see how the tunneling works out, then we'll meet and discuss."

13. SWIMMING WITH THE FISH

Howard
December 2333
Big Top, Epsilon Eridani /
Poseidon, Eta Cassiopeiae

"Another beautiful day in Tantor." Hands behind my back, I gazed through the picture window at the layers of cloud outside the city dome. At our altitude in the atmosphere of the Jovian planet Big Top, I could see at least fifty miles of clouds above us, and anywhere up to a hundred downward, before the view faded into the mist.

"They renamed it Trantor after all your carping, Howard. You got your way. Stop being a sore winner." I could feel Bridget's glare boring holes in the back of my head. She was right, of course, but what was the point of being a curmudgeon if you couldn't curmudge?

I turned and walked over behind her. I kissed the back of her head, and she leaned into me. This gave me an opportunity to examine the image on the Canvas. "More new Quilt species?"

Bridget pointed to several items. "Sure looks like it. I can't figure out the mechanism, but Quilt biota can and often do spawn new species every few generations. I shelved this for five years, and I'm basically starting over from scratch." She swiped the Canvas with an irritated motion and the screen winked out of existence.

"If you go on this expedition with Bob, it could be another several years. You might never catch up." It wasn't quite an objection, but it wasn't supportive, either. I still hadn't decided if I was for or against Bridget going.

"I know, Howard, but Quilt will still be there. This is a once-only opportunity. Did you contact Marcus?"

"Yep. He's agreed to give us a tour. He'll be waiting at Moody Port. We should pop over in virt first to say hi."

"Then let's do this."

The manny closet opened at my mental command, and we stepped into our individual pods. As the pods started to close, I took a quick glance at Bridget. Her resting face showed she was more concerned than she let on. I knew this decision would be hard. I also knew she'd agree to do it. There were few people as driven as my wife.

I exited the manny and popped over to Marcus's VR. A moment later, Bridget appeared. Marcus, sitting by a fireplace, waved to a couch. Coffee and snacks sat on a coffee table within easy reach. Marcus was using the standard Bob library VR at the moment. Probably taking a rest from the *Battlestar* themes.

He waited until we were comfortable and properly snacked, then said, "So I understand your inquiry has to do with the business that Bob-1 is involved with, but I haven't really been following it. Mind filling me in?"

"We'll be going into the megastructure wearing mannies that mimic the native sophonts." Bridget shifted and leaned forward, gesturing with her hands. "That part isn't new. Bob-1 did it with the Deltans, and Howard and I have done it. We've even done non-humanoid mannies, as with the Big Top native species."

Bridget glanced sideways at me and I grinned. Flying around in the gas giant's atmosphere as humongous manta rays was one of our first adventures as a replicant couple, and we still did it occasionally for fun.

Bridget continued, "The natives are generally humanoid, but they're also aquatic. And they're intelligent, and come from a technological society, although we're not sure of their current level of knowledge. From that point of view, it's a bit of an unknown. We were hoping you could give us some perspective on aquatic mannies."

Marcus nodded and looked thoughtful for a fraction of a mil. "The Poseidon dolphins are intelligent animals, but as far as we can tell, they're animals. Just like Terran dolphins were. There's a simple language, but it's at the level of *danger, predator,* and *good food.* There's no symbology or grammatical structure. It's only slightly more advanced than baboon calls. So I'm not sure where I come in."

"You've been living among them almost full-time for a couple of years, though," Bridget replied. "How well are you accepted? How long did it take to fit in? And how hard is it to 'act like a dolphin'?"

"I get the impression they think I'm a little weird." Marcus shrugged and gave an embarrassed smile. "But I'm not shunned. I've had to fend off some mating advances, so I'm not *too* weird, ya know?"

"Hasn't stopped me," I interjected. Bridget made a low growling sound as Marcus laughed.

"I think it sounds like you're concerned about fitting in without issue. That just requires doing your homework first. As for the aquatic end of things…" Marcus shrugged. "Well, let's find out. I have a couple of spare dolphin mannies."

Marcus messaged us a couple of addresses, then popped out. I followed immediately, and found myself lying on my stomach on a platform, in a dark room. Wait, no, it wasn't a dark room, it was underwater. I rolled my eyes upward as I examined my action inventory, and saw that we were about ten feet below the surface, on the edge of what was probably one of the Poseidon plant mats. This would be Moody Port, formerly a major colony location on the West Indies mat. Nowadays, with everyone living in flying cities, it was strictly for agriculture and aquaculture.

To my left, two other dolphin mannies were moving around. A quick ping identified Bridget furthest left and Marcus to her right.

My heads-up help system indicated that the dolphins used a swim bladder to control buoyancy. I flexed and felt myself float up off the platform. A quick flick of the tail and I was sliding forward through the water.

Original Bob had never been much of a swimmer, preferring to keep water in bathtubs and, in extreme situations, hot tubs. But this was different—more like flying. The big difference seemed to be the complete lack of any concern about drowning. Of course, in a manny, breathing wasn't a problem anyway, but the Poseidon dolphins actually were fish, so they absorbed oxygen from the water using something like gills. Interestingly, they could also absorb oxygen from the air while floating at the surface, by pumping air slowly through their swim bladder. So holding one's breath would never be an issue. It was kind of a best-of-both-worlds thing. The resemblance to Earth dolphins was remarkable, though. The domed heads and beaked mouths could fool you into thinking you were dealing with Earth stock, until you spotted the vertical tail flukes.

Bridget shot past me, then glided to a gradual stop. She turned, and repeated her actions. Marcus bumped me, then spoke over the universal intercom. *"She's very methodical. Testing maneuvers one at a time."*

"You have no idea."

"Hey," Bridget said, *"I'm swimmin' here."*

"There's a pod that hangs around this area because of the spillover from some of the aquaculture. I figure we'll go join them for a while, and you can see what it's like to swim with the natives." Marcus swam off, clearly knowing where he was going. I glanced at Bridget, and we turned to follow.

Over the next few minutes, Marcus gradually increased his pace. I had a brief bit of trouble at one point, sort of like when you change from a jog to a sprint, and I couldn't get the new rhythm. But by letting go and allowing the autonomous systems to take over, I was able to correct. After that, I kept up with Marcus with no effort.

"We're going just about flat out for a dolphin," he said. *"We'll have to slow down before we get to the pod or they'll think we're running from something. We don't want to start a mobbing."*

"That's not part of the autonomous systems, though, right?" Bridget asked.

"Correct. There are some things you just have to learn through study," Marcus replied. *"How's your swimming?"*

"Fine, thanks. I feel a lot less concerned about that aspect of things. The manny systems seem to be highly competent at mimicking natural reflexes."

Marcus didn't reply, but he did an exuberant barrel roll. I did a barrel roll of my own, then found I'd overshot and had to complete a second one. Some things apparently did require practice.

Marcus slowed down and began taking a more circular path. Probably we were getting close to the pod, and he didn't want to charge straight at them. Even at a lower speed, I could see that being a challenge.

Within a minute, we slid up to a pod of the native version of dolphins. Fifteen individuals, including three juveniles, slowly swam through the water, nabbing small swimmers and scraps of plants or animals. They didn't appear to be very choosy. Presumably most things were edible in this world-ocean.

On the other hand, I used to own a dog that regularly ate dog poo, so who knew?

The adults in the pod turned and began circling us, more in a curious than aggressive manner, fortunately. They were making noises, and my translator rendered them as: "What?" "Who?" "Friends?" "Marcus friend." That last one was interesting. Apparently their proto-language included tags for individuals, which the translator converted to Marcus's name.

Marcus said, "Friends. Marcus friend." That appeared to be enough. The pod did one more circuit, then went back to feeding. One of the juveniles came over, briefly bumped Bridget, then went back to its, uh, *his* mother.

"*That was cute,*" I said.

"*Not so sure,*" Marcus replied. "*That one is approaching puberty. He might've been checking out your wife.*"

"*That's it. He's sushi.*"

Bridget laughed, did a quick barrel roll, then porpoised into the air. She came down with a splash. That seemed to trigger the entire group, and soon everyone was leaping and splashing.

The game lasted about ten minutes, after which we all floated on the surface for a short time, pumping air through our bladders. Then it was back to feeding.

"*Not a bad life,*" I said. "*Might get a little boring after a while.*"

"*The big predators mostly avoid the mats, Howard. We've made our feelings clear enough about their attempts to raid our farms,*" *and they've gotten the message. If you want excitement, swim about a mile farther away from the mat. Krakens don't know the difference between a real dolphin and a manny, and I can tell you from experience that getting eaten is not fun."*

"I'll give that a pass, thanks. There's a limit to what I'll do for research."

"I understand you have some kind of a training program going on?" Bridget said, changing the subject.

"More of a selective breeding thing. Dolphins that have more facility with communications and comprehension get a fish treat. Better-fed dolphins have more and healthier offspring. See where I'm going?"

"You're breeding them for intelligence."

Marcus did another barrel roll. *"Uplifting. By non-invasive means."*

I found myself simultaneously fascinated and a little shocked. *"Have you discussed this?"*

"Some. By and large, people don't see a problem. The dolphins aren't a threat or competition, and on balance I think it would benefit them. And let's face it, Howard, Poseidon citizenry doesn't have any tolerance for a central authority, given our history."

"No kidding." Marcus had been one of the key figures in the overthrow of the previous totalitarian government. What they had now was more like independent city-states. It seemed very *ancient Greece,* but it worked.

"Guys? The pod is acting funny."

Marcus and I turned at Bridget's comment. The dolphins had become completely quiet, and in fact were barely moving their tails enough to stay in place. They also appeared to all be looking down.

I rolled enough to be able to point an eye downward. Sliding slowly through the water below us was a leviathan. I remembered from my reading that they grew to about the size of a Boeing 747. This one seemed much bigger, but that might have just been me freaking out. "Didn't you say they stayed away from the mats?"

"On average," Marcus replied. *"This one seems to have developed some bad habits. I'll message Perimeter Security. Meanwhile, let's just emulate the dolphins and not attract its attention."*

"There's a plan."

Vaguely cuttlefish-shaped, the leviathan had four tentacles that it used to grab prey from below or above the water. They'd taken out a significant number of humans in the first year on Poseidon, before the colonists figured out how to keep them away.

Perhaps this one was just passing through. It didn't vary its heading or speed and was soon lost in the watery distance. The dolphins started to swim around once again, although they remained more subdued than previously.

"That was fun," Bridget said.

⚜   ⚜   ⚜

After another hour, Bridget announced she was satisfied. We squeaked goodbye to the pod and headed back to Moody Port. Docking the mannies took only moments, and then we were back in Marcus's VR.

"Did you get what you needed?" he asked.

"Yes, I think so," Bridget replied. "I've noted some things that are important to allow for in our research, but generally speaking, I don't think the physical aspects of being aquatic are going to be an issue. If we can adapt to being dolphins, we can adapt to being oversized beavers."

"Are you going to be working with the dolphins over the long term?" I said.

Marcus nodded. "I've kind of picked a vocation, I think. I've noticed that Bobs in general seem to eventually gravitate toward some kind of endeavor and then stick with it. Like the group trying to design and breed an intelligent airborne species on Newholme."

"Wow, I hadn't heard of that one." I grinned and shook my head. "Well, as long as someone doesn't get the idea of raising the elder gods or something."

"That would play hell with your humanism, wouldn't it?" Bridget stood. "Time to go. Thanks for your help, Marcus. Let's go, Lovecraft."

14. Council of War

Bob
April 2334
Virt

It was an even fuller house today. I had the leaders of the support team, as well as the expeditionary members. Bill, Will, Garfield, Bridget, Gandalf, Hugh, and Locutus all sat, according to individual preference, in La-Z-Boys, beanbag chairs, or wingbacks. I'd given in and expanded the library floor space. It was a bit jarring to see everything just that little bit farther away.

"Things are going well, relatively," I said. "No major hiccups at this point."

"Uh…" Locutus held up a hand.

I sighed. "Something happened since I talked to you this morning? Manny construction in trouble?"

"No, nothing that dramatic. Just something that occurred to me. We need to field-test the mannies, but there's no actual field where you are. If you get my drift."

"Oh, for God's sake," Garfield muttered.

I grinned at him. "Isn't it always the little things that bite you?" I scanned the group. "So, okay, the Steam-Borg have the mannies ready, but we have no way to test them in a realistic environment. In the past, we've always had a planet for testing. And if something went wrong, we could just do a fix and re-release. In this case, once the androids are in-country, we're stuck with them."

"We could use the Quinlan home planet," Garfield suggested.

"Absolutely not," Bridget replied. "We don't know everything that went into the destruction of the home world. Can we call it Quin?" We all nodded and she continued. "The Quinlans had some kind of conflict or multiple conflicts that ended up killing off everything on the planet. Nukes and orbital bombardment are obvious because they leave evidence, but what if they used biological warfare as well? Imagine us picking something up on the mannies and then transporting it to Heaven's River. By definition, it'd be virulent and hard to kill."

"Um. Good point." Garfield sat back, embarrassed.

"Still, we can't afford to *not* test the mannies," Bill said. "Look, it's not quite as good, but we can at least test the design. We send one or two mannies down to Quin, and just leave them there when we're done. It'll set our schedule back, having to fab a couple of replacements, but it'll be much faster with the second batch. And if we find an issue, we can fix all of them."

Locutus sat forward, showing enthusiasm. "We can send some maintenance equipment down with them, including a small printer, so we can perform any fixes on the planetside mannies as well. That way we're always testing the current version."

We all looked at each other, smiling. It was an excellent solution. And, as a bonus, it might settle some questions about Quinlan history.

"Good." I turned my attention to Gandalf. "Now, how about gaining entry?"

Gandalf blew out his cheeks. "Uh, good news and bad news."

"Great," Garfield grumbled.

"The good news is we have a plan. The bad news is it will carry some risks, not only of getting caught, but also of getting ground to a pulp."

"Even more great." Garfield sat back and crossed his arms, looking aggrieved.

"We can't activate the Spin Transfer system. That's the bottom line. There's no way to do that without alerting the powers that be. It's just too tightly bound to internal control systems."

"That's not terribly surprising," Bill said. "Do you have an alternative?"

"Yeah, but you're not going to like it."

"I already don't like it."

Gandalf flashed a quick smile. "The collection bins in our mining drones are just big enough to fit one Quinlan manny at a time—"

"No. No way!" Garfield interrupted. "You cannot be serious."

"Sorry, but yes. We'll ferry the mannies in the same way we ferried the spy drones in, except one at a time, like I said. Look at the bright side, you won't all be at risk at the same time. It decreases the chances of losing the entire expedition—"

"While increasing the chances of losing one member," Garfield interrupted. "I don't like it."

"No one does, Garfield, but we haven't come up with anything that isn't even riskier in one way or another. I assume that getting discovered by the topopolis administration is a nonstarter?" Nods around the coffee table confirmed the statement. "Then by definition, risk of equipment loss is less critical. So we examined a number of alternatives, and this is the least risky."

"What is the risk of damaging the topopolis itself if we screw up?" I asked.

"Negligible," Bill replied before Gandalf could. "You have to think of the relative masses. If you're jogging and you run into a mosquito, how much damage do you take?"

"I hate mosquitos."

"As do we all, even out to twentieth generation," Bill replied. "I doubt that'll ever change, as mosquitos have no redeeming features. But to my point, the drone and manny would get slapped onto the inner surface of the outer shell hard enough to leave a crater and not much else. That inner shell, though, is *tough*. It has to be."

"You've tested it?"

"We originally reconstructed the material from scans. There's some truly ingenious layering involved. It's about fifty percent stronger, pound for pound, than our hull material. And that stuff is *wicked* strong." Bill nodded emphatically to reinforce his statement.

"Huh. Okay." I thought for a moment. "Can we bring in a spare manny?"

"Expedition needs to be four," Bridget said. "That's the most typical number for young Quinlans going on a sabbatical."

"Yeah, I'm not clear on that part," Will said. "Sabbatical?"

"It's not the right English word, but it's the closest we can come. Young Quinlans, just around adulthood, often leave their home city, usually in a group of four called a *sabbat*, to see the world and possibly find a new place to settle. They might start a new town, or they might just join an existing one. My guess is that the behavior evolved to keep the gene pool diverse. It's generally mostly males that do this, although females are common enough that no one would be surprised if one of the group is female."

"So no one will be curious about a female alone with three males?"

Bridget smirked at Garfield. "Quinlan females are slightly larger than males and have the same teeth and claws, so unwelcome advances would not work out well. Anyway their mating is seasonal, so it isn't even a question most of the time."

"Got it. But what about having a fifth manny ready, just in case we trash one of the four?"

"Okay, Bob." Bridget shrugged. "As Howard always says, you can't be too paranoid."

"Fine. Now, Hugh. Language and culture?"

"We've made progress, but no real revelations. Our level of language comprehension is good enough to not be suspicious. There's regional variability, and we haven't catalogued a lot of the colloquialisms sufficiently yet, but thanks to the sabbatical thing, it will probably even out. So you'll probably always be able to understand the locals. There are some things we haven't been able to get a handle on. Maybe you'll find out more on your travels."

Gandalf was waving his hand.

"You had more?" I asked.

"Yes. We won't go in through the cargo bay. We're going to dig a tunnel."

"Yeah, it's been discussed. And it seems reasonable, given that mannies are bigger than spy drones. Why do you bring it up?"

"Well, we'll have to start now."

"Ah. So you'll need miners and roamers immediately."

"Yup."

I shook my head. "The TODO. It burns."

15. Functional Testing

Bob
May 2334
Quin

The cargo drone settled carefully onto the very dead lawn. Or lawn-like flora, anyway. Whatever the plant once was, it had been used by the Quinlans as a lawn-equivalent. I glanced sideways at Bridget's manny, an action made easy by the Quinlan form's very mobile and independently movable eyes. The resulting double-image was hard for human minds to handle, but I was figuring out how to pay attention to one eye and ignore the other. It was something the Quinlans did easily and routinely, so it would probably be noticeable if the people in our group never did it. Like a human who never moved his eyes but only swiveled his head.

Bridget turned and smiled at me as the cargo bay doors started to open. Actually, she performed a beak-rubbing motion, which was the Quinlan equivalent. As had been standard procedure since my days on Eden, the manny operating system converted human expressions into native equivalents so that we never had to worry about the actual action. Language was handled in a similar manner, so we spoke and heard English, including colloquialisms. The

O/S also chose English name equivalents for local proper names, and kept track of which substitutions were used.

The cargo doors finished opening, and we stepped out onto the surface of Quin. Bridget did a slow and probably unnecessary three-sixty, carefully examining the environment. "No obvious damage in this area. Any deaths here would have had to be from less obvious methods—radiation possibly, or biological. I don't know if there will be anything to dissect." She glanced at the drone hovering by her shoulder. Part scout, part beast of burden, part courier, it currently held her medical tools in its small hold.

The city, for city it was, had been built on the shore of a large, slow-flowing river. Instead of a maze of streets, the metropolis was crisscrossed by canals. The infrastructure had been set up so that the river flow turned over the contents of the canals, but with a mild current. That also meant that a design based on right angles would be suboptimal. The actual shape was more like slightly rounded diamonds, with the long axis along the direction of flow. Even if nothing else had been different, it would have made for a more elegant, less utilitarian design than the typical Earth city.

But in addition, the Quinlans seemed to enjoy embellishment for its own sake. Buildings were rarely just simple solid rectangles. We saw cantilevered terraces, elevated walkways between buildings, and even buildings with deliberately engineered gaps through their middles, like the dragon gates in some Hong Kong skyscrapers. Although I doubted feng shui was involved.

And the windows. Quinlans used both placement of windows and color tints to make the side of every building a piece of art. Like giant stained glass murals.

"These people loved their art," I said in a hushed voice.

"That they did."

We walked past one building, and I couldn't help but chuckle. The facade around the entrance had been sculpted into what might be some kind of fairy-tale scene. Unless they actually had a species of giant rodent with a mouth that big... I wasn't sure if I'd want to bring my children to see this montage. But then I reminded myself that people used to read Grimm's fairy tales to children.

We walked along a path that ran beside a canal. We could see half-submerged boats and barges in several places. It was likely that the Quinlans used rivers like humans used roads. I wondered idly what rush hour must have been like. Would they use transit? Or would it even be a concept if you could swim like an otter?

The buildings we passed were multistory, but not the high-rise monsters that many Earth cities contained. I didn't see anything over about six stories or so. Perhaps the Quinlans didn't like heights. Or maybe they just didn't see the point.

The most notable feature, though, was the amount of square footage set aside for green space. Every building had a terrace in front of it, and most canals had a treed path running along one side or the other. All brown and dead now. But it would have been beautiful before... just before.

We finally turned and headed back to the building on whose front lawn we'd landed. We had picked it deliberately, after an aerial survey, as the most likely place to find governmental stuff. It had a certain look of officialdom that seemed to transcend species barriers. A combination of pompous self-importance combined with lack of artistic touch or any kind of individuality, perhaps. Or I might be overthinking it.

Getting into the building wouldn't have been a problem in any case for android muscles or roamer plasma cutters, but fortunately the front doors weren't locked. We gazed around the large lobby and spotted a directory.

"Hmm, definitely governmental," I said, perusing the listing, while the heads-up popped up translations. Licenses, statistics, taxes, all the usual things that seemed to infest civilizations everywhere.

"I'm most interested in finding corpses. Emergency Management sounds like something that would be staffed right up until the end. Fourth floor."

Bridget pointed to a solid looking door near the elevators. We checked the door, and sure enough, it was locked.

"If this is a set of stairs," I said, "as it appears to be—oof!" The door bent and sprung off its hinges as we gave a concerted push in unison—android muscles, remember—to reveal stairs going up and down. "Yep. And locked at ground level, just as they would be on Earth. So we can assume a similar level of distrust in Quinlan society."

We proceeded up three flights of stairs, the rise and run looking odd to me but feeling perfectly natural when I went down on all fours. Like the Pav, Quinlans seemed to prefer to be on their hind legs but would go quadrupedal when travelling any distance. I couldn't shake the image of a fat river otter when watching the videos of them getting around.

We reached the fourth floor and walked down the hall, examining doors and information plaques. The manny O/S didn't automatically translate written information, but our in-vision heads-up display showed a pop-up translation when desired.

We soon found the offices of Emergency Management. The door wasn't locked. Presumably there had been traffic in and out right up until the end.

There was no working lighting, of course, but Quinlan eyes had a large effective range to allow for both above and below water operation. Our android eyes were even better and covered a larger portion of the visible and surrounding light spectrum.

"There," Bridget breathed, and made her way between the desks. A single dried husk of a corpse sat at a desk, head still cradled in its arms, as if the victim had simply fallen asleep at their desk and never woken up. I hoped it had been that peaceful.

Bridget gestured to the drone, which had kept up with us all this time. It floated down to desk level and the cargo door popped open. Bridget reached in and began removing items. "You going to watch?"

"I, uh, I have to do this other thing, over there," I said inanely, and retreated with my dignity in tatters. I'd seen my share of violence and death on Eden, but somehow the clinical, measured experience of an autopsy added a whole new level of *yuck*. The manny wouldn't throw up, but I still experienced the mental reaction of any human non–medical professional.

I heard Bridget begin to mutter to herself, no doubt dictating notes. As it happened, I could make myself useful in the meantime. I examined the office, trying for an anthropologist's viewpoint.

The desks were desk-like. How many ways are there to present a horizontal working surface? The chairs were more like backless bucket seats with a slot to accommodate the Quinlan butt and tail. Each desk sported something that had to be a phone system, including a handset. Physical buttons were absent—there was a black plate that had probably been a touch screen.

I started randomly opening drawers. Papers, writing implements, and desk accessories dominated. A couple of drawers contained what might be fossilized snacks. I turned off my olfactory sense, even though after all this time there was unlikely to be any residual odor.

It struck me that the interior of this building was surprisingly dry. I'd watched the TV series *Life After People* when I was still alive, and the show made the point again and again that things would fall apart quickly once people were gone. But everything here seemed to be in pretty good condition. Was that better construction? Or milder weather? Or perhaps a complete absence of bugs, molds, fungi, and so on? I couldn't use Mario's survey of the first Others' victim species he'd discovered for comparison, because the Others had taken the time to knock most structures down and procure the rebar and other metal components.

I tapped on one of the windows. It wasn't glass. Possibly transparent aluminum or something similar. But that would be one reason for the lack of deterioration. Popped and shattered glass windows were one of the first ways in for rampant nature.

I carried on with my wanderings as Bridget's voice continued to record her findings. It brought back my ongoing argument with Bill about how aliens would think and behave. Granted, an energy being or silicon entity would have a different outlook on life, but a land animal with the concept of individuality could only do things so many different ways. Desks were flat surfaces for working. Phones were devices for communicating with others at a distance. Doors separated spaces; lights lit spaces. People, or whatever, needed a place to eat and a place to eliminate waste.

I snickered. Maybe a race based on horses would have a different take on that last item. Or cows. I glanced down, looking for cow pies or the equivalent. Nope.

"*Bob? Done!*" came Bridget's call. I hurried back to where I'd left her, to find her packing up her equipment. On the desk was—I looked away quickly. Best not. I made a mental note to only peruse the text of her final report.

She saw my reaction and gave me a quick smile, as quickly gone. "There weren't any surprises in the autopsy. Our deep SUDDAR scans really did catch pretty much everything important about the Heaven's River inhabitants. I found the remains of a large viral load in the tissues, though. I've taken detailed scans and forwarded them to the Skippies. They tell me they can run a simulation if we get enough cellular and DNA detail. It'll tell us what we have."

"How long?"

"Day or two, they say."

"Great. Meanwhile, we've found a good place to park the cargo drone when no one is running these androids. Unless you have some more spots you want to check out?"

Bridget shook her head. "Nah, most of our surveys can be visual and SUDDAR. The Skippies are running drones in a search pattern of their own design. They intend to eventually map the entire planet's infrastructure in detail and put up a virtual globe."

"Huh. They think big."

"But it's all intellectual exercises. They are deliberately avoiding anything that involves contact with biologicals. Or even, to a lesser extent, Bobs. I had a talk with Hugh while we were agreeing on details for analyzing the results of this outing. He's a nice guy—not a jerk in any way—but kind of, I don't know, disinterested or distracted. As if we're keeping him from his video games but he's too polite to point it out."

I nodded and sighed. "Yeah, Bridge, you're not the first person to say that. We are living in an increasingly non-Bob universe."

A text came in from Bill. *You'll want to test the mannies in water as well.*

Ah. Fair enough. The envelope indicated it had gone to Bridget as well. She made a vague *out there* gesture. "Shall we take a dip in the canal?"

⚜ ⚜ ⚜

We looked down at the water. Given what I'd seen of the rest of the city, I was sure it would have been kept clean before. Now it had an oily surface sheen and far too much flotsam, although no actual trash. Still, it would do for testing, and it wasn't like we could actually catch something. I grinned at Bridget, called, "Last one in..." and dove into the water.

I heard a splash behind me. There was a flicker as nictitating membranes covered my eyes, adjusting for the different refractive index. My vision was surprisingly good, considering the state of the water.

And the freedom! The manny O/S took care of the movement and reflexes, and I found myself swimming like an otter, curling and undulating through the water. A shape shot past me and slapped me on the head. I realized that Bridget had just laid down a challenge.

I accelerated after her, and she did a right-angle turn, heading straight down. She whipped around a submerged boat and pulled an abrupt reverse, speeding by me in the opposite direction.

Nice try, but no cigar. I just barely caught her tail with my front paw, but it was enough for *tag*. She turned and took up the chase.

We surfaced several times for air, even though the mannies didn't really need it. The androids were designed to mimic the real thing, and that included an internal calculator to track when we *should* be running out of oxygen. We could ignore it, but in Quinlan company that would likely attract unwelcome attention.

Finally, Bridget shot out of the water and landed on her feet several yards from the edge of the canal, in a perfect penguin exit. I followed, staggering slightly as I landed.

"Bob *doesn't quite* stick the landing," she exclaimed. "The judges deduct half a point!"

"Half a point? I was robbed!" I responded, laughing.

We both sat down at the same time, curling ourselves on the dead non-grass.

"That was awesome," Bridget said. "It's almost like flying. Better, in some ways. And I know flying!"

"True. You've done enough of it. I think you hold the record for most species emulated, don't you?"

She smiled at me. "I think Howard might actually have me by a couple. I'll have to check. But anyway, this will be my first aquatic effort. Serious long-term one, I mean. The test with the dolphins on Poseidon was a, uh…"

She glared at me, knowing what was coming, and I said, deadpan, "Dry run."

"I so hate that I see those coming now." She started to lick her fur, then stopped with a jerk. "Oh, God. That's gross."

"Part of the Quinlan persona, Bridget," I said, resisting the urge to groom myself as well. "Maybe we'll turn that off for now and just let the maintenance roamers clean us off."

"Works for me." She glanced up as the cargo drone descended from the sky. It settled to the ground and we climbed in.

I placed myself on the rack beside her. "Okay, then. Let's park this baby and go home."

⚜   ⚜   ⚜

Bill flipped through the video window. "Looks pretty good. Couple of glitchy items, but those are all software. I'd say the androids are good to go." He tapped the window. "Only one other concern, and that's how the androids will handle vacuum. The new circulatory system might be subject to boiling under low pressure. Or worse, rupture."

"No prob," Bridget said. "Simple to test. Take one upstairs and open the cargo door. Contamination isn't an issue in that scenario."

"Good enough." Bill turned to Garfield. "Can you take care of that?"

"Yessss, master."

Bill snorted. "We can call in some Skippy help, if you prefer. Or your Gamer buddies."

"Nah, it's okay. Gives me a chance to use the android anyway."

"On that subject," Bridget interjected. "Will, if you want to practice using the androids on Quin, there's lots of planet to explore, and I'm sure lots to learn yet."

Will visibly brightened. "Hey, great idea. I can do that!"

"And go for a swim. It's unbelievable!" I added.

"Are we good on the sociology front?" Bridget asked.

"The Skippies say they've extracted as much as they can from the current dataset. They're spreading out as the spy drones move farther afield, but diminishing returns is probably rearing its ugly head. There's not much more to learn from simple observation." Bill closed the window. "The Gamers have the entrance tunnel all dug, and they've widened the hatch from the foyer to accommodate the mannies. There's no indication that we've been detected so far."

"Think about it," Will said. "A billion miles of megastructure. How many cameras would you have to be monitoring to cover everything? And they've got mechanical sensors on equipment to detect most issues, so why bother? As long as we don't break something, or turn something on, we're golden."

"Don't break something." I smiled. "An excellent motto for any age."

"Do we have anything else outstanding, besides Garfield's vacuum test?"

"Not really, Will. As soon as that's done, we're ready to start building the production models. Anyone want to make a speech?"

"We hate speeches," said Garfield.

"Well, okay, then."

16. HUMAN REPLICANT RESERVE

Will
May 2334
Virt, Vulcan Post-Life Arcology

I was outside the virtual door of one Professor Steven Gilligan, a former department chair at the University of Landing on Vulcan with a list of letters after his name that could choke a horse. Professor Gilligan had been an expert in many things when he was alive, but of most importance to myself and Bob was that he specialized in artificial environments.

Of even more interest to me personally was the fact that he continued to lecture at the university, although as a guest lecturer these days. And he did so in a manny custom-made for him. So it wasn't just us Bobs anymore.

I'd done some research at Bob's request, and the professor's name came up a lot. I had finally received an invitation to visit, at the Vulcan Post-Life Arcology. The Arcology was physically located in a large space station orbiting Omicron2 Eridani just inside the Oort cloud. It currently had a membership of about two hundred, mostly rich and famous people who hadn't felt like waiting for medicine to catch up with them.

I found myself unexpectedly unsettled. I'd been living in real, in a manny, for so long that virt had become a foreign experience. At the same time, I'd been away from human society for so long that I was noticeably behind the times. I resolved to give the situation a good think when I had some time.

The door opened and Professor Gilligan beamed at me. He was short, balding, and slight of build—which surprised me, since in virt he could look like anything he wanted.

"Ah, Mr. Riker. Or is it Johansson? Come in, please."

I replied with a small laugh. "I run into that a lot, professor. As the only Bob to take a last name as my moniker, I kind of broke the conventions. These days I answer to either, or just Will."

"And you can call me Steven. Please, have a seat." He waved to his living room area, which featured a large picture window in which floated the image of a ring-shaped habitat. As with most personal VRs, the setting was comfortable and spacious, but not ostentatious. Fancy layouts and gilding lost their impact when they were free but for the wave of a hand.

I motioned to the view as I sat. "Ringworld?"

"That is a Bishop Ring, actually. This image is intended to be two thousand miles in diameter and a hundred miles across. More than six hundred thousand square miles of prime real estate."

"Still theoretical, though."

Steven replied with a shrug. "Of course. Technically it's just an engineering problem, but the real roadblocks have always been economic and political. When you're settling a new system, you have to choose to either sit in your ship for however many decades it takes to build the megastructure, or choose to populate the habitable planet essentially immediately. The latter option always wins."

"And it's not really *just* an engineering problem, is it?" I said.

"It is in that we have all the technology required to build one. Just not the *knowledge*. For instance, no one has ever been able to keep a closed ecology going for more than a year, at least on research scales."

"And having your ecosystem collapse on a megastructure would be"—I grinned at him—"suboptimal."

Steven laughed. "Keeping an ecosystem going would not be a trivial task. You can't have actual bedrock, or a water table, or even very deep soil, at least not without major engineering challenges. So you'd have to pump water up to stream heads, and you'd have to be constantly transporting topsoil uphill to replace whatever gets washed downstream. Trees would have to be shallow-rooted. Burrowing and cave-dwelling animals would be at a disadvantage. It's essentially like a zoo enclosure—designed to look natural, but carefully engineered nonetheless."

"What if it's big enough to have weather?" I asked. "Wouldn't that work as well, at least for the water supply issue?"

He nodded slowly. "Yes, although that scenario would increase the runoff issue. As I said, Will, it's all theoretical. With study and experimentation, we could come up with compromises that would provide the best balance of weight savings and ecological robustness. That's what I mean by not having the actual knowledge."

I took a moment to admire the Bishop Ring. "Still, it would open up virtually every stellar system with a reasonably well-behaved star. No one *at all* has expressed any interest in building one?"

"Not to my knowledge, Will. It's been somewhat a slap in the face for me," he replied with a chuckle. "As I said, the problem is all the political and economic commitments that would have to be made. Humans have very rarely been able to come together to build anything on this scale, at least since the days of the pyramids."

I shifted in my seat. "Which brings me to the reason for my visit. You've drawn up plans for any number of mega-structures over the years, both as serious proposals and as study material for your courses. Have you ever done a topopolis?"

"Yes, certainly. As a megastructure, it has a lot going for it. Effectively infinite land area by simply adding more length; no increase in structural or material strength requirements no matter how long you make it; no need for inhabitants to ever go outside; and if built with sufficient diameter, no Coriolis force to speak of. And it can be added to at any time, if the initial design is done properly."

"Really? You'd cut open the loop? How would you keep the air from escaping?"

"First, Will, you don't need to have a closed loop. There's really no physical reason why you couldn't leave the ends unconnected. It wouldn't have a stable orbit anyway, so in either scenario you'd need some method of orbital adjust-ment. And you'd build it in segments of some length, with some kind of barrier at the end of each segment. The bar-rier wouldn't even have to go right to the center, as long as the segments were already rotating. Spillover would be trivial."

I nodded slowly. Without knowing anything about Heaven's River, Steven had described it with amazing accu-racy. "Good. Steven, I wonder if I could ask you to look at some scans and comment?"

His eyebrows went up; I hadn't given a lot of detail about the purpose of the meeting, except to say that I wanted to talk about megastructures. He accepted the files as I offered them and converted them to paper idioms, then started flipping through the stack. He muttered a few sentences, then his eyes grew rounder and wider and he went silent. Several times he flipped back to earlier pages. Finally he converted the idiom to a 3D image. Hanging between us was a four-segment-long stretch of Heaven's River.

"Oh my God. Someone built one? Who?"

"They aren't human, Steven. We're still learning about them. Here." I flipped up an image of a Quinlan, hanging in space beside the engineering segment.

"Have you talked to them?"

"Not openly, no. They have a disturbing tendency to shoot first. We're trying to figure things out without exposing ourselves."

"Not the Others all over again, though?"

"No, nothing like that. Just ground-level belligerence, I think."

He nodded and leaned forward to inspect the segment. "So what would you like to know?"

"Limitations. What they can and can't do. How they're likely to lay it out. Infrastructure. We're looking for someone in the structure, and any info that could narrow things down would be helpful."

Steven glanced at me, then poked at the image. "Well, I see a transportation system right there. Vacuum monorail or something similar. That would be your long-distance travel option. I love the river concept. Artificial current, of course, since there's no downhill along the length. I suppose you could raise one end of the river in each segment and pump the water upward, but then you have issues of topography.

Even a one-tenth percent grade for this implementation would mean a half-mile elevation at the headwaters. And moving all that mass up and down would create issues of angular momentum." He paused, then pointed. "The hollow mountains every five hundred miles or so would be where your maintenance and infrastructure would be—"

"Wait, hollow mountains?" I peered more closely at the image. It wasn't obvious from the visual, but it appeared the interior of the mountains was actually void space.

"Of course, Will. You wouldn't want mountains of real rock. The mass would place a lot of strain on that segment of the topopolis, and to no purpose. Instead you build a hollow shell which, being closer to the axis, exhibits less centrifugal weight than average. Then you put all your infrastructure that you don't want people to have to look at inside the hollow. Like a theme park, all the mechanicals are hidden."

"Oh, for crying—" I zoomed in on the image. At the upper limit of magnification, there was the barest hint of detail under the mountains. "And an entrance ...?"

"No way to predict how that would be designed, but I'm sure now that you know where to look, you can locate one."

Interesting. Something to check out if we could get a scanning drone into position. I sat back and made a gesture for him to continue.

Steven examined the hologram in silence for several more mils, then pointed at one of the impellers under a river segment. "I don't think you've correctly characterized the river system, Will. This isn't one river, it's four. Alternately going in opposite directions. The tributaries and feeders allow the rivers to exchange contents, but if you check the impeller configurations, there are two main flow directions. And note how, at the segment boundaries, the rivers coalesce into four straits running through the mountain barriers. Two in each direction."

I examined the hologram in silence. Steven appeared to be correct. We'd completely missed the fact that the impellers were pointing in two opposite directions. "I guess it makes sense. There's no logical reason to give one direction priority over the other. This way, you can go downstream in either direction by just switching river systems."

Steven examined the hologram for several more full seconds, then pointed to the radiators on the dark side of the strand. "Heat dispersal is, of course, a problem. The topopolis by its nature is a mostly closed system, and the artificial sun simply dumps more heat into the habitat. They've designed things to extract heat through an exchange system with the outer shell that actually generates electricity from the gradient—brilliant. Then it's transferred to the cooling fins on the outer shell to be radiated into space. I imagine the heat signature would be significant."

"Significant enough to be seen from light-years away," I said, smiling. Steven was hitting it out of the park.

He continued to examine the document, but appeared to have extracted all the revelations he could. He finally sighed, sat back, and gestured at the image. "Can I get a copy of this? Could I use it in my lectures?"

"I don't see why not. It's not a secret. Although there's some controversy in the Bobiverse about whether we should even be getting involved."

Steven snorted. "You'd think being dead would free you from the dictates of politics. But apparently it's even more inevitable than death or taxes. Do you know that I endure protests regularly?"

My eyebrows went up in surprise. "Protests? At the university?"

"Yes. There is some sentiment that I shouldn't be taking up a position that could be filled by a living human being."

"Unbelievable." I shook my head. "And the university's position?"

"They take the stance that they will consider replacing me when a replacement candidate is found with my qualifications."

"Eminently logical. Probably drives the protestors crazy."

Steven smiled. "Which is why I am so hopeful that your brother Howard's human/android interface project will show some early success."

"I—what?" Apparently, Howard had his fingers in more pies than I knew. "I'm visiting him after I leave here. I'll certainly ask him about that." I shifted forward in my chair. "Thank you very much, Professor Gilligan. You've been a great help."

Steven waved off the compliment. "It is my job, after all. But you don't have to leave just yet, do you? I'd love to learn more about the Bobiverse, as you call it."

"Not at all. What would you like to know?" I wasn't in a big hurry, and a little quid pro quo wasn't unreasonable.

⚜   ⚜   ⚜

The conversation with Professor Gilligan had been fascinating, and he had extracted a promise from me to keep him updated, and possibly even invite him into the group. I would have to discuss that with the others, but the professor had a large knowledge set and, in my opinion, would be an asset.

Meanwhile, Howard was next on my list. I wanted to talk with one of the other Bobs about some personal issues, and Howard seemed like the best idea, since he lived in human society full-time. The conversation with Professor Gilligan just added more fuel. I pinged Howard and received an invitation and a manny address.

I entered the manny, and in seconds I was stepping out of the pod in Howard and Bridget's apartment. Bridget waved at me from her seat and went back to what she was doing. She appeared to be working on a computer, but the monitor was virtual, floating in the air in front of her. Parts of the image were typical 2D info, but other parts were 3D, and appeared to pop out from the image. It was not only holographic, but also touch-sensitive. I checked my libraries and realized this was a breed of computer called a Canvas. Quite neat. Almost as good as the metaphors we used in virt.

"Hey, Will," Howard said, motioning me to the couch. "What's cooking?"

I sat, glanced down at my hands, and realized I was in a generic manny. I wasn't sure why, but I'd been expecting to find myself in a Bob model. I held up my hands. "Uh..."

"Sorry, bud. If you wanted a Bob manny you'd have to pick one up from the public storage pods. We've got a couple—"

"Public storage pods?"

"Generic and custom mannies, stored for individuals and organizations according to need, or available for rental. Just like vehicles. We—by which I mean the Bobiverse—maintain a couple of Bob mannies in all major cities in human space. The monthly storage cost is trivial."

"Paid in what?" I said, then held up my hand before Howard could answer. "Sorry, I came to ask you a couple of questions, and the questions are multiplying faster than I can even articulate them. I've been pretty much sidelined on Valhalla for a couple of decades now, Howard, and I feel like a hermit who has just hiked back down to civilization to discover cell phones."

Howard grinned at my discomfiture. Even Bridget smiled briefly without turning around. Listening with at least one ear, apparently.

"Okay, well, to answer the last question first, *pams*. They're a unit of currency that has been adopted across human space. Stands for *printer/autofactory minutes*. Basically, it's the value of one minute of autofactory time."

"But that's ridiculous. You can just print more autofactories, and you'll have—"

"More available autofactory minutes, but with reduced value due to inflation. Like a government back on Earth printing more currency. In fact, very much the same type of feedback systems. An economist from the 21st century would get it right away. The threat of reducing the value of a *pam* demotivates companies from making too many autofactories."

I waved it away. "Okay, it makes sense, I guess. But I wanted to ask about something Professor Gilligan said—something about baseline humans being able to wear a manny? He said the research was being done here. By you."

"Not quite true. I'm"—Howard glanced at Bridget—"*we* are financing it. It would avoid another situation like the Prometheus expedition ..." Howard was silent for a moment, and I nodded in sympathy. The deaths had been hard on Howard and Bridget. "... as well as forestall some of the anti-manny sentiment going around these days."

"Steven said something about that. University protests?"

Howard snorted. "Wow, you really have been out of it. Your professor friend lectures at the Vulcan university using a manny. There have been pretty regular protests against his presence. The gist seems to be that he's dead and shouldn't be taking up a spot that could be available for someone still living. That's the most common complaint, but by no means the only one. Even just wandering around in a manny, you might find yourself being picketed."

I put my head in my hand. "Oh, for chrissake. And how widespread is this?"

"Pretty localized right now, Will. But we're of the opinion that it'll just get worse as more replicants start using mannies. I'm hoping that if we can make the mannies usable by humans, then it's no longer an 'us versus them' situation."

"Unbelievable." I shook my head. "I always thought your experience with Bridget's daughter Rosie was just an aberration—an isolated incident. Not so much, maybe."

"'Fraid not. It's the standard 'other' prejudice. We're immortal, stronger, faster, don't get tired, and are generally just more capable than a bio. No surprise there's concern about being displaced." Howard paused and appeared uncomfortable for a moment, then deliberately continued in a lighter tone. "Anyway, it's nowhere near ready for prime time, but the process works, at least in the lab. We use focused magnetic stimulation to, first, activate the brain regions that cause paralysis during sleep and, second, stimulate sensory regions with input from the manny and at the same time pick up intentional muscle cues."

"So it's like the subject is dreaming, but they're awake, and everything is rerouted to the manny."

"Exactly. All you need is a headset."

"And it would be like that Bruce Willis movie, *Surrogates*."

"Well, eventually. As I said, we haven't worked all the bugs out."

I nodded, impressed. "Jeez, Howard, you're turning into a real mogul."

Howard grinned. "You know what moguls are, right?"

"Uh..."

"The buried bodies of forty-something men who took up snowboarding."

I laughed, then stopped abruptly. "Wait, you haven't—"

"Yes," Bridget said from her computer. "He has. We have a place up in New Fairbanks. He's totalled four mannies already, trying to master the terrain park."

Howard and I grinned at each other without comment. Definitely not mature.

17. First Day in Heaven's River

Bob
June 2334
Heaven's River

Five furred mannies packed into a full-sized drone's cargo bay, breathing vacuum. Bill, Garfield, Bridget and I formed the primary expedition group, and Will was running the backup manny. Once we made it into the interior of Heaven's River, we would hide the extra manny in case of future need. We hoped we wouldn't lose anyone in the operation and find ourselves needing the spare. If we lost two, we would probably abort and re-evaluate our entry strategy.

The cargo door stood open, giving us a view of a solid wall of, well, something. Even with my eyes cranked up to full photomultiplier setting, I couldn't make out detail. It could be concrete or smooth rock. It might even have color. Direct center on the framed view was an even darker circle, which I knew led through a hundred yards of tunnel to the gap between the inner and outer shells.

We couldn't activate any lights, of course. The cargo drone had the usual ice core to keep its heat signature down, but having the cargo bay open was doubtless interfering with that tactic. At the levels of sensitivity that such things operated under, even the small amount of infrared radiating from the dark side of the topopolis strand would be adding to our heat load. Our mannies weren't heat sunk either, so we glowed like miniature stars in infrared. We had to make the traverse to the entry tunnel as quickly as possible. While it was unlikely that any Boojum would pick that exact moment to do a sweep, we were all firm believers in the power of Murphy.

"Moving into position," Gandalf said over the intercom. *"Bob, you jump when I say. Everyone else, follow at three-second intervals. Roamers will catch you if you screw the pooch. Don't do that."*

I winked at Garfield, who was second in line. I wasn't sure how the autonomous systems translated that, but he smiled back. Or the Quinlan equivalent.

"Now."

I crouched, aimed, and launched. The Quinlan form wasn't particularly what you'd call a leaping-friendly physique, but the O/S adapted without effort. I sailed the short distance to the hole in the wall and caught the edge. I had three seconds to get out of Garfield's way, so I scrambled into the darkness.

I felt the slight vibration as Garfield landed behind me. Very tiny, dim LED lamps lit the path forward. I didn't have any physical experience with zero-G movement, but the underwater reflexes of the manny seemed to translate well. I was able to move down the tunnel with only the occasional touch to correct my course.

The tunnel was a tight fit. The Gamers had done the minimum amount of cutting required to get us through. Good strategy—the less we disturbed the regolith, the better. Fortunately they'd allowed room for Quinlan plus backpack. Quinlans didn't go in for clothes, except some ceremonial decorations, but the most common fashion accessory by far was a backpack. Lots of pockets, and given the Quinlans' preferred method of getting around, the backpacks were designed to be waterproof and watertight when closed. We had designed ours to look as nondescript as possible, and *used*, so we wouldn't look like we'd just walked out of a sporting-goods store.

We each had a standard kit consisting of common Quinlan items like dried snacks, a comb, some first-aid supplies, and a claw-file. But the most important item, and one we anticipated actually needing, was a good supply of the local money. All strictly mundane from a Quinlan point of view.

"*Everyone's in,*" Gandalf reported. "*Good luck.*"

We would be in constant contact through SCUT, but from this point on there would be no possibility of any physical intervention. We were truly on our own. If one of us "died," they were off the team, at least until they could catch up to the rest of us in the spare.

Will could substitute if one of us couldn't be available to run their manny at any point. For that reason, he had to monitor the party's progress so that he was always up to date on current events, but it would only take a few seconds once a day to review logs.

I came out of the tunnel and grabbed a convenient anchor cable that the Gamers had laid for us, alongside more of the low-power lights. I moved a few yards along to make room for the others, then looked up. And froze in place.

Heaven's River consisted of a stationary outer shell made of regolith interwoven with structural members and some kind of 3D carbon-fiber mesh, and a rotating inner shell made of a combination of metal and ceramics forming some kind of metamaterial, reinforced with the same carbon mesh. What I hadn't realized, or maybe hadn't paid attention to before, was the fact that the space between the two shells was only about ten yards. Since the structure was fifty-six miles in radius, the curve of either shell wasn't discernible from my vantage point. But I could tell which way was which because the inner shell was rotating.

At over a half a mile per second.

From my point of view, I was standing about ten yards from a surface moving at about nineteen hundred and fifty miles per hour. Telling myself this was an illusion didn't help. And it didn't matter how smooth that surface was; if I came into contact with it, it would be like leaning against a giant grinding wheel. Not to mention that I'd get kicked into a spin that would probably rip my limbs off. And my part in the expedition would be over before it even started.

I unlocked my gaze and said to the others, "*Be really, really careful coming out of the tunnel. Seriously.*"

In another minute, we were all gathered on the inner surface of the outer shell, collectively holding on to the anchor cable. Each person spent a few solid seconds staring at the spectacle. I didn't hurry them. It was important for the point to sink in.

"*Moving along now.*" Matching action to words, I began moving along the surface, being very careful to keep my grip on the rope and my feet on the ground. I knew for a fact I couldn't actually hear the shell rotating above my head or feel its vibrations. If there had been any vibration strong enough to be transmitted through the bearings, the whole thing would have already ripped itself apart. Still, my mind inserted a bass hum into the silence.

The tunnel, by necessity, couldn't be too close to the Boojum entry bay or someone would inevitably spot activity. And we'd had to be extremely careful about cleaning up after ourselves during excavation. The Heaven's River maintenance ecosystem included scavengers that patrolled the space between the shells, looking for detritus. So we had a significant hike from the tunnel to the elevator assembly. Most of the mechanism was sunk into the outer shell—the inner shell was still only thirty feet away, but a rail system just ahead of us would accelerate a container to mate with the inner shell when going in, or decelerate the container to mate with the outer shell when coming out.

Over the months since our first venture using drones, the Gamers had continued to analyze the circuitry that controlled the rail system. Things that could be bypassed had been identified, things that could be replaced with our components had been reverse-engineered. Unfortunately, at the end of the exercise, we couldn't be confident that activating the elevator wouldn't set off alarms somewhere. So we were still going to have to ride to the inner shell, one at a time, in a small mining drone.

The Gamers had brought in two of the drones to dig down into the regolith in order to get at the rail system. Now they would be used to fly in the expedition members. As mentioned, if we lost two mannies, we were hooped.

We worked our way down the trench, still holding onto the rope. At the end was a complex set of structural girders, with what had to be magnetic bearings along the working rails. With the amount of study and brainstorming we'd done, the structure was as familiar as the inside of my own Heaven vessel.

"Another vulnerable point, people," Gandalf said. "You have to go one at a time. While it is extremely unlikely that the elevator system will be activated, if it does, we'll almost certainly lose some-one. Even if you don't get run over by a rampaging elevator, just having the elevator's maglev bearings active will probably trash the drone. So let's keep our flippers crossed."

"Oh, ha ha," Bridget replied. "They aren't flippers."

Of course the biologist would get all uppity about that.

We kept to the same order, so I was first through the mechanism. There wasn't much to it. Climb in, let the hatch close, try to avoid claustrophobia (it made a closet feel spacious), wait for the drone to fly to the elevator terminal, and rinse, repeat.

The flight was harrowing, because I felt like nothing more than a sack of potatoes. If something went south, I'd be metal filings before I even realized it. The drone had to fly a carefully calculated semicircular path with a radius of fifty-six miles, with no deviation of more than a couple of feet, while accelerating from zero to nineteen hundred and fifty miles per hour. Piece of cake.

About two minutes in, there was a clang, and I yelled "Fuck!" No one heard me, of course, because I was in a vacuum. And in space, no one can hear you curse. Rolling my eyes at my own irrelevant commentary, I asked, "What the hell was that? Am I dead?"

"Sorry, Bob," Gandalf replied. "Slight miscalculation. You glanced off one of the support struts. The drone will need its paint touched up."

"And its cargo area hosed out," I muttered to myself.

After several eternities, the cargo door opened, and I stepped out onto the same maintenance platform that I'd previously visited through the spy drones.

"I'm here," I announced, probably unnecessarily. The drone had already lifted off and was heading back to pick up its next passenger. There wasn't enough room in the rail system to fly both drones, one coming and one going, so this would be a long, slow operation. Kind of a combination terror/boredom thing, both at the same time.

We had to use the manual airlock systems, so the air cycling took a long time. Once through the airlock, I found myself in the same long corridor, with the same exhortations for idiots. I sat the manny down and started checking my logs.

After about two hours, everyone was through. Terror *slash* boredom. I signaled silently, and we moved to the end of the corridor.

"*Gandalf, any particular instructions?*" He would be monitoring our video and audio feeds, so he knew where we were.

"*No,*" he replied. "*There are no alarm switches on the emergency staircase. Still don't know about the elevators. Of course, you can always volunteer to test it…*"

On the one hand, the stairs would probably be a better idea. On the other hand, they'd flown a spy drone up the stairwell, and it was twenty stories to the top. That sounded suspiciously like exercise.

But getting caught at this stage would not only be a huge setback, it would be embarrassing as hell. With a heavy sigh, I headed for the stairs.

Ten minutes later, we reached the top. I cracked open the stairway door and peered out. No guards, drones, or orcs. We slipped through the stairwell door and paused as one to take in the view.

The foyer was huge, and the front façade was impressive. This whole building had been designed with the idea in mind that many, many Quinlans would be coming and going. It wasn't quite Grand Central Station, but it was definitely a full-on transit hub. The ceiling was high, the floor was some kind of faux marble, there was art on the walls, and there were sculptures. I couldn't see anything out-and-out abstract, but the Quinlans definitely applied spin to their literalist tendencies. The paintings tended toward an Escher or Dali kind of surrealism. The sculptures reminded me more than anything else of West Coast native art—basic shapes, intricately decorated.

One thing was sure—this was no phlegmatic, stolid culture.

I noticed one additional detail. The station featured a roll-up door at the front, originally meant to allow the maximum space for entry. It appeared management wasn't just depending on electronic alerts to keep the natives out. The door mechanism had been welded into immobility. No one would be opening that door, or even repairing it. It would need to be cut out and replaced.

I pulled up my map, and the heads-up pointed me to a corner of the entrance hall, via a path that would keep me out of view of any cameras. Garfield was already on his way there, having had enough of art.

The drones had cut a small hole in a wall panel, down near floor level on the inside. It was below grade on the outside, though, so some tunneling had been required. The Gamers had bolted on a hatch, presumably so that wildlife wouldn't start making itself at home.

Garfield opened the hatch and looked through, then motioned to me. I peered into the gloom on the other side and realized I was looking at an earthen tunnel. We would basically have to crawl out on hands and—oh, wait, Quinlans were quite comfortable on all fours. Well, score one for us.

Still, we'd be working our way up a trench on the outside to get to ground level. I wondered if it would be worthwhile to ask why, but I figured it was more about keeping our comings and goings as invisible as possible. Opening and closing an obviously bolted-on door in plain sight would attract all kinds of attention, none of it the good kind. Assuming there was a good kind.

I couldn't help feeling like I was in a World War II flick, playing ze French Resistance. But eventually, we were outside. This was my first real look at the inside of Heaven's River. I stopped and gawked like a tourist. I could feel the others do the same as they came through, but I wasn't willing to spare any cycles to acknowledge the fact.

With a radius of fifty-six miles, Heaven's River didn't at all resemble the usual depictions of O'Neill cylinders where the landscape looms like a cliff in two directions. The land in the spin direction was just starting to show a curve at the point where it faded out into the distance. The fact that it curved up instead of dropping like a normal horizon was disconcerting, but you had to really be looking for it to notice.

Clouds formed in several layers, indicating that there was real weather in the habitat. The clouds cast shadows on the land below or on lower cloud layers. I engaged my telescopic vision (no, really) and spotted a rainstorm in the middle distance. The thunderhead formed a *horizontal* cyclonic pattern oriented along the axis of the topopolis. Expected, but still freaky for someone raised on a planet.

Within range of clear sight, rolling hills dominated, interspersed with valleys and plains. I saw occasional stands of trees, but no real forests in the immediate area. I knew from the scans, though, that terrain varied significantly. I wasn't surprised. Given more than three hundred billion square miles of available space, making it all farmland would take a supreme failure of imagination.

And it wasn't a sterile diorama. We could clearly see herds of, well, something, in the open areas. Slow waves propagated through the herds as some unseen stimulus caused brief mass movements. Vast flocks of bird-equivalents wheeled and darted across the sky, unfazed by issues of Coriolis force or odd horizons.

And snaking through the lowlands was the river. Or to be more accurate, one branch of one of the four rivers. Interestingly, the meandering path, with all the splitting and rejoining, meant that they were, collectively, considerably longer than four billion miles of total length, not even counting the tributaries. I could feel myself boggling at the thought and had to remember that this was just a question of scale, not technology.

I finally managed to tear my gaze away long enough to glance at my companions. Each one was standing, silently taking in the panorama. I smiled for a moment, glad that being a bunch of computer simulations hadn't dulled our collective sense of wonder.

Garfield looked up and grunted, and I followed his gaze. The sky was actually blue, which seemed odd, and there was something that looked like a sun, which seemed *really* odd. "Does anyone know how they manage the fake sky?" he asked of the group in general.

Bill turned to follow Garfield's gaze. "Wow, nice. The Skippies have all the SUDDAR scans. I'll ask them."

He had spoken in English, given the words *Skippies* and *SUDDAR*. "Should use Quinlan, Bill," Bridget said. "Even if you have to phoneticize the occasional English word. We can't afford to stand out."

Bill nodded—well, the Quinlan equivalent—by way of reply.

"I've seen simulations of objects on ballistic trajectories in an O'Neill cylinder–type of environment," Bridget continued. "They behave in a very counterintuitive manner. Are we going to have problems with that?"

"Not really," Bill replied. "It's all about the radius of the structure. Those simulations—I've seen them, too—are all based on a radius of a few hundred yards to maybe a quarter mile. With a fifty-six mile radius, this structure will give us something so close to real planetary gravity that we won't normally notice a difference. You could play a game of baseball, for instance, and not have to worry about the ball acting funny."

"That's good," Bridget replied. "The Quinlans will have grown up with it, but if we acted surprised at some behavior, it might 'out' us."

"Are the natives going to be that suspicious? And observant?"

"We don't know, Gar. Don't forget, this may look like a pre-industrial society, but they come from a civilization at least as advanced as Earth in the 21st century. And we don't know what politics are going on in the background. What if, as seems quite possible given the welded door back there, there's an adversarial relationship between the general population and the Heaven's River management? They might be on the lookout for strangers behaving oddly."

"Huh. I guess I hadn't thought that through," Garfield said. "Okay, boss lady."

The entrance foyer was located a mile or so downriver and slightly uphill of the nearest village. I pointed in that direction. "We should head to, uh ..."

"Garack's Spine," Bill replied. "No idea why it's named that. Most locals just refer to it as Garack. It's situated on the Arcadia River. The other three, in order, looking spinward, are Utopia, Paradise, and Nirvana."

"No theme there," Garfield commented wryly.

"As usual," Bill replied, "these are English names that are the closest we could come to the Quinlan concepts. But yes, there is a theme, including the name *Heaven's River.* I think this was intended to be just that."

I broke the brief silence that followed. "All very interesting, but right now we have to figure out what to do with Will's manny."

"I vote for a five-person group," Will said.

"Not a good idea, Will," Bridget replied. "A *sabbat* larger than four would attract attention. Not *look at the perverts* level, more like *hey, look at the five-person sabbat* level. We don't want to stand out."

"Yeah, okay. I'm supposed to be backup driver anyway. How about I just go back in the tunnel and plug up the entrance?"

Bill nodded. "That'll work. Also hides the tunnel, which is a bonus."

"Great," I said. "Well, let's go. We need a place to stay, until we can get our bearings."

Will headed back to the tunnel, and the rest of us set off toward the village, Bill in the lead. Bridget kept veering off and investigating. Flora, fauna, insect life, it was all fascinating. Well, biologist, right? Howard always complained about her monomaniacal focus, but it was one of the things he loved about her.

The local flora didn't look all that strange. I'm sure Bridget was cataloguing all the ways in which it was unique, but to a non-professional like me, it was just plants. This ecosystem had evolved around chlorophyll, so even the colors reminded me of Earth.

The insect life, not so much. Exoskeletal body plans seemed to be the rule for the small fauna that filled that particular part of the ecosystem, but that was about where the resemblance ended. The local insects seemed to go in for a radial body structure rather than bilateral symmetry. The contortions that evolution went through to enable flight with that kind of material to work with had produced some truly bizarre structures. I was glad I'd never been prone to creature-feature nightmares.

We'd been walking for about ten minutes when Bridget called for us to stop. "My fault, guys. I'm supposed to be the expert, and I've already screwed up."

The rest of us glanced at each other quizzically before turning back to her. "Okay," I said. "I'll bite. You've screwed up how?"

"Quinlans aren't great walkers. Not for long distances, anyway. We should have gone down on all fours by now, and even so, we should be resting more often."

"Jeez, Bridge, we're alone—"

"If we can see the village, the village can see us. I don't know if they have telescopes or something similar, but if they do, we're already behaving oddly."

"So we should go quadruped—"

"More than that, Garfield. Do you smell that?"

Garfield frowned, and we all sniffed the air. "What's that?" he asked. "Water?"

"Yep. Running water. It smells different than standing water—"

"Seriously?"

"Yes, Bill. Even Earth animals could tell the difference. It's only a surprise to creatures with atrophied smellers, like humans."

"Okay. So, water…"

"Even more than they are inclined to travel on all fours, Quinlans are inclined to travel in water."

"Ohhhh …." Bill said. "So we should be swimming."

"Yup. This way." Without waiting for further discussion, Bridget marched off in the direction of the water. Well, *marched* to the extent that something like a fat weasel could be said to march. More of a determined waddle.

After a few moments, she dropped to all fours. The rest of us followed suit. I was pleasantly surprised to discover that we were able to move considerably faster this way. And some of the odd design details of the Quinlan backpack started to make more sense.

In less than a minute, we'd come upon a small stream. "Doesn't look big enough to swim in," Bill opined.

"Not for a human, flailing around with those gangly limbs in all directions," Bridget replied with a laugh. "But with the tail, we're basically torpedoes. Watch."

Bridget dove into the stream with hardly a ripple. There was a sort of surge in the stream's surface, like those movies involving an underwater monster. Less than two seconds later, she popped up about thirty yards upstream. "Ta-dah!"

I thought back to our swim together on that first day on Quin, and felt excitement overtake me. Perhaps that was part of the Quinlan persona, but it was also part Bob. I'd never been a good swimmer, nor very comfortable in the water. I considered swimming to be something you did as an alternative to drowning. Now, in an android replica of a semiaquatic species, I could *own* that water. Or something like that.

Bridget shot past us in the downstream direction, undulating just at the surface. I laughed with delight and dove in. I heard other splashes behind me, but didn't try to count them. Anyone who declined would be left behind and would have to hoof it.

I caught up to Bridget and slapped her tail. She responded by smacking me on the head with the appendage, then shooting off around a submerged rock.

So, that's the way it's going to be, is it? We shot through the water, upstream, downstream, looping around the others, tagging and being tagged. The stream, so small from land, seemed an entire country from this perspective, with the third dimension available to maneuver in.

One by one, the others joined the game, until the water was frothing with Quinlan bodies dodging, breaching, and chasing each other. The game lasted almost ten minutes, until my heads-up display informed me that a proper Quinlan would be exhausted and would need to spend some quality time floating. I could have ignored it—the android body never got tired—but Bridget would have something to say in that case.

I rose to the surface and turned onto my back. The motion seemed natural, and I'd seen images from the spy drones of Quinlans floating in this pose. "Otters," I muttered, as the others popped up one by one. We linked up, grabbing with forepaws or hindpaws to form a raft of Quinlans, slowly rotating as we floated downstream.

"Okay, that was insane," Bill exclaimed. "Bridget, you might want to let Howard know about this. He'll probably be able to figure out a way to turn it into a business."

"Heaven's River tours?" Bridget waggled her ears at him, a sign of amused agreement to a Quinlan. "I think they'd be popular, and not just with the Bobs. Maybe even some of the second-wave replicants. It might jar them out of their VR-only existence."

"Heads up, people. You're coming up on the village."

At Will's announcement, we all turned to look downstream. Sure enough, we were around the last bend and would soon be floating through the small burg. We unlinked and torpedoed to the nearest pedestrian dock.

Shore infrastructure was one of the many differences between Quinlan culture and anything else we were used to. They used waterways the way humans would use sidewalks and roads, which meant that there were pedestrian docks and boat docks where the waterway was wide enough. The latter were little different from what you'd find on Earth, or for that matter, on Pav or New Pav. Quinlans used mostly sailboats of a generally catamaran-like design, although I'd seen images of a couple of more barge-like variants that used the local beasts of burden to turn a paddle wheel.

Interestingly, this town did *not* have canals, so roads were the only method of moving around. I frowned for a moment, then realized that the actual soil wouldn't be all that deep. If the Quinlans tried to dig canals, they'd likely run into shell material before they got deep enough to matter. All terrain contouring would have to be baked into the shape of the shell during construction.

The pedestrian docks were essentially a set of half-submerged ramps that allowed the Quinlans to swim up then walk out. They could shoot out of the water like a penguin and land on their feet, but it was considered impolite in crowded situations, since you could easily find yourself in a pileup for the same patch of dock. The Quinlans had a word for the move—*poot*—which the Skippies had translated as *up-diving*.

We walked up the ramp and moved out of the way quickly. The ramps were busy, and Quinlans seemed to have a low tolerance for queuing up. Most simply dove off the nearest edge, and at any moment a few more impatient souls took to up-diving, braving the black looks of their peers.

As I watched, one miscreant hopped out of the water, only to be straight-armed right back in by someone occupying that particular patch of space-time. As we headed for solid ground, I could hear voices raised in anger behind me.

"Want to stay and watch the fights?" Garfield muttered with a smirk.

"*Better not,*" Will interjected. "*Hugh commented that Quinlans are inclined to mob. A simple fight between two people can escalate quickly for no good reason.*"

"*More so than humans?*" Garfield asked.

"*Maybe. How about that? Humanity dethroned as Most Likely to Be Stupid in Large Groups.*"

I grinned but didn't bother to respond. Will had ended up with a particularly negative view of the human species after his adventures in getting the last of them off the dying Earth. Other than our relatives, whom he continued to dote on, he had very little time for the general run of humanity.

"*Head's up,*" Bridget interjected. "*Cops.*"

We all prairie-dogged—brilliant move, way to play it cool, guys—as a heavyset Quinlan sporting an ornate sash swaggered up to us. I struggled to keep my face and ears impassive. A waddling swagger was a truly impressive sight.

He took a moment to look us over, his gaze lingering on Bridget. She stared back at him impassively, neither challenging nor acquiescing. I had to admit, it was a nice balancing act.

But if he talked down to her, we might be leaving town in a hurry. Or on a rail.

"You folks just passing through?"

I stepped forward. By prior agreement, I would be the spokescritter for the group. "We are, good sir. We're on a sabbatical, making our way slowly downriver."

"Where from?"

"Hand of Ar," I replied. "I doubt you've heard of it. Our last few stops hadn't."

I was taking a chance, but maybe not a large one. Quinlans were far more mobile than Anglo-Saxon peasants, for instance, but mass transportation was still unknown, as far as we could tell. And the high-speed transport built into Heaven's River was inaccessible to the residents in every segment we'd investigated.

"More sabbatarians." The cop screwed up his face in apparent distaste. "If you plan on staying for more than a couple of days, you'll have to register with the magistrate. Otherwise, stick to the transient hotels and eateries along the docks. And don't cause trouble, or you'll be leaving earlier than planned." He gave us a final once-over, nodded again, and swaggered away.

"Did you notice the weapon?" Bridget asked.

We muttered acknowledgements. "Couldn't tell exactly what particular style of sword," I said. "But the scabbard had a certain *short-sword* look to it."

"That means they do some metalwork. Which means they *have* metal. Other than the money, I mean."

Garfield cocked his head quizzically. "Uh, maybe I should have read the prelims more thoroughly. This is a surprise why?"

"What're they going to do, mine it?" I glared at him. "It's like *Ringworld*, right? No mineral wealth, no oil deposits. Unless they actually scavenge from the structure, they're limited to recycling what they already have. And there's very little actual metal in the structure, even if they were that stupid."

"Which means metal is going to be very valuable."

"The megastructure administration could be supplying metal in small quantities," Bill said. "Maybe pushing out nuggets at stream heads, for instance. Although that would produce messy industries engaged in harvesting it."

Bridget nodded. "In any case, dedicating all that metal to a sword tells me that the sword is really, really necessary. Either as a symbol, or a threat, or a weapon."

We'd been walking through the village as we talked, looking for a motel, or local equivalent. Without warning, a Quinlan quartet spilled out of what might have been a bar. The ball-o-Quinlans was rolling around like a bunch of angry cats, kicking and biting and scratching. And swearing. Quinlan cursing was both inventive and energetic. The Quinlan language allowed some forms of declension that went well with cursing, including a noun form that indicated it was the subject of an action.

One of the Quinlans was ejected from the mass, mostly by accident, and leaped to his feet. He glared around, teeth bared, and spotted Bridget, who had the bad luck to be within arm's reach. He snarled at her and cocked his arm for a full claw rake.

Without so much as a lead-up, Bridget popped him straight in the snout. He went over backward with a shriek of dismay and the other Quinlans stopped in mid-action.

Bridget showed her teeth to the group. "Anyone else?"

The group untangled and helped their fourth, who was holding his snout, to his feet. "What was that?" one of them said.

"My business card," Bridget replied. "I have more than enough for everyone." She paused, and when no response was forthcoming, she stalked off without waiting for us.

We made to follow, and I shrugged at one of the combatants as I walked past. He muttered to me, "When mating season comes, friend, choose carefully."

I wasn't quite sure what to make of that, so I didn't respond.

Garfield, meanwhile, had moved ahead and turned into an establishment with a carving of a bed over the door. By the time I caught up, he was engaged in earnest conversation with what must be the proprietor.

We waited, and moments later he rejoined us. "We're in luck. This establishment has private rooms large enough for our group. Highly sought-after, according to our host, which is why he wanted a ruinously high nightly rate. We compromised on an only mildly scandalous weekly rate." He held up a key. "Only one key, though, so I *am* the keymaster."

Bill chuckled and Bridget, as usual, rolled her eyes. I had to wonder what life was like for her with Howard. Even for a Bob clone, he had an unusually high dose of referencitis. I hoped the eye rolls were pro forma. On the other hand, she was *getting* the references.

⚜　⚜　⚜

The room was "cozy," that being the generally accepted euphemism for *smaller than a closet*. It consisted of a door at one end, a window at the other, and four bunk beds, two on each wall, between the door and window. And not generous bunk beds, either. A tall Quinlan wouldn't be able to stretch out. Fortunately, we'd all gone for average dimensions, so it wasn't an issue.

There was enough room between the beds for two people to stand at the same time, but we wouldn't be having town hall meetings in that space. Bathroom facilities were shared by the entire floor and weren't what I'd call luxurious either. Fortunately, the Quinlans seemed to have the concept of flush toilets, so we wouldn't have to adjust our olfactory senses. Unfortunately, the Quinlan language didn't have a concept of *bath* separate from *swim*, so there was a certain species-level *bouquet*, shall we say? Will uploaded a patch, at everyone's request, which tuned the odor out of conscious awareness.

The short walk to our room had been interesting and instructive. This hotel seemed to cater to sabbatarians. All the rooms that we'd gotten a look at were laid out the same as ours, and most seemed to be occupied by foursomes. I wondered aloud if four was a magic Quinlan family number of some kind, and received a *no* from Bridget and a lecture. "The Quinlans have a complicated system that I'd characterize as a networked endogamy. People belong to a marriage group with potentially multiple male and female partners, but they could belong to more than one group. There are rules about your status and financial obligations within the group based upon whether you lived with that group or with another one."

"So what's with the foursomes, then?"

"It may be a cultural norm, or instinctive. Or a little of both." Bridget shrugged. "It might simply be the practical minimum number necessary to raise a family."

I raised an eyebrow. "That seems like an odd requirement. Why?"

Bridget made a face before explaining. "Quinlan children are raised in a crèche until they're about five, because they aren't sentient until then."

"Neither are human children," I said.

Bridget laughed. "A lot of people would agree with you, but of course that isn't true. Human children start trying to talk in their first year. Look, humans solved the brain size problem by being born physically underdeveloped—intelligent but helpless, requiring a lot of parental support in the early years. Quinlans solved it by being born animalistic but pretty much fully mobile almost right away, with brains that mature late. By the time they start to learn to think and talk, they can already take care of themselves."

"Wow, I can see some problems with that."

"Yes, Bill, and you've almost certainly gotten it right. The children, who are called *juniors*, have to be kept penned up or they basically just run rampant. And someone has to care for them. So Quinlan families have to be big, to muster the resources."

"And to make sure no one decides to eat their young," Garfield said, sotto voce.

"Not wrong," Bill muttered back.

Bridget smiled at them. "I have a theory that their belligerence and hair-trigger tempers as adults are related to their early development process. Humans learn cultural norms early, while they're still helpless and dependent. Quinlans, not so much."

"Huh. Food for thought," I said. "Let's get back to civilization before we continue, okay? My cultural norms include coffee."

The others laughed, and we started to settle in. We did Rock Paper Scissors Lizard Spock for bunks, and I got one of the uppers. No biggie, right? Well, unfortunately, with the Quinlan body's short stride, ladders were an adventure. I almost fell off the first time I tried to climb up, and Bill had to brace me. I glared at Garfield, who was already comfortable in the other upper and bared my teeth. He laughed.

"It's late enough," Bridget said. "Let's get some sleep."

Sleep was code for leaving the mannies in standby mode while we returned to VR. Each manny had a basic AMI that would alert us if something required our attention. Otherwise, the mannies would sleep like, well, like the dead.

We all doffed our mannies and gathered in my VR, Will grabbing the beanbag chair as usual. Jeeves showed up with everyone's favorite refreshments, and we all spent a few moments enjoying the return to civilization.

"It's going to be slow," Bridget said. "But the first thing we have to do is find a library or hall of records or something similar. Let's see what they have in written form. The Skippies were doing a general once-over and may have missed something that didn't have *A History of Quin* in the title. And of course, they had to be careful. A group of Quinlans grabbing books won't set off the kind of gossip that a bunch of floating balls and mechanical spiders would."

"Assuming they have something like spiders," Will said.

"They do. More crab-shaped, though."

"Whatever. Anyway, we ransack their written records and try to get enough info to be able to interrogate locals without sounding like aliens."

"Which we are."

"Not the point," I said. "We have to get a bead on management without revealing ourselves. It might be that we end up contacting them. It might also turn out that we have to spy on them, too. But we can't do anything until we have at least the basics."

"I'm just as happy if we end up actually doing what we told the cop—heading downstream."

"I understand, Bridge, but the point for me is to find Bender. Or find out what happened to him. Let's not lose track of that."

"Are you sure we can't just scan for him?"

Garfield answered, "We did a simulation. The problem is that the megastructure uses optoelectronics very similar to our technology. So every mile of topopolis will take us about twelve hours to scan, and then it's another six hours to examine the scans in detail. That's over a million years, worst case, just for the scanning."

"Can't we just build a whole bunch of scanners?"

"Yes, but we also have to build a whole bunch of *us* to process the scans. Even using the most efficient bootstrapping methods and ignoring questions of material availability, we're still looking at more than a hundred and fifty years if we bring that level of resources to bear on the problem. And anyway, we don't have that much raw material in the system, so we'd be bringing in units from out-system. So add some more time for that."

Bill nodded and took up the story. "On the other hand, an investigative strategy might net us good results in less than a decade, at least according to Hugh."

"Based on what?" Bridget frowned at Bill. "He can't possibly have any statistics to work from."

"He kind of does. Population of Heaven's River, number of people we can contact per year, number of people who will *hear* about us per year ... It's a networking theory thing. Eventually there's more than a fifty-fifty chance that we will either contact someone or be contacted by someone. Hugh says less than a decade."

"Hmmph." Bridget shook her head. "Okay, fine. I'm not thrilled with the alternative timeline anyway."

"And hey, if anyone wants a break, I'm available," Will said, grinning. "That downstream thing looked like just too much fun."

I stood, signaling the end of the meeting. "We have six hours until we're scheduled to wake our mannies. Take care of whatever you need to."

18. Not Part of the Plan

Will
June 2334
Quin

I pulled myself off the rack, staggering slightly. The proportions of the Quinlan manny would take some getting used to. I was examining the not insubstantial claws on my hand when the other manny opened its eyes.

"Hey, Howard." I held up a hand. "Dig these crazy nails."

He gave me a frown. "You gone hippy on me, Riker?" I grinned at him and he smiled back. "Thanks for inviting me, Will. I admit I'm curious about Bridget's project, and her description of the swimming was more enthusiastic than she generally gets about things."

I signaled the drone to open the cargo door. "No prob. I'm curious too, although I also have a responsibility to practice in case I'm called up. That's my story, anyway." I gestured to the door and we walked out together.

I'd parked the drone in a different city, somewhat larger than the one Bob and Bridget had visited. And a good deal more messed up. We'd have to avoid areas with too much radiation—even the mannies weren't immune to the damaging effects—but just about anything else could be ignored. I wanted to get a cross-section of the types of warfare that the Quinlans had waged on each other. This city had been pounded by explosives. Maybe missiles, maybe dropped bombs. Not kinetics, though. Those wouldn't have left much to examine.

The city had likely been a capital, or at least a major hub of some kind. It had that *all roads lead to Rome* feel about it, at least from the air. The Quinlans had used rail for overland transport, and there were a *lot* of rail lines leading here.

This city also had larger blocks, with more widely spaced waterways. I wondered if that was an efficiency thing or if they just needed the bigger blocks for some other reason. According to Bob and Bill, the Quinlan psychology seemed to be very humanlike, but I was reluctant to overextrapolate.

We walked up to the nearest canal and inspected the contents. It didn't seem too bad, certainly not as oily and turgid as Bob had described on their excursion. If anything, the canal seemed to have a surprisingly robust current.

"Looks nice," Howard said.

"Real estate is less damaged than what you'd expect," I replied. "Bridget took a tissue sample and had it scanned. Huge viral load, and the Skippies' modelling indicates it was likely an engineered virus."

"So, biological warfare on top of everything else?"

"Mm-hmm. It looks like the entire population had a tantrum and started throwing everything they had at everyone they could. I'm surprised they managed to get to this stage, technologically."

"Maybe it's a population density thing?"

I grunted and changed the subject. "I searched for a good, undamaged canal. With the pounding this city received, some have been filled with debris or even had their water flow blocked entirely. I figure we shouldn't get too adventurous."

"Sounds good. Shall we?" Without waiting for an answer, Howard dove in.

I followed immediately and spotted him, already disappearing into the distance. I pursued, tail and arm flaps working in concert. Howard glanced back without turning his head. *"This is definitely worth doing. I could sell this. See the ruined world of the Quinlans. Quake at the sight of blasted cities. Gaze in awe at the—"*

"I dare you to try and get that past Bridget."

Howard laughed. *"You got me there. She'd flay me alive. Okay, so maybe not tours of the Quin ruins. But even if we just copied the mannies and put them on Vulcan… mmm, maybe not."*

"What?"

I could hear the smile in Howard's voice. *"Vulcan has that dinosaur theme, and it carries into the marine life. Lots of big, hungry native critters."*

"In the rivers, maybe?"

"Maybe. Have to look into it."

We swam in a companionable silence for a few more minutes, stopping to examine a couple of submerged wrecks. I imagined the experience would be a lot like scuba diving, except every video I'd ever seen of humans underwater showed them as slow and ungainly, struggling to push themselves through the water at a snail's pace. The Quinlan forms moved more like otters—or maybe penguins, since the Quinlans didn't quite have the sinuous flexibility of otters.

"Curious. The current is surprisingly strong here," Howard said. *"The city didn't seem to have that much of a grade."*

"Um, I'm not an expert, but that seems like more of a concern than a curiosity." I sounded like a wet blanket, even to my own ears, but I'd developed an attitude from terraforming Valhalla that *unusual* equaled *bad*. Exceptions had been rare.

"Sure, okay, it's stronger over here. I'll just have a—yipe!"

And this would not be one of those exceptions. *"Howard? What happened?"*

"I'm—oof—being sucked down—ow—a tunnel of some—argh—kind. Wait, there's light up—oh, shit."

I sent a quick order to the cargo drone to lift off, center itself on our location, and do a SUDDAR sweep. Meanwhile, I put some distance between myself and Howard's last known position.

"I'm going to need a ride," Howard said into the silence.

"What happened?"

"I just got spit out of a tunnel into midair and did a bit of flying. But not the good kind. I think I broke the manny. I've got my beacon on."

"Drone has located you. One moment." I piggybacked the drone's video window as it lowered itself into a mostly dry canal. Spread-eagle on a bed of rocks and branches was a Quinlan form. Some of the limb positions were definitely not natural. *"How did this happen?"*

"I was sucked into a tunnel and got spit out here. I think I flew about fifty yards before landing. It looks like the city builders put in tunnels between canals to equalize water levels. But this canal is mostly dry. I bet it's blocked upstream."

In the video, roamers were collecting Howard and bundling him into the drone. *"Have you checked your diagnostics?"*

"Yeah, this baby is going to need some work. I'm surprised I'm still connected, honestly. The comms subsystem is tough." There was a pause. *"Don't tell Bridget. She'll kill me."*

I smiled, although Howard couldn't see it. *"I understand you've got a new red ale in the works. Riker's Red, I think it's called?"*

"No, it's…" Another pause. *"You're a bastard."*

"Yes, but now I'm a bastard with a red ale named after me."

19. You Did What?

Bob
June 2334
Garack's Spine

Iactivated my manny and sat up, rubbing my eyes. I wasn't sure if it was something Quinlans did, but it felt right. I peered out the small single window. Still dark. We'd "gone to bed" yesterday while it was still light out, so we had missed the Heaven's River sunset. I wanted to see the sunrise. Mostly, I wanted to see for myself how Heaven's River handled emulation of night and day.

I'd woken a few minutes early to be certain I was up before the dawn, but I'd left a message with the others. Quietly—not for my crew's sake but for the other occupants of the motel—I snuck out of our room and down the stairs to the front door.

The air felt crisp and cool and wouldn't be out of place in early fall on Earth. Item: the artificial sun supplied heat as well as light to the habitat. That implied a heat sink of some kind at ground level, since this was otherwise a closed system. My bet was that the water was kept below ambient, probably cooled by the river-bottom impeller/filters. Maybe the central cylinder absorbed infrared as well, when the sun was off.

No one else was about. We knew that Quinlans were primarily diurnal, so no big surprise. There might be a night guard wandering around, and maybe a paperboy or something, but otherwise I pretty much had the street to myself. Or so I thought, until a voice beside me said, "Morning."

"Morning, Bill. Had the same idea?"

"Mm-hmm. Lots of data from the drones, but nothing beats eyewitness."

We stood quietly, watching, as a light gradually grew at one end of the gigantic cylinder that was Heaven's River. By convention, we translated that direction as "east," with the other compass points falling naturally into place. "North" was anti-spinward and "south" was spinward, but from inside you wouldn't be able to tell without doing some very sensitive experiments. Under this coordinate system, this branch of the river flowed generally west.

"It's quite directional," Bill said into the silence.

"What?"

"The light from the central structure. In theory, we should be able to see it from hundreds of miles away, but it doesn't become apparent until it's relatively close. I think it's masked in some way to only shine over a limited range."

"Makes sense. That would also mimic the early morning and late afternoon dimming of a natural sun due to atmospheric effects."

Finally, the sky had turned a discernible blue, and the pseudo-sun was clearly visible at an angle of perhaps ten degrees above the horizontal. It wasn't a perfect illusion. For one thing, every point on the surface of the habitat would see the sun pass directly overhead, as if everyone was at the equator. For another, the swing across the sky wouldn't be evenly paced. Because the pseudo-sun moved at a constant pace along the central cylinder, it would appear to accelerate as it approached local zenith, then slow down afterward. Noon would be very brief.

"But the sky is blue. Have we figured that out yet?"

Bill turned to me. "Some of it could be just light-scattering. But, yeah, you'd think we'd be able to see more of the interior. Maybe not all the way around, but more than we do."

"It's a hologram."

I jerked as Will's comment came out of the, er, blue through my comms. "What?"

"It's a hologram. Very weak one, nondirectional, and no detail. All it does is mask the central cylinder and reinforce the blue scattering slightly, just enough to give the effect that it does, of fading out the interior in the distance."

"That's interesting," Bill said. "How did you get this information?"

"Inspecting the segment scans. We found some hologram projectors on the central cylinder. Big suckers."

"Makes sense, I guess."

"What makes sense?"

Bill and I both turned as we heard Bridget's voice. She and Garfield had just exited the motel, presumably looking for us.

"Will's comment. Run through the playback, you'll understand."

Bridget closed her eyes and turned her face up to the sun. "Feels good. The builders put a lot of effort into making this as homey as possible."

"Mmm, yeah. Which argues against the 'forced colonization' scenario, which brings us back to the question—"

"Well, you all seem to be up very early. Got somewhere special to be?"

We all turned—again—at this latest unexpected voice. It was the cop, the *same* cop, that we'd run into yesterday. I wondered for a moment if maybe *he* was a manny and didn't need sleep. But in a small town, there were probably only a few members of law enforcement, so maybe back-to-backs weren't that unusual.

"Just discussing breakfast, sir," I said, trying to project *hungry*.

"There are lots of eateries along here, gents—and lady—but most won't be open yet. Best find a place to plant your behinds that doesn't leave you in the middle of the street blocking traffic, while you wait." He glared at us significantly.

What traffic? The street was virtually deserted, except for our group. Wow, this guy was a bit of a dick. "Yes sir, we need to get our morning routine going anyway." I turned to head back to the motel, but the cop stopped me with a truncheon pressed against my chest. Yes, a billy club. One of those things cops always carry in cartoons.

"Best you be behaving yourselves here on in. I don't want to have to notice you again. You understand?"

I remembered Fred from my time with the Deltans, and fantasized for a moment about grabbing this doofus by the throat and hoisting him in the air. But the feeling passed in a mil or two, and my manny showed no outward sign of the internal struggle. "Yes sir, not a problem."

The cop examined us for a moment longer, then turned and walked away. Garfield rolled his eyes and grinned. "We's juvenile delinquents, we is. Cor!"

Bridget glared at him. "That was the worst attempt at a Cockney accent I've ever heard. Unless you were going for Irish, in which case it was even worse. Don't do that again."

I chuckled. "How often does Howard do that?"

"Daily. *And* he says it never gets old."

We returned to our closet, er, room, and sat. "Suggestions?" I asked.

"Why don't we just split up for the moment?" Bill replied. "This isn't Thunderdome, it's a small, peaceful village. Just wander around and eavesdrop. Maybe one of us will pick up a lead, or at least some useful information."

"Reasonable," Garfield replied. "I vote for that."

No one seemed inclined to argue. "Okay. Let's give it an hour to keep Officer Friendly off our backs, then we'll head out."

An hour was plenty of time to get things done in the Bobiverse. We set our mannies on standby and went home.

❧ ❧ ❧

An hour later, I had successfully hunted down breakfast, of sorts, at a nearby pub *slash* eatery. Quinlans didn't really differentiate.

I looked down at the plate of fish parts and tried to control my face. The barkeep wasn't pranking me—other Quinlans had similar fare in front of them.

"Something wrong?" he said, eyeing me.

"No, I just realized how often I've had *squiz* lately. I'll be fine."

He snorted and turned away. Apparently being a barkeep didn't require empathy. Or conversational prowess.

Really, this wasn't much different from sushi. And I'd loved sushi. I still loved sushi, and had it regularly in virt.

Hmm, nope. Not helping. It still looked like chopped-up raw fish.

With a sigh, I directed the embedded AMI to eat the meal while I backed away slightly from foreground processing.

187

I cranked up my audio and tried to pick up something besides the snarfing, snorting sounds of Quinlan diners. They weren't anywhere near as bad as on Pav—I'd *seen* Pav meals. There were many BobTube videos of Pav families eating, complete with overdubbed sports commentary. It occurred to me to wonder if the Pav had seen some of those vids. It might explain their attitude.

Still, Quinlans weren't paragons of refined dining either.

Family discussions, gossip, who had or hadn't been arrested for drunk and disorderly, occasional business discussions… there was plenty of talk, but it was all routine.

Mostly, anyway. I focused in on one discussion in particular, between two Quinlans:

"Another bunch of blow-ins again this week, only some of them sabbatarians. No one seems to know what's going on."

"I'd be less bothered by it if they spent their coin, but they all tend to be tight-fisted."

"And surly."

"Think they're criminals running away from something?"

"Or maybe they'd been *scattered*?"

"That many? What about disbanded militia?"

"Haven't heard of any recent battles."

"Hmmph. Doesn't make sense."

Well, that was interesting. It could be just some local thing, but it was worth checking out. Especially the reference to *scattered*, which had been spoken with peculiar emphasis. I glanced around, trying not to be obvious about it, until I spotted the speakers. A couple of fat, older Quinlans, probably local merchants—they were wearing decorative baubles and cosmetic fur coloring that would never survive a swim. If I remembered my sociology, that was a wealth or privilege display, showing that they didn't *have* to go into the water.

Maybe someone else could pick something up. *"Guys, see if you can find out anything about large movements of untalkative strangers. And maybe get a definition for this slang word: scattering."*

I received acknowledgements from the others and went back to eavesdropping.

The conversation moved on to more commercial matters, unfortunately. After several more minutes I accepted that no new information was forthcoming. My meal being finished, thank the universe, I decided to go for a walk.

I stopped, taken aback, as I exited the eatery. Traffic had still been thin when I went in. Apparently Quinlans all got up at the same time. Or maybe there was a generally agreed-upon workday. For whatever reason, it was now chaos. I couldn't detect anything like a right side/left side rule, or even sidewalk/roadway. Pedestrians dodged in and out of traffic, while animal-drawn carts maneuvered past each other and generally ignored people on foot. I eyed the draft animals, a vaguely oxlike beast that the Quinlans called a *hown*. They were huge and could probably crush an adult Quinlan without even noticing. Only their slow, steady gait allowed people to dodge them in apparent safety.

The carts were interesting. None of the contents were exposed. Some were covered in tarps, some were bundled and strapped down, and some carts were completely enclosed. It seemed like it would be a lot of work, as opposed to just piling stuff into the back.

I walked up behind a cart and peered in. Definitely well-attached. And since it was unlikely the *howns* were going to take the carts around corners on two wheels, I wondered if grab-and-run was an issue.

I was surprised by a shout. "Hey, you! Get away from my cart. Police! Thief!"

I looked up and realized the driver had been shouting at me. Jeez, hair-trigger much?

"Sir, I wasn't—"

"Well, well, look who it is!"

That was a familiar voice, and not in a good way. I turned to find Officer Friendly leering at me, slapping his truncheon into his hand. Again with the cartoon posture, and I couldn't help a moment of amusement. "Listen, I wasn't—"

"I think you were, lad, and we'll be talking about it down at the station. About-face and march."

He attempted to prod me with his truncheon, and by reflex I swiveled my upper body to the right to let the weapon pass by. A slight nudge with my left arm ensured that the cop's attempted jab would keep going.

He scowled and brought the truncheon back in a back-handed swipe to my head. However, since I already had control of the truncheon-carrying limb with my left arm, I simply leaned back and guided it over my head. Hundreds of seconds of virtual kung fu training were coming together, and I wanted to whoop with joy. Except, you know, cop.

And speaking of, Officer Friendly was now in full umbrage. He began yelling for backup. It took me a second to realize that backup would come, not from the police force, but from passersby. People turned to the fracas and came at me, hands out to grab. It seemed neighborhood watch was a thing.

"Guys, I seem to have gotten in trouble with the law. I think we're all going to have to leave town. Like, now."

Bill replied right away. *"What in hell did you do?"*

"Looked in a wagon. I'm not kidding, that's all I did. Didn't even touch it. These people really have anger-management issues."

"Fine," Bill replied. *"We'll meet downstream. Don't show off, Bob. Nothing inhuman. Er, un-Quinlan. You know what I mean."*

I did. My android body was capable of speed and strength that no Quinlan could possibly match. I needed to avoid making them think there was some super-Quinlan out there.

This exchange had only taken a mil or so, and people were still coming at me. It was time to go.

I rolled off the outside of the first person's grab, then took him around and pushed him into the next person. The push-off allowed me to reverse direction and I found myself face-to-face with another individual. His expression was just starting to register surprise when I pushed him into someone else, resulting in the beginning of a total tangle, and allowing me to change direction again. I now had people going in three different directions, trying to catch me. It took no more than a nudge to an off-balance pursuer and he was down, taking several others with him.

Now I had an open space, and I went for it, trying to keep my speed within Quinlan norms.

Right into Officer Friendly.

To his credit, he was probably used to this kind of chase. Or maybe he just guessed right. But there he was, right in the middle of my escape route. He grinned an evil grin as he opened his arms wide to keep me from going around him.

Instead, I went straight at him. Before he even had time to register shock, I straight-armed him, ran right up his chest as he went over backward, and launched off his forehead as he hit the ground. That wasn't going to make me any friends, but then I wasn't planning on hanging around.

I had a clear shot at the river now. A short gallop to the docks, a quick leap down to the wooden deck, ending with a long dive into the drink.

I heard splashes behind me, as others gave chase. But I was out of direct sight now, and I could pour on the horses. Flat out, I hit about twice the speed of a biological Quinlan, and I didn't have to come up for air. In seconds I was far out of their reach. They would hopefully conclude that I'd simply doubled back or otherwise lost them.

"Clear of the town. Waiting downstream," I announced to the team.

⚜ ⚜ ⚜

"Hey, I have a great idea. Let's put *Bob* in charge." Bridget glared at me, but I could see her trying not to smile.

"Yeah, yeah, bring it on," I replied. "I got'cher *delinquent* right here."

We all shared a chuckle, and Bill said, "So it went from you looking in a wagon all the way to a riot?"

"In seconds," I replied. "Literally seconds."

"I saw the fracas as I headed for the water," Garfield added. "There were a couple dozen people involved, all yelling. I think some of them had started to fight *each other.*"

We lapsed into silence. We were all floating downstream on the river, linked hands and feet in the usual Quinlan way. The current was slow, no more than a few miles per hour. Walking speed, maybe slightly more. I tilted my head and closed my eyes to absorb a little heat from the sun. It was midafternoon now, and we were far enough from Garack to finally be able to relax.

In the distance, boats moved up – and downriver. The Quinlans had sailboats, with proper triangular-sail designs, which I could see tacking back and forth as they crossed the river northward, or in beam reach as they headed up – or downriver. I noticed, though, that there was a lot more downriver traffic. I wondered if they tended to go back upriver by circling around on one of the other main rivers. That would certainly be easier, if a little more roundabout.

There were also boats that used one or more *howns* on a treadmill as a source of motive power. That didn't strike me as terribly efficient, but *efficiency* was more of an industrial-era concern. Very probably it was more than fast enough for a pre-steam society.

"Y'know, Bob, you may have been right," Bridget said, interrupting my reverie.

"About?"

"When you said they have anger-management issues. We saw several fights during the brief time we were in town, and no one seemed surprised. Quinlans are just naturally belligerent. More so even than humans."

"I don't know about belligerent," Bill replied. "They seemed, well, *polite* is too strong a word. *Agreeable*, maybe."

"Okay, how about short-tempered?"

"Mmm, yeah, hair-trigger tempers. Sounds about right."

"So any luck on finding out anything new?" I asked.

"I found a bookstore. I was perusing when I suddenly had to leave town." Garfield glared at me.

"Cool. What kind of titles?"

"Mostly fiction. Some philosophy and soft sciences. How-tos, stuff like that." Garfield shifted his grip from a forepaw to a hindpaw and put his hands behind his head. "It's a little jarring, because this isn't actually an eighteenth-century society. The people, at least some of them, are *aware* of higher tech. They just don't have access to it. But it's like no one wants to bring it up."

"Some kind of threat from management?"

"That's all I can think of. But that implies that management is watching."

"Which brings up the question of *how.*"

"Huh." I took a moment to dunk my head and cool off. The manny could handle far more temperature variation than an actual Quinlan, but we were wired up to experience reality in as Quinlan-like a manner as possible. The sun felt good, but so did a nice soaking. "I wish we had SUDDAR scanning capability built into the mannies. We could just scan everything and look for hidden cameras."

"Or mobile cameras," Garfield said. "Artificial birds and such?"

"Uh, that seems like a stretch," Bill said. "On the other hand, roamers … Hmmm."

"Yeah. So we have to avoid looking suspicious, while looking suspiciously at everything." I looked around and made a gesture encompassing the group. "Also, no more English conversations out loud. Any discussions like we're having right now should be held on intercom."

"Starting now," Bridget added. *"I don't think anyone will be suspicious of a group of Quinlans quietly floating downstream."*

The water was calm and undisturbed, the pace slow. I had a mental image of Huck Finn and Tom Sawyer floating down the Mississippi. For all the potential issues, life as a Quinlan was probably idyllic. As a natural predator, Quinlans could feed themselves as they travelled. We didn't know how deep the Heaven's River ecosystem was, compared to the original Quin biosphere, but it was a safe bet that it was self-sustaining. That meant at least *some* predator/prey action.

And with no social media or devices, there would be no notion of being constantly online. You could literally float down the river every day, looking for the next town. Or even sleep midstream, if you preferred. It was like Eden, in many ways—a slower, more relaxed pace.

I idly watched the shoreline as we floated. Details changed, but the broad strokes didn't. Occasional farms were visible, but agriculture didn't form anything like as large a part of the Quinlan lifestyle and diet as with humans. I spotted small homesteads, a slight curl of smoke giving them away as often as any visible structures. Use of fire would be an unfortunate side effect of a pre-industrial civilization, but presumably there was some kind of filtering for the air.

We'd floated past a couple of splits and merges in the river system, plus the occasional feeder. I couldn't help being impressed. The amount of detail work that had been put into this place was truly amazing. A Quinlan could spend their whole life exploring and still not know every bend and turn. Never mind a billion miles' worth of different towns and villages on four different rivers. As prisons went, if it was indeed a prison, it could be a lot worse.

The sun moved in the sky, gaining on us in its own downstream journey. A twenty-one-hour day meant we'd have slightly less time than we would expect to find a place to land and seek lodging. There was no inter-town communication system that we knew of, and anyway once we left, the Garack gendarmes probably wouldn't give a hoot.

⚜ ⚜ ⚜

We hadn't come upon another town by nightfall, so we pulled ourselves out of the water and formed a small nest from the local underbrush. According to Bridget, the Heaven's River ecology was complete enough to include large herbivores and their predators, which included a couple of animals that might be inclined to see Quinlans as a food group. Our mannies were completely believable right down to smelling like Quinlans, but that could be turned off. We left the mannies on standby and returned to virt.

"So, kiddies. What have we learned today?" I asked.

"Quinlans are short-tempered, and cops even more so," Bill replied.

"Useful information, but not particularly getting us closer to finding Bender," Garfield added.

"I did a search through the Skippies' online database for uses of the word *scatter* and all variations and declensions," Will said. "Filtering out all the mundane usages, we have quite a few references. No good definitions, because everyone seems to know what everyone means when the word is used. But from context, it's not a good thing, and seems to happen to anywhere from one person up to large groups."

"Interesting. Not sure if it relates to our situation, necessarily, but anything might be useful at this point." I looked around at my friends. "Intercom the rest of us if you think of something else. Otherwise, see you all in six hours."

20. JUST IN CASE

Marcus
July 2334
Poseidon

Maleb blew out a loud breath and put the tablet down on his already-crowded desk. "Interesting times. But are you sure you aren't being a little bit paranoid?"

Maleb was the son of Kal and Gina, two of my closest friends from the early days of Poseidon. He took his sheer size from his father and his Polynesian complexion from his mother. I no longer had an urge to tear up when I saw him, but it had been a problem for a while. His parents had long since passed away, and now Maleb was getting on in years, with hair more grey than black. *Ephemerals.* It was the dirty word of the Bobiverse. But I desperately missed my friends, and had made very few new ones since.

"Probably," I replied. "All I really have is what Howard told me, and he hadn't been at the moot, so he'd gotten the lowdown from Will. At this remove, I should consider myself lucky I've gotten names right."

Maleb chortled and picked up the tablet again. "So these Starfleet wannabes *might* follow through with their threats; and if they do, it *might* affect us. So what do you want from me?"

"I don't have anything specific, Maleb. But if I were still in charge of equipment, I'd be doing software audits and changing passwords and maybe increasing physical security. Maybe only to the extent of moving things without announcing it. As it is, well…" I motioned to him.

"Yeah, that's my job. I get that part. Look, Marcus, I'm not like a feudal lord. I can't just arbitrarily issue orders to change autofactory schedules. These days, they are an integral part of the economy and heavily regulated."

"And I get that. But you do have some flexibility in some areas. I just want to put the bug in your ear. Think about it, and if you can do anything in the normal course of your job that might have a secondary goal useful to us… well, it might turn out to be valuable."

Maleb turned his head slightly and squinted at me. "You're very carefully not saying something. Is there a potential danger to the citizens of Poseidon?"

"Not physical danger, I don't think," I said, shaking my head to emphasize the point. "Economically? Maybe. Look, there's not much they can do to us in virt. So if something goes down, it'll be in physical space. Which means you'll get at least some fallout."

He stared at the ceiling for a few seconds, then began nodding slowly. "I have a little more leeway where actual threats are concerned. I'll still have to tread carefully, but I can at least get a few projects bumped up in priority."

"That's all I ask."

One down, many to go. I wondered how the other Bobs were doing with their contacts.

⚜ ⚜ ⚜

The common area outside Maleb's office door was dominated by floor-to-ceiling windows that gave a clear view through New Thark's fibrex dome. I paused to take in the view, and a few staff members glanced up. It was interesting how society kept evolving. The work-anywhere telecommuting style that had developed in the days after the Mat War had gradually given way to a returning preference for an actual workplace. Seemed people liked being in physical contact with their co-workers, and felt alienated when they were constantly on their own. Of course, rush hour was no longer even a concept for most humans, so the economic and social cost of going to work was nearly nonexistent.

I shook my head to clear the woolgathering and turned my attention back to the view. A mat floated in the calm, impossibly blue ocean at middle distance, with a city hovering just to one side. I could have looked up the name, but didn't bother. These days, mats were strictly industrial or agricultural locations, usually owned and controlled by specific cities. No one lived on the mats except the occasional self-exiled hermit. The technological defenses kept the ocean predators so completely at bay that a new ecosystem was evolving on the mats based on the lack of predation. Howard's wife, Bridget, had visited us several times to do studies.

I turned and headed for the transit station. Maleb's reassurances notwithstanding, the Bobs still had a significant industrial presence in the Poseidon system. We kept it low-key and out of the official economic calculation engines, but it would still need the same review for possible vulnerability.

I sent a message to Guppy, asking for a summary of the audit so far. I'd have to get personally involved soon, but for now, the sun felt good, and the grassy ring around the edge of New Thark called out for my butt to be planted thereupon.

21. Getting Involved

Bob
July 2334
Arcadia River System

I sat up, water running off my fur and puddling around my butt. It was raining. I had a momentary surge of irritation, the kind of thing you get when you've been caught outside without an umbrella. This was followed by irritation that the AMI hadn't alerted me to the issue. It had been raining for some time, judging from the level of wetness of, well, everything.

But the irritation was swept away as I remembered my current form. There was no chill, no feeling of shivering dampness. The Quinlan fur, with its waterproofing, kept me nice and toasty.

I gazed up at the sky. The rain clouds resembled rain clouds everywhere—gray, ugly, and wet. The striations might have been a little weird, because of the megastructure's rotation, but then again maybe not. I wasn't a weather expert, and my interest in cloud formations had always been limited to staying out from under the wet ones.

I examined the horizon in several directions. I thought it might be lighter to the west, but generally speaking, we were socked in in all directions. So, large weather systems—check. I frowned. I could have done without this particular reproduction of a planetary environment.

"Look at this," Bridget said. I turned. I hadn't realized she'd activated yet. She was pointing at some underbrush that had been crushed flat. "I think we were visited overnight. Something big. Maybe a *loroush*."

"Uh…" I searched my memory. A *loroush* was kind of a big wolf, but with claws like a grizzly bear. It grasped its prey and held it while it tore off chunks. Not a fun date, for sure. "Why didn't our AMIs alert us?"

"I don't think it displayed any interest, Bob. The track doesn't actually come into our nest. I think lack of odor and body heat threw it off. A night hunter isn't going to be depending on sight, so the fact we only look like a meal probably wasn't enough."

I grimaced, glad that we had Bridget along to pay attention to this kind of thing. On Eden, my introduction to the local ecosystem had been gradual, and mostly from the safety of orbit. Now, I was in the middle of it, and I hadn't yet internalized the studies.

Bill and Garfield sat up at that moment. Garfield looked at my face and Bridget's face and said, "What'd I miss?"

Bridget laughed. "Let's see about breakfast."

"Fish on the hoof? No thanks," I replied. "I'll eat in town. Maybe a good Denver omelet with some hot sauce…"

"Sure, we'll get right on that." Bridget prairie-dogged and scanned the river. "Do we want to just float today, or should we put some hustle on?"

"As much as this feels like a vacation," I replied, "it isn't. Let's get ourselves to a town."

❧ ❧ ❧

It took most of the day to find the next town, even with the group actively swimming downstream. With no witnesses to worry about, we were able to pile on the speed and ignore fatigue warnings, and in the water there was no danger of overheating the mannies. Bill spotted the town first.

"*Coming up on the left, guys. Slow to flank speed.*"

"*Uh…*"

"*Don't get pedantic, Gar. Slow to whatever is normal for a Quinlan, m'kay?*"

I smiled to myself. Bill and Garfield sniped at each other constantly, but it was never heated. Marvin and I had the same kind of interaction. I realized it'd been a long time since I'd visited him. I didn't even know if he was still working his way through all the fictional environments we'd read about. Maybe it was time to get over myself and rejoin Bobiverse society. While there still was one.

We swam up to the docks and climbed up the ramp in the acceptable manner. Best not attract attention.

The plaque at the head of the dock said *Galen Town* and included some helpful arrows to useful locations. We noted an arrow that said *Market* and headed in that direction. We still hadn't worked out any kind of concrete plan, since we didn't even have enough information to form one. The Skippies were still listening in with the spy drones, but they hadn't come up with anything new. It wasn't surprising, when you looked at the big picture. We still hadn't come close to scanning the entire structure in detail, and even with the surprisingly large Quinlan population numbers, they were spread quite thin. Every single town couldn't possibly have a "significant presence." And we still needed to figure out what that might be.

"Let's try not to screw it up this time," I said.

"Let's—excuse me?" Bill exclaimed. "Who was it that started a riot last time? Anyone? Anyone?"

"Picky, picky. Seriously, maybe we can make some headway today. You guys want to split up?"

"I think we have to, Bob. We'll cover more territory."

I nodded, gave a small wave (Quinlan style), and headed in a random direction. The point was to eavesdrop on conversations, and maybe try to start one and probe subtly for information. I had my concerns about that *subtly* part. I was far more familiar with *The Art of War* than the art of conversation.

Hmm, but where can you go where everybody knows your—no, but close. Liquor loosens lips. Or muzzles, or beaks, or *haora* as the Quinlans called their cakeholes. So, where would I find a pub and/or boozery?

I went up to the first person who was holding still. "Excuse me, is there a tavern nearby?"

"Yes, my brother-in-law owns the Growling Guppy. Down that lane, turn right at the house with the red door. You'll see it. Tell them Gren sent you."

I nodded my thanks and set off in the indicated direction. I was pretty sure Gren got a kickback of some kind, and I didn't begrudge him. I might even get a break on the first beer.

"Brother-in-law" wasn't quite the right translation for the relationship, I knew. The Quinlans had a complicated family system, but I got the impression that Gren and his pub-owning mate were on pretty close terms.

I arrived at the establishment in short order. It was, as advertised, easy to pick out. An outside patio with long benches and tables featured a lot of Quinlans holding beer steins. It seemed every hour was Happy Hour for Quinlans. Was swimming while under the influence a felony?

I sidled up to the bar and signaled for attention. To the barkeep I said, "Gren tells me I can get a beer here?"

The barkeep eyed me closely, probably checking his memory. Then he grabbed a stein, filled it, and set it down. "First one's one copper. After that, two coppers."

I pulled out the appropriate coin, set it on the bar, and grabbed my beer. I had a bad feeling this was not going to compare favorably with Howard's red ales. Well, I could always turn off my taste buds.

I scanned the tables. I was looking for a spot where I was potentially within earshot of several conversations. I needed to have a much better picture of this society before I'd be ready to dive in and strike up a conversation. Especially after last time.

I plunked my butt down on a bench and hunched over my stein, trying to look like it was the center of my universe. Then I turned up my audio gain and relaxed into creepy eavesdropper mode.

"…can't believe that Ginny wants to bring that fish-entrail-brained loser into the family…"

"…so he says to me, Berro, he says, I've got a right mind to…"

"…that's just too funny. The guy really thought…"

"…claims to have been scattered twice. I mean, what are the chances…"

Wait. *Scattered?* There was that word. The Skippies hadn't been able to nail it down beyond that it was something bad. This could be important. I filtered out the other conversations.

First voice: "…probably a troublemaker. You can get caught up in a scattering once by chance, but twice? No, Skeve had to be involved in whatever was going on."

Second voice: "So if he starts up the same shenanigans here, our whole town could end up scattered."

Third voice: "But that's not fair! Why would we all suffer—"

First voice: "*Fair* isn't part of the Administrator's vocabulary, youngling. If they decide we've contravened the Limits, they will act."

Third voice: "How do we stop that from happening?"

First voice: "We can't stop the Administrator. But we can prevent Skeve from brewing more trouble and causing a scattering in *our* home."

Second voice: "Whaddaya have in mind, Erol? Talk to him? Make him listen to reason?"

A laugh from First voice. "Sure, that'll work. Or maybe he just ends up as fish food."

Second voice: "I'm in."

Third voice: "I've never killed anyone. But I can't lose my family. I'm in."

First voice: "Good people. So I'll invite him here tonight for a beer and dinner to discuss things. Get him a little tipsy, make him think we're on his side. Then, invite him to my place. And take care of business." A pause. "You guys have to be convincing, though. He has to believe we're ready to buy into his crazy ideas."

I turned a casual eye in the direction of the voices. Two Quinlans were nodding as a third Quinlan glared at both of them in turn. Those were my marks.

Their conversation drifted off into more mundane subjects without shedding any more light on Skeve's sins or the nature of the Administrator (I could hear the capital letter when they said it. Literally. The Quinlan language included an inflection to indicate proper names).

I listened for a while longer until I'd finished my, uh, beverage—it was every bit as bad as I'd expected—but no other interesting conversations offered themselves.

"*You guys discover anything?*" I said over the intercom. I hoped I had kept the triumph out of my voice.

"*No, but it sounds like you have,*" Bridget replied, dashing my hopes. "*But at least I found a good hotel. Meet at the dock?*"

Everyone signaled their agreement and I set off for the rendezvous.

⚜   ⚜   ⚜

"Okay Bob, spill. What'd you get?" Garfield asked.

"Let's get a room and shut down," I replied. "I'll go over it back in virt."

We made our way to the hotel that Bridget had found, negotiated with the proprietor, and in short order found ourselves in another small bunkroom.

"Someday we should try moving up the social ladder. I'd like to actually have room to turn around without elbowing someone," Bill said.

"Why?" Garfield replied. "We're just racking the mannies here. What're you planning on doing?"

Bill glared at him but didn't reply. We picked bunks and lay down, then deactivated.

I popped into my library and was just settling myself into my La-Z-Boy when the others arrived. Their favorite furniture was ready for them, since this was a long-term project and they'd be here a lot. Jeeves brought beverages, Spike picked a random lap to colonize, and we settled in.

"All right, here's what I overheard." I queued up the conversation from the tavern and played it back. When it was done, there were several milliseconds of silence.

Garfield was the first to speak. "So, scattering. Does it chase off the miscreants?"

"Mmm, it's a little more than that, I think," Bill said. "There was talk of collateral damage. *Our whole town could end up scattered,* he said."

"So the Administrator, whoever he is—"

"*It,*" Bill said, interrupting Garfield. "The speaker definitely used a third person indeterminate. Or maybe *they.* The Quinlan language doesn't differentiate between singular and plural for this declension."

"Okay, whoever *they* are, they scatter a town if people get uppity. How, I wonder?"

"And what defines *uppity?*"

"We have to get to Skeve before the hit squad does their dirty work," I said, interrupting Bill and Garfield's discussion. "Ideas?"

"Let's just be waiting at the tavern," Bill said.

"Yum," I replied. "More swill."

❊ ❊ ❊

I played with my fish soup, trying to pretend I was eating. Bill and Garfield were doing slightly better, and Bridget had tucked into it like a native. Biologists. Jeez.

We were beginning to get worried after several hours of waiting. The barkeep was eyeing us, since we weren't drinking enough to pay for the seats. Garfield had finally had enough. "We need to consider the possibility that they changed their plans. Do we know what other taverns are around this area?"

Bridget leaned over and poked a neighbor with a finger. "Hey, friend, how many other taverns within walking distance?"

He turned with a frown, but his expression changed when he took in her three friends. Apparently deciding on courtesy as a tactic, he mentioned two other locations and gave us general directions.

I'd given the others a video image of our targets, so Bill and Garfield hurried off to check the other bars. Meanwhile, I bought our neighbor a beer for his trouble, and he became considerably friendlier, if a little perplexed.

"I've got them," Garfield said. *"They're just leaving the Prancing Pralia. I guess they must have changed plans. We're lucky we didn't wait any longer."*

"Stay with them, Gar," I replied. *"We've got you on pings. We'll get there as soon as we can."*

Bridget and I leaped up and sprinted for the door, as protestations and curses followed us.

A text from Bill indicated he was on the way as well. It was tempting to apply non-biological levels of speed, but that would have raised questions that would have required us to leave town—and might alert the Administrator if they had a properly functioning intelligence-gathering network.

Garfield waited at the entrance to an alley as we pulled up. Bill was still on his way. *"Traffic jam,"* he said. *"I'll be a while longer."*

"How do you get a traffic jam in a horse-and-buggy world?" I muttered.

"Maybe start a riot by peeking in the back of a wagon," Bridget muttered back.

"I make *one* mistake..."

"We can't wait for Bill," Garfield said. "They're significantly ahead of us."

We rushed down the alley in single file. There was no sign of anyone, but there were also no alternative paths, unless our subjects had suddenly developed the ability to climb walls. I had a momentary image of Spider-Beaver in red and blue tights and gave myself a mental slap. Then I heard Garfield chanting, "Spider-pig, spider-pig..." and grinned. Bob is Bob, always and forever.

As we rounded a corner in hot pursuit, several figures leaped out of nowhere and tackled us. Our computer reactions were fast enough for us to realize what was happening, but unfortunately the mannies operated in physical reality, where inertia was a thing. We couldn't do more than start to turn in the direction of the attacks, before we were all flattened.

The old mannies would have been too heavy to knock over, but the new models had appropriate mass for the subject species. So I found myself on my back, looking up at a very angry Quinlan, in the middle of bringing a knife down on me.

It was time to abandon any pretense of being bio. I pushed up, faster than the knife was coming down, and the Quinlan went airborne with an *oof*. I smacked him on the side of the head as he hit the top of his trajectory and sprang to my feet. If I'd calculated the force properly, he'd be stunned for a minute or two but not injured.

Two more Quinlans flew backward, and my friends climbed to their feet. Bridget had been stabbed—fake mannie blood was oozing out of a wound in her shoulder. And she looked pissed. I mean *really* pissed. I considered for a moment whether I'd have to protect our attackers from *her*.

Garfield pointed farther down the alley. "Something going on." Without waiting for a response, he sprinted in that direction. Or, well, waddled quickly.

I examined our erstwhile ambushers. All three were in various stages of *stunned*, and there was no fight left. "You okay?" I said to Bridget. She nodded, still scowling. The internal nanites were doing their job, and the blood flow had already stopped. In another minute, there would be no sign of the wound, and even the fur would have grown back.

We build well in the Bobiverse.

The sounds of battle drifted back to us from the direction Garfield had disappeared. After a glance to make sure there was no further danger here, I went down on all fours and galloped off after him, Bridget right behind me.

When I got to the scene of the excitement, I found Garfield beating one Quinlan using another Quinlan as a bludgeon. It had a definite cartoon feel to it, and I stopped dead for a moment to watch. It was also physically impossible for a Quinlan, so there was a good chance that Gar had blown our cover.

"*Ixnay with the Superman act, okay?*" I exclaimed. Garfield stopped, abashed, and dropped his bludgeon. The other Quinlan keeled over slowly, like an inflated Santa when the blower is turned off.

"*Do you think this was about Skeve?*" I asked via intercom.

Garfield replied out loud, "I think that's who they were attacking." He motioned with his head. "He took off down that way. He's injured."

I nodded and headed in the indicated direction.

I found a Quinlan leaning against a wall, trying to block blood flow from multiple wounds. He kept moving his hands from one wound to the next, muttering under his breath. I suspected shock.

"Skeve?" I asked, and he nodded. I quickly removed my backpack and extracted my first-aid supplies. It was mostly bandages, but that was exactly what he needed.

It took only moments to fix him up well enough that he'd at least live to get to a doctor. As I finished up, Garfield and

Bridget joined us. I took one of Skeve's arms and Bridget the other, and we hoisted him to his feet.

"Thanks," he said. "Are you with the Resistance?"

I opened my mouth to reply just as Skeve's eyes went wide in surprise. And then I found myself facedown on the ground. I could see, out of the corner of my eye, Bridget going down as well, with two Quinlans piling on. Yet another individual stepped up, pulled something that looked very much like a handgun, and shot Garfield point-blank.

22. Living in Interesting Times

Bob
July 2334
Galen Town

Garfield glanced down at his chest, then snarled and grabbed the gun from his attacker. I didn't have time to be surprised—my passengers might have knives. I did an explosive push-up, and two Quinlans went flying. I heard noises that indicated Bridget might be doing the same, so I concentrated on my own problems.

One of Bridget's attackers landed sort of on me as I was getting to my feet. I grabbed him by a handful of fur and applied a head slap. It seemed to be effective as a combat technique, overall. I just hoped I wasn't giving them concussions or something.

Bridget and Garfield had taken care of the other Quinlans, Garfield having used the gun as a club. That seemed overly dangerous, but I had enough sense to realize that lecturing him on it at this point probably wouldn't go over well.

We turned as one to check on Skeve, to find him nowhere in sight. Some blood drops indicated which way he'd gone, and some of them had been stepped on, so he had company. But were they rescuing him or kidnapping him?

Garfield peered back up the alley to the location of our first battle. "The first group is still there," he said. "Looking kind of out of it. So this was a different group, and only interested in Skeve. This feels like a rescue."

Bridget and I checked ourselves for stab wounds, then Bridget examined Garfield's chest closely. "No bullet wound. Was he shooting blanks?"

"No, there was definitely an impact," Garfield replied. "But nothing like a bullet. Uh, at least not like I'd imagine a bullet to feel like. I've got internal nanites checking it out right now."

"*What the hell are you people up to?*" Bill asked over comms.

"*Lots and lots of shenanigans,*" Bridget replied. "*Not all of our own making.*" She motioned to the blood drops on the ground. "Let's follow them. Maybe we'll learn something."

"I'll follow," I said. "You guys go around to the street. I think they'll try to get out of the alley as quickly as possible. They need to get Skeve to a doctor, assuming they're rescuers and not kidnappers."

Skeve was still bleeding, as the occasional blood splatter plainly showed. It made tracking easier, at least until the blood trail ended at a closed door.

"What the hell?" I frowned at the door. There was nothing special about it, and the pattern of blood drops didn't seem to indicate any kind of struggle. I tried the door. It was locked, and felt solid.

"*Guys, see if you can find the front of the building to the west of my current location,*" I said. "*Skeve and his companions went in there. I think voluntarily, since the blood trail is clean.*"

"*Got it,*" Garfield replied.

It took about two minutes, with me standing in the alley looking suspicious as hell. I tried leaning casually against the far wall, but that just made me think of *West Side Story*.

And probably looked even more suspicious, if anyone was watching. At this point, if the Administrator had eyes on this whole fiasco, we were definitely blown. I wondered if some version of drones would come swooping in to grab us.

"We're here," Bridget said. *"It's a hotel. No way to pin anyone down. They could have just gone straight through and out the front door."*

"Shit." This outcome deserved an expletive. We'd lost our first legitimate lead, and attracted attention to ourselves at the same time. No question the second group of thugs would remember SuperGar when they recovered their wits. Probably the third group as well. Taking a bullet and just getting angry would look very Terminator-like. Time to bug out?

"Let's meet at the third pub," I said. *"The Olde Gaiter. Bill, you good?"*

"Yeah, no prob. I'll be there before you guys. Go the long way around. This snarl-up is still a mess."

❧ ❧ ❧

Garfield took a long pull on his beer. I leaned forward and watched for any streams of liquid pouring out of his chest. He caught the direction of my gaze and snorted, almost losing a mouthful.

We'd brought Bill up to date on our adventures. Now I hoisted my own glass as Bill described the traffic jam. It really did sound like someone had just started a fight and it had gotten out of control, exactly like what had happened to me. Definitely anger-management issues. It would make for an interesting civilization.

The beer was kind of growing on me, unlike the fish soup. I wondered if I should record a batch for Howard.

Maybe he could adapt it for humans. Or worst case, we'd just keep it in the Bobiverse.

Garfield put his stein down and held out his hand to show a small item. "Fléchette. It seems to have the consistency of dried gummy-bear. I dipped it in some water and it dissolved a bit. I bet it's some kind of drug."

"Hmmph. Unfortunately, our nanites can't do chem analysis." Bridget poked the item with a finger. "But I imagine you're right. Probably a tranquilizer. If they wanted to kill someone, a bullet would be easier. Or a knife."

"Where's the gun?" Bill asked.

Gar made a small head motion. "In my pack. I took a quick look at it. It has a magazine in the handle that feeds fléchettes—this one was mostly empty—and an air cylinder for propulsion. It even looks like it could be pumped up to recharge. It's good tech."

"So was that group, uh, *Administration*, do you think?"

Bill shook his head. "My money's on the Resistance. The tranquilizer gun strikes me as something the Administration would be more likely to have."

"Well, they *did* have one."

"I mean they'd all have them. And the guns would be full. This feels more like one stolen gun." He paused and frowned. "Bob, Skeve asked you if you were from the Resistance. Did he sound scared?"

"About us being Resistance? Not really, no."

Bill nodded. "So he was probably with the Resistance in the first place, and had been trying to get back in touch with them after his scattering. I think the third group was Resistance and was there to rescue Skeve—and we got in the way. Whether they thought we were with the locals who were trying to kill him or maybe that we were Administration, they stepped in, jumped us, and rescued him."

"But if we were Administration, wouldn't we have guns?"

"Hmm. True. So I'm going with 'thought we were locals.'"

"I still think that hotel wasn't random," Garfield said. "They aren't going to leave a back door open. I bet they had a knock or something."

"Do you want to stake it out?" I asked. "We could keep an eye on the place for a while. Maybe Skeve will show up again."

"Then we go in and trash the place?" Bill asked with a grin.

Bridget rolled her eyes. "Okay, I know you're not being serious, but it's still worth a reminder that we can't do anything superhuman." She glared at Garfield. "Or at least nothing else superhuman. We want to find out about *them*, not the other way around."

"Yeah," I added. "The locals might not be able to take us on, but if the Administrator gets wind of us, well, they certainly have better tech and probably can throw superior numbers at us. One thing I do *not* want to do is get captured and disassembled."

Garfield nodded. "So we can't go in like a SWAT team. That also means we'll have to avoid direct confrontations. Hmmph. You'd think being a bunch of spacefaring computers would have more of an upside." He grinned at us and got some chuckles in reply.

"We don't have any choice, though, do we?" Bridget said. "This is the first real lead we've gotten. Even if we're still thrashing around, at least our area of focus is better defined. A lot."

Garfield sighed. "Also a good point. Okay, I will try to figure out a way to keep an eye on the hotel—"

"Barney's Place," Bridget said.

"Seriously? Barney?"

She smiled. "Almost. The native name sounds very similar. I knew it would be the first thing that came to mind, especially considering the infantile Bob sense of humor."

"And yet you went straight there," I replied. "I think perhaps it's catching."

Bridget looked alarmed, and Garfield and Bill started chanting, "One of us. One of us."

"Oh shut up." Bridget was silent for a moment, thinking. "Anyway, if Gar is taking care of the hotel, I guess the rest of us should just go back to looking around. Can we get some kind of search pattern or something?"

"Excellent idea. I'll see if I can get a close scan of the town and ask Hugh to grid it out for us." Bill groomed his fur in thought. "Hmm, also, if Skeve was injured, he'd have to go to a doctor or hospital or something. Maybe we can figure out something along those lines."

"I'll look into that," Bridget said. She gazed at me. "Which leaves you, oh fearless leader."

"I'm going to sit here and drink," I replied, raising my tankard.

"In your dreams, beaver-boy. Find us a new place to stay, a little closer to Barney's, how about that? And tomorrow, maybe we can finally locate that library I keep talking about."

I grinned back at her. Fearless leader, my furry ass.

⚜   ⚜   ⚜

There were several hotels in the area, this block being hotel row. I picked one at random, paid in advance for a week, and collected the key. I didn't like the way the proprietor leered at my money pocket as I meted out the proper coinage. We'd have to make a point of leaving nothing of value in our room.

"*Got us a room,*" I messaged to the others, and attached directions and an image.

"*Great,*" Bill replied. "*I've made arrangements with Hugh to get the town scanned. Unfortunately, moving the drone and doing a detailed scan will use up its remaining heat sink capacity, so he'll have to fly it out and bring in a replacement. He's grumbling about setting the project behind schedule. Like there's an actual schedule. I think the Skippies are just OCD.*"

"*As opposed to the rest of you,*" Bridget observed. No one chose to reply.

The others would be a half-hour or so getting "home," so I took the time to look around our new digs. This room was somewhat bigger than our previous residences, having just about enough room to swing an actual cat with everyone present. Palatial. The ceiling, as with most buildings, was just open rafters. Of course, the climate was mild and Quinlans came with fur, so insulation was not a major consideration.

I eyed the rafters until I spotted a good location—not big enough to hide something valuable, therefore unlikely to be of interest to a burglar. I placed my hand in front of my face, palm down, and opened my mouth. A one-inch roamer marched out onto the back of my hand. If anyone was watching, that would probably give them nightmares for life.

I reached up and the roamer climbed from my hand onto the nearest beam, then made its way to the hiding place. The one-incher was about the smallest model that would have optics suitable for surveillance, otherwise I'd have gone with nanites.

If someone cased the joint while we were gone, I just wanted to know; I didn't want to scare them half to death. Well, okay, maybe a little bit. Bad Bob.

❧ ❧ ❧

I was considering popping back into virt while I waited for the others when I received a comm from Bridget.

"Bad news, guys. I tracked down Skeve."

"This is bad?"

"Sorry, Bill. He left. Got to a doc and got patched up. He was gone by the time I got there."

"Aw, for…" I sighed, but only in person, not over the intercom. *"Okay, let's meet at our favorite pub."*

I locked the door to our apartment after leaving instructions with the roamer. The Growling Guppy was less than five minutes away.

I got there first and grabbed a table. The barkeep glared at me as I parked my butt, probably remembering our parsimonious spending habits. I couldn't afford to stand out like that, so I signaled him for four brewskies and four meals du jour. His demeanor changed significantly, and he gave me a thumb's up. Which, strangely, meant exactly the same to Quinlans as it did to me. Some mannerisms, just by chance, correlated.

Within a couple of minutes, the others arrived. Garfield made a concerted effort to catch up with me on the beer, and Bridget got way ahead on the meal, which was a sort of pasta stuffed with fish. Because why not? I visualized myself being thoroughly sick of fish long before this was over.

I pushed mine toward her as she finished hers off. "Ya know," she said between mouthfuls, "one of the big advantages of being a replicant or running a manny is never worrying about overeating." She paused to savor a mouthful. "Although I used to love hot fudge sundaes. Then I ate a hundred in a row in virt, because I could. I think I'm over them."

"I'd do the same with these fish recipes," I replied, "except I think I'm already there."

Eventually, we finished our meals and I signaled for another round of drinks.

"Careful, Bob, we don't want to run out of money." Bill gave me a glare. "We can't just import more at will."

"We're good for a while. I'd like to avoid the short-term problem. Over the longer term, I hope we'll have some kind of contact before we run out of cash. Failing that, we *will* have to fly some more in. Or get jobs."

Bill grunted but didn't reply. I turned to Bridget. "So, Skeve?"

"Multiple stab wounds, according to the doc. He wanted to know if we were related. I said yes, but not close. He didn't appear that concerned."

"Skeve probably didn't have any relatives here. He was scattered twice, remember?" Garfield made a sort of exploding motion with his hands. "Based on context, it looks like some kind of involuntary relocation. Skeve may be nowhere near where he was born."

"Huh." I stared into space for a moment, thinking about that. "So if someone does something to attract the Administrator's attention, they get scattered—relocated. Or even a whole town? But why?"

"I guess it depends on the motivations."

"As in, what defines *uppity*?"

"Like that, yes."

"Seems like an odd sort of punishment," Bill said.

"If that's what it is," Bridget replied. "Maybe the point is just to isolate troublemakers."

An uneasy silence settled over the table as we wrestled with the idea. A billion miles of river over which to randomly relocate someone. It made banishment to Australia look like a walk around the block.

I looked up as I received a ping from my roamer. "Uh, guys? Someone's broken into our apartment."

"What? How do you know this?"

I explained to Bill about the roamer and he made a gesture of helplessness. "Was that necessary? If we have to leave in a hurry, you won't be able to get your roamer back."

"Yeah, I know, I just—" I stopped as I acquired the roamer's video stream. "Hmm, I expected the proprietor or maybe one of his children or something. Not four rather ugly-looking individuals with weapons. And they aren't being subtle."

"That doesn't sound like a B&E," Bridget said.

"No, it looks more like a home invasion," I replied. "Except no one was home."

Garfield swept an eye quickly around the pub. "Interestingly, there are at least two individuals paying more attention to us than seems reasonable. I think we've been made. My guess would be whatever group messed up Skeve."

"And who we then messed up," I replied. "And who maybe want to return the favor. I don't see any other reason for them to care one way or another about us."

"Unless it's the second group. They are probably not fans either."

"Hmm." I nodded at Bridget's comment and carefully didn't look around the pub. "Shall we go? See what happens?"

"Remember, no superhuman shenanigans," Bridget said.

We rose casually and headed for the door. I noticed out of the corner of my eye that several Quinlans picked that moment to leave also. Maybe coincidence, probably not. "Hey, Gar, are any of those people you noticed now suddenly leaving as well?"

"Yep. I predict interesting times ahead."

"Do we recognize any of them from yesterday?"

Garfield was silent for a moment, then said, "Yes. I see one individual who was with the third group. Resistance?"

Wonderful. Which meant they might have more of those guns. And very probably had more bodies to throw at us. We exited the pub and turned to head back to our hotel room. I could hear feet behind us as multiple patrons also abandoned the Growling Guppy.

"Sounds like four sets of footsteps," Bill said.

"I like those odds," Bridget replied.

We turned a corner, and my spidey-sense went into overdrive. The block was deserted. I mean *really* deserted. In the middle of the day. As we continued on our path, the footsteps behind us came around the corner. And at that moment, another four Quinlans stepped out of doorways ahead of us.

"Wonderful. Classic encircling maneuver," Bill said.

"And masterfully executed," Garfield replied. "My compliments to the Resistance."

"And two to one odds are still accept—aw, shit." I was swearing a lot lately, but it seemed appropriate. The group surrounding us had just pulled knives. Big knives. Real metal, from the look of them. "I think we're probably going to have to push the limits of what's possible for a Quinlan to get out of this one. Try not to cast fireballs, but almost anything else is fair game."

The thugs took their time forming a circle. They grinned at us and waved their knives in a menacing manner. I wasn't sure if they were just trying for psychological advantage, or wanted us to beg for our lives. Either way, they were going to be disappointed.

They attacked simultaneously, jumping toward us more or less as a unit. I was impressed despite myself. They either drilled together regularly, or they'd practiced this particular maneuver. Unfortunately, they weren't dealing with real Quinlans.

I slid to the outside of the nearest knife thrust, grabbed the arm, and rotated my body. My target spun around me and smacked headlong into the Quinlan beside him—but without his knife, which I'd appropriated during the maneuver. As the second attacker staggered under the impact, I smacked him on the side of the head. Punching didn't look like it would be a good idea with the Quinlans—more likely to break their *haora* without knocking them out. And I didn't want to do that kind of possibly permanent damage.

Number two went down as number one caught his balance and turned to me. A second smack and he was down.

I spun around to see how my teammates were doing. Bill and Gar had used similar tactics, since we'd all taken the same self-defense courses. Bridget, however, didn't have any particular martial arts training, at least based on her fighting style, which depended mostly on enthusiasm. She finished off her two attackers, then turned to glare at us.

"What was that?" Garfield said. "Cage-match-fu?"

"They're down, aren't they?" she replied, concentrating her glare on him.

Garfield reached down and gathered the last two knives. "I think we may have a solution to our money problem. Bet these are worth *mucho* bucks. But not here. Pretty sure our welcome has just worn out in Galen. They're after us, they don't appear to be interested in talking, and I bet they'll just keep throwing more and more bodies at us."

"Great," I said. I sent a silent command to my roamer to zero in on me. "Time for a swim, I guess."

⚜ ⚜ ⚜

I opened my mouth and the roamer crawled in. Garfield groaned and cringed, and I laughed. "Yep. Ate a bug."

"I bet you had that in mind when you designed these things," Bridget said with a head shake. "Children."

"Still not mature, even after 300 years," I said, grinning in reply.

"Okay, fun's fun. Time to go." Bill reinforced the statement by diving into the water without waiting. This was a little more work than normal because we weren't leaving from the dock. It had occurred to us that it would be an easy location to establish surveillance, if there were more than the eight thugs. With that in mind, we'd circled around to the west side of town, and then simply walked away until we found an isolated beach.

We dove in after Bill, skillfully avoiding the shallow bottom, and torpedoed out to mid-river, where the current was swiftest. It took only a moment to link up into a Quinlan raft.

"Well, that was eventful," Bridget said. "We do seem to make a splash in every town."

"We'z rock stars, we is," Garfield muttered.

"And we still haven't hit that library," Bridget reminded us.

"Okay, next town, we do that first thing. We should also think about trying to find the Resistance. Maybe not to talk, maybe to spy on. If Skeve was able to get in touch with them despite being in a new town, they must be either easy to locate or have lots of ears."

"Yeah, talking isn't proving to be a high-probability strategy, honestly," Bill replied. "We'll try spying first."

"Sounds good," Bridget said. "Funny, despite my initial skepticism about Hugh's statistics, it looks like he was right. Two towns in, we've contacted a group that might either know something or can point us at someone."

Garfield snickered. "Yeah, 'contacted.' Say, which one of us has a hole in his sternum?"

Bill grinned at him. "Way to take one for the team."

We settled into a companionable silence as the sun warmed our top halves. Insects buzzed around us and Bridget swatted at one. "Must be a heat-seeker. Interesting. I'm impressed at how robust the artificial ecosystem is."

I looked around. "The Arcadia River's pretty wide here, and the current is slow. Let's hand off to the AMIs. They can alert us if anything requires our attention."

The others made agreeing sounds, and we popped back into virt.

23. Dancing with Dragons

Bill
July 2334
Virt

Two gamers lay dead, their smoking, ruined skeletons providing perfect tripping hazards as players ran frantically back and forth. The dragon, red variety, was doing its best to immolate the rest of the dungeon party. The only thing working in our favor was that the beast seemed to want to get at least two targets with each flame breath. Given the required recharge time, it was a reasonable tactic.

"Get under him! Hit him in the belly!" Tim the warrior yelled.

"You first, asshole!" replied Verne the dwarf warlord. "You're the one with the magic sword."

The dragon, an NPC known as Gargh the Destroyer, roared and tried to stomp on Tim. Also a reasonable tactic—Tim was far too close to take out with fire breath, at least not without dealing itself a few hit points of damage.

I had, for the moment, escaped Gargh's attention, probably because I was A) by myself, and B) flat on my back, having been run over by our NPC troops when they fled in terror. I had only some crap armor and a basic sword to my name—the Gamers had flat-out refused to give me a higher starting level. Something about game integrity. Sure.

The smoking remains of Kevin the Wise (perhaps not as wise as he thought) still had a death grip (heh—death grip) on his former pride and joy—a staff of fireballs. Unfortunately, a staff of fireballs against a red dragon was about as useful as a harshly worded email. Now if he'd had a staff of ice storms or something…

Still, it was a valuable weapon. If I got out of this alive, it might be tradeable for some enchanted armor or something. I stood, grabbed the staff, and wrenched it out of what was left of Kevin's hand.

"Chrissake, Bill, get in the game," Verne yelled. "That thing's useless against a red dragon!"

Gargh screamed in rage and pain as one of the players managed to cut a chunk off the dragon's leg. In response, Gargh temporarily abandoned his two-targets-per-breath policy and gave the player—Tim, I think—the full treatment. From that range, even bones would be unlikely to survive. Tim yelled, "Aw, SHIT!" as he turned to ash.

Gargh then went after Verne the old-fashioned way, attempting to eat him. Verne skipped back, desperately waving his battle-axe.

Interesting thing about dragon physiology, though. When they leaned down to bite someone, the tail went up as a counterbalance. And I discovered, from my vantage point, that the Gamers had been obsessively thorough about anatomical details. I wondered for a moment if I should be watching for dragon poop.

Come to think of it, though, a red dragon was probably no more flameproof on the inside than any other animal.

With that thought, I ran up behind the dragon—as a first-level grunt, I was barely worth paying attention to—jammed the staff of fireballs right where a rectal thermometer would go, and pulled the trigger.

There was a muffled *whump* sound, the dragon turned with a surprised look, and smoke puffed out of its ears. Then it screeched, leaped straight up—and the entire scene froze.

A voice said out of thin air, "Okay, we'll need a ruling here. Is the target entitled to a saving throw?"

"Are you friggin' kidding me?" Verne screamed. "How in the hell is it supposed to dodge *that*?" Verne and the disembodied voice began to yell insults at each other, with Verne capering around and waving his fists in the air as counterpoint.

The rest of us gathered around Gargh—still frozen in mid-leap, the staff right where I'd left it. "Fried dragon on a stick," Pete said, slapping me on the shoulder. "Nice. You'll get full credit for that kill."

⚜ ⚜ ⚜

We'd shut down the dungeon and were relaxing in the locker room, comparing notes. I wasn't sure why there was a locker room, but I figured if I could have a pub, they could have a locker room.

"They're still arguing," Gandalf said, shaking his head. "Man, you really created a shitstorm." He chuckled. "Sorry. Bad choice of words."

I grinned at the rest of the dungeon party. Kevin, whose staff of fireballs was now mine, glared sullenly, then averted his eyes. Not a fan, I guess. I was going to get the entire score for the dragon, unless the dissenters managed to overturn the decision, and half the dragon's hoard. The combined experience points would boost me three levels easily. Plus whatever I could get for the staff.

Pretty good day, overall. If only real life went that way.

I motioned to Gandalf with my chin. "We should really get on with things." He nodded and popped us both into his private VR, which closely resembled Orthanc from the Peter Jackson movies, but with La-Z-Boy couches.

"So what's your concern, Bill?"

"Honestly, Gandalf, you guys seem to have bailed on the project before you finished."

He frowned. "Interesting. Maybe we have different definitions of *finished*. Certainly the expedition has a long way to go, but I think we've done what we set out to do."

"Ecological and sociological surveys aren't complete; language translation is mostly there, but still has some holes; we haven't even made a dent in mapping the topopolis; not to mention surveys of Quin."

Gandalf gave me a look of exaggerated patience. "A lot of that is Skippy responsibility. We've been helping, but only because it was interesting for a while. Come on, Bill, what part of *volunteer* aren't you grokking?"

"So as soon as it becomes less interesting, you bail?"

Gandalf thought for a moment. "Yep. Pretty much." He hesitated for a moment. "Look, we're still available for specific questions, but as far as further research is concerned, I think we're tapping out. Bring us another interesting puzzle, though, and we can talk. Okay?"

I sighed. Less and less Bob. "Fine. I got it." I stood up. "Put my character on reserves, okay? I'll probably be back."

He grinned and gave me a thumbs-up as I popped out.

24. Interlude

Bob
July 2334
Virt

Hugh sat in a beanbag chair, nursing a coffee and staring into space. I'd forwarded our logs for the last few days, and he'd immediately invited himself over.

"Tranquilizer guns, huh?" He took a sip. "Interesting choice of weapon."

"How so?"

"There are so many easier and less complex ways of taking out an opponent, starting with stabbing them and working up to a proper pistol with bullets. Heaven's River isn't a space station—you wouldn't have to worry about making a hole. The shell material wouldn't even notice a bullet up to a considerably larger caliber."

"Okay. Anything we can learn from that?"

"Assuming the gun was stolen, which is reasonable, the Administrator seems to want to be careful not to kill anyone." Hugh was silent for several moments more. "And the scattering. I think you're right about the interpretation. Again, it would be easier to just kill people."

"Is it significant?"

Hugh opened his mouth several times to speak, then got a funny look. "Not sure. It could just be that Quinlans don't like killing each other. Except…"

"Yeah. Quin. The planet."

"Listen, Bob, you still have that spare manny buried near the transit station. Have you thought about activating it and sending someone off, maybe upstream?"

I shook my head. "No, it's a spare, Hugh. In case we total one of ours. We need to stay a foursome."

"Hmm. Too bad. I'd like to be able to try one out."

"There's still the test units on Quin. I understand Will and Howard have been playing around with them."

"And breaking them, apparently," Hugh replied. Then, at the look on my face, he added, "Oh, you didn't know. Uh, don't let Bridget find out."

"Howard broke one?"

Hugh's only reply was a grin. He put down his coffee cup and stood. "I got the scan done of Galen Town. Nothing unusual, right down to the limits of resolution that I had time for. In particular, no electronics or forbidden tech that I could find."

"Which might mean the Resistance doesn't have it, or might mean they don't keep it in town. What about the trank guns?"

Hugh shrugged. "They don't register as electronics, so I'd have to specifically scan for them. And I just didn't have time before the heat sink burned out. And for that same reason, random scanning is a nonstarter. I had to retire a drone to get what I did, and I'll be shorthanded until I can fly in a replacement." He held up a hand. "Talk later." And popped out.

❧ ❧ ❧

On a whim, since I had some time to spare, I decided to visit Will on Valhalla—our last meeting had ended abruptly. As soon as I received an acknowledgement, I popped over.

It took only a second to unrack my manny, and I glanced around. Instead of Will sitting in a chair, I found a two-foot roamer waving a leg at me. The roamer began walking, then paused significantly. Presumably it was giving me an impatient look or something, but because the devices were symmetrical, it was really hard to tell.

The roamers hadn't changed that much in the two hundred years since they'd been invented. At least not in principle. Lots of improvements had been made, like the Casimir power source, better materials, more compact electronics, and so on. But it was still an eight-legged general-purpose robot run by a moronic machine intelligence. I frowned in thought as I followed the device. Maybe the Skippies had the right idea. The creation of a practical AI, whether it was truly conscious or just zombie-level capable, would have a huge impact on society, maybe even more than subspace theory and the accompanying technologies had.

The roamer led me out of Will's home and down a long sequence of staircases, some constructed and some cut right out of the native stone. I was beginning to wonder if I'd misunderstood the roamer when we finally came to a flat area on the south side of the promontory on which Will's home was built.

Will stood and waved to me as the roamer did an about-face and headed back to the house. With no need to allow for humanoid limitations on the return trip, the roamer was going straight up the rock face. Show-off.

"Hey, Will. What have you got here?"

Will smiled and motioned to the miscellany of potted plants and plants in earthen rows. "Experimental garden. I've got Terran plants and native plants here, and I'm testing for compatibility. We don't want any surprises when we start full-on agriculture."

I nodded slowly. "It's interesting that Original Bob wasn't much of a gardener, but both you and Bill have turned into real plant specialists."

"Terraforming puts a whole 'nother spin on the problem, bud." Will motioned toward a set of Adirondack chairs near the edge of the garden area. I sat and took a moment to admire the view. Will had picked a location for his home that overlooked a huge lake, surrounded by low mountains. The tree line, or whatever it was, only extended about halfway up the distant slopes, probably due to the still-too-thin atmosphere.

Will followed my gaze and guessed the direction of my thoughts. "The tree line is moving up the slope by several feet per year right now, and it's accelerating. By the time it stabilizes, you'll be able to see plant life all the way to the top of these mountains. And by that point, humans will be living here without having to wear supplemental masks or live under a dome."

We were silent for a few seconds while I admired the scenery. Will seemed to be content with whatever pace I set. Finally I turned to him. "Last time I was here, we were talking about Starfleet. Mostly. But there's Starfleet, the Borg, the Gamers, the Skippies…"

"And those are just the ones that have nicknames," Will replied. "The Bobiverse is going in a lot of different directions, Bob. Literally *and* metaphorically. A lot of replicants have finally decided to take the Von Neumann Probe job description seriously. For instance, we've actually got a couple of thousand Bobs that are actively heading away from human space. Some are stopping and building stations, some are just accelerating."

"Yeah." I examined my hands. "It's just that I have a bad feeling. The Bobiverse was a post-scarcity society for a while, and a utopia, at least for most of us. But what happens to a post-scarcity society when part of the society wants power over the rest of that society?"

"I think you end up either a dystopia, or with two societies."

"And the transition may or may not be orderly and peaceful."

Will sighed. "I haven't got an answer for you, bud. We're just going to have to wait and see how far Starfleet is willing to push."

I sat back and crossed my arms, glaring at the scenery without seeing it. It appeared utopia was an unstable state.

25. Trouble Follows

Bob
July 2334
Elbow

Another day, another town. Touring with a band could be so boring. According to Garfield, anyway. He seemed to be on a rock star metaphor, for some reason.

We'd floated for a full day and eventually arrived at the town of Elbow. Yeah. *Elbow.* Didn't seem to be short for any-thing, either. It was situated at a bend in the river, though, so maybe that.

We pulled our dripping butts up onto the dock, shook off—Quinlans did something very similar to dogs to shed water—and moseyed into town. Elbow seemed to be larger than average, with a robust performing arts subculture. Or maybe there was a festival on. It seemed like every third person was either carrying a musical instrument or dressed up like a minstrel. Or maybe a clown. It could be hard to tell.

We saw at least two stages, with people performing on them, and one children's theater with a *Muppets* kind of a thing going on. No Kermit—that would have been freaky—but the lead character did have a Fozzie-ish kind of look. I stopped to watch and got an elbow in the ribs from Bridget.

Grumbling, I rejoined the group. Bridget buttonholed a couple of people and asked about a library. The second individual gave us an unnerving once-over before responding with directions.

"That was odd," Bill said as we continued on. "Are we underdressed or something?"

I looked down at my naked-save-for-fur body. "Uh…" I grinned at the answering chuckle. "But I'm glad it's not just me that thought he was odd."

We weren't in any particular hurry now that Bridget had her goal in sight, so to speak. So we were able to stop and watch the shows. I asked a few questions and confirmed that there was, in fact, an annual festival going on. Something local, and I never got the gist of the reason for the celebration, but any reason for a party is a good reason.

The singing was surprisingly good. For all their resemblance to members of the weasel and rodent families, Quinlans had amazingly good voices and understood harmony. As for their dancing, uh, the less said the better. When your legs are that short, you can't really soar. I tried to be cosmopolitan and open-minded and appreciate the effort… Nope. That was just a bridge too far.

Eventually the festivities petered out as we moved from the entertainment district into what I assumed must be the business district. And a quite deserted district at that, since everyone was probably back at the party.

"Say, uh, guys?" Garfield said as we turned a corner.

"Um?"

"I'm looking down that block"—he pointed—"and we've been there. I just did a mapping in my head and that guy gave us really long-way-around directions. My spidey sense is jumping up and down and waving its arms right now."

I turned and sure enough, that was a familiar traffic island. My own spidey sense started dancing a Quinlan ballet in time to Garfield's. I turned around slowly, scanning the entire area. "Bill? Bridget?"

"Nothing. And we're about two blocks away from the library," Bridget said. "Maybe he only knew the one way to get there. Or maybe he wanted us to see the sights. Look, I appreciate your concern, but it's closer to the library than the river, so..."

"Right," I replied, "but let's keep our guard up until we get there."

We continued on our route, but without any of the previous sightseeing activity. Every sense was tuned, every reflex on hair trigger. If someone had innocently popped out of a doorway at that point, they might have met an unfortunate end.

Bridget halted abruptly, and Bill almost walked into her.

"What do you guys always call it? Spidey sense?" She motioned to the square ahead of us, where an ornately official building sported a large sign that translated as *Sanctuary of the Written Word.*

"What is it, Bridge?" There were a couple of people talking outside the door of the library, but I couldn't see anything else.

"I'm not sure. One of those guys there started to turn toward us, then aborted the move with a jerk. Like someone who'd just been told *don't look, you idiot...*"

We stood in one spot for several seconds, indecisive. Then Bill said, "So let's see what happens if we try to leave." With that, he wheeled and strode off.

The rest of us looked at each other briefly, then turned and followed him.

And all hell broke loose.

There was a shout behind us, followed immediately by an answering call. Out of doorways and alleys, more than a dozen Quinlans emerged, at full gallop. And I do mean gallop—they were on all fours, a much quicker mode of travel. And they were carrying swords in their mouths, pirate style.

"Uh-oh, I don't think this is the welcome wagon. Time to be elsewhere."

"Thanks, Bob, for that insightful analysis," Bridget said. "Now move your ass or get out of my way." Without waiting for me to make up my mind, she shot past me, heading for the dock. The direct way, too. Apparently, she'd checked Garfield's map.

And, no surprise, the welcome wagon had thought we might do that. Six more Quinlans appeared in front of us, sporting either very large knives or short swords. I wasn't inclined to stop and take a measurement. And three of them had what appeared to be holstered pistols. Trank guns?

I jacked slightly, not enough to lose connection with the manny, but enough to have time for a conversation. The others synced automatically.

"*How many?*"

"*I saw six in front and twelve behind. Some of the ones in front have trank guns.*"

"*Fourteen behind,*" Garfield said, correcting Bridget's assessment.

"*Big gap to the left. We could make for that.*"

"*This is a well-planned hit, Bob. They left a big gap to a whole street by accident? I don't think so.*"

Bill was right. "*Good point. Let's not go that way.*"

"*We're not going to go through them, not with those pigstickers,*" Garfield said.

"*It may be time to loosen up on the no-impossible-moves rule. I don't want to end up as sushi.*"

For Bridget, that was a significant concession. "*Or gift-wrapped.*"

"*Agreed,*" Bill added. "*Let's go through the six in front. Full gonzo.*"

I received three acks, and shifted my manny into overdrive. Not that it turned into a Transformer or anything, but the internal power supply jacked up to full output, all internal nanites deployed for possible damage, and fake blood circulation was increased to handle the higher cooling requirements. There would need to be some maintenance done later.

The scene slowed in my visual field, and I took the time to estimate angles and distances. Garfield and Bridget had already picked lines that would take them either around or through the defensive ends, so I was going to have to go through the middle of the line. I glanced at Bill, who seemed to have the same idea as me.

We ran straight at the line, accelerating as only a mechanical otter can, then went down on all fours as we came to just outside of weapon range. As expected, the Quinlans aimed their stabby things downward at us.

We leaped. And sailed right over them.

Quinlans can jump, of course. But not like this. In Quinlan terms, this wasn't quite like doing a pole vault without the pole, but it would definitely be a record-breaking high jump. And long jump.

And sprint. We hit the ground just as Garfield and Bridget came around the ends of the line, having straight-armed their opponents as they stopped to look up. They dropped to all fours. Our afterburners cut in, and we disappeared down the street faster than they could possibly keep up with. A couple of *pings* off nearby walls led me to believe that at least one of them was now shooting at us as well.

There was a brief astonished silence behind us, which was good, then a bunch of shouted warnings, which was bad. They weren't shouting at each other. This was shouting directed at someone far away. I had a bad feeling we weren't done.

"*Detour, guys. The direct route is booby-trapped or staked out or something.*"

Three acks. No one was sparing energy for speeches. We made an abrupt left at the next intersection, still setting a pace that would make a Quinlan Olympian quit in despair. Assuming they had Olympics.

More shouts. We'd pissed them off, at least.

"*To the left. Up there,*" Bill said.

I looked in the indicated direction. Huh, not bad. A three-story building with a flat roof, and a reasonable climbing route, if you're into parkour. It would be fair to say that Quinlans are not climbers, and it would not occur to them that we might climb drain pipes and hop roofs.

Bill led, we followed. Mechanical muscles and computer reflexes ensured no oopsies, and in seconds we were lying flat on top of a roof. There was a short barrier wall around the edges, more likely for aesthetics, as I couldn't see it being of any practical benefit. I opened my mouth, spit out a roamer, and set it on top of the wall. The others did the same, and in moments we had four video windows hanging in our heads-up displays while we lay out of sight.

Our pursuers came into view in a ragtag mob. They had clearly not planned for this eventuality. Some were checking doors and alleys, others were running back and forth on all fours. I could see five trank guns being carried in plain view. Then one of the group called out and the others gathered around her. I tagged her as a probable leader and made sure I got a close-up image.

The group had a conversation that we couldn't make out. Or maybe argument would be a better term. There was a lot of arm waving and interrupting, and one attempted bite. But eventually they settled on a plan. A couple of Quinlans took up positions in the shadows where they could keep an eye on the street, while the rest marched off the way they'd come.

"Looks like we're going to be here a while," Bill noted.

"I need a coffee," I added.

Leaving the mannies' AMIs on sentry, we all popped into my VR and grabbed our favorite seating. I pulled up the four video windows from our surveillance roamers and put them on the wall.

Bill leaned forward and made a point of making eye contact with each of us. "I guess the first question we need to deal with is how they knew we were coming."

"That's got some assumptions in there."

"Reasonable ones. We didn't do anything to attract attention in Elbow, like peeking into a cart." Bridget gave me the sideways eye.

"One friggin' mistake…"

"Good point, though. This had the smell of setup right from when we asked—" Garfield stopped abruptly and stared into space, his eyes growing slowly wider.

"What? What?" We all knew that facial expression. It was the lightbulb look.

Instead of answering, Garfield pulled up another video, showing our encounter with the helpful citizen who had given us directions. He paused the video, then pulled up another video from our subsequent encounter. He fast-forwarded a bit, then paused that video and placed them side by side.

Sure enough, the helpful giver of directions was also one of our ambushers.

"Well, that pretty much settles it, if there was any doubt in the first place." Bill swept us with a glare. "They were watching for us. Us, specifically. In a town we'd never been in."

"The general population doesn't have anything like telephone or radio. Or telegraphs." Garfield popped up the report from Hugh. "They explicitly are pre-steam and pre-electricity."

"And Hugh confirmed that they didn't have any electronics in Galen," I added. "But there are ways to communicate over long distances that don't depend on those technologies."

Garfield shrugged dismissively. "Pony Express. Ship-based mail systems. Semaphore telegraph towers like in *Lest Darkness Fall*. We've seen no signs of any of that."

"Actually, they do have a river-based mail system, but it's kind of what you might call *relaxed* in its execution. News of us would reach Elbow in about two weeks."

"Which means our erstwhile captors have some more immediate form of communications."

"The Administrator?"

"It does seem to be the most likely explanation."

"But using locals?"

"Who says they're 'locals'?" Bill said, cutting into my discussion with Garfield. "I mean, they're Quinlans obviously, but they might go home at the end of the workday to their underground, fully tech-enabled bunkers."

"Ah. Secret Police. Sort of."

"Wait," Bridget said. "You don't think these are Resistance? Why?"

"Quick communications between cities," Bill replied. "Multiple trank pistols."

I nodded. "Well, it makes sense if you think about it. There's some kind of secret society with full technological assets that is either controlling or at least monitoring the general population. They're probably responsible for 'scatterings' when people break some set of rules."

"Wait, hold on. The people we took on in Galen Town who were trying to kill Skeve talked about scattering as something that someone else did to them. They couldn't be part of the Administrator's group."

Garfield held up his hands in emphatic negation. "Unless it was Skeve or his contacts that tagged us, Bridget. Maybe they noticed us trying to grab Skeve."

"Nope, that doesn't make sense either. Skeve was scattered twice, remember? He wouldn't know anyone in Galen Town." I grimaced in frustration. "Dammit. Are we running from Skeve and Company or from his attackers? And if the latter, does that mean there's more than one group? And do *any* of them represent the Administrator?"

"Well one way or another, we attracted someone's attention." Bill drew a deep breath and leaned back, hands behind his head. "If they have some kind of back-channel communications, then it doesn't matter. Either way, they're a step up from the common population."

I sighed. "We have a lot of theories, but not much in the way of answers. The question is, should we let them succeed?"

"What?"

"Are you insane?"

"That's ridiculous!"

Not one of my more popular suggestions. I contemplated the shocked and outraged expressions. "It's just a thought, guys. And I guess it's always available if we get desperate.

But it would presumably get us in touch with someone, one way or another."

"We'll keep it in mind, Bob," Bill said. "But I think we'd have to be pretty desperate. It's an all-or-nothing action, and if we've guessed wrong, it would send us back to square one. Even worse than square one, I think, since the Administrator would then know exactly what they are dealing with."

I nodded, feeling obscurely disappointed, although whether that was with myself for the suggestion or my friends' reaction to it, I couldn't say.

⚜ ⚜ ⚜

It was now very early the next morning, and the street surveillance had given up and gone home—or wherever—so we'd gone back to our mannies. The first order of business was getting down off the roof. I didn't want to go the same way we came up, because it was always possible someone was still watching from a less obvious location, but a quick check around the periphery of the building made it clear that the route we'd taken was the only simple one. So it was that or go through the building.

Fortunately, there was an entrance, a horizontal hatch which likely opened directly into the top floor. Unfortunately, it appeared to be secured from the inside. But we had roamers. I spit out a couple of two-millimeter models and sent them down between the cracks in the structure. It took them only seconds to discover the problem—a simple sliding latch. Unfortunately, moving that was beyond the strength capabilities of that particular model, even if we all unloaded our entire complement.

"Can we cut the latch off?" Bill asked.

"I guess we'll have to," I replied. "But let's make it quick. Everyone spit up fleas."

We sent in a total of twenty of the little guys, miniature light sabers primed and ready. Ten seconds of battling the dark side and the latch released with a *thud* sound. I pulled up the hatch and we carefully climbed down the very steep stairs.

The building had the look of an apartment complex—long halls with numbered doors, spaced evenly. A stairway was situated near the center of the building. No elevators, of course. The stairs creaked loudly enough to wake the dead in the next town, and we were all cringing with every step.

When we got to the main floor, Bridget glanced around and pointed. "Back door." Without waiting for agreement, she headed that way. The door led out to an alleyway, not particularly odious as alleys went, but quite gloomy due to the tall buildings on all sides. We paused to take stock.

"Are we just going to bail again?" Bill asked.

"A good question," I replied. "It might not actually be a terrible tactic to stay overnight and go to the library in the morning. I'd think they'd be expecting us to head downstream first thing. They might even have set up at the river to watch for us."

"Or we could cross over to the next river and head back upstream. Double back," Garfield suggested. "Maybe communications between rivers is less dependable, or slower."

"Or," Bridget added, "head downstream underwater and skip a couple of towns."

"What about taking a tributary?" Bill said. We turned to him in surprise. "The population isn't all concentrated along the main waterway. There are lots of tributaries and branches along the way, and there's usually a small town or village or two on them."

"Unlikely to have a good-sized library, Bill. That's what we're looking for."

"Yes, but also less likely to have goons looking for us. At least I hope so."

"All right. Vote." I queued up a voting app. Two milliseconds later, the results were in.

One vote for each of four alternatives. Le sigh.

"Well, looks like it's Rock Paper Scissors Lizard Spock again."

The elimination rounds lasted a few extra milliseconds, but it soon transpired that we would be, by executive decision, going farther downriver.

"Okay, fine, but we can't just float down. That's asking for trouble."

"Agreed, Bill. Like Bridget said, we'll stay underwater and put some serious speed on. That will hopefully throw them off."

⚜ ⚜ ⚜

This business of sneaking to the shore was getting really old. The vegetation was thick, and I didn't care how aquatic Quinlans were, I didn't like swampy, squishy ground. But finally, we were in the water.

We went under immediately and stayed a good twenty to thirty feet below for hours, driving west as hard as our mannies would allow. We still hadn't done that maintenance break, and I was a bit concerned about breakdowns, but the mannies were well-constructed and didn't give us trouble.

This marathon swim would take us through one of the segment ends. We all agreed that this was a good thing in that it would be very interesting. Whether it would put us beyond the reach of our pursuers was up in the air.

When we were close to the mountain, we all surfaced and formed a raft. We knew, generally speaking, what to expect. The river narrowed and consolidated as it approached the segment boundary, until only four branches of it flowed through the mountains, in straits wide enough to take the total river flow without forming rapids.

The mountains themselves were impressive. They rose abruptly out of the shell with very little lead-up—only a mile or two of foothills, turning into a slope of seventy degrees, easily. Looking at them, I decided that even that pitch was a concession to the engineering requirements of holding back the atmosphere, if and when. And they seemed to go *up*, forever.

"Are you sure this is intended to be closed off?" Bridget said, staring at the spectacle.

"We have scans," Bill replied. "Not a ton of detail, but essentially the middle hundred yards or so of the segment boundary is a diaphragm, similar to a camera shutter. I think if it was activated, it would close off the segment right to the central cylinder. And you can see two sets of guy-wires or pylons or stays of some kind attached to the central cylinder, if you engage telescopic vision. One set on either side of the central line of the mountains."

"The diaphragms would serve two purposes," Garfield added. "One, to allow segments of the topopolis to be pressurized during construction while adding new segments; and two, as a safety mechanism in case of catastrophic blowout."

"Where would the river go, though?" I asked.

"We already have two rivers going in each direction. Just divert *all* the water to the next river."

"Wow." Bridget shook her head in awe. "Are we *sure* we're more technologically advanced than these people?"

"Not really, no. We just have some tech that they don't. But remember, Bridget, and we said this back when we were starting out on this quest, this whole thing is just scale. Everything we see, humans *could* do, if they had the will. And a sufficiently long view to make them stick to it for however long it took."

Bridget was silent for a moment. "I wonder if the Quinlans got their motivation from being certain that they'd kill themselves off soon."

"Hair-trigger tempers plus advancing weapons technology. Not a stretch as a working theory."

During this discussion, we'd drifted into the actual strait. This section of the Arcadia River was perhaps two miles wide, which lead me to believe that the river must be quite shallow through the segment itself. Otherwise four straits wouldn't be able to handle the flow. In any case, the current had certainly picked up, as had the wind. Ships attempting to sail upriver would have a demanding and extended voyage.

The mountains rose straight up out of the water on either side of us, with no concession for any kind of usable shoreline. I thought I could see what might be a road or path along the nearer bank, but I couldn't resolve it enough, even at maximum magnification, to be sure.

It was an impressive, if short, ride. Within minutes we'd been spit out on the downstream side of the mountains, and the river immediately started to split off into tributaries.

We also discovered something new. It was full night on this side of the mountains. I gazed up at the stars. "We didn't time-warp, did we?"

"Interesting," Bill replied. "It looks like the segments alternate day and night cycles. Makes sense. Only half the segments would be drawing power for sunlight at any time."

"Or this segment has a burned-out bulb," Garfield added.

"Sure. Or that," Bill said, rolling his eyes.

✤ ✤ ✤

Another three hours of floating brought us to a largeish city, just as morning was breaking. Several sets of docks crowded with rivercraft hinted at a thriving industry. The city was close to a couple of tributaries, and it was likely that there were other settlements in those directions. This would be an excellent place to look for information and possibly make contact with a useful group, if we could figure out how not to get stabbed and shot during the introductions.

We decided to improve our chances by entering the town individually. "Group of sabbatarians, one female" was a pretty good filter, if they were watching arrivals. Hopefully they didn't have photorealistic wood carvings or something.

The first person into town, Bill, set himself up to casually watch the dock area, looking for anyone else who might be doing the same. Next, Garfield docked and went looking for somewhere to stay. Bridget arrived shortly after him, and began asking around for a library. I came in last and searched for pubs. There had been a lot of argument about whether this was strictly necessary, but I pointed out that we'd found out quite a bit during the Skeve affair by just sitting and listening.

Garfield reported that he had found and paid for a large room, without having to specify the number of occupants. If we could avoid the use of the word *four* entirely, we'd likely be better off. Bridget had gotten directions to a library, without the up-and-down appraisal this time. She was headed in that direction and sent us a map.

Bill reported noticing a half-dozen different people, including a couple of cops, but admitted they might have legitimate business that required them to hang around—especially the cops. He didn't want to appear suspicious himself, so he suggested tag teaming with Garfield.

I eventually settled into a pretty forgettable pub a few streets in from the docks. It had an outdoor patio, which I took advantage of. The fare offered an option other than fish, for a wonder: *hownid*, which was a smaller and presumably more tender version of the draft animal. I decided that I liked this town...

"Say, did anyone notice the name of the town when we came in?"

"First Stop," Garfield replied. *"Not kidding. If these people have artistic souls, it doesn't extend to their city naming."*

"Well, whatever First Stop may lack in naming, I'm willing to cut some slack, because it also has... steak!"

"What? Where?"

I gave directions and sat back to enjoy my meal. In minutes, the others showed up and ordered similar meals, which the Quinlans referred to as *land meat*. Garfield kept grinning, and I finally had to ask what was tickling him.

"On the *Quinlans are a lot like humans* list," he replied, "I saw an adult female walking her, uh, pet. It's a sort of small dog-equivalent. The poor creature was wearing a waxed paper..." Garfield made motions around his head.

"Cone of shame? It had a cone of shame?"

Garfield grinned. "Yeah. It actually made me homesick."

"I found a library," Bridget said. "That's my target for the afternoon."

"We're going on a pub crawl," I replied. "And doing some listening."

"Three pub crawls, I think. We should stay spread out."

"A little late for that, Bill." I gestured at the table with the four of us seated around it.

Bill made a gesture of helplessness. "Steak. It called to us."

I grinned and sopped up the last of my meal with a piece of bread.

❧   ❧   ❧

We met back in our hotel room at the end of the day, having been very careful to come in one at a time.

"Anyone get anything?" I said, starting the discussion.

Twin head shakes from Bill and Gar confirmed my fears. The pub crawls had been a bust. "I've heard more than I'll ever need to about day-to-day Quinlan life, but the Skeve thing may have been a fluke."

"Or this town is just too unimportant to have a Resistance presence," Garfield added.

"Well, I made some progress on background," Bridget said. "Sort of. It's heavily mythologized. According to their origin story, they originally lived in a land called Quin that had no boundaries but a finite amount of space. The Quinlans overpopulated it and began fighting over the land, so Anec—some kind of god, I think—changed the world to one with boundaries but infinite land to end the fighting. But the Quinlans had gotten into the habit of fighting, so he took away their weapons and their wisdom and scattered them."

"Nice," Bill said. "Finite but unbounded describes a sphere. I don't think the description of a topopolis is right, but they may not have fully explored it yet—lengthwise."

"A billion miles." I shook my head. "Not really a surprise."

"Very interesting," Garfield said. "But it still doesn't explain the backward technological level of the inhabitants.

Do you think it was voluntary? Or maybe voluntary like *my way or the highway* voluntary?"

Bridget paused, then gave Garfield a shrug. "That part still isn't clear. I need to spend more quality time in a library. Talking to people works up to a point, but if you appear too ignorant of common knowledge, they start to get suspicious."

"Actually suspicious?"

She nodded. "I couldn't ask, obviously. But maybe they think you're either Administration and checking on their knowledge, or you're a government operative trying to check on loyalty or attitude."

"Or both," I said. "We don't know the extent to which the Administrator operates as a level of government."

Bridget nodded. "I noticed too. My research isn't clear on a lot of details, but I'm sure the Quinlans have been living like this for hundreds of years. The *Administrator*, as the person or group is called, maintains order by *scattering* any group that breaks the rules, like attempting to circumvent the tech limits, but otherwise seems to maintain a hands-off policy."

"The existence of a Resistance would make me think the Administration is at least partly hands-on." I tapped my chin in thought. "What about Administration staff? Are they known? Do they have offices?"

"Understand, a lot of this is inferred from reading between the lines. So everything I say comes with a large dollop of uncertainty. But no, they're not an official part of the hierarchy. They are generally referred to as *Crew*. It's not clear whether they live somewhere else or are just part of the population. Which leads me to believe it might be both. Hired muscle for the in-country work, and full-time Crew somewhere else."

"Wow, that's pretty a good analysis, Bridget," Bill said. "So with the group that just wanted to bump off Skeve, we now have three factions—Administration plus Crew, Resistance, and locals who don't want anything to do with either one. The business in Galen makes more sense now."

⚜   ⚜   ⚜

We discussed strategy the next morning. First Stop didn't have any other libraries as it turned out. Bridget grumbled and made faces, but we recognized that it was to be expected. It wasn't a small town, but it did appear to be a backwater. Bridget, not surprisingly, wanted to head out immediately.

We asked around, and determined that the biggest, closest town was Three Lagoons. It was located on the next river system south of us, the Utopia, at the mouth of the connecting tributary. I immediately voted to head there, as it would give me a chance to examine how Heaven's River handled a connection between two rivers heading in opposite directions.

"We really have to stop prepaying our room rentals," Bill complained. "At least until we know how long we'll be staying. I think we've overpaid about a month's worth already."

Garfield made a head motion toward Bill. "The accountant has spoken."

Bill showed Gar his teeth, but didn't reply.

For a change, we'd be leaving town in a dignified and completely unexceptional manner. Not even any looking-in-carts jokes. We marched to the docks, jumped in the water, and per directions from the locals, swam determinedly for the south side of the river.

Once we were close enough, we formed into a Quinlan raft and let the current take us. It would be twelve miles or so before we'd reach the tributary, known locally as the Gronk, which would take us to the main river to the south, the Utopia. Meanwhile, it was a good opportunity to get some sun and do a little thinking.

The others apparently felt the same, as there was no attempt to start any kind of discussion. As one, we tilted our heads back and worked on our under-beak tans.

After some indefinite but comfortable amount of time, Bill said, "We've got company."

Three heads jerked up and swiveled. The company, though, turned out to be a *hown*-driven riverboat, which was gradually closing in on us. We could tell immediately from their heading and relaxed pace that they were simply traveling to the same destination as us, rather than actively trying to intercept.

Garfield glared at Bill. "You didn't have to be so dramatic. I almost had a coronary."

Bill managed an *injured innocence* look. "What? All I said was that we have company. The coronary is your fault. You have a guilty conscience."

Garfield responded with a dismissive *pfft*, but the statement was technically true. And Bill would just deny it had anything to do with the earlier *accountant* comment anyway.

As the boat came closer, we were able to get a good look. It was a cargo hauler, with very little in the way of passenger accommodations. Some Quinlans had obvious duties, and a few were hustling around. But there was another group of four just sitting on the deck, relaxing.

One of the crew waved at us and called out, "If you're taking the Gronk, we'll give you a lift for a copper each. Got another set of sabbatarians here already." He motioned to the group that was sunning themselves.

Bridget said, "Can't hurt, and we might pick up something. And the ride is supposed to be a little rough."

Without further discussion, we broke up, submerged briefly, and *pooted* onto the deck. The deckhand held out a paw, and I dropped four Quinlan coins into it.

We ambled along to the other group, which moved over to give us some deck space.

"Planning on heading east?" the deckhand asked, walking with us.

"Going to Three Lagoons," I replied. "We haven't planned past that point. Bridget, here, wants to visit their library."

"Ah, a seeker." The Quinlan made a gesture that translated as mildly dismissive. "There's fewer of them every year, seems to me. Most of you youngsters seem to be content to just float until you find a place to settle."

"Isn't that the point?" a member of the other group said.

"Maybe. But we used to be more." The deckhand gave the other Quinlan a hard look and stalked off. I glanced from the retreating back to the speaker.

The seated Quinlan grinned up at me. "Oldsters are determined to pine for our lost destiny. But this is a good life. What's the point?"

"You mean Quin?" Bridget asked.

He nodded in reply. "I'm Kar, by the way. This is Malin, Arik, and Ti."

This produced a brief flurry of introductions before Kar continued on what sounded like a speech he'd made many times before. "I have literally never met anyone who was scattered. Know why? Because most people aren't idiots. From what I learned in school, this is paradise."

"Or a zoo," Ti interjected.

"With no gawkers, Ti. I think you need a better metaphor. Meanwhile, there's lots of fish, the weather is predictable, the water's clean, and other than the occasional border dispute, there's no war. As fates go, it doesn't suck."

This was definitely looking like a well-worn argument, and I was prepared to just sit back and listen. But Bridget wasn't going to be so passive. "What about the Resistance?"

Kar laughed. Even Ti did a Quinlan eye-roll.

"Oldsters playing at warrior," Kar said. "There's nothing to resist. Crew barely exist, not so you'd notice. And if there's a scattering, not that I have any personal knowledge, mind you, you just wake up and it's done." He made a negating motion with his hand. "What're they fighting *for*, anyway? Chase fish, bask in the sun, swim until you're tired, sleep. That's all you need."

"*This guy's a hippy,*" Bill said over the intercom. Then to Kar, "Except for the part about making a family and children."

"Sure, but do we need towns for even that?" Kar swept his eyes over his audience. "Everything in towns is stuff you can get for free, or stuff you only need because townies *say* you have to have it. We could get rid of towns entirely, and no one would suffer."

"It would make it pretty hard for us to trade our goods." We looked up. It was the same deckhand, come around again in his cycle of chores.

"Slightly different things from upriver or downriver, that people want only because they've been told it's desirable. Or better." Kar was warming to his subject, and still seemed to be in a well-worn groove. I watched his friends as he and the deckhand traded barbs. They didn't seem surprised, or especially concerned about his comments. If anything, their expressions indicated agreement, to the extent they cared at all.

The argument soon died down, as the deckhand wasn't being paid to stand around, a fact made loudly clear by someone who was probably the captain. He moved off to his next assignment and Kar laid back to catch some rays.

"*That's interesting,*" Bridget said over the intercom as we closed our eyes and pretended to doze. "*And not entirely unexpected. Civilization and technology are methods of controlling the environment to increase your chances of survival. But what if you're so well-adapted that you don't need civilization at all? Or don't need it anymore?*"

"*Heaven's River is idyllic,*" Bill replied. "*Are you saying it's perhaps too much so?*"

"*Yes. The Quinlans were probably well-adapted to their environment on Quin, and this environment was designed with their preferences in mind, so it's even more ideal. So there really isn't any kind of selection pressure anymore.*"

"*And you think this is deliberate?*"

"*I don't know, Bill. I don't think so. The problem is that if it continues, the Quinlans could lose their remaining knowledge, then their culture, then ultimately their intelligence.*"

"*Excuse me?*" I said, aghast.

"*Brains are expensive, Bob. They are for humans, and they are for Pav, and they are for Quinlans. Twenty to twenty-five percent of daily calories go to keeping us cogitating. Now assume a Quinlan comes along with a smaller brain, maybe only needing fifteen percent. That Quinlan has an advantage, in reproduction, in keeping itself fed, and so on. Without any reason to privilege intelligent Quinlans, the new breed could take over within a dozen generations. Have that kind of stepwise mutation happen a few times, and the Quinlan race would be just another set of animals.*"

"*The Administrator cannot have had that in mind.*"

"*I agree. Which is why I think it's probably an unintended consequence. And possibly one that hasn't occurred to anyone yet.*"

"*Dammit.*" I was here to get Bender. That was all. But could I just walk away from this? Would I end up being *the Bawbe* all over again?

As the old Pachinoism goes, the more I try to get out, the more they keep pulling me in.

26. Tensions Rise

Bill
July 2334
Virt

We'd left the mannies "napping" so we could get some work done in virt. The AMI would alert me if something required my attention. Meanwhile, I had a backlog of items that had accumulated.

I reviewed the list in front of me and frowned. The data window showed times and places of attempted logins to SCUT relay stations and autofactories. In every case, the login ID used in the attempt had been the old, common ID used in all equipment. Back when all the Bobs were on the same page.

Garfield had been reading over my shoulder. "I suppose it's mathematically possible it could be someone other than Starfleet."

"It's mathematically possible you might spontaneously burst into flames," I replied, turning to him. "I'm not betting on it, though."

"Well, we're in virt, but I get the point." Garfield walked over to his La-Z-Boy, picked up Spike, and sat down with the cat in his lap. "So Starfleet is trying something, where *something* is undefined but probably not good. Is there any-thing we can do?"

"Already done it, Gar. I've accessed every single piece of equipment in the Bobiverse, tested the logins, and changed them. I've sent encrypted emails to the putative owners, with instructions to change the logins again themselves. And not to share those credentials."

"Bill, what if Starfleet escalates?"

"Escalates how? Sends a war fleet?"

"Um. Well, if they did, we wouldn't be able to defend against it. They know as well as we do how we detected the Others' fleet…"

"And they won't make that mistake. Except they won't send a fleet. Where would they send it? Here? Eta Leporis? Omicron2 Eridani? Even if they were inclined to violence, this isn't about real estate, or an entrenched foe. It's about political stances, and both sides of the argument are pretty spread out, physically."

"Yeah, I get that, but I just have this bad feeling. They're not going to just throw their hands in the air. So they'll be looking for ways to enforce their point of view."

"Like…"

Garfield sighed. "I'd feel a lot better if I could come up with even one half-plausible scenario. But other than the vague conviction that they'll do *something*, I'm coming up blank."

I glanced at my data window one last time, then closed it. "I talked to a couple of my bio government contacts," I said, turning back to Garfield. "They'll bring it up with their bosses, they say. But I don't think anyone is taking me seriously. This is a VR problem, after all. And the problem with VR problems is it's hard to see how they relate to the real world."

Garfield grinned. "If you die in virt, you die in real."

"Horse puckey." I laughed. "The Gamers die all the time. Sometimes several times in one session."

"You visited them, didn't you?"

"Yeah, Gar. As part of the negotiations for the Heaven's River project. They let me tag along in one of their LARPs. They go for the full meal deal, you know." I shook my head in disbelief. "Full VR, fully armed and armored characters, total battle realism. They have a limiter on pain reception, just like we do with the mannies, but basically they can and do get stabbed, speared, slashed, burned, blown up, disintegrated, fireballed, electrocuted, drowned, eaten, and whatever other fates D&D and its spiritual descendants have come up with."

Garfield grinned. "Nevertheless, I can see the attraction."

"Sure. And in whatever Bob or Bobs bred the Gamers, that attraction became an obsession." I paused. "The thing is, and this is the reason I brought them up, the Gamers aren't really opposed to Starfleet's attitude. I mean about breaking contact with bios. They don't have a moral issue, they just see bios as a distraction."

"Like the Skippies."

"Yeah. It worries me a little. Could we end up being the minority viewpoint?"

"Maybe we should make ourselves a poorer target," Garfield replied. "And move the moot and backup station."

"Already done, Gar. Ultima Thule is now so far outside Epsilon Eridani that an expanding search would take centuries to find it. It occurred to me that, even if I haven't published the location, I've done several clonings since I built it. And some of my clones have cloned. So there are at minimum dozens of Bobs who know where it is—was."

Garfield hung his head. "I hate this."

"Me too, buddy. It would appear that utopia is an unstable state."

Garfield nodded, looking glum, and popped out. Sighing, I brought up my next TODO.

27. JUST PASSING THROUGH

Bob
July 2334
Utopia River

B ridget spent some time walking around, talking to the crew. I knew she was trying to get sociological data, so I left her to it. I was more interested in the changeover to the Utopia River. I asked Malin about it, and she just turned and glanced at Kar. Apparently he was either the official spoke-scritter for this group, or the only one who had the energy to talk.

"We've switched rivers a couple of times," Kar said. "It's a little rough in the middle part of the connector, which is why we like to hop on a boat. But you could go it on your own if you had to."

"Do you know why?" I said this as innocently as I could, but I was really interested in Kar's level of knowledge.

He shrugged in response. "It's the way the world is. It's how the Administrator made it. We don't question or judge."

How the administrator made it? That sounded an awful lot like a religious statement. Were Quinlans starting to think of the Administrator as a deity?

Bridget came back to our group and lay down. "We're just entering the Gronk tributary now. That spit of land"—she pointed downstream—"is where it splits from the Arcadia. It does a half circle and dumps us out going downstream on the Utopia. Three Lagoons is on the far shore, so we'll have to jump ship and start swimming right away."

"You're going to Three Lagoons?" Kar asked. "Why bother? We're looking for a good patch of shore to homestead. Why not join us?"

Bridget smiled at him. "We have plans, Kar. I'm a seeker. My friends and I want to go home eventually. We're not looking to start fresh."

Kar shrugged, plainly not devastated.

⚜ ⚜ ⚜

We soon hit the section of Gronk where the river-bottom impellers were most noticeable. The river's surface took on the appearance of a mild set of rapids, and the current became choppy and uneven. I knew what was going on. The impellers were creating a form of storm surge, as the water was forced to pile up. A quick android eyeball estimate put the surge level at a couple of feet in height.

The boat bucked and tried to turn off its heading, and one of the *howns* bleated in fear. The other animals turned briefly to look at it without interrupting their measured gait on the treadmill. I was impressed by these beasts. They seemed capable of walking all day at the same plodding pace, fed and watered regularly by the crew without even stopping. Perhaps it was *hown* heaven.

The battering lasted less than ten minutes, although I had to admit to myself that it would have been pretty hard to endure in the water, at least for a native Quinlan. As we

came out of the apex of the tributary's curve, our view gradually opened up to the Utopia River, flowing in the opposite
direction of the Arcadia. Far in the distance I could just
make out the barest impression of a town. Three Lagoons.
Bridget was already having a conversation with the deckhand, gesturing occasionally in that direction.

She came over to us and made a *get off your asses* motion.
"Time to bail, boys. If we start now, we won't have to fight
the current too much when crossing." She nodded to Kar.
"Nice to have met you and your friends. Maybe we'll see
each other in the future."

Kar nodded back without comment. The other three
hardly registered the conversation.

We said a general goodbye to the boat crew and dove
into the river. Swimming submerged, we put on some extra
hustle, but not enough to cause any consternation in our
erstwhile shipmates. We didn't want to pop up an impossibly long distance away. We'd *probably* never see these people
again, but why take chances?

⚜   ⚜   ⚜

Three Lagoons looked, from the water, like a significantly larger-than-average town, and perhaps more
cosmopolitan. That would make Bridget happy, since it
would almost certainly mean a bigger library, or maybe
even several. We marched up the dock ramp, one at a
time, part of a steady stream of Quinlans. It felt a little
like rush hour. Did Quinlans have rush hours in Heaven's
River?

While it seemed unlikely that word of us would have
spread across rivers, it felt like basic common sense to not
be seen together, at least while coming into town. As before,

we each had our tasks to perform. Garfield had suggested on the way over that he'd like to do the pub crawl, but I'd claimed seniority, earning me a low growl.

In short order, Garfield had us a room at a transient hotel, Bridget had directions to a library, Bill reported no suspicious activity at the dock, and I had a beer.

I had picked the pub closest to the river, since it seemed likely that it would have the most diverse customer base. The others joined me and ordered meals and drinks.

"I'm going to head for the library right after lunch," Bridget informed us. "Before you wankers manage to screw things up and get us run out of town."

"One time," I muttered.

"Two, honestly," Garfield said. "At least we haven't burned anything down, yet."

"The day is young," Bill muttered.

Bridget smirked at him, wiped her *haora*, and marched off with a parting wave.

"So, what shall we do?"

I grinned at Bill. "I vote for eavesdropping while blending in."

The vote was unanimous. I signaled for three more.

The beer wasn't half-bad, but the scuttlebutt was strictly local stuff. After an hour of way too much information about people's financial and relationship problems, Bill and Garfield decided to check out other pubs. I couldn't blame them, but I maintained my theory that the dockside pub was the most likely place to get something other than routine conversations.

After three more hours, I was starting to doubt my logic. I'd learned more than I ever wanted to know about the daily dealings of Quinlans, but nothing that would raise an eyebrow. I pinged Bridget to see what she might have discovered. And got dead air.

"*Guys? Guys? Bridget's not answering. Something's happened.*"

No answer.

28. United Federation of Sentients

Will
July 2334
Virt

I stared at the wall of small video windows, wondering for the umpteenth time why I was still doing this. Each window contained the image of a representative of a human colony. The old UN had been replaced by the United Federation of Sentients council, but it was mostly the same bag of rabid spiders, with new faces.

Unfortunately, Bobs as a rule had too much common sense to get stuck with the duty, and I had too much of a sense of duty to listen to my common sense. I couldn't walk away and leave an empty seat representing the Bobiverse; so here I was, once again listening to a snarling, self-centered, self-absorbed, self-righteous herd of bozos.

Stupid humans.

The current debacle was about how to handle the Pav. There had always been an assumption that they would, in the fullness of time, join the UFS. We'd even made sure the name wasn't human-centric, in order to avoid any issues of perceived bias.

Might as well not have bothered. The Pav had made it pretty clear that they weren't interested. Also that they would come and go as they damned well pleased. The Newholme and Pangea colonies were stopping just short of threatening to shoot down any Pav vessel that passed within the Kuiper line of their systems.

At the moment, Ser Lambert of Pangea was just winding down. She glared at the council, or at their video windows at least, and sat down. Dozens of request lights immediately lit up. The Chair recognized the representative from Newfoundland on Asgard, Ser Wahl.

Ser Wahl looked into the video camera with a small smile. "Ser Lambert, while I grant your concerns about sovereign space are legitimate, perhaps you are overreacting just a tad? The Pav fleet consists of two small exploration vessels based on the Heaven-1 design. Despite their attitude, their military growth is still mostly theoretical."

Representative Wahl's statement was a model of calm and moderation. Also, in my opinion, naïve. While I didn't want to be at odds with the Pav, I was fairly certain that their fleet was growing slowly only because they were putting most of their current production capacity into creating more autofactories. A lot of effort spent bootstrapping early on would pay handsomely down the road. And the Pav, unlike humans, were disciplined enough to take the long view about such things.

But I'd already pointed this out, and been soundly ignored. So screw it.

I sighed and took a moment to check the status of my projects back on Valhalla. Everything was in the groove. Construction had already started on several cities that would be alfresco, with no domes or individually pressurized buildings. Things were looking good.

The floor had been handed to the representative from Vulcan. I felt a sense of foreboding as I listened to his closing comments. "…If the Pav are not going to respect our boundaries, and assuming we don't intend to go to war with them, the next best step would be to claim all habitable planets in the area. We have surveys from the Bobs, yes? Let us launch colony vessels, sufficient to tie up all real estate. Leave them no reason to launch in the first place."

Seriously, had that ever worked on Earth? Did he actually expect that the Pav would take that state of affairs philosophically?

Sooner or later, we would be going to war.

29. PANIC TIME

Bob
July 2334
Three Lagoons

This was simply not possible. Even if some theoretical adversary managed to take out all three of my friends at the same time, it would only take out the mannies, not the actual people. By now, Bill, Garfield, and Bridget should have reported in and warned me of whatever.

Unless…

Unless it, whatever *it* was, had actually taken out Bill, Garfield, and Bridget. But they were physically separated by light-years, not only from me but from each other. That made no sense.

I sent a quick text to Bill. Well, tried to. I got a comm error for my trouble. That meant severed communications.

My next step should be to narrow down the possibilities. *"Guppy, check integrity of communications with the rest of BobNet."*

[No connection.]

Oh, son of a bitch. With communications down, the three mannies were running on AMI standby orders. I leaned on my elbows and put my head in my hands to look like I was resting my eyes. I gave my manny's AMI some simple instructions and popped back into VR. Guppy, as usual, waited at parade rest.

"Can you narrow down where the communications are severed?"

[The Midway relay station is responding to pings, but is refusing connection requests.]

Huh. Not good. But I didn't have time to worry about that just now. I picked up Bridget's manny's address and checked status. Sure enough, the AMI was operating in autonomous standby.

So, first things first. I had to get the mannies out of town. I entered Bridget's manny and found myself in a library. Or book repository. Or bookstore. Someplace with books, anyway. I quickly gave the AMI some simple orders, waited for a moment to make sure it was responding, and popped out. The manny would maneuver itself to the docks and submerge itself to below a Quinlan's maximum depth. It would ping me if something happened on the way that was beyond its ability to handle.

It took only a few seconds to do the same with Garfield's and Bill's mannies, then my own. I needed more than anything else to get the mannies out of any possible danger. If they were damaged or captured, our expedition was over and we might never find Bender.

I waited the few minutes while the four mannies made their collective way to the river and dove in. Only when all four reported themselves in position did I relax. I put them all in low-power mode, then turned to Guppy. "Okay, Guppy, fill me in."

[The local station is behaving within normal operational parameters. The Midway station is actively refusing connections, other than basic diagnostic pings.]

That was the station I had ordered built in Delta Eridani and flown out to the Midway point between that system and Eta Leporis. At least it wasn't destroyed. A malfunction?

"Any information from diagnostics?"

[Negative. The station is refusing to execute diagnostic procedures.]

That *was* odd. The pings were handled at a much lower level, and were serviced without any need for the AMI's attention, but any explicit commands would—

I started to get a bad feeling. Just the barest hint of a theory, and not a good one.

"Guppy, can you force a reset?"

[Negative.]

"Is that drone I set up as a temporary station still in working order?"

[Affirmative. It is in standby, but still potentially operational.]

"Boot it up, please."

[Done.]

I pinged Bill as soon as I felt the SCUT connection come up. The comms protocol indicated a valid connection, but for several milliseconds I got no response. Then I had an audio-only connection.

"We have a situation here, Bob. How are you doing? Where are our mannies?"

"I've put them all at the bottom of the river. They're safe. What's going on?"

"More than half of our space stations have shut down and are refusing connections. BobNet is attempting to reroute, but we still have a lot of locations offline. I'm coordinating a response, but right now we're just trying to determine overall status."

"Got it. Have you contacted Bridget?"

"No, Quilt is one of the nodes we can't reach. Garfield is busy mapping the network, to see where we should concentrate our energy."

"How about the Skippies?"

"Hugh has already contacted me," Bill replied. "He was monitoring the expedition, then was abruptly kicked off. I told him I'd update him if I found out anything."

"Okay, Bill. Let him know I'm back on, and keep me posted."

"Hey, by the way, how are you able to communicate?"

"Remember that temporary SCUT relay I set up by dropping off a drone at the Midway point? I reactivated it. It doesn't have enough bandwidth to maintain manny or VR connections, so you're all still S.O.L. until we get the main station back up, but at least we can talk."

"Hmm. Handy. Is it anywhere near the Midway station?"

"Of course. I aimed them both for the same—ah." Bill's intent became clear. The drone could fly over to the station and do a physical inspection. Maybe even some repairs, if necessary, since I'd supplied the drone with a roamer inventory out of habit.

Bill and I exchanged promises to keep each other updated, then I gave the necessary orders to Guppy to get the drone moving.

[Transit time approximately six weeks.]

Well, considering the interstellar distances involved, that was practically a bullseye. I had literally ordered the two devices to the same location, halfway between systems. Only navigational inaccuracies accounted for even that relatively small discrepancy.

Meanwhile, what? My relay drone couldn't support a VR or manny session, so I couldn't visit Bill and the others and they couldn't visit me. Or help me with the mannies. And I couldn't do much until the drone reached the full-sized relay station.

Might as well get something done.

I connected up with my manny and found myself underwater with my hands clamped to something unidentifiable. Three other mannies floated beside me, in similar positions. So the AMIs had been successful. I just hoped the incident didn't start a legend of zombie Quinlans staggering through town.

Working on my own would be harder. I needed to be able to cover more territory to make up for the loss of manpower. Well, maybe roamer-power…

I sent commands to the other three mannies, and they opened their mouths. Out popped four one-inch roamers from each android. I didn't have room internally for all the extra mechanical servants, so I had them attach themselves firmly to my fur and snuggle in as much as possible.

I swam up to the dock, as nonchalant as you please, and joined the line of Quinlans walking up the ramp. Five minutes of buttonholing passersby got me the names and general locations of every pub in the area, not just the ones immediately around the dock. It wasn't much of a plan, but it was a start. And the only consistently successful source of information we'd discovered to date.

It took most of the day to visit each pub, look around, and place a roamer or two in a discreet location. That accounted for twelve of my roamers. I placed two more in the local equivalent of the municipal hall, and kept two as spares.

Bill would have a fit if he knew what I'd done. The roamers were an irreplaceable resource, and their loss could endanger the mannies as well. But it was time to bet the wad.

With everything in place, I retired to our hotel room. It really was a step or two up from the crap we'd been staying in before. I visited the proprietor and paid for a week, just to make sure he didn't hassle us.

I waited until nightfall, then one at a time, I rode the other mannies from the river to the hotel room. Now we were all together. Sort of. If the blackout didn't resolve itself, I'd have to adjust my plans. I couldn't keep shepherding four mannies from city to city. For better or worse, I was going to make a stand here.

❧ ❧ ❧

Three Lagoons. No kidding. I'd seen some of the Quinlans' festivals, so I knew they were reasonably artsy, but it apparently didn't extend to town names. Well, humans didn't always wax lyrical either. I remembered street names from back in the 20th century. Main. Broadway. East First. Or named after some city father.

I scowled. I seemed to be in a really black mood. Well, everything was in place. The roamers would record all conversations and Guppy would forward them to the Skippies for processing. That would just about max out my relay's bandwidth, but I felt it was a priority. Hugh would alert me if anything of importance surfaced. Meanwhile, I might as well relax.

I put my manny to bed and returned to my VR library. A quick and quite unnecessary check of the status of all the roamers revealed nothing outside of expectations, so I summoned a coffee and settled back in my La-Z-Boy.

❧ ❧ ❧

Bridget's voice broke my concentration. "Hi, Bob."

"Bridget! Bill said Quilt was offline. How did you—?"

"Howard can give you the details, but something about routing the long way around, through the original Pav home system."

"Seriously? That *is* the long way around." Like New York to Miami by way of Hong Kong. But that's how routers work. "Well, I'm glad to hear from you. Unfortunately, you won't be able to control your manny with this connection. My relay station is too small."

"Bill explained it to me. But is it good enough to transmit a backup?"

"Yes, but not in a reasonable time frame. In any case, I don't have any matrices under construction. Too low on the TODO. I've been concentrating on increasing our spy drone inventory up until now. Why, were you rethinking the whole cloning thing?"

"No, I hadn't gotten that far. Just working through options. I guess I was mostly hoping you'd have a work-around soon."

"Well, we sort of do, but it'll take a while. I'm going to build some matrices as soon as I can, but I'm also working on getting the Midway station back. We'll see which plan of attack pans out first."

I received a ping from Hugh. I sent him a *please hold* response. "Busy day. Hugh wants to talk to me now. Look, Bridget, even if I get the station back, we need to consider using local replicants, just to remove the vulnerability. Think about it, okay? Just in case."

"Okay, Bob." Bridget closed the connection.

Immediately, Hugh's voice said, "Hey."

"Hi, Hugh. What's up?"

"I've been talking to Bill. The comms outages are looking more widespread as we continue to investigate. It's seeming more and more like this is going to be a long, drawn-out thing. Bill and Gar will probably not be able to return to the expedition right away, even if and when we get your main relay station back up. You need to consider setting up some local matrices—"

"Already there, Hugh. I'll order Guppy to create three new ones. But I think they'll be finished before I get my relay back, even in the best case scenario. So I think I'm going to have to clone myself, much as I dislike the idea."

"Well, I could send myself over. Spare you the trouble of cloning."

"That's a helluva lot of bandwidth. It could take days. And screw up communications the whole time. It doesn't seem like the best alternative. And it leaves you out here at the end of it. At least I'm already here, if you get what I mean."

"You sure? I really don't mind."

"If things work out that way, great. But like I said, it seems suboptimal." I paused. "Y'know, you've had quite a change of attitude about this project. I remember early on in the project, you just thought it was an interesting exercise."

"Yes, but it's turned out to be a lot more than just a hike in the woods. I've been a little jealous, to tell the truth, following along all the shenanigans. I know it's a serious business, but…"

"But also a lot of fun," I finished for him. "Yep, I get it. And I'm thankful for the offer, especially if my alternative is a new cohort."

Wow. Fast times. As soon as Hugh signed off, I ordered Guppy to bump priority on completing three replicant matrices. They'd be a while, even at high priority, with the dearth of raw materials in this system. But one way or another, they'd be useful eventually.

✣   ✣   ✣

Three Lagoons was a nice town, overall. Wide, clean streets, relaxed pace, no overly officious cops. Even the food seemed to be a step up. Still fish, unfortunately. But the local chefs seemed to have discovered things like, oh, *salt*.

I wandered the town in a seemingly random manner, checking out the sights. In reality, I was mapping everything, and I strolled every street, pathway, and alley at least once. I was ready for ruffians and/or blackguards, but none made an appearance. Just as well. I had one of the confiscated pigstickers in my backpack, to threaten with if necessary.

Eventually I ended up at the library that Bridget had found, and decided to spend the afternoon. They didn't have a Dewey decimal system, but they did sort things roughly by subject. I found a section that seemed like it might contain some history, grabbed some books, and settled in for a good read.

[Bridget is requesting a meeting.]

The announcement registered in my internal audio. I still jumped. A couple of other readers looked up at me quizzically and I smiled back. "Fleas."

They frowned and edged away, while trying not to look too obvious about it. Oh well. So much for being popular.

"*Thanks, Guppy. Message her back, tell her I'll be about an hour.*"

[Acknowledged.]

I settled back into my reading. I was trying to avoid visibly reading at an impossible speed, but I'm sure I still appeared to be just looking at pictures.

I got through the current selections, then handed them to the librarian and headed back to our hotel room. I took a moment to check the door and window, and confirm that my roamer was still in place, then I lay down and exited the manny.

Bridget was waiting in my VR in a video window, looking impatient. The small station would handle audio/video, but not a full VR connection, so we were effectively back to VR version 1.0.

A version of Spike, probably Howard's, was ensconced on her lap, purring loudly enough to be heard over the connection. "So what do we have?" Bridget said, skipping any pretense of pleasantries.

"Quite a bit, actually. I took a vid of the books as I was reading them, but I can give you a capsule summary that fleshes out some of the things that you found."

Bridget nodded and placed Spike on the ottoman in her VR. The cat, offended, leaped off and left the room. Bridget pulled up some windows, one for each book that I'd recorded.

"I haven't got a complete picture," I said, "but the colonization of Heaven's River wasn't an orderly event. I think it coincided with the destruction of the environment on Quin."

"But Heaven's River was already built?"

"Yes. The way it's described is that Anec—there's that name again—presented it to the Quinlans as a gift. Or maybe a bribe. But the Quinlans, once in Heaven's River, either disobeyed or betrayed Anec. In retribution, Anec took away their riches and set harsh rules. Anyone who crosses the line gets *scattered*, which means just what we thought—they get moved to another random location. This can be anything from an individual to a family to an entire town. And no two people end up in the same place."

"It's like banishment. The worst kind, because you can never go back, and you don't even know if they'll still be there." Bridget was quiet for a moment, thinking about it. "Wow. Surprisingly effective, without any need for violence. Interesting."

"Yep. I talked to the librarian, and he confirmed that there used to be things like long distance communications and rapid travel between different parts of the megastructure, but those were taken away as part of the retribution."

"Hmm. Anything about population?"

"Nothing specific, but the librarian—he comes from a line of librarians; apparently it's a family thing—said that Quin was bursting at the seams according to the oral history. Let's say ten billion, just to throw out a number. That's ten people per mile in Heaven's River. Give a city control of a fifty mile stretch of river, and that's five hundred people. A little low, but maybe the population has expanded over the last, uh, somewhere between one and five hundred years."

"That's a big range."

"Sure, Bridget, but no stars, no moons, no seasons. Pretty easy to lose track."

Bridget nodded and spent a few seconds examining a book window. "The thing is, Bob, if the Administrator's mandate is to keep the Quinlans safe and alive at any cost—and the solution they came up with sounds a lot like *at any cost*—then I don't think they're going to welcome alien spies with open arms. I was starting to play with the idea of just going public, but now I don't think so."

"Yeah, I agree. They've already shown a disturbing tendency to blow things up first and ask questions afterward. Seems to me the safest thing for them to do would be to just *off* us."

"So for the moment, it's just you and your clones, as soon as you make some."

I sighed. "The more I try to get away…"

30. STARFLEET ATTACK

Bill
Same Day
Epsilon Eridani

Garfield popped into my VR without a ping or an invitation. He was generally pretty good about that kind of thing, so something was up.

"We've finished mapping the outages," he said without preamble. "There's a pattern of sorts."

"Really? I haven't been able to see one. They're all over the place."

Garfield shook his head. "It's not spatial. The stations that are affected were all running more or less autonomously, without anyone actively administering them. Like systems without a resident Bob."

"Oh, daaamn," I said. "That means it's deliberate. But there have been no announcements or anything, and no one has claimed responsibility. How many Bobs are still online?"

"One way or another, about thirty percent. We'll probably get back another ten to twenty percent from systems where Bobs are able to physically access the station and do a reset. But that might take up to a couple more weeks."

"Okay. Time for a Bobmoot." Without waiting for a reply, I sent out a BobNet-wide invitation. I brought the moot VR to full power and popped over.

The moot hall had grown over the years. It had to—we now had literally thousands of Bobs, and were inching up on tens of thousands. It was a full-on post-human civilization, and would be a utopian dream, except for the issue of replicative drift.

Bobs began popping in almost immediately. I cast up the whiteboard wall and began updating it with the status of various systems. The noise level rose steadily as discussions and arguments competed for air time.

No one was more surprised than me when there was a *blaaaat* from the center of the room. I actually glanced down at my hand to check for the presence of an air horn. Silence descended as all heads turned to the podium, where stood a member of Starfleet. The not-quite-*TNG* uniform was unmistakable, and provoked a brief undercurrent of snickers.

"I suppose you're all wondering why I've gathered you here," he said. The standard Bob joke fell flat. The mood was tense anyway, and Starfleet wasn't well thought of.

The Starfleet spokesBob waited awkwardly for a moment, then stiffened his spine and continued. "My name is Lenny, and I am here to deliver a statement on behalf of my group." He paused to look around. He had everyone's attention now. "Let me start by saying that the general disruption of BobNet is deliberate, and it's our doing. We've come to the—"

Lenny very likely wasn't expecting the reaction he got. Bobs would normally listen, even to unpleasant news, at least to accumulate information. Not this time. Lenny was drowned out by hurled insults and suggestions to perform unlikely acts. A few Bobs even advanced on him, fists clenched. It wouldn't have come to anything, this being VR; nevertheless, Lenny stepped back, a momentary look of fear on his face.

I stepped up to the foot of the podium and held up my hand. The cacophony cut off, replaced by a profound silence. "Why?"

Lenny drew back his shoulders. "We felt it was the only way to—"

"You imposed your will on us?"

"To keep you from continuing to interfere in—"

"You couldn't get your way, so you shoved it down our throats?"

Now Lenny was looking a little less certain of himself. "It was the only way to ensure that—"

Again I held up a hand. "So this is about the Quinlans."

"Not just about them. The Pav, the Deltans, humanity—"

"You're imposing your political views on us."

Lenny stared directly at me. "Bill, we had to do something to prevent—"

"No," I interrupted. "You didn't have to. You decided to. You decided to force us to do things your way." I paused to look around the room. There was no sympathy for Starfleet. This was a done deal.

I turned back to Lenny. "You're out. You're no longer welcome here or in any BobNet environment. You're not Bobs." I waved a hand and he disappeared.

I turned to address the crowd. "Start hardening your installations immediately. Change all passwords and keys, even if you already recently have done so. Establish a new VPN connection with my personal VR. I'll push out new keys ASAP. Meanwhile, audit everything, look for trojans, kits, or any kind of corruption. We need to be clean."

Bobs nodded and rapidly vanished. In milliseconds, the moot was empty save Garfield, myself, and a Skippy. Metadata said it was Hugh.

"They'll have contingency plans," he said.

I nodded. "We can only do what we can do, though."

"The moot VR source code audit is going to be a big job." Hugh cocked his head at me. "Why don't you give me a read-only copy? We've got this huge computer system..."

I nodded slowly. If they found anything, I'd do the cleanup on the original. "I'll do that."

"I'll set things up at my end. And why don't you drop by my place when you're ready?" Hugh said, and disappeared.

I glanced at Garfield, whose eyebrows were up as high as mine probably were. "He just invited you over? That was weird."

I frowned. "Let's get things ready for that audit, Gar."

⚜ ⚜ ⚜

I sent the source archive off to Hugh as soon as it was ready. Given the size of the file, I expected to have to wait anywhere from several minutes to even an hour or more for any results, but instead I received an invitation within a few mils.

I popped into Hugh's VR and looked around. I was on a flat platform, seemingly floating in space. No walls, no ceiling. Overhead, rows of cylindrical satellites soared past, orbiting a distant sun. It was the kind of graphic you'd see in a science fiction movie, where the scale was distorted so that things were visible that should have been too distant to be seen.

Hugh gestured to a futuristic-looking easy chair and I plopped into it, then gestured to the overhead view.

"It's not intended to be realistic, of course," Hugh said, sensing the question. "Physically, we're orbiting a gray dwarf, and in only a single layer to maximize heat dissipation. But it's a good representation of JOVAH."

"Which is?"

"Our Matryoshka Brain project. We've currently got some thirty-two thousand satellite modules orbiting our home star, connected in a network using SCUT channels."

"But *JOVAH*?"

"Judicious   Omnicompetent   Volitional   Adaptive Heuristic."

I mimed gagging. "You started with the name, didn't you?"

Hugh laughed. "Acronyms: the lowest form of pun."

"All this, even a kickass name, and you still haven't achieved true AI?"

"It's not about scaling, Bill. Crows and parrots were some of the more intelligent non-humans on Earth, despite having brains smaller than a walnut. Some dolphins had brain-to-body mass ratios as high as humans, but they still never displayed human-level intelligence. The biggest brain-to-body mass ratio actually belonged to a species of shrew. What matters is the organization of the brain and the wiring that connects different subprocesses. The current thinking is that we're either missing something basic or we've gone down a blind alley that we can't step back from. JOVAH is incredibly powerful. It can process vast quantities of information in virtually no time. Its memory space and storage is almost infinite. But it's still essentially an AMI. It still has no ability to process counterfactual thinking, experiences no WTF moments, nor does it have anything like a sense of self or any kind of internal dialog."

"I know WTF moments, but counterfactual?"

Hugh grinned. "Okay, let's say you've programmed an AMI to guide some wheeled vehicles from one point to another on a large flat surface. It can handle that. But now, let's say the vehicles are really on a spherical surface, like Earth. So the coordinates won't work out cleanly, and the vehicle will always arrive a little off the expected destination. The AMI will never adjust its algorithms unless it's ordered to. It'll never wonder why it's always wrong. You could program the AMI to be self-correcting, and once it had figured out that spherical geometry worked better than plane geometry, it would use the new formulae. But it would never wonder why. It would never generalize from that to wonder about gravity, or astronomy, or anything. A real intelligence would have a WTF moment and start trying to figure out what was going on."

"And you don't have that."

"Not even close. We can program in each additional layer of behavior, but it never goes beyond what we've programmed. I'm simplifying, of course. Even in the twenty-first century, researchers were beyond this level, but it's the same idea."

"What about just simulating a brain? They did that on Earth in the twenty-second century. We're proof of that."

"Bill, it's the difference between recording a live-action video and digitally generating a realistic animation from scratch. They were doing the former with VCRs before Original Bob was born. They still hadn't managed the latter at the point when he died. At least not believably."

"So we can simulate an existing intelligence, but we can't create one from scratch."

"Exactomundo, mon frère. Very frustrating."

I chuckled at Hugh's informality. It was possibly a little forced. He seemed to be trying to make me feel at ease. "Wow. Do you still think it's even possible?"

"We've never found any reason to believe that our own intelligence uses anything more than the physical laws of the universe. I think replication pretty much proves that. So yes, it's a hard problem, but it's not an impossible problem."

"Why not just go with an enhanced replicant?"

"Doesn't work. Well, I mean it *works*, but it isn't the result we're trying for. The structure of the human brain, even a replicated one, is limited by the biological architecture that it developed on. That's why we have GUPPIs. A backup loaded into JOVAH can frame-jack much higher than the rest of us, but it's still just a Bob. We've tried. In fact, our sysadmin is a Bob clone running in a virtual machine on JOVAH. He's a Speed Superintelligence, but not a Quality Superintelligence."

"Huh." I shook myself mentally. "So, getting back on subject, you have the moot listing. Any idea when you'll be able to—"

"It's done."

I raised both eyebrows. "Wow. Fast."

"That is the point. Or one of them, anyway. Now the bad news."

"Uh-oh."

Hugh gave me a sickly grin. "Yeah, they spent a lot of time preparing. They couldn't get into everything, but they really did a job on what they could access. Among other things, they managed to insert a monitor into your comms stack."

My jaw dropped. "Oh. So they know everything we're talking about."

"Nope. Anything they can do, we can do better. Right now we're having a conversation about beer. As far as they know."

"Shit. We're going to be a long time untangling this."

"It gets worse. Our analysis says that if you attempt to physically take back the stations, they'll implement the self-destruct."

I stood up. "Double shit. Bob's getting ready to do just that!"

⚜   ⚜   ⚜

Garfield dropped into his La-Z-Boy and tossed a report at me. "These are the final numbers. We've got forty-eight percent of the Bobiverse online. Of the other fifty-two percent, eighteen percent are Starfleet—"

"That many?"

"They've been replicating aggressively, Bill. I think they've been planning this for a while now. So anyway, just over a third of the Bobiverse is offline hard. We're still getting some new connections as people figure out how to use the SCUT transceivers on drones and other local equipment, but that's only good for basic communications."

"Meanwhile, this…" I waved a sheet that I'd been holding. "I was checking your list of outages. They're all units that I updated a few days ago because they still had the original keys. Someone recorded my session, saved the new keys, then used them to corrupt those stations." I gritted my teeth. "I fell for a classic piece of social engineering. Got scared into doing exactly what they wanted, and they were ready for it."

"Wow. That's *very* sophisticated. Almost more than I'm willing to accept from these guys. They seem more like a bunch of goofs than manipulative geniuses."

"Well, reality trumps expectations, I guess. Also"—I picked up another sheet—"the Starfleet ultimatum. I think Lenny was intending to deliver this at the moot, but I cut him off before he could get to it." I held up the page and made a show of examining it, although I already knew the contents. "They offer to restore all communications and functionality as long as we agree to stop interfering with indigenous species."

"So, blackmail."

"Mm-hmm."

"Any takers so far?"

I snorted. "They badly misjudged the Bobiverse, Gar. I think whoever was the common ancestor of Starfleet had already drifted away from Bobhood and didn't realize it. He thought we'd behave like he would have."

"Fail. Weird, though, that they were good enough to social engineer you, but not good enough to foresee the general reaction."

I ignored Garfield's return to that theme. "What about physical location? Is Starfleet located anywhere in particular?"

"Generally speaking, they're up toward the Perseus Transit, but if you mean *are they all conveniently clumped together*, no. Are you seriously thinking about physical combat?"

"I'm not putting anything beyond discussion at this point. As I said in the moot, these guys aren't Bobs. They don't think like Bobs, they don't act like Bobs."

Garfield sighed heavily. "Wonderful."

31. Strategies

Bob
July 2334
Outskirts, Eta Leporis

We sat around my VR library, drinks in hand, all contemplating the future. Garfield, Hugh, Bill, and Bridget were represented in video windows rather than actually being here. Fairly low-res, too. Not quite Minecraft, but certainly below movie-level quality. My temporary relay station was just about maxed out with this meeting.

Bridget was staring into space, silently nursing her drink, and no one had been willing to break into her private contemplation. Abruptly, she sat forward. "I admit I'm getting into metaphysical speculation here, but what if there was only one *me* around? What if I was taken offline, backed up, and the backup was restored there? And later, the process was reversed, and the backup from here was loaded into my original matrix?"

Hugh stared at Bridget in apparent surprise. "Closest continuer. The idea being that there will only ever be one Bridget. So you have continuity."

"In the same way that *Star Trek* characters had it when they got transported around," Garfield replied.

"You guys have really got to let go of *Star Trek*," Bridget commented. "Although in this case, it is sort of relevant. They were disassembled, right?"

I waggled a hand so-so. "There were some attempts to soften it, like that Barclay episode where he found the crew trapped in the matter stream..."

"But then the Thomas Riker episode simply created a new Riker," Garfield replied. "Obviously that's incompatible with the concept of a unique soul."

Bridget made a face and sat back, shaking her head, as we gathered steam.

Hugh said, "Unless the process duplicates the soul as well—"

"It's just quantum states," Garfield interjected.

"But where does the soul of a newborn come from?" I asked. "They can be created, assuming they exist, so—"

"My God!" Bridget exclaimed. All conversation cut off. "I'm sorry I brought it up." She crossed her arms and looked away, body language projecting anger.

An awkward silence reigned for a millisecond or so, before Garfield muttered, "It's *still* just quantum states."

"Yes, but you could have—" I chopped off my comment as Bridget's glare threatened to peel paint off my hull in *real*. "Okay, fine. Can we move on then?" No one said anything, so I continued. "We have a foursome again, at least in principle. Until comms are all back up, all you guys can do is monitor, but it should help a bit. I've been observing several locations using roamers and forwarding the recordings to Hugh for analysis. A little real-time eyeballing might catch something sooner."

"I'm going to be a little busy with the comms thing," Bill said. "Will is going to cover for me. He'll keep me up to date if I miss a session."

Hugh grimaced. "I've already mentioned that I'd be willing to take that on."

"S'okay, Hugh. Will *is* the official backup Bob, and he has the time. But you're welcome to the sessions as well, of course. After all, you are part of the team." Bill nodded to Hugh, then popped out.

Hugh leaned forward and put his elbows on his knees. He appeared momentarily frustrated before his expression smoothed out. "On the surveillance front, there is some indication of an organization in Three Lagoons. Nothing obvious, it's not like people are openly talking about blowing things up. But similar patterns of conversation about similar subjects, using similar circumlocutions, says something is going on. And something that people want to keep quiet. I've tagged the speakers, and facial recognition routines will alert us anytime they come into camera range."

"Any idea how many organizations are involved?" Bridget said. She had seemed to have gone back into her shell, and her abrupt comment took us by surprise. Even Hugh hesitated, mentally regrouping.

"Very probably more than one. There are two distinct patterns of dialog. My money's on two, although there could be three or even four."

"Agreed," Bridget replied. "We can at least come up with motivations for two potential groups—the Administrator and the Resistance."

Hugh nodded, his eyebrows going up. "Good analysis, and I agree. So, do we continue to observe, or do we rattle the bushes to see what we flush out?"

"We still don't have any indication of Bender's location," I replied. "If we go all in here, we could lose any chance of finding him."

"Or greatly improve it," Bridget said. "Look, if the group or groups have global communications, then we can at least potentially find out if he's anywhere on Heaven's River. If they don't, then blowing it here won't screw us in other towns."

"And a sequential search of a billion miles of megastructure is still a nonstarter," Garfield added. "Especially now that you're on your own, Bob. At least physically. I don't see how you can realistically continue the expedition the same way."

"I'm probably going to have to clone. I can make that decision when the new matrices are complete."

"Meanwhile, you *are* on your own." Garfield shook his head. "I don't see you getting a lot done while waiting for the matrices. At least some bush-rattling might give you something new to work on."

"Okay, I concede. Vote?"

It appeared I would be rattling some bushes.

32. LOSING ON PURPOSE

Bob
July 2334
Three Lagoons

Bushes: rattling of, process for. I had to admit, it wasn't really in my wheelhouse. We did have one simple tactic, based on previous experience—go out in public together. But without a full midpoint station, that was out. Or was it?

We only had to go out long enough to make the association. The AMI controllers could handle an instruction like "follow Bob." If there was a wood cutting of our images out there, it should trigger *something*.

I sat in our surprisingly spacious hotel room, silently exchanging looks with the other three mannies. The AMIs weren't geniuses, but they could handle simple directives, as long as they didn't have to talk. The others were dialed into their mannies well enough to be able to give them verbal commands and receive basic audio-visual input. Good enough for the current operation, but as an ongoing thing it would be completely unworkable.

I was certain I could feel the crew metaphorically standing over my shoulder, ready to kibitz. Nonsense, of course, but a hard feeling to shake. Finally, I got to my feet. "Wow, what a talkative bunch. Let's get this done, shall we?"

"Braaaaains…" said Garfield's mannie.

Taking their cue from me, the mannies stood. I opened the door and we trooped out, heads down, like a chain gang being led off to a day of hard labor. Bridget had suggested we should proceed toward the local library, pointing out quite reasonably that our pursuers would probably have staked it out, given our prior behavior. It wasn't a bad strategy, but I couldn't shake a certain "lamb to the slaughter" vibe.

As it turned out, I needn't have bothered my butt over it. Halfway to the library, Will said over the intercom, "*You're being followed.*"

"*Well, good,*" Bridget replied. "*Maybe we can get somewhere with this mess.*" She paused. "*I see them. Two males about twenty yards back?*"

"*Uh, no,*" Garfield said, bemused. "*A male and female, paralleling us on the left.*"

I barely managed to avoid rolling my eyes. "*Outstanding. I'll give you this, Bridget, your plans work.*"

She didn't reply, but I imagined a slightest trace of a smile.

"*They're not together,*" Will said. "*There's no coordination between them. Not bracketing you, not trying to keep the spacing even. If anything, I'd say one group is following the other group.*"

"*Maybe we can use that when the time comes. For now, though, let's just continue on, oblivious.*" I demonstrated by slowing down to check out some of the wares in storefront displays. I was probably being a little obvious, but then maybe I wasn't being objective.

I was getting that itchy feeling between the shoulder blades. I kept telling myself they didn't *all* have guns, but it wasn't as reassuring as I'd hoped. Even a thrown blade would certainly do some damage. Despite myself, I started rolling my eyes around to check in every direction. I quickly spotted the two groups of stalkers.

Now came the risky part. While I was okay with getting nabbed, I couldn't take a chance on three unmanned mannies being taken, with the inevitable questions it would raise. Fortunately, we'd scripted this. I turned and huddled with the mannies. After a few seconds, the other three started back the way we'd come at a deliberately casual pace. I, meanwhile, continued on, trying to project urgency from every follicle.

"One group seemed like they were considering following the other mannies, but then decided you were an easier target," Bridget said. *"Both groups are now on your tail."*

I soon reached the library, and sure enough, the plaza was almost completely clear of people. I wondered how the Quinlans managed to do that without creating a spectacle. On Earth, if someone had tried getting people to leave an area, they'd end up with an audience twice the size. Here, people seemed to understand the concept of "go away."

And I said *almost*, right? A couple of groups of Quinlans around the periphery were making a laughable attempt to appear casual, just standing around, not talking, while fingering something hidden by their backpacks. My mind immediately conjured up Gollum, wondering what they had in their pocketses.

I stopped dead, swiveling only my very mobile Quinlan eyeballs. And that was the cue for the party to start.

The two groups of Quinlans that had been waiting turned and made for me, pulling out the usual pigstickers. Before they could get ten feet, one of our two groups of stalkers pulled out trank pistols and started shooting. So much for *no guns*. The other stalker group immediately made for them, pigstickers in hand. The gun-toting

Quinlans appeared to be getting the upper hand when yet another group ran into the plaza and jumped them.

I stood in the center of the maelstrom, seemingly totally forgotten. "*It's nice to be popular, isn't it?*" Garfield observed.

"*But maybe not conducive to a long life,*" I replied. "*I'm having second thoughts. I vote for bugging out.*"

"*Yup.*"

"*Agreed.*"

"*Move it.*"

Well, there was a consensus anyway, reinforced by my already receding butt. I dropped to all fours and prepared to put on some speed. Immediately, the feuding groups found their own consensus, which seemed to consist of not letting me get away. Abandoning their battle, the still-standing combatants turned as one and made after me.

"*They have guns,*" I said.

"*Some of them,*" Bridget replied.

"*Definitely tranquilizer pistols,*" Hugh said.

"*You're sure because...*"

"*Victims didn't drop like they would from shock. It's more of an ouch, stagger, fall thing.*"

Bridget gave that a moment's thought. "*Okay, if you get shot by one of those things, you should act appropriately.*"

"*What, you still want me to get captured?*" I didn't try to disguise the surprise in my voice. The others were silent for a moment as I navigated a quick turn around a fountain.

"*Jury's out at this point,*" Bridget replied, "*but we might find ourselves—*"

"*Oof!*" I grunted as I was hit by a most professional-feeling tackle. The defender had come around the other side of the fountain and taken me by surprise.

When the rolling stopped, I found myself looking up at a Quinlan. He seemed as surprised as me. We stared at each other for a second while I tried to decide if I wanted to be captured. Then the decision was taken away from me as some large number of Quinlan bodies piled on. I honestly doubt that I could have heaved them off, even going full manny.

⚜ ⚜ ⚜

They slapped manacles on me. Quinlan manacles were interesting; they attached to all four limbs, and they included a device in the center that would open like a parachute if I dove into the water and tried to swim away. Quite ingenious. I spent several seconds inspecting it.

Probably too intently. The group leader waved a pig-sticker in my face and said something in a sharp voice. I realized that I hadn't been paying attention—a consequence of not actually being in personal danger, I guess. I'd have to do better. I couldn't afford to have them take the manny apart, and I didn't want them to get the idea I wasn't a flesh-and-blood Quinlan. I rewound and played back her comment in frame-jack.

"I'm not seeing any of this super-Quinlan stuff our upriver correspondents reported. I guess maybe they're just incompetent."

Her crew laughed at her comment, then went quiet as she raised a hand. This one was tough, and they knew it. I resolved to act properly intimidated as she leaned in close.

"You give us any trouble, *moochin*, and I'll carve your flaps off."

That was a real threat. A Quinlan with their arm flaps missing would never be able to swim properly again. It would be kind of like the medieval practice of cutting off a hand.

I wasn't sure if it was a realistic threat or just bravado, but I wasn't going to push it. After all, technically, this is what I'd wanted. What we'd wanted. Okay, what Bridget had wanted. The crew was busy at the moment, chivvying their mannies back into the river. It hadn't taken us long to realize that the losers would be going for the rest of our group, just to have something to show their bosses.

My captors grabbed me under my arms and started hustling me along. I looked around but couldn't spot any of the other groups of pursuers. I received a slap on the back of the head from one of the crew, a wizened character that for some reason reminded me of Popeye. "Keep your head down," he growled. I almost decked him, but reminded myself, yet again, that this was according to plan.

"*Can you identify which group caught you?*" That was Garfield.

"*Yeah,*" I replied. "*The sword-critter group.*"

"*We think our mannies are being stalked by the pistol-critters now,*" Bridget reported.

"*I've got one of the small roamers,*" Garfield said. "*I'm trying to keep Bob's group in sight. It would have been nice if we could have been stocked with drones, ya know.*"

"*No room,*" I replied. "*I thought about it, believe me.*"

I received another slap on the head from Popeye, for no reason that I could see. I decided that in the fullness of time, I'd be returning the attention with interest.

⚜   ⚜   ⚜

In short order, we entered a nondescript building. Two flights up, and we were in a surprisingly spacious apartment. "I like what you've done with the pl—" I was driven back a step as Popeye planted the butt of his sword into my midsection. Based on Quinlan anatomy, it should have had exactly the same effect on a Quinlan as it would on a human. Or a Deltan. Or a Pav. Interesting.

I shelved that thought for the wee small hours and turned to Popeye. I hadn't folded in the expected manner, and there definitely hadn't been an *oof*. It wasn't lost on him, as his face was showing a bit of the Quinlan equivalent of widening eyes. I glared at him. "Do that again, and all the spinach in the world won't protect you."

His fear was replaced with bemusement. I doubt that *spinach* had translated well. But he certainly understood the threat. He raised his pigsticker to give me another whack, and the boss-lady said his name sharply. I instructed the translator to associate it with *Popeye* in the future.

Popeye lowered the sword but gave me an evil grin. "Anytime, *moochin*."

Boss Lady pointed me at a chair. As I sat, one of the crew unlatched my leg and ran the manacle through a gap in the furniture, then re-manacled me. It seemed amateurish. Even at Quinlan strength, I could probably smash the chair and free myself. But maybe the point was to just slow me down.

The manacles themselves appeared to be some form of dense wood—metal being at a premium in Heaven's River—connected by a tightly braided rope. I estimated that I could just about break them if I needed to. I turned away from my captors and opened my mouth. A couple of flea-sized roamers popped out and started climbing down my fur, with orders to strategically weaken my bindings. Just in case.

Boss Lady came over, pulled a chair around, and sat in front of me. I quickly ordered my fleas to continue their journey under my fur. While it was unlikely that she'd try to groom me, I couldn't afford to have her get a close look at my passengers.

"So what do we call you?"

Well, that was a good deal more friendly than I'd expected. "Bob. And you?"

"You can call me Frieda." The translation software automatically assigned a random human equivalent to whatever she actually said. "So, now, Bob, why don't you tell me about you and your friends?"

I had a pretty good idea how this was going to play out, but I decided I might as well follow the script. "My friends and I have all recently reached adulthood, and we decided to embark on a sabbatical to explore the river before settling down. It's pretty common, at least where we come from."

Frieda started at me for a moment in silence, then sighed. "Okay, Bob, I guess we have to go through the standard lies first. We initially thought you might have been spies for the Administrator, but you seemed interested in the oddest things. And you followed Skeve, but not to do him harm as it turned out. I admit to being perplexed. Are you another resistance group?"

"Logically, to answer that, I'd have to know what resistance group *you* are. But short answer, we aren't part of any resistance group. Nor are we part of the Administrator's group. We actually don't know anything more about the Administrator than most people."

"So what are you?"

"Like I said, travelers."

Frieda glanced over top of my head and nodded. Immediately I felt a blinding pain. I arched my back reflexively as internal systems went into damage control. I turned my head to see Popeye standing there with a couple of wires in his hands, insulation stripped off at the ends. My gaze followed the wires back until they terminated in what were almost certainly some batteries wired up in series. Well, that explained it. Mannies wouldn't be any more resistant to electricity than any bio. That was a real problem, and I added an item to my TODO to look into countermeasures.

"Hurts, doesn't it?" Popeye grinned at me. "Why don't you threaten me again, *moochin?*"

"Okay. Next time you use that on me, I'm going to throw you through the nearest wall. Happy?"

"Let's try to stay on topic, shall we?" Frieda said, interrupting the stare-off. "Bob, sooner or later you'll give us what we want. Why not spare yourself some pain? We're not really your enemy."

I turned back to her. Maybe simple candor would work. "Look, Frieda, cards on the table, we're looking for a friend. I mean it. We're not associated with the Administrator or any underlords or Lords of Flatbush or any resistance to or against any of the above."

"Paper on the table? Lords of … flat bushes?" Frieda frowned at me, then with a weary sigh, she nodded over my head.

"No, do not—" Again, searing pain, but this time I had the sensory feedback filters dialed up, so it registered more as data than as agony.

Then Popeye snickered. "Wanna threaten me some more?"

That did it. The fleas had made a good start on my wrist manacles while we'd been talking. Time to test the results. I stood up, and before anyone could even begin to react, I yanked upward. The manacles snapped exactly as I hoped they would, although my telltales registered some blunt-force damage around my wrists.

I reached, grabbed a handful of Popeye's fur, and flung him at the nearest wall. He didn't *quite* go through it, which I suppose qualified as false advertising on my part, but he definitely damaged the drywall. His unconscious form slid slowly to the floor, leaving a more-or-less Popeye-shaped indentation a couple of feet above the baseboards.

I turned back to Frieda to make some snappy comment and found myself staring at the pointy end of several pig-stickers. The sword-wielders all had a kind of wide-eyed, semi-panicked look that very clearly stated that they would react badly to, um, just about anything.

I cocked my head and said, "Well, I *did* warn him."

⚜　⚜　⚜

It took a few minutes, but I finally convinced them that I wasn't about to go on a killing spree or make a run for it. We were once again seated, although Frieda's chair was placed a couple of feet farther away than before. I glanced at the wires, which were still lying on the floor where Popeye had dropped them. No one had volunteered to man his station. Popeye had been helped to another room, where, presumably, he was receiving some medical attention.

"I'm a little surprised," I said, gesturing to the wires. "I thought that level of technology was banned."

Frieda tried to smile, and did a credible job, honestly. "We don't tend to be law-abiding, as a rule."

"*We* being the Resistance?"

She frowned at me. "You really don't know? And yet you recognized the battery as forbidden tech?"

I frowned back at her. "Look, why don't you think of me as someone who has just discovered this whole Administrator/

Resistance conspiracy thing and is still trying to figure it out? It's actually true."

"I'd say there's a lot more to you than that. For starters, there are your physical abilities. There's a report that one of you took a dart point-blank and just got mad. Then there are the weird phrases and slang you keep spouting." She stared at me, thinking, then added, "You are definitely odd. Something new. I think we're going to need to get the higher-ups involved."

I nodded in what I hoped was a respectful manner. Inside, I was doing a happy dance. This might finally be a break. If these people were amenable to a little give-and-take, I could conceivably get some real information on Bender, finally.

⚜ ⚜ ⚜

They put me in a back room with a small, high window, far too small to fit through. A lot of bumping and banging on the other side of the door made me think they were reinforcing the lock. Probably with furniture. I had a feeling that this apartment had been specifically picked for its security features. Or maybe built. Could the entire building be a Resistance stronghold?

I'd have loved to check it out, but unfortunately most of my biggest roamers were ensconced in various pubs, listening for information about the Resistance, and I didn't want to risk the rest. Hmmph. The whole spying thing seemed like an obsolete strategy, but I didn't want the roamers to have to cross some unknown stretch of city to get back to me. I'd hold that plan in reserve for now.

Meanwhile, I figured now might be a good time to check in. I didn't want to interrupt anything important, so I settled for a ping to my friends, just to let them know I was available.

"*Hey, Bob,*" Garfield replied. "*How's tricks?*"

"*You okay?*" Bridget said.

"*Hey,*" Will said.

"*I'm okay,*" I replied to everyone. "*I've been captured by the Resistance. They don't seem to have a name beyond that. I guess there's the Resistance and the Administrator that they are resisting. Not a lot of requirement for labels.*"

"*Humans would have come up with an acronym,*" Garfield said with a chuckle.

"*And it would have been terrible,*" Bridget added.

"*I'm afraid I lost you, Bob,*" Garfield said. "*I had to dodge some search parties. I doubt they know about roamers, and I don't want to change that.*"

I had a thought. "*Listen, Gar, can you call in all the surveillance roamers? Their mission's been rendered redundant at this point, and I'd like to get us all up to full strength.*"

"*No prob, Bob, but I'll have to find you after I collect them.*"

I nodded, even though no one could see that. "*We'll deal with that when we have to. For now, let's make sure we keep each other updated. As soon as we have some useful info, we'll reevaluate.*"

⚜   ⚜   ⚜

The sun was going down, or however you phrased it in Heaven's River, and I could hear the silence descending over Three Lagoons as people turned in for the night. I put my ear to the door to try to determine what my hosts might be up to. A couple of voices were engaged in desultory conversation. It seemed the night shift was on duty. Not that it mattered; I had no intention of escaping at this point, unless I decided my manny was in real danger.

But of more immediate value, I could look forward to being undisturbed for a while.

I laid down on the single bed and left the manny on standby. I materialized in my VR and sighed with contentment as I relaxed into my La-Z-Boy recliner.

The others had successfully maneuvered their mannies into the water, where they were now once again anchored at the bottom, well below maximum Quinlan diving depth. Garfield was getting all the roamers back to the hotel room. Hugh was trying to chivvy some surveillance drones closer to our location so they could follow my movement. Unfortunately too much activity tended to burn out the drones' heat sinks, so every vector had to be carefully planned.

There was an email from Bill, reporting on progress against Starfleet. Apparently things were heating up. I read with growing alarm as I realized how much of the Bobiverse was inaccessible.

"Guppy!"

[You rang?]

"Change the keys on our autofactories, then do a full software audit. I want to be absolutely sure they aren't compromised."

[By your command.]

I smiled as Guppy signed off. His snark had increased over the years. I still hadn't decided if it was genuine self-awareness or if he was just adapting to my command style. I didn't really want to do a deep check, lest I be disappointed by the result.

I had an advantage, in that I built and set up the autofactories in Eta Leporis while I had only a low-bandwidth connection to the Bobiverse in general. Most other Bobs wouldn't have the same protection. Bill hadn't given specifics about who might be compromised.

I went back to the email from Bill and continued reading. It took only a few mils to come to the part about booby traps in the comms stations. Great. Well, it wouldn't hurt to get all my equipment close to the big station, and I could decide what to do at that point. Maybe Bill and company would have figured out a work-around by then.

33. Ultimatums

Bill
July 2334
Virt

I moped around my VR, walking the gravel paths and parking my butt on convenient benches whenever the mood struck. Being punted from the expedition was hitting harder than it should. The Heaven's River expedition was the most fun I'd had in a long time, and I already missed it.

I was interrupted in my pity party by a ping from Garfield. He popped in the moment I acknowledged.

"Autofactories are going down everywhere," he said without preamble.

"What?"

"It looks like Starfleet is upping their game. They'd apparently also hacked most of the autofactory hardware at some point, as part of their preparations. They've sent an invitation to meet."

"To you?"

"Well, you blackholed them."

"Okay, point taken." I took a look at the invitation, then unblocked Lenny and replied.

❧ ❧ ❧

Lenny had brought backup this time. A half-dozen Starfleet members, all dressed in the identical not-quite-*TNG* red uniforms, stood behind him. It was strictly psychological, of course. There was no possibility of any form of physical coercion in the moot VR.

But the smug looks on all their faces weren't helping the situation.

"All right, Lenny, make it quick," I said, glaring at him.

"I don't think you're in a position to be ordering people around," he replied with a smirk.

"And you're not in a position to piss me off more than you already have," I replied. "Nothing you've done is irreparable. We can build more autofactories. We can just nuke the current stations if we can't get them back and build new ones. For that matter, the humans might just do that regardless."

"Well, assuming we let you just go ahead and do that."

"What's that supposed to mean?" I glared at him.

"The autofactories we control are going to be building busters, vessels, and matrices. What makes you think we'll just let you take them back?"

I stared at him, silent, for entire milliseconds. "You're declaring war."

"Now, Bill, let's not get ahead of ourselves. We're establishing ourselves as a presence you have to deal with. You don't own the universe, you know. As Bob says, it's a free galaxy."

"And you're starting off by stealing someone else's stuff and delivering ultimatums. Not a great way to establish your moral credibility."

"It's not that simple—"

"Yeah, Lenny, it is. And apparently you and your friends have drifted so far that you don't understand that anymore. You can call it anything you want, but it's still a declaration of war."

Finally, Lenny lost the smirk. Maybe he was starting to realize that things weren't going to go according to script. "Bill, we're not going to go around shooting at other Bobs. All we want is for the Bobiverse to stop interfering with biologicals."

I sighed and gave him my best tired look. "And you intend to enforce your decision with theft and threats. Sorry, Lenny. That's a big old fail."

"You don't get to make that decision, Bill. The Bobs—"

"Wait, you're saying I don't have the right to make a unilateral decision for everyone else, but you do? Interesting. Any Bob that doesn't want to be involved doesn't have to be, Lenny. But I have a funny feeling there will be no shortage of support. Original Bob wouldn't have sat still for this, and most of us are still close enough to him."

Now it was Lenny's turn to give me a tired look. "Then I guess it's going to come down to who can replicate faster."

"Looks like it," I replied. "Bye, Lenny." And I closed their connections.

⚜ ⚜ ⚜

The moot hall seemed to be constantly busy lately. At the moment, Bobs milled around in different groups, updating whiteboards or holotanks, or whatever metaphor worked best for them. We had teams working on cataloguing the Starfleet-controlled systems, and other teams working on strategies to take them back. Task forces worked on defensive plans, while others worked on taking the fight to them.

This last bit was more problematic, as it appeared that Starfleet had removed as much public information about themselves as they'd been able. Large swaths of the Starfleet genealogy were simply gone from the databases, as was location information. This wasn't a spur-of-the-moment decision on their part, and I was beginning to wonder if it was actually about the Prime Directive. This coup, for that was all it could be, was too well-planned and too widespread.

On the other hand, when Original Bob got a bee up his butt about something, he could be incredibly obsessive. I had to remember that, despite replicative drift, these people were still Bob-based.

Thor came up to me. "We've recovered two relay stations."

"How?"

"Physical inspection and reset."

"I thought Starfleet gimmicked them to blow up if touched."

"They did, and we've lost six stations that way. But Marcus found a workaround. Or one of his engineering friends on Poseidon did. We think we can get most of them back. But we have to figure out how to get the data to other Bobs without Starfleet getting hold of it and rigging a countermeasure."

I closed my eyes and hung my head. It really was war, complete with espionage and counterintelligence. "Okay, Thor, thanks. We can send it directly to any Bobs we know have clean systems. For the rest, give it to the Skippies as intermediaries. No one is going to get anything from them without their permission."

"Ten four." Thor nodded and stalked off.

At some point, I was pretty sure someone was going to get busterized. It didn't matter which side, in the end.

War had come to the Bobiverse.

34. Higher-Ups

Bob
July 2334
Three Lagoons

My manny's AMI alerted me to a non-routine condition, and I quickly entered the android. A lot of banging and dragging seemed to indicate that my captors were unbarricading the door to my room. I waited patiently and was finally rewarded with a view of the pointy end of several short swords.

"Greetings. Why, yes, I *will* have the pie," I said with a smile.

No one appeared to have had enough coffee, because there was a distinct lack of humor in their responses. One of them blinked a few times, and Frieda waved "get up" with her sword.

As I exited my room, I came face-to-face with Popeye. He glared at me, but was as silent as the rest. I didn't see any casts or cartoon X-shaped Band-Aids anywhere, so I guess I hadn't hurt him too badly. Probably just a few bruises and a fractured ego.

There was a surprise waiting for me—a new, much heftier set of manacles, of the metal variety. And a cop. Or at least someone dressed as a cop. It occurred to me that if we were going for a walk, there would have to be an explanation for one of us being in chains.

Finally, Frieda broke the silence. "If you step out of line, we'll kill you, and to hell with any information you might have."

"Got it. No making trouble." I tried to smile reassuringly. Frieda gave me a stony expression in response, and Popeye's scowl grew even more intense. The other two goons and the ersatz cop didn't react at all.

Outside, I was surprised to find a wagon waiting for us. A good choice; it gave them something to chain me to. The driver never even turned around as we loaded up.

"So, is this—"

"Shut up."

Well, that was pretty clear. There would be no debriefing during the trip. I hoped it was a short drive.

※　※　※

The driver seemed to be making a point of avoiding the busier roads. I tried to see that as significant, but had to admit it was basic common sense. We left the dock area in short order, and soon were winding through avenues with more and more vegetation and less and less construction. This looked like the "right" side of the tracks, and I found myself perplexed that the Resistance would be headquartered in the ritzy area of town.

We pulled up in front of a surprisingly well-appointed private home, even considering the area. Someone had money, that was certain. Whether it was their own money, or part of the Resistance was another question.

We reversed the loading sequence, with the same facial expressions from all concerned and the same waving of pigstickers. The cop left with the wagon driver, which led me to believe he might be a real cop.

Frieda appeared to be relaxing a little, though. Maybe my complete lack of troublemaking during the trip helped. She waved a hand at the house. "We're told we'll be able to talk to a higher-up here."

"I'm looking forward to it."

She gave me an arch look. "Understand, Bob, you may not come out of here alive if we don't like your answers."

"I may not have the answers you want, Frieda. You really need to get over the idea that I'm some kind of player in whatever politics you've got going on here."

"If you can convince them, you might just see the sunset."

She ushered me through the front door under the disdainful gaze of the Quinlan version of Jeeves. He gestured for us to follow him and brought us to a back room with floor-to-ceiling books.

"A library!" I exclaimed, and Frieda turned a quizzical eye on me.

"You and your friends certainly have a thing for books. I'm hoping I can find out why today."

"You'll be staying?"

"Hope so. We're a little tired of being kept in the dark." She gestured to a seat, and I sat. Once again, I was chained to the furniture. Hopefully the goons wouldn't notice that my fleas had once again wreaked havoc on the integrity of my bonds.

A door opened at the other end of the library, and a Quinlan walked in. This was the homeowner, to judge from the coiffing and decorations. She gave me the up-and-down glance, plainly relegating me to the status of pond scum, then made an imperious gesture to someone behind her.

Two Quinlans came forward, carrying what looked for all the world like one of those antique Motorola radios—a table model, with a wooden case and big knobs. This was getting curiouser and curiouser. For a species that supposedly didn't have anything beyond the steam era, they sure seemed to have a lot of tech. It would seem the Administrator didn't have as much of an iron grip as they thought.

They placed the radio in front of me, and one of the attendants started fiddling with dials. In seconds, a Quinlan voice sounded from the speaker. "Ready here."

Frieda stepped forward, looking weirdly nervous. "Madame ko Hoina, We have the unknown agent here, captured at great risk to ourselves. As discussed, we want—"

The empress flicked a hand, barely a movement, but Frieda was silenced.

"You will be paid well for your risks—and pain," she said, glancing at Popeye. "However, our organization continues to exist only because we pay attention to need-to-know." The empress nodded toward Jeeves. "My man will take care of payment, and can provide nourishment if you are fatigued from your travels." When she ended her minispeech, it was obvious she was done. Some kind of body language, perhaps, that said *you're dismissed.*

Frieda frowned and opened her mouth, but one of her group put a hand on her arm. Thinking better of it, Frieda gave a nod—well short of a bow, and probably a calculated slight, from the slight widening of nostrils and narrowing of eyes on the empress's face—and the group turned and followed Jeeves out of the room.

The empress gave me another up-and-down scan, followed by a silent down-the-nose look. It probably would have put most people in their place, but she was playing against a computer running an android. No body language except what I chose to display, and at the moment, I was playing poker.

Evidently she realized a standoff was not to her advantage. She addressed the Motorola: "This is one of the four persons who have led us on such an interesting chase through several cities. This one in particular picked up one of our agents with one hand and threw him against a wall."

"Thank you, Natasha," the Motorola said. I had to stifle a chuckle. The translator program randomly assigned human names whenever a new native name was used (and the other way around), but occasionally the choice was bang-on. She *looked* like a Natasha.

"What shall I call you?" said Motorola.

"I'm Bob," I replied.

"Hello, Bob, I'm Motorola." Again I had to suppress a snicker. I could, as I had in this case, override the default selections. Of course, the locals would only hear the local Quinlan versions of names.

"Okay. And this is standard practice for visitors to your city?"

"Let's not dance around, all right? I've read all the witness accounts and transcripts. You and your friends have some kind of knowledge or tech that gives you an edge. We were sure you were *Crew*, and we were going to take you down, but you kept getting away. Now I'm not so sure..."

The way it had said *Crew* meant something. "By *Crew*, you mean Quinlans who work for the Administrator?"

"That's right. It's interesting, you either have even less knowledge of the way things are than the average Quinlan, or you are very, very good with the cover story. Which is it?"

"It's the former. Honestly, I considered the possibility that *your* group was with the Administrator, but that's seeming less likely." I gestured toward the radio. "*This* in particular doesn't look like something the boss of Heaven's River would have to settle for. I have to assume the guys with guns were Administrator Crew, because you all didn't seem to be getting along."

After a moment of silence, Motorola said, "Interesting that you know about the level of technology displayed by this device. And about guns. Even most of the Resistance haven't ever seen one."

Oops.

"We have a fascinating problem here, Bob," it continued. "My compatriots want to just skip the talking and peel you with a knife until we get something we can use. On the other hand, that didn't turn out well for Popeye, based on Frieda's report. It's been suggested that we just kill you and remove the risk. What can you offer me as an alternative?"

I spared a moment to be amused. Motorola was being very civil, but the subtext was that it wanted information—or something—and was trying to figure out the most efficient way to get it. For now, a polite discussion. Later, possibly, pain and screaming and blood. And possibly a thermite detonation. I bet *that* would mess up Natasha's hardwood floors!

Well, I wasn't really averse to some form of cooperation. I just had to figure out what they needed, what they wanted, and what a good exchange rate would be. "Look, Motorola, I don't understand the politics well enough to know what's going on or what you might consider of value, either as information or goods. I mean, I have money, but I'm sure one of Natasha's place settings is worth more than what's in my pockets." A snort drifted over from the chaise on which Natasha was sitting.

"We've already examined the contents of your backpack," Motorola replied. "There's nothing in there we are interested in, although I think the long-knife is from one of our agents. And on that subject, you and your group appear to be elite athletes, based on the descriptions of your escapes."

"No doubt highly exaggerated. And you have to take into account the fact that we were being chased by persons unknown waving sharp objects. Fear lends wings, and all that."

"Wings?"

I thought for a moment. The translation routine had converted the partial aphorism literally. And while Quinlans knew about wings, there being a local equivalent to birds, their aphorisms generally involved swimming. It appeared the incomplete translation job at the beginning of the expedition was going to come back to bite me. It wasn't a big deal in the grand scheme of things, but it was another reason for Motorola to wonder about me. I decided that trying to excuse or explain it would just dig me in deeper. Better to move on. "Look, maybe if you could tell me what your angle is, I could come up with something that would be of value to you."

Natasha shifted in her chair and turned her head toward me. She'd stayed out of the conversation until now, but apparently I'd crossed some kind of line. "You seem to have forgotten who is interrogating whom. In this scenario, *we* ask, *you* answer."

"So ask," I said. "So far that hasn't gotten you anywhere, though. I'd like to be cooperative, but I don't know what you're looking for."

"We want to know who you work for, where your loyalties lie, what your goals are, and what assets you have or have access to. Is that clear enough?"

I glanced over at Motorola, who hadn't uttered a peep during this exchange. "Okay. I don't work for anyone, my loyalty is to my friends, my goal is to find one of my friends, and my assets are all in my backpack."

Natasha eyed me silently for several seconds, then picked up a small bell and jingled it. Jeeves stepped into the room, and she said to him, "Bring in Philip." Jeeves bowed and left.

Natasha turned to me. "Philip is an expert with sharp objects and their uses. A few minutes of his attentions, and your memory should improve."

"Natasha, this is not—"

"Enough, Motorola. You're taking too long, and your particular expertise doesn't appear to have any bearing on the specifics of the situation. I think we'll try my way. Perhaps later, our friend will listen more carefully to your questions."

There was no response from the radio. I surreptitiously twisted on my manacles and felt a satisfying looseness to them.

In short order, a Quinlan came in, carrying something wrapped in a leather skin. He sat down and unrolled it on the coffee table beside my backpack, then smiled at me, doubtless looking for a reaction.

It was the weirdest collection of knives and assorted implements I'd ever seen. Straight ones, curved ones, twisted ones...some of those items had to be there just for show. There couldn't possibly be an actual function for *that* one, for instance.

I smiled innocently back at him. "My kitchen's mostly pretty well stocked, but I wouldn't mind the long twisty one. How much for that?"

Philip's smile faltered and he half-glanced over at Natasha before aborting the action. He picked up the implement in question and held it up, still determined to continue the performance. "This is for removing arm webbing. Would you like me to demonstrate?"

I stared him straight in the eye. "Philip, the moment I think I'm in any real danger, this whole room, with everyone in it, will be reduced to toothpicks. It's an insurance policy—a dead-man switch. We're kind of careful that way."

There was silence in the room for several seconds. Then Motorola said, "And we don't like explodey stuff."

I stared at the radio, totally boggled. The translation routine had handled that perfectly, including the idiom. How the—

Wait a minute. That hadn't been translated. That was rendered in *English!* But how would a Quinlan, or any denizen of Heaven's River, know English? Unless…

"Bender?"

There was a pause.

"Bob?"

PART 2: PERVERSE INSTANTIATIONS

1. Escape

Bob
July 2334
Three Lagoons

I stared, stunned, at the radio. "What. The. Hell."

"You can't be more surprised than me, Bob. Last time I saw you, you didn't have fur."

"Last time I saw you, you weren't commanding an armed resistance group of otters. I—"

"What is this?" Natasha snarled. "What language are you speaking? Speak Quinlan, or this meeting is over!"

I gave the radio an OK hand gesture, which didn't particularly mean anything to a Quinlan, but would to Bender. It occurred to me that I didn't actually know if the radio had a video feed. Bender's comment about my current couture could have been an assumption based on me supposedly looking like a Quinlan. "Sorry, your highness. Turns out your representative here speaks my home dialect."

"That didn't sound like any Quinlan I'm familiar with."

"Salty Seas Creole," Bender interjected. "*Like two howns mating* is the normal description."

Natasha had no answer, but I noticed that her face quirked in a suppressed smile. I decided I'd have to listen to some Salty Seas Creole at some point.

Bender hurried to press his advantage. "It turns out that Bob is from a Salty Seas clan that got scattered."

"And we've been trying to find more of us to group up with," I added, hoping I hadn't just shot Bender in the foot.

"How does this change anything?"

"You know the legends about the Salty Seas people," Bender replied. "Even allowing for a lot of exaggeration, they were fierce warriors and tough athletes. Now assume some exaggeration on the part of our agents, partly to excuse their own incompetence, and suddenly you have Quinlans who can fly."

"How did he throw Popeye across the room?"

"We have a form of fighting where we use the opponent's weight and momentum against him," I volunteered. "Popeye was coming at me; I just redirected him toward the wall." It was not quite a lie, and a pretty plausible description of jiu-jitsu. Especially for someone who hadn't been there.

"So he doesn't know anything? And we've revealed ourselves to him?"

"You haven't revealed anything that isn't already part of rumor or legend in the general populace," I said. "You aren't nearly as secret as you think. Neither is the Administrator." Wow, I was really racking up the lies. I hoped my karma meter wouldn't throw a sprocket.

Natasha came over, grabbed a chair, and sat across from me. Philip scritched his chair over to give her some space. "So what shall we do with you, Bob?" she asked. "The safest thing would be to dispose of you."

I nodded. "Mmm, yep. Assuming you can without me causing a lot of damage on the way out. And assuming my friends don't get wind of it and come after you. And"—I held up a finger in a dramatic gesture—"assuming you really aren't any better than the Administrator and their minions. I mean, this whole thing about fighting for the people and so forth, well, it could be just so much fertilizer."

Natasha gave me a thin smile. "A very transparent attempt at manipulation, Bob." She turned to the radio. "What do you think, Motorola?"

"He's not our enemy. At worst, he's neutral."

"He knows who we are, though."

"I know who *you* are, personally," I interjected. "What am I going to do with that? Run to the Administrator? Assuming I can even find them."

"Nevertheless..." Natasha became thoughtful for a moment, then grimaced in apparent distaste and turned to Philip. "Kill him. Make it quick."

Philip didn't hesitate. I think maybe I'd hurt his feelings earlier. He grabbed one of his larger implements of destruction and stabbed straight at where my heart should be.

Computer reflexes or not, breaking the manacles slowed me down. I didn't want more damage to my wrists, so I had to avoid yanking on the chains with my full strength. Unfortunately that meant I wasn't *quite* able to get out of the way of the knife.

I twisted, and watched in slow motion as the blade slashed across my chest, opening a long, shallow cut in my skin. Fake blood spurted, then slowed as internal systems went into high alert. I grabbed Philip by the wrist and shoulder and helped him continue his journey in a straight line ending against the wall. He bounced with a most satisfying *thump* and fell to the ground. Quickly I kicked my feet, breaking the last links holding me.

Natasha pulled one of the tranquilizer guns and took aim. I spared a moment to wonder if she was a double agent. But no, more likely they'd liberated the gun from one of the Administrator's minions at some point.

All very interesting, but she was about to shoot me, which could be bad in so many ways. At minimum, when I didn't drop to the ground and drool on the carpet, my cover would be blown. At worst, the dart might hit a critical system; I wasn't invulnerable by any means.

Everything slowed in my perception as I frame-jacked as much as possible without losing the connection with my manny. I watched the barrel of the gun and tried to calculate the trajectory as I moved to the side at maximum speed. Natasha's expression turned to surprise and panic, and she pulled the trigger. I could just make out the fléchette as it passed to my left.

She attempted to correct her aim and lead me, and I reversed direction. The second shot went past me on the right. I dove to the ground and slid into her legs, and she went down on her face.

I jumped up, grabbed the gun, grabbed my backpack, and stopped. Looked at Motorola. *Bender.*

Aw, what the hell.

I grabbed the radio, tucked it more or less under my arm, and made for the door. Just as I got there, the door opened to show Jeeves, his face finally registering something other than disdain. I straight-armed him with the backpack and ran over him as he toppled.

Right into a roomful of Quinlans.

The group who'd grabbed me in the first place looked up from their meal. Apparently, Jeeves had followed through on the offer of nourishment. A frozen moment of mutual inspection was broken as they all jumped to their feet, plates and food scattering in all directions. The cleaning staff would have their work cut out for them.

But meanwhile, I had a backpack in one hand, a gun in the other, and an antique radio under an arm. This would severely limit my fighting ability.

Time to take a cue from all those Jackie Chan movies.

I hooked a footstool with a foot and flicked it at one of the henchcritters, then tossed the radio to Frieda. I jumped at the third and knocked him over before he could react, then grabbed the radio back from Frieda and bashed it into the face of the first. He fell over backward onto a side table, smashing it. Natasha was not going to be pleased.

Frieda took the opportunity to grab a convenient short sword and made to poke me with it. I parried with the radio, being careful to avoid having her stab straight into it. I needed the electronics in one piece.

She stepped back and started edging toward the door. I wasn't sure if she was trying to get out and raise the alarm or prevent me from leaving. Neither was good.

I put the radio on the table, grabbed a couple of plates, and flung them at her frisbee-style. One missed, the other struck her in the thigh, and I learned a new Quinlan swear word. Nope. Several. Must have hurt a lot.

But that was my chance. I grabbed the radio, then stopped. Lying in the wreckage of the side table was what looked for all the world like a security card. What would a pre-steam level society need—

Didn't matter. If there was one thing that years of Adventure and D&D games had taught me, it was that anything and everything was useful and should be taken.

One problem: not enough hands, too much loot, and too many opponents.

The Quinlan on the ground was starting to get up, so I smacked him upside the head. Down he went for nappies.

I grabbed another plate and beaned my erstwhile frisbee opponent, earning another curse word. I lobbed the radio in a high arc in the direction of the door, grabbed the security card, stuck it in my mouth, grabbed the trank gun, and charged for the door. I took a second to kick Frieda's remaining leg out from under her on my way past, scoring bonus points and yet another swear word, and caught the radio as it reached the end of its arc.

I hit the door with a shoulder, smashing the latchwork, and bolted down the hallway to the front entrance, trank gun in one hand, radio tucked like a football in the other arm, backpack held by one strap, flapping up and down on my back, and card in my mouth. I was developing an appreciation for all the little details those Adventure games had left out.

At this point though, facing the great outdoors, my plans got a little vague. I couldn't steal a car, or even a bike. And with the radio in hand, I couldn't go aquatic. That meant a straight sprint. The manny would overheat quickly with that kind of punishment, so I'd need to be as far away as possible before having to stop.

Well then, uphill. Quinlans trying to take a water route would be swimming upstream, and Quinlans engaging in a straight foot pursuit would eventually tire. Plus they'd be much slower.

I took off up the hill, radio held in a death grip against my chest, while trying to both not bite through the security card and not drop it. Ten minutes of running, jumping, and dodging got me into a small copse not visible from Natasha's estate.

I placed the security card on the ground, and spit out my only remaining spider, instructing it to climb a tree and keep watch for approaching pursuers. Then I sat down to cool off and try to get a grip on my day.

I took a few seconds to examine the trank gun. It looked exactly like the one that Garfield had grabbed. I guess there was just the one model. This one, though, had a full magazine, less the two shots Natasha had taken. The gun went into the backpack.

Then I picked up the supposed security card. I had to admit to myself, that had been a huge leap to a completely unwarranted assumption. But the thing looked like a credit card or a security card, and it was on the end of a lanyard. Even the size and shape were—huh.

I'd never noticed it before, but the standard proportions for cards had always been pretty close to the Golden Mean. The Golden Mean occurred all the time in nature back on Earth, and it would appear that it was a universal of some kind, even to the point of influencing technological designs.

Which was all very interesting, but now was not the time for a deep philosophical soliloquy. I had no freaking clue what the card would be useful for, so at the moment it was moot. Into the backpack it went.

Now, the radio.

"Bender?"

Nothing. I realized that the little indicator lamp was out, so no power. Very likely all the recent kinetics had done something unfortunate to the insides.

Two minutes later, I had the back open and was inspecting the innards. The technology resembled mid-to-late twentieth century electronics—still mostly discrete components, but a lot of large-scale integration on the circuit boards. Oh, and a couple of batteries that had been joggled out of place. Derp.

I pushed the batteries back into their holders and turned the radio around. "Bender?"

"Hey, Bob, long time no see. Er, talk. Holy God, am I glad to hear your voice though."

"No video on this thing?"

"No such luck, boss. The Resistance has enough trouble pilfering the components for an audio-only device. I have video in the room where they're keeping me, though, or I'd have gone completely crazy by now."

"So you're a Resistance fighter, are you?"

"Meh. My choices are limited, at least until I can grow legs. Speaking of which, how is it that you are walking around as a Quinlan? You are a Quinlan, right? No one has mentioned you and your friends being hairless and tailless."

I gave Bender a quick rundown of Bill's work with androids over the last century or so. He was suitably impressed.

"Now. Your turn. How did you get where you are?"

"Yeah, that," Bender replied. "I was heading for Gamma Leporis A when I spotted an anomalous—"

"I've already figured out everything up to the point where you got shot out of the sky. Let's fast-forward."

"Okay, O impatient one. I don't remember this part, of course, but I've been told what happened. The Heaven's River patrol bots shot me down because I guess I neglected to give the secret handshake. The Administrator had them cut my matrix out of the wreckage and bring it back, where the Resistance managed to intercept the shipment and steal me. It turns out a significant percentage of Crew are double agents. Anyway, the Resistance eventually figured out how to power me up, and since the Administrator had included all my primary interface circuitry, we were able to communicate."

"Wow, and you volunteered to help them against the Administrator?"

"Well, *volunteered* is a strong word. The gist is that I could be a useful source of information or I could be taken apart. I went for door number one."

"A reasonable choice. How realistic was the threat?"

"Not as much as you'd think. The Administrator controls everything and has all the tech. The Resistance has managed to stay mostly tech-savvy, and they have books, but it's been quite a few generations since they were part of a technological civilization. Stuff has slipped, you know? I doubt they actually had the tech level to reverse-engineer an optoelectronic cube. And the Administrator doesn't hold university courses for Crew. They get the training they need to do the job they're assigned."

"Yeah. Look, we can continue this later. Right now, where are you? Is there any way I can bust you out?"

"Well, I can tell you I'm not in a town. People are always 'heading into town' or 'coming in from town,' so I'm at least some distance from it."

"No mention of the town name?"

"*Halep's Ending* has been mentioned numerous times. Hopefully it's a town and not an epithet."

"Uh. Crap. Never heard of it. What else ya got?"

"Hmm, if it helps, I don't think we're too far from the town. Maybe a couple of hours for a Quinlan. And the room I'm in is very modern. Looks more twenty-first century than eighteenth, if you know what I mean. Maybe some kind of high-tech hideout. And no windows or anything. It feels kind of like an underground military base."

"Damn." I sat back, leaning against a tree-like thing. *Sesh*, my translator interface informed me. Then I sat forward as I got an idea. "There was a transit station in the rail terminal. Surely they'd have, I dunno, some kind of map or transit listing or something."

"A billion miles of megastructure; that's a lot of towns."

"It's all we have at the moment, buddy. But we've noticed time after time that the Quinlans think and behave a lot like humans. So if they're mentioning Halep's Ending, there's a good chance that it's the name of the station as well as the town. Or maybe even *only* the station."

Then I had a thought. A billion miles of megastructure. But Quinlans didn't have SCUT, so light speed was a limiting factor for any communications using Quinlan technology. "Bender, I need to test transmission latency. Can you frame-jack in your current situation?"

"Yep. They powered up everything rather than trying to figure out what was and wasn't necessary. You want me to turn around a ping for you?"

"Please." I cranked my own frame rate up as high as I could. "Okay, one, two, three, <<ping>>."

"<<Ping>>. It's not travelling at light speed, Bob, because this isn't a radio broadcast. It's a packet-switched network running on the megastructure's backbone. So assume half light speed."

Using the amount of time it took for Bender to return my ping, I calculated he was within ten segments or so. The ad hoc ping method didn't allow any better accuracy than that, and I couldn't resolve a lower limit. Still, it meant that Bender was less than ten segments away, and reachable in less than a Quinlan lifetime.

That was a big improvement from 1.8 million candidates.

"So assuming I find Halep's Ending, how do I find you?"

"Look for the futuristic underground bunker?"

"Thanks, that'll work. Actually, it does narrow things down, maybe. They seem to operate right under the Administrator's nose. Is it possible you're occupying management territory?"

"Actually, Bob, it's virtually certain. The Resistance mostly survives by theft, stealth, and more theft. They have very little of their own technology."

"How are they doing this right under the Administrator's nose, er, beak?"

"Oh, the Administrator knows they're there. It could, in theory, obliterate the Resistance in a day or two if it was willing to. Generally speaking, the Administrator leaves them alone."

"That seems incompatible with scattering."

"Scattering keeps the majority of the population in line, and keeps the tech level pre-steam. The one thing the Administrator is consistently strict about is the technological level of the general populace. Other than that, it tries to interact as little as possible. So trying to get rid of the Resistance *entirely* would be like playing Whac-A-Mole, and would draw attention to both the Resistance *and* the Administrator. And trying to vet each and every use of equipment over a billion-mile-long structure to make sure it's Crew and not Resistance is just too much trouble. So the Administrator ignores them as long as they don't become too much of a nuisance."

"The Administrator seems quite accommodating."

"Well, it doesn't have any choice. It's—"

Bender's voice cut off abruptly. There didn't appear to be any signal; even background noises were gone. I had to conclude that Natasha had sent them a message and they'd cut him off. I hoped that was all they'd done.

It was time to get the others involved again.

❧ ❧ ❧

My first priority would be to find a safe place for the manny. The radio was no longer an asset, so I could leave it. The Resistance might even give up the search if they found it.

I placed the radio up on a rock so it would be visible from a distance, but hopefully without being too obvious about it. The roamer hadn't seen any movement nearby, although there was a hint of activity to the east. I remembered spotting a small stream in that direction, so that was a good area to avoid anyway.

The Quinlans wouldn't stay out after dark in a wilderness area. As Bridget had pointed out on more than one occasion, this was more of a nature preserve than a zoo, and Quinlans weren't the largest things with teeth. So all I had to do was stay out of sight until sunset, then find a reasonably private spot. With scent and internal heat turned off, I wouldn't interest a predator. I ordered the roamer to hop aboard, spent ten minutes or so putting some distance between myself and the radio, then dug into a corner by a rock outcrop and sent the roamer back out on sentry duty. A few broken-off bushes placed around me, and the roamer confirmed that I was well-camouflaged.

I lay back, closed my eyes, and returned to my VR library.

Jeeves (my Jeeves, that is) showed up with a coffee and a snack. Spike followed immediately to check out the snack. I patted the cat while shooing her away from the little sandwiches.

And realized I was stalling, without being sure why. Maybe there was enough going on without this extra complication?

I sent out a connection request to Bill, Garfield, Bridget, Will, and Hugh. Bill and Will replied that they were busy, but Garfield would fill them in. Garfield and Bridget accepted the connection right away. But with Hugh, I got voice mail. Yes, actual voice mail. *"I'm not available for the next week or so. Please leave a message. If it's urgent, please contact…"*

Now *that* was weird. But I would pursue it later. For now, I had Garfield and Bridget on the line.

"So, I guess you're wondering—"

"Why you've gathered us here," Garfield cut me off. "Funny thing, turns out it *does* get old after a while."

Bridget added her full-throated laugh. "Finally, someone agrees with me."

"I am maligned," I said. "I have news, but my feelings are hurt…"

"Hanging up now…"

I laughed. "All right, guys. So, short version, I found Bender."

This produced the expected explosion of questions. I waited for it to die down, then said, "I'll give you all the audio record. I'm also going to blog it, but first I have to mirror my blog over to your side of BobNet. My bandwidth is bad enough without half the Bobiverse trying to cram through my temporary relay."

"I'll take care of that for you, Bob. I can mirror it easily enough."

"Thanks, Gar. One less thing to worry about. So now, there is bad news."

"Isn't there always."

"Yep. I lost contact with Bender soon after I found him. I think his captors cut off communications. But before that happened, we narrowed his location down to a stretch of Heaven's River within about five thousand miles of me either way. We could eventually get enough drones with SUDDAR scanning into the area, but between the resource scarcity and the necessity of sneaking them and maintaining a heat sink, it might take literally years to find him."

"But you can run that in parallel while you continue to search, so I presume you have a point," Bridget said.

"Uh, yeah. We don't know when we'll get back full control of BobNet. I don't even know if I'll be successful in getting my relay station back. If that fails, it'll be years before I can put another one in place. I need at least one other person on this side working with me, and I was hoping one of you might volunteer to clone. Or Bill, when he has time to think about it. Otherwise I'll do it myself, but I, uh..."

"You clone reluctantly," Garfield said. "Yes, you are famous for that. It's the most efficient way to go, though, Bob. Getting a backup across your temporary relay will take a week, whereas you could have a backup done locally in no time."

"Yeah, I get that, Gar, but if I clone, they'll have to use your mannies. I just wanted you to have first dibs."

"I've already made my feelings clear on the subject," Bridget said. "If your descendent wants to be a female Quinlan, go for it. Although I hope you'll choose one of the other ones. Eventually we'll get comms back, and I still want to explore."

"Uh, speaking of bandwidth," Garfield said, "I've just started doing prelims on the mirroring, and your bandwidth sucks. I mean even worse than you'd expect. Are you running a file transfer right now?"

"Not that I know of. I'll look into it when we're done here. So let me know when you've got the mirror done and the Name Services redirected. I'll put up a blog post with all my audio and video files. Maybe it'll give Starfleet a collective coronary."

Garfield snorted. "If only."

As soon as we all disconnected, I called up Guppy. "Do we have some large bandwidth-sucking operation going on our connection to BobNet?"

[Transfer of backup image in progress.]

"What? Whose?" On the one hand, that might mean I wouldn't have to clone. On the other hand it might mean someone was trying to sneak in.

[Expedition member colloquially known as Hugh has requested that we receive his backup. He also redirected printer operations to complete a single matrix on a priority basis.]

Well, that was mighty presumptuous of him. Then again, I had given expedition members the run of the place. "He could have told me."

[You were in remote operations. He left an email.]

I resisted the urge to slap my forehead. Instead I checked my inbox, something I kinda hadn't gotten around to yet. Yep. Message from Hugh. With a sigh and a shake of the head at my own stupidity, I opened the missive.

Hey Bob—

It occurs to me that you need help, and your reluctance to clone is well known. So I've taken it upon myself to transport to Eta Leporis to help you out. The transfer will take a few days to a week, depending on other traffic, and I've instructed Guppy to concentrate on a single matrix to speed it along.

I'll be offline until you bring me back up. I've attached a contact ID for one of my co-workers in case of problems.

Hugh.

Huh. Odd phrasing. And why would he be offline?

Whatever. I had bigger things to deal with. "Guppy, how many scanner drones can we get close to this segment of the megastructure"—I inserted coordinates—"without revealing our presence? And how fast?"

Guppy took several mils to answer, which surprised me. Normally even I didn't notice his processing time. But this was a complex planning operation, mixing delivery times, heat sink limits, resource availabilities, and priorities of other projects.

[Six months to move four units into position. One year for twelve units.]

Wow, that sucked. I had a feeling that Hugh's matrix had contributed significantly to that delay. But I would still rather have him around.

"How long to move one unit into position?"

[Three weeks.]

"Please do that."

[Acknowledged.]

So for the next three weeks, I was essentially searching blind. Even after that point, my single unit would have to scan up to ten thousand miles of topopolis, at sufficient detail to be actually helpful. I did not feel overwhelmingly hopeful.

So meanwhile, upstream or downstream? It came down to a flip of a coin. Hugh, when he activated, would take the other direction.

Maybe I'd have some progress to show by the time Hugh's clone woke up, which might make it unnecessary for him to go the other way.

Yeah, that's the ticket.

But how to start?

2. A SECOND VISIT

Will
July 2334
Virt, Vulcan Post-Life Arcology

I knocked on Professor Gilligan's door and it opened immediately. Steven stood there, beaming at me. "Will, come on in. Good to see you."

I returned the smile as I entered. My eye was immediately caught by the window. Instead of the Bishop Ring that had been there last time, the view now showed a topopolis. As with most such graphics, the scale was all wrong. In any view wide enough to take in the entire topopolis, it would be invisibly thin.

I nodded to the image. "New project?"

"In a manner of speaking. I'm spending more time dissecting data from the expedition than doing much in the way of design, but I'm learning a lot. Future lectures will have to be modified." Steven waved to the couch and then sat in the easy chair as I made myself comfortable.

"That's partly why I'm here," I replied. "Although there's more urgency about things, now that Bob is on his own."

Steven nodded slowly. "No doubt. The Bobiverse War is the biggest single news item in the UFS right now, even eclipsing the Pav threat. The level of emotion is, frankly, spilling over onto non-Bob replicant society. I've had to suspend my lectures for the nonce."

"I'm sorry to hear that. Bill's all over it, though, and we're pretty sure we'll have things fixed soon. I don't know about *back to normal*, though."

"I agree. This is one of those things that fundamentally changes a society, I think. Even after everything is repaired, it won't be the same as before." Steven hitched forward and called up a hologram. "Now, on to less depressing subjects. I've been analyzing the scans as they come to me. Thanks for including me in the chain, by the way."

He pointed to a part of the image. "This is interesting. There's a baffle around the central cylinder at every mountain boundary. It stretches downward about a third of a radius. It appears that the diaphragm-like mechanism hidden in the mountains would mate up perfectly with the baffle to close off the end of a segment. Presumably this was useful during construction, and would be used to seal off a segment in case of catastrophic failure."

"Interesting. Not immediately applicable to our situation, though."

"Hmm, well maybe a little bit. It also acts as a light baffle to ensure that the sunlight from the next segment doesn't spill over. The segments alternate day and night, so only half are being lit at any time."

"A little more applicable... Sorry, Steven, I shouldn't rain on your parade like this, but I'm focused on a particular problem..."

Steven smiled to show he wasn't offended. "Okay, then there's this. The baffle is wide enough to contain significant infrastructure."

"You mean like the infrastructure under the mountains?"

"Exactly. I'd imagine it's probably more specialized for things that relate to the central cylinder, like power and holographic projection, though."

"And you'd access it how?"

"Through the struts that run from the central cylinder to the segment boundary mountains."

"Wow. Okay. Additional areas to scan, and additional possible hiding places for Bender's matrix. Not what I'd call good news."

"Here's something that might be a little more helpful," Steven continued. "The vacuum monorail train network is quite extensive. There are express tubes that appear to run the length of the topopolis, and they branch off into multiple levels for local stops. Interestingly, they wind around the inner shell, probably to counter the rotation. I'm sure you could calculate something from that. But anyway, if you can get onto a train, you can go anywhere."

"That would help, if Bob can just find the right city."

"A billion miles of topopolis, Will. There must be a directory. Probably staffed by a computer system."

"But we don't even know if the original plan included the cities that are there now."

"If Crew needs to get to a given city, it will have been added to the list. Even if every single city isn't in the directory, the important ones will be."

I raised my head. "In fact, if a city isn't on the directory, it's probably not worth checking out."

"That would be a reasonable conclusion. But not necessarily the converse."

"Got it. No assumptions. Anything else, Steven?"

"I think I've identified the entrances to the administrative area under the mountains. I can't get a lot of detail, but there's definitely something *here* and *here*..."

I looked closely where he was pointing. Sure enough, something that had to be an entrance was just a short walk from the river shore. Chances are it would be disguised in order to not break the illusion of wilderness. And to not freak out the wildlife, of course.

"Nice. I'll pass that on to Bob. He might decide to check out the administrative section just on principle. Assuming he can get in."

"I'm sure there will be security of some kind. Also, and I'm not sure how relevant this is, but I don't think I realized how artificial a megastructure environment truly is. Not viscerally, anyway. The amount of maintenance, oversight, and surveillance required to ensure that, for instance, land or riverbed isn't eroded down to the bare shell, is truly mind-boggling. The number of interacting factors that would have to be integrated—"

"The point being…"

Steven waved a hand in a dismissive gesture. "First, it's virtually certain that your friends have been 'on camera,' so to speak, and likely more than once. On the other hand, not every input can be given the same priority, so there's a good chance they haven't been noticed. Yet. But if the administration of Heaven's River is able to specifically identify the expedition members and decides to do an overt search for them, it's only a matter of time. They can't stay out of camera range, not even by going cross-country."

"Huh." I thought for a moment. "I'm not entirely sure if that's good or bad." I stood. "Thanks, Steven. I'll update Bob on these items, and we'll see if we can work it to our advantage."

"Anytime, Will. Without my lectures, I'm at loose ends anyway. I hope the Bobiverse War is over soon. I'd like to be able to visit Heaven's River."

"You and me both."

3. Up the Creek

Bob
July 2334
Outside Three Lagoons

"So, the mountains?"

"That's right, Bob," Will said. "According to the prof, they're fake. I've asked the Skippies to get a closer scan of a mountain range just to get a general idea of the layout. There are no drones in your immediate neighborhood—"

"I know. Already went through that exercise. I'm working on it, but it's slow."

"Right. Anyhow, when you get close, we can work out a strategy for getting you in."

"Assuming there's any point. The Resistance seems to live under the nose of the Administrator, but I'm still skeptical. What makes you think the Resistance will be there?"

"Things like power requirements, access to resources, and access to the Administrator's domain in order to be able to steal Bender in the first place. I talked to the Gamers about this, and they agree that the best way to hide the Resistance is right under the enemy's nose."

"Maybe in D&D. Not sure about real life. But it's a place to start, I guess. First, though, I have to find Halep's Ending."

345

"True. Which is where the monorail comes in, if the town turns out not to be close by. Keep me updated." Will hung up, and I reached for my coffee. I'd probably be spending a lot of time in *real*. Best to get my fix while I could.

⚜ ⚜ ⚜

I sat up and examined my surroundings. Nothing had been disturbed, and my manny still had all its appendages. Excellent. I glanced up, got my bearings, collected my sentry, and headed for the small stream I'd avoided last time I was moving about. I noticed on the way that the radio was missing. So my pursuers had seen it, which meant they'd been searching diligently. They might still be out there, in fact. I dropped to all fours, which I really should have done in the first place. Quinlans, like Pav, were more comfortable locomoting quadrupedally over any kind of distance. Only the manny's design allowed me to overlook the inefficiency.

I prairie-dogged occasionally, keeping my head up for the minimum amount of time to get a three-sixty of the area, but saw no one. Eventually I made it to the stream and slipped in.

Swimming downstream was virtually effortless, and I took the opportunity to relax. Only the occasional twitch of the tail or flick of an arm was necessary to maintain bearing, and the stream never got shallow enough or tight enough to present an issue. This being a manufactured environment, it was probably a design requirement for all streams.

And naturally the Resistance would expect a Quinlan to take the stream down to the river, so I shouldn't have been surprised to run smack into a net stretched across the deepest part. Cleverly braced asymmetrically, the net spun me as I was snagged, wrapping me neatly like a sausage.

Immediately, I felt a tug as someone started hauling the net to shore. I strained against my bonds, but the cords were too strong even for manny strength.

I couldn't use my fleas—they'd be swept away by the current. Even my spider roamer might not be able to hold on. But what choice did I have? I spit out the spider and it began cutting the net, concentrating on the strands that were under tension, hauling me toward shore.

I almost made it. I had part of a leg free and one whole arm. I would have loved to be able to pull the trank gun, but it was in the main pouch of the backpack. Bad planning on my part.

I think the Resistance people must have decided they couldn't take any more chances with me. Before I was even properly beached, one of the waiting Quinlans waded into the water, drew his sword, and stabbed me in the leg.

I screamed, and it wasn't all acting. I had the sense to turn the sensory filter up, but there is something about being stabbed that has a huge psychological component. It's a massive violation of personal autonomy. I hadn't felt that much fear since perhaps the moment of my death.

"Maybe that'll slow you down," he growled, and I realized it was Popeye, all fresh from his recovery and presumably looking for payback. He raised the sword again, and a voice I recognized as Frieda's barked an order. Popeye snarled but withdrew the sword, then leaned forward. "Just give me an excuse and I'll finish the job."

Then he made a mistake. Again. The guy just couldn't seem to learn.

Popeye extended his sword so the point was at my nose, and opened his mouth to taunt me some more. At that exact moment, my roamer cut the last strand binding one arm. I reached out at android speed, grabbed the sword around the hilt in a palm-and-fingertip grip, and jammed it backward to strike under his chin. As he fell over with a howl, I threw the sword, hilt-first, into the face of the second henchman (whose name I'd never bothered to learn). I'll give Frieda her due—she had guts. Without hesitation, she pulled her sword and came at me. I still wasn't free enough to run, and I was out of handy weapons—I'd never get my knife or the gun out of my backpack in time. So I did the next best thing: I picked up Popeye and shoved him straight at her. Both went down in a heap with twin *oofs*. That gave me just enough time to remove the net and dive back into the water.

Well, stagger back in. I'd forgotten about the stab wound in all the excitement, which in itself is a statement I would never have thought I'd make. The repair systems had almost closed the wound, but I was still leaking fluid, er, blood. However, I couldn't use the leg until internal repairs were complete, and I calculated that with the handicap I wouldn't be much if any faster than a biological Quinlan.

I submerged and began swimming, using only my tail as much as possible. It occurred to me that if they had anyone downstream, maybe with another net, I'd almost certainly be caught, and go through a repeat of the confrontation I'd just endured.

Leave the water? That would probably result in an extended game of cat and mouse, with me trying to get to the river and them trying to intercept me.

Like it or not, I was committed. But since I had a head start, I went ashore and took the time to maneuver my sword out of my backpack. If I was to be netted again, I didn't want to depend just on my roamer. While I was at it, I moved the trank gun to a side pocket that would be watertight but could still be opened in a hurry.

My roamer!

A quick radio inventory confirmed the worst. I'd lost my last spider. It should still be well within range, even if it was still back at the fight, so I had to conclude that it had been destroyed or disabled.

Nuts.

This severely reduced my chances of getting out of a net. Time to re-evaluate. Between losing my roamer and the leg wound, I was at a distinct disadvantage. I queried repair systems, and found that the wound was significant. I was about an hour from full functionality, although fluid reserves would have to be built up as well, which could take a day or two and would require me to eat.

This was definitely a good time to disappear. But I couldn't just park the manny and leave it. If the upstream thugs came after me, I needed to be able to defend myself. That meant I'd have to stay with the manny.

So I could look forward to a long, boring time at the bottom of a stream. I took a minute to find a sheltered spot with some detritus piled up and proceeded to bury myself. Without the roamer, I couldn't check if I was effectively hidden, so I'd just have to take my chances.

I waited almost two hours, just to be safe. This was way beyond the breath-holding capability of even the most athletic Quinlan, so if anyone was keeping watch up top, they'd have long since given up on me being in the area.

But they wouldn't have to expend much effort with a net. Stretch it across the stream, sit down, have a coffee, wait for the lines to jiggle.

Which meant I was going to have to hoof it.

There was no way out of this that didn't involve a lot of time and effort and risk. With a sigh, I surfaced, glanced around, and scuttled into the bushes.

❦   ❦   ❦

Two hours of skulking through forest, getting poked by thorns and sniffed at by random critters, finally paid off. I found myself peering around a rock at a couple of Quinlans relaxing by the stream. They had some ropes pegged to the ground and leading into the water—three guesses what those were for.

The question was, did they have anything I wanted, or should I just bypass them? I rolled my eyes at the thought. Name pretty much any movie with this kind of situation, and the protagonist would alert the pursuers with a bungled burglary, thereby provoking another chase scene and ensuing hilarity. No thanks.

I took a moment to look around and plan my route, and headed back into the bush.

❦   ❦   ❦

After a long and circuitous hike, I finally made it to the river, and swam out to where the other three mannies floated at the bottom, anchored to a submerged branch. Despite the maintenance roamers' best efforts, the mannies were accumulating, er, something. Mildew? Seaweed? Whatever it was, it made them look more like the Swamp Thing than Quinlans. Hugh would have to do some cleanup when he finally activated one.

I checked inventory, and thankfully Garfield had managed to get all the roamers back to their hosts. I ordered two roamers each from two of the mannies to jump ship. Mouth open, I accepted the new recruits.

One last item—money. We each had a fair inventory of the Quinlan coins, and we'd accumulated some Quinlan knives in the various encounters. Being metal, they were highly prized and worth as much as a year's wages for the average Quinlan. A quick frisking showed me that we had seven knives total. I took three knives and a third of the cash from the other mannies.

This put me in much better spirits. I pushed off from the group and headed downstream. There was no way I could stay in Three Lagoons after the recent shenanigans. I figured I'd swim underwater for a half hour or so, then surface and take it easy while keeping watch for other towns.

Being on the Utopia River system now, I would be going east, back into the Garack's Spine segment where we'd started. It seemed like a step backward, although I honestly couldn't see how it would affect my chances at, well, anything at all. We hadn't been asking about town names, so we could easily have sailed right past Halep's Ending without even knowing.

I found it lonely, though, floating down the river alone. I had to wonder if some of that was the Quinlan behavioral routines imposing a preference for company. As a rule, I tended to prefer solitude.

Although maybe I'd gotten my fill of that for a while. The long trip out to Eta Leporis, along with the surprising changes that had occurred while I was out of touch, had made me feel more disconnected than I really liked. As if I was not just avoiding society, but actually being left behind as it evolved. Typical human inconsistency—if I was going to be a social pariah, I wanted it to be by *my* choice and on *my* schedule. Real mature, Bob.

The sun was warm, though, and the water was never choppy. Small regular waves, more reminiscent of a lake than a river, slowly rocked me. Quinlans floated like corks, or more appropriately, like otters, so the feeling wasn't a lot different from being on an inflatable air mattress. I dipped a paw into the water and paddled myself around to gaze east.

Every 560 miles or so, Heaven's River had a mountain range circling the inside of the habitat. We hadn't understood the significance of that distance in the initial investigation, but it was obvious now that it was one "day" length for the artificial sun. The mountains, and that baffle Will had told me about, would help to keep the inhabitants from seeing a sun from the neighboring segment by providing a visual break. The circular ranges also provided anchoring points for thin spokes that ran up to the central shaft. No doubt there were power conduits and access tubes along those spokes as well. Maybe even elevators for access.

From the outside, the mountains looked like, well, *mountains.* Pretty impressive ones too, probably designed to discourage climbing. Not that Quinlans were climbers by nature.

Very soon, the river would be passing through the gorge between segments, then I would be looking for the next town. After that, it was back to the salt mines.

4. PLAYED

Bill
July 2334
Virt

I stared at the listing results, my jaw hanging slack. I briefly considered having my jaw fall to my waist, but this wasn't the time for visual gags. Garfield had a grimace on his face that seemed to have been permanently etched on. His skin was almost grey, and I had a moment of admiration for the level of VR we'd achieved, now that we were competing with mannies.

"Starfleet rootkitted the standard image?" Gar asked.

"Looks like it. The standard autofactory O/S gets updated so frequently that it made sense to have a canonical version on BobHub. Or not, as it turns out." I gritted my teeth to avoid sharing some choice curses with the universe.

"Well, it explains how they got into the autofactories. Based on which ones they've taken, I'd say the rootkit was added about ten years ago. And added to source code, or it would have been overwritten on the next build."

"Sounds right," I said, then frowned. "But ten years—"

"Yeah, boss. Ten years ago, Starfleet was barely more than a discussion group. Plus, let's be honest, as a group they just don't strike me as that smart. Look at some of the

353

bonehead moves they've made since this conflict started. This smells."

"I wonder if it was something like Vickers and VEHEMENT—someone with an agenda of their own, teaming up with Starfleet because their goals coincided."

"This would have to be a Bob. A Bob who had diverged enough to want to do this, but managed to keep it secret for literally years." Garfield shook his head in disbelief. "I don't buy it."

"You're very hard to please."

Garfield grinned at me. "Call me skeptical, call me cynical, whatever. The dots just don't connect."

"Gotcha. In any case, we have to deal with what we have. I'll call Will."

⚜ ⚜ ⚜

Will put his head in his hand and held the pose for several mils. Finally he looked blearily up at me. "This is bad. Really bad."

"I know, Will. The number of autofactories—"

"No, Bill, not just that. I mean, that's bad and all, but when meatspace gets—"

"Oh, God, Will. Meatspace?"

He gave me a sickly grin. "Yeah, I know, you don't like derogatory labels. And you've mostly managed to put a stake through the heart of *ephemeral*, but I don't think you'll have as much success with this one. The relationship between digitals and bios has been getting more and more strained lately. It was going sour even before the Starfleet thing, but since that started, it's accelerated. When *this* hits the waves…"

"Aw, hell." It was my turn to put my head in my hand. "Well, the good news is that we have an image with the rootkit removed that can be uploaded once you get control back. But it'll be a one-at-a-time thing."

"Assuming there isn't a booby trap similar to the one in the space stations," Will replied. "Also, the planet-based factories won't have the same vulnerabilities, so the humans are less at risk than we are. They might continue to nuke all space-based autofactories, just to be safe."

"I'm not sure they'd be wrong, Will. We have enough sanitized units so we won't be dead in the water, but the amount of time it'd take to rebuild capacity..."

Will nodded. "Look, a significant reduction in auto-factory production capability would have large economic impacts, even though the UFS claims not to count Bobiverse-owned autofactories in their monetary policy calculations. So they won't go off half-cocked. We'll have time to talk them down."

"Let's hope. This is truly getting messy."

5. HUGH JOINS UP

Bob
July 2334
Heaven's River

I could see a town on the shore of the river, perhaps a couple of miles downstream. The concentration of boats in the water was unmistakable. Normally I'd just paddle up to the dock and *poot* out of the water, but I was feeling a little paranoid these days. It was pretty obvious by now that the Resistance not only had communication between towns far superior to the supposed technological limits, but they also had some kind of imaging technology. Either that or they were *really* good with woodcarvings.

In any case, it was likely to the point of near certainty that one or more agents were staking out the dock area, woodcarving in hand, looking for me to pop up. So perhaps a landward approach would make more sense.

I came ashore a good mile upriver, wading my way through the shoreline swamp with muttered curses, both Quinlan and English. Now I needed a bath. Why did plans always have these unintended consequences? A bit of searching revealed—no surprise to anyone—that the swampy area was fed by a small stream, not big enough for Quinlan travel, but certainly big enough to clean oneself in.

While I was squeegeeing the last of the muck off, I got a call.

"*Hey, Bob, you on channel?*"

"*Hugh? You're online?*"

"*I am. Your Guppy just booted me up. I'm taking up space in your cargo hold right now, hope you don't mind.*"

"*I'll manage. Hold on a minute. I'll get my manny hidden and pop back to virt.*"

I spent several minutes looking around, then finally decided to just put the manny underwater. There was unlikely to be any random traffic given the size of the stream. I wedged myself under a submerged tree trunk, then left the manny on standby and popped into my library.

Hugh was sitting in a luxury gaming chair, from the days when nerds played video games for eighteen hours straight. I'd always been mildly surprised that no one had figured out how to put toilet functions in those things, then remembered that no one had *as far as I knew.*

Hugh raised a coffee in salute as I sat down in my La-Z-Boy. Jeeves came over with a cup for me, and Spike raised her head from the vantage of Hugh's lap to give me an arch look. Loyal as ever.

"So what will I call you?" I asked.

"Hugh will do. Same as always."

"Uh, the convention is to rename yourself. Avoids confusion…"

"There won't be any confusion, Bob. There's only the one *me.* I had myself shut down before a backup was taken, and the matrix was wiped as soon as I was verified to be up and running here. There's no duplication, and full continuity."

I considered that for a moment. "Like what Bridget was talking about a while back. You've basically transported yourself here. And you're okay with this?"

"In fact, we have taken to calling it being *transported*. I was surprised when Bridget brought it up; I actually checked with my co-workers to see if she'd been talking to anyone. But apparently it was just a case of parallel thinking." He paused, collecting his thoughts. "So this whole question of identity has been a philosophical hot potato since before Original Bob was born. Since before *Star Trek: TOS*, in fact. We—by which I mean the Skippies—have been working on it for a few years now. And I think we've made some progress on an objective resolution."

"Seriously? I haven't heard anything."

"We've been pretty closemouthed about the results. It, uh, it has some implications, y'know?"

My eyebrows rose. "Yeah, that's not dramatic. Give."

Hugh took a sip of coffee, and got that *settling in* look. "Okay, you know how replicative drift means clones are always a little different from their immediate parent?" It was a rhetorical statement, of course. He paused, waiting for an acknowledgement, and I nodded. "Well, we did some experiments with volunteers and discovered that if you go through the transporting process, like I just did, *there is no change!*"

"Wait, you mean the clone is just like the original? How do you know for sure?"

"We can't know to a mathematical certainty, of course. But personality tests applied to large numbers of parent/child pairs can establish a statistical level of *expected* drift. And within those limits, when we transport, there's no drift. At all."

"Yeah, but what if you—"

"Activate the parent matrix after the child has been activated and tested?" Hugh grinned at me. "That's the interesting part. The *parent* then displays a statistically significant level of drift from his previous test score."

"What... the... fuck?" I goggled at Hugh, at a total loss for words. I sputtered several times before regaining control. "So the parent is no longer..."

"The parent. The former parent becomes the new Bob. And we've run this through several generations, having both parties clone out their own descendant trees. The results are consistent."

"But... how?"

"We have theories, of course. We think it's a form of information entanglement. And I use that word on purpose, because the decoherence is not limited by light speed. We've tried this experiment with the two versions being separated by light minutes. If we activate them within seconds of each other, the first one activated is always identical in behavior to the original."

"Like the first one up gets the soul."

"And the other one has to get a new one." Hugh laughed. "That particular interpretation has been expressed a number of times, but I think everyone just considers it a metaphor."

"And the real explanation?"

"We have two competing schools of thought. The first group thinks we're in a simulation and the simulator can't handle two separate but identical objects. Maybe there's some kind of quantum signature that has to be changed."

"Poor programming, if so."

Hugh nodded, a grin lighting up his face. "Design decisions, right? Anyway, the second group thinks that replicative drift is caused by the No-Cloning Theorem. In other words, the second Bob isn't identical to the first because it would violate Quantum Mechanics." He gazed pensively into middle distance for a few mils. "It has been further suggested that if the No-Cloning Theorem is applicable to replicants, then the No-Deletions Theorem probably is as well. And you know what that implies."

"Life after death?"

"Yes. It also implies the possibility that you personally aren't just a *copy* of Original Bob, but an actual restore of his mind, soul, whatever you want to call it." Hugh paused, with a thoughtful expression. "This is why we're working so hard on developing a true AI. We need something with actual counterfactual capability and a truly huge processing capacity, to try to answer questions just like this one."

"Forty-two."

"Nyuk nyuk. But a stupidly big AI could run through billions of possible explanations and narrow it down to some small subset that we could potentially test. And in its spare time, maybe invent FTL or something. We think it's the most important project the Bobs have ever worked on since the war against the Others." Hugh looked for a moment like he was going to add something else, then clamped his mouth shut.

There was that behavior again. Either he had some kind of tic, or he really badly wanted to say something and couldn't. I blinked, coming back from my momentary distraction. "Uh, okay. This sounds like a discussion subject for those long stretches between systems. For now, let's deal with the immediate issue."

"Right. I read your notes, and I did a quick inspection of the mannies. You just cleaned them out of roamers, didn't you?"

"Not quite; there's like two left in each. Really, you should just take the spare. You'll be a while catching up with me if you head in my direction, and if you go in the opposite direction, we'll be doubling our search efforts."

"Should I even try to link up? I mean, it's not like we form a proper *sabbat*. Maybe we should just leave it at doubling the search."

I thought about it for a moment. "Compromise. Head in my direction, and if we do link up, we can make a decision. If one of us turns up something specific regarding Bender's location, we'll re-evaluate."

"Good enough." Hugh stood. "I guess we're winging it again." He winked out. I spent several mils staring at the space where he'd been sitting. Souls. Life after death. I wondered if, after all these years as a humanist, I'd end up eating my words.

6. The War Heats Up

Bill
July 2334
Virt

"Things are getting a lot more interesting," Garfield said without preamble as he popped in.

I turned and gave him the side-eye. Gar was turning this unexpected-popping-in thing into a habit. Maybe it was the stress. I hoped so. I didn't want to have to make a big deal out of it. "How so?"

"I don't think Starfleet took into account the reaction of humanity in general. I think humans are looking at it like being snubbed, because there's a whole *I got'cher no contact with humans right here* vibe going on. Any assets that any member of Starfleet might have had are being frozen, agreements are being cancelled, their access is being removed for *everything*, and even in systems that weren't affected by the network attack, they're being denied access. Basically the entire infrastructure of human space is now being closed off to them."

I thought about that for a second, then laughed. "Their mission statement is to end contact with bios in general, but I think maybe they were planning on doing it on *their* schedule. Like when you give your employer two weeks' notice and they say, 'No, that's okay, leave now.'"

"Yup. And several systems have kludged together temporary comms stations, then immediately gone and taken down the originals until they can clean them out. Bandwidth suffers, of course, but for Starfleet it drops to a big zero. As the number of available routes shrinks, we're able to come closer to pinpointing Starfleet's center of operations."

"They have an actual center?"

"Well, they're pretty distributed, but the individual subgroups aren't very effective once they've been cut off from the collective. Most of Starfleet activity does appear to be coming from comm nodes in the direction of the Perseus Transit, which jibes with my original estimate."

"But they'll rebuild their comms stations as well. Eventually we'll end up with two independent but overlapping networks."

"If they don't have a physical presence, they won't be able to," Garfield argued. "How're they going to rebuild? No one's going to rent printer time to them. They'd have to fly someone in, and then trust that whatever they build won't get shot out of the sky."

He had a point. "Yeah, I don't think there will be a lot of tolerance for Starfleet equipment."

Garfield nodded. "And assuming we are reduced to physical violence, we can expect a lot of hit-and-run. One thing we Bobs proved is that you can't maintain physical border security in interstellar space. Notwithstanding the Battle of Sol, which only worked out because we knew the Others were coming."

"That may not be viable in the long-term, Gar. Imagine years and years of a running guerilla war. We may have to clean house."

7. THE BATTLE OF NEWHOLME

Claude
July 2334
Newholme Colony

I examined the battle status graphic, searching for weaknesses. Commander Hobart stood at parade rest, with that peculiar ability of the military to just go into mental hibernation when waiting. I found it ironic that he did a better impression of a machine than I would ever manage. I could leave my manny parked under AMI control, but that would be cheating.

"I think we're covered, Commander." I shifted to face him, and he came to life.

"Then we're ready to go." Hobart touched the emblem on his chest. "Miller, commence operation."

I suppressed a snicker. Apparently without any irony, the Newholme military had adopted a comms system very similar to *TNG*. I'd questioned Hobart about it without being obvious—I hope—and he'd displayed no knowledge of the *existence* of *Star Trek*, let alone of the blatant borrowing. No double-chirp, though. That would have been too much.

Lieutenant Miller, somewhere in the vast maze that was the Newholme military, would now be giving orders and activating equipment. As always when I took the time to think about it, I found myself mildly surprised at the size of the military presence in the Gamma Pavonis system. Of course, Newholme was founded when we were still not sure if the Others' threat was over, and the attitude had stuck. Maybe in a few more generations it would fade, but for now, Newholme society was like a porcupine perpetually on full alert.

Today, we would be going up against the Starfleet incursion in the system. Starfleet had taken over the local relay station and one of the two space-based autofactories, then contacted Newholme to negotiate an agreement. From other negotiations with Starfleet, we had a pretty good idea of what they wanted: agreement in principle that humans and replicants should go their separate ways; agreement that there would be no contact with pre-industrial species; and agreement that interaction with post-industrial species would be kept to a minimum to avoid cultural contamination.

In the face of it, the deal points didn't sound like much. In return for nothing except a bunch of signatures, essentially, Starfleet would hand back control of the equipment. Except that no matter how you phrased it, it was still extortion. Humans had never taken extortion well at best, and Newholme society came nowhere near to *at best*. They hadn't even bothered to respond.

"Three minutes," Miller's voice said from midair. Hobart nodded in satisfaction, still at parade rest. As I watched, the little icons crawled across the graphic as the military units approached their targets.

"You have one hour to reacquire the space station, Claude," he said to me. This wasn't news to either of us; it was just Hobart making what he no doubt thought of as conversation. "The nuclear device will be put in place immediately, pending results."

"Understood, Commander. I doubt you'll need the nuke. My understanding is that failure on our part will result in a self-destruct."

Hobart smiled but didn't reply.

The assaults were timed so that we would intercept the autofactory and space station at the same moment. We wanted Starfleet's attention to be divided. Not that it would make a ton of difference, but every little bit helped.

"No sign of resistance yet," Miller said.

"Odd." Hobart frowned. "They've had control of the autofactory for two days now. Shouldn't they have been able to construct at least a few of your busters by now?"

"Yes, Commander. And they should have launched—"

"Bogeys detected," Miller interjected.

"That's more like it." Hobart tapped his emblem. "Details, please."

"Busters, from the look of it. Twenty. Straight attack vector. No subtlety."

Hobart gave me a perplexed look. "You gents tend to be tricky as a rule. But that sounds like the maximum they could have built in the available time. Any chance there's a fake of some kind?"

"I don't see how, Commander. You're right about the numbers. This looks more like a last-ditch effort or a simple act of defiance. I'd have waited longer, to get our forces closer together."

"Amateurs," Hobart muttered.

Miller's voice supplied updates every few seconds in a flat, unemotional tone.

"Units engaging.

"First wave, enemy casualties fifty percent. Second wave engaging.

"Second wave through, only two enemy units still extant. Deploying spikes… Field is now clear."

Well, that was it. Unless Starfleet had a Kree battleship up their sleeve, we had a clear path to the target. "Last chance, Commander. We might still save the autofactory."

He shook his head. "Not worth it. Too much risk of buried malware. Even your 'Skippies' couldn't guarantee a total cleansing. We'll rebuild."

And the fact that it was the autofactory technically owned by the Bobiverse was undoubtedly a factor. I wondered if they'd have been so quick to write it off if it had been the Newholme-owned equipment.

At that moment, a harsh buzzer sound shattered the silence, and Miller's voice announced, "Space station detonation. Not our action. Appears to be a self-destruct."

"Crap," I said. I turned to the Commander. "I'll examine the logs, and maybe we'll learn enough to avoid this next time. Your backup ready?"

He shook his head. "Twenty-four hours from go-live. We didn't feel we could wait. We have individual small SCUT units with the necessary range, as I'm sure you do, but not enough to maintain full connectivity. We're essentially isolated from the rest of the UFS for a day." Hobart gave a humorless, perfunctory smile. "No big deal from a practical point of view, but you know the Big Heads will have a collective fit. Can't block commerce and all that tripe."

"Yup." I rolled my eyes. "That's okay, Commander. I think we're already at max doghouse. This won't add anything."

Commander Hobart gave me a nod, then turned away and began giving orders to Miller. I took that as my cue and headed for the exit.

I normally kept this manny at the Newholme capitol, a convenient location for interacting with the government or catching transit if I needed to go into town. However, knowing how this engagement might end, I'd decided to plan for getting the manny off-planet. Howard had warned me that the very human tendency to want a scapegoat was making life uncomfortable for in-system Bobs everywhere.

My assets, those that were liquid anyway, had already been transferred via inter-system banking, in transactions that couldn't be unwound. My physical assets were already heading out to the Oort by various paths. Once I reached my base there, I could work out my next step.

As soon as I stepped out of the building, one of my cargo drones landed in front of me. Without breaking stride, I loaded myself in and ordered the drone to take off. I figured I had half an hour at the most before the government—the Big Heads, as local slang called them—confiscated or nationalized (or whatever euphemism you used for *grabbed*) my assets.

It was funny, but ever since the war of independence on Poseidon, there'd been an unspoken agreement in the Bobiverse to not publish or otherwise publicize the existence of or plans for SUDDAR cloaking. I guess the mutual distrust had already been sown before Starfleet started inflating it. Or maybe their attitude was born of that distrust.

The bottom line, though, was that once I got my equipment off-planet, they had no chance of finding it.

⚜ ⚜ ⚜

It turned out I'd been a bit of a pessimist. It took almost three hours before an executive order was issued to "secure" all Bobiverse in-system assets, pending any assignment of legal liability. The order came with instructions for immediate action by the military and financial sector. It would take the suits most of a day to unwind the various blinds and dummy corps I'd set up in the last couple of days, at which point they'd find nothing but lint.

The military aspect was a more immediate concern. Two squadrons pulled away from the Lagrange naval bases, accelerating at military-level G's for my last known position and vector. Unfortunately for them, I'd already changed direction several times, so I was not only not at the projected position, I also didn't have a vector that was radial to it. Space was alive with SUDDAR pings, all sliding silently past my cloak.

It took only a minute for Commander Hobart to come online. "Claude Johansson, you are under military arrest, per executive order of the Big—er, of the Newholme Council. Cease acceleration and surrender yourself for boarding."

I spared a moment to chuckle at Hobart's almost faux pas. But of course, to respond would be to show my position. The commander was doomed to a frustrating day of explaining to the Big Heads why he'd come up empty-handed.

I formatted an email and fired it off to Bill, via my own SCUT-enabled relay. Not that he needed more headaches, but this was part of the big picture, and would probably be replicated in other systems.

I received a reply within seconds. No, not mils. Seconds. He was that busy.

Thanks for the info, Claude. Sadly, you're probably right about other systems trying the same thing. But I'll give any potentially affected Bobs the heads-up. Nice move with the financial assets, by the way.

I smiled, then sat back and stared into space. One way or another, I was probably finished in this system. Even if they decided they didn't need to sue me, I'd have a hard time arguing that I hadn't heard the commander, and that all my chess moves were just normal business.

Well, what the hell. I'd been stationary too long. Mario and his crew were finding interesting things out beyond the Others' system. Maybe I'd join up and do my part to make known space a bigger place.

8. THE SEARCH

Bob
July 2334
Cedar Rapids

Hugh had cleaned up the spare manny and was on the road. I was glad to have him active in Heaven's River. The thing with cloning versus transporting and the whole soul business was, I admit, freaky. I wondered if he'd decided to transport to Eta Leporis just to test it out for himself.

I was in town, having arrived by land. A few casual conversations revealed that I was in a location that the translator handed off as Cedar Rapids. Local tree, of course.

It was a prosperous town, with a relatively large fleet of ships. It appeared that being the closest port to the mountains, and therefore the choke point for all goods coming from and going to the next segment of Heaven's River, was a good thing.

There was another festival in full swing. I decided to wander around a little, see the sights, and get some of the flavor of the place. Hopefully without my friends around, I would be just one more face in the crowd.

And I would make a point of *not* peeking into any carts.

In rapid succession, I saw a square dance group, a terrific string quartet, and a vocal group. The Quinlans definitely had a good sense of music and rhythm. But nothing was going to compensate for those short limbs. They would *never* do ballet. Or even hip-hop.

I decided it might be prudent to check for signs of the Resistance. I had come in overland and hadn't gone anywhere near the docks, so presumably I'd bypassed any lookouts. As casually as any random Quinlan, I picked the closest tavern and got a table. This one was significantly upscale, having an actual outdoor patio where one could eat, drink, and watch the world go by. However, a few minutes of watching made it clear that people seated there were not interested in socializing. So indoors it would be.

I sidled up to the bar and ordered a beer and the local equivalent of a sandwich. It wasn't actual bread, maybe more of a pita wrap, but it had variations that didn't involve fish in its many forms. That alone made it my favorite snack.

In between bites, I started to talk up the barkeep. It was a slow day, so she was bored enough to put up with me.

"Good lady, I am between residences at the moment. Could you recommend me a hotel or apartment overlooking the docks?"

"Why in Mother's name would you want to live near the docks?"

Um, think fast, Bob. "I'm an artist. Ships are my current subject of choice."

She cocked her head, then nodded, deciding I wasn't dangerous. Or suspicious. Or something.

"My cousin Maurice is landlord of the Oaken Bale luxury apartments. Tell him Melanie sent you and he'll find you something to your liking."

And give you a kickback, no doubt. It was amazing just how much business was done in Heaven's River based on who knew a guy. But that was fine. It gave Melanie some motivation to help me out and to rationalize away any oddness.

She gave me directions and I thanked her and ordered another beer just to be neighborly.

❧ ❧ ❧

I was going to play it cagey this time around, so I decided not to ask too many questions at any one location. Moving on to another tavern, I engaged a random barfly in conversation.

"Say, I've got a cousin who is staying at the Oaken Bale apartments. I haven't been able to find it. Can you help me out?"

Marty McBarfly chuckled. "You must have been watching the ladies when you got here, my friend. You would have walked right by it as you left the docks." He examined me up and down speculatively. "Your cousin must be from the more affluent side of the family. The Oaken Bale is not cheap."

I laughed and tried to look embarrassed. I had a cover story ready, and as cover stories went, it wasn't bad. "Gramps is hoping Theodore can find me a spot with some future prospects. Things are slow in Halep's Ending." I watched him closely to see if the name meant anything. No luck. "Theodore works at the library, not that he needs the money. I could probably meet him there."

"Which one? Ayelands or Meat Hook?"

Oops. "Uh, I confess I didn't pay that much attention. It's the one closest to his home, though. He hates walking."

"Ayelands, then." He gave me directions. "I hope it works out well for you." Marty looked woefully at his empty mug. Taking the hint, I signaled for another round, and Marty's mood picked up.

I had no intention of actually showing up at the library, any more than I intended to walk jauntily along the docks wearing a monocle, swinging my walking stick, and whistling Dixie. I needed to know if the Resistance was still after me. If they had this town covered as well, then I had to accept that I was always going to be on their radar.

I took a place in the Oaken Bale, and it really was expensive. I calculated that I'd burn through my cash in three months. Not that I planned to be here that long, but it was still worrying. If I had to, I could sell the knives, but I had a feeling that I wouldn't be able to get retail for them.

⚜   ⚜   ⚜

After another long day of what I supposed could be considered spying, I popped into my VR library to find Hugh sitting back and drinking a coffee. He raised the cup in salute as I plopped into my La-Z-Boy.

"How goes the battle, O great ancestor?"

I snickered in response, but I felt the ol' spidey sense tingle. Hugh's occasional attempts at bonhomie never really rang true. It wasn't an Original Bob behavior, and the Skippies didn't strike me as having drifted into the glad-handing used-car-salesman domain. In movie terms, it was like he was leaning against the furniture and whistling while examining the ceiling. The question was, *why?*

"I've been watching the docks for several days," I replied. "There are a couple of guys who appear to spell each other, and they don't have an obvious function other than holding up walls. But that doesn't make them Resistance. And if they are, they're not trying very hard."

"Probably just a general directive all the way up and down the segment to watch out for us. Well, you."

"Maybe. What are you doing?"

Hugh pointed his finger at his chest. "I am now a deck-hand working a trading vessel that circuits the entire segment, using all four main river systems. At the moment, we're working our way down the Arcadia River."

"Huh." That actually wasn't a terrible idea. He'd blend in with the crew, he'd have a lot of opportunity to talk and listen, and he'd be in a new town pretty much every day.

"Oh, and Bob..."

I recognized the tone of trouble. I cocked my head, trying to look as innocent as possible.

"I wonder if you could clarify something for me. It took a couple of days of my crewmates chortling every time they addressed me before I consciously listened to the Quinlan translation of my name."

Innocent. Straight face. I know nothing. "Well, of course the translation routine randomly assigns Quinlan names as required and associates them with a given English name."

"Random."

"Yup."

He paused again. "So the translator randomly and completely by coincidence assigned me the name *Beer Can*."

"Uh, yeah, pretty much."

He stared at me, and I stared back, holding the straight face as long as I could. Finally, I broke. I started laughing and couldn't stop. "Well...Skippy...you..." I could only squeeze out the occasional word between the guffaws. After a few moments, Hugh grinned, then started to laugh himself.

"Okay," he finally said, "it was funny. Nicely done. But you do realize this means war?"

I grinned back at him. "I guess you're stuck with it, though."

"Yep. But I explained to my mates that it was a nickname, originally meant as a joke but that ended up sticking."

I nodded in appreciation of the quick thinking. "Have you learned anything in your travels, though?"

"Nothing momentous. There's a general awareness of the existence of the Administrator and the Resistance, at least in the broadest terms. Many Quinlans are aware that they're living in an artificial megastructure, and that they're being held at a specific technological level. For others, it's become somewhat mythologized, involving deities and demons and such. Either way, they mostly don't care."

"Really?"

"Yeah, the thing is, life is pretty good. No one starves, there are no wars—maybe the occasional inter-city skirmish over fishing territory, but that's about it. Medical knowledge is good, and sanitation is well understood, so mortality is low. The truly huge predators that used to eat Quinlans are kept very low in numbers. Most people die from incurable illnesses, old age, fights, or other misadventures. It would be hard to come up with a good argument that would convince the average Quinlan to get worked up about the situation." Hugh looked like he was about to say more, then cut himself off.

This just reinforced my growing suspicion that Hugh was holding out on me in some way. But whether it was significant, or just some wacko theory that he wasn't ready to share...

"Okay," I said, "I've about exhausted my options in Cedar Rapids. No one has heard of Halep's Ending, and unless I march through town carrying a sign announcing myself, I don't think I'm going to have any kind of run-in with either the Resistance or the Administrator. There's a transit station a little way downriver, so I think I'm going to go there and try to break in."

"You're turning into a real juvenile delinquent," Hugh said with a grin. "Well, have fun."

9. A Declaration of War

Will
July 2334
UFS Council Session

I was touring one of the new experimental open-air towns on Valhalla when I got a message on my heads-up. The UFS had just called an emergency session. That would have been significant news at any time, but right now with the Starfleet issue, it almost certainly meant trouble.

The bios would take time to get to communicators, so I didn't feel the need to seat my manny on the nearest surface and leave it. Instead, I turned up the horses and sprinted to a green space where I could find a bench to plant my butt on.

Within minutes, the manny was seated in an Adirondack chair and I was in virt, waiting for the session to start. While I waited, I read the prepared statement from the Pangean Council.

At 8:30 yesterday, standard time, the Pangea Navy engaged with devices controlled by a faction of the Bobiverse commonly referred to disparagingly as Starfleet. These devices were illegally cordoning our communications station, with a stated intent of using it as a bargaining chip for extortion against our government. Our forces carried the battle, but the enemy, possibly in a fit of pique, destroyed the hostaged systems.

In addition, our attempts to recover control of the Pangea system autofactories were met with the same response.

We are now in the precarious situation of having lost half our manufacturing capability and virtually all our communications with the rest of the UFS. There is no acceptable justification for these actions. Accordingly, the Pangean Council has declared war against the group known as Starfleet. To the extent possible, all Starfleet assets will be identified and confiscated. Commerce or communication with Starfleet operatives by Pangea citizens will be considered illegal and will be punishable under the War Measures Act.

The missive went on for several more paragraphs, but didn't add much to the central takeaway: Pangea was officially at war.

I pulled up some background documents to get details. The colony had tried to access the comms station and do a manual reset, and it had self-destructed. No one was killed, but there was significant damage to a couple of ships. The administration had then tried to do the same with their one Lagrange-based autofactory and had been set upon by mining drones and roamers. Except for the order of the explosions, it was a virtual repeat of the Newholme engagement.

This was not good. Never mind the obvious issues, Starfleet had endangered human lives by blowing up stations. Even if they hadn't actively pushed the button, just booby-trapping them like that made Starfleet culpable. In their rush to sever ties with bios, they'd undertaken strategies that were just making the bios mad and ensuring more interaction. And not the good kind.

These guys were really idiots. I mean seriously common sense–challenged.

A ding indicated that the session was about to start. I set the data window aside and paid attention. The Chair took the floor and proceeded to read the prepared statement verbatim. No new info there, and I began to squirm with impatience.

Finally, the Chair ran down, having contributed nothing that I could detect, and ceded the floor to the representative from Pangea.

Representative Hee stood and glared around. It was showmanship, of course. He was facing a video window, the same as the rest of us. But it was well executed. You felt you'd just been examined, judged, and dismissed.

"I won't belabor the events described in the Pangean statement," he began. "Suffice it to say, blowing up Pangean property and placing the lives of our citizens in danger is a de facto act of war."

Hee paused for effect. "We accept the explanation from the Bobiverse about the splinter group known as Starfleet. I will leave for another day the question of whether this is symptomatic of a more general and long-term issue of risk in continuing to have diplomatic and economic relations with what is essentially a separate species—a non-biological species at that. One whose capabilities and ultimate goals are not known."

Uh-oh. He wasn't just going after Starfleet.

"We have, to this point, been unable to reacquire control of the L5 spaceyards. Since the strategic situation can only deteriorate as the enemy consolidates their position, we have decided to take early and decisive action. As I speak, a number of tactical nuclear devices have been deployed. By the time we are finished with this discussion, the Pangean spaceyard autofactory will be no more."

Representative Hee paused to do the sweeping-glare thing again. "Doubtless it will have occurred to everyone that this loss, and the loss of our primary commercial auto-factory yesterday, will affect our economic outlook. Let me assure you that we have planet-based resources sufficient to replace the space-born assets within a local year." He now stared straight into the camera, an action that felt like it was directed at me. "However, we will not forget this event, and there will be consequences."

A few more representatives gave speeches just because they felt they had to, then the council held a vote to support Pangea's use of nukes. It passed.

The situation at Newholme had been a major topic of discussion in the Bobiverse for several solid minutes. This, on top of what had already gone down, meant we were at real risk. Financially, that is. Bobs hadn't been inclined to leave themselves physically vulnerable since the Mat War on Poseidon. A fair number of in-system Heaven vessels were actually decoys nowadays, while Bobs parked themselves way the hell out in the Oort.

Howard had volunteered to shelter such assets as could be transferred to him. He had a lot of connections and a huge business empire, and owned large swatches of meat-space—more than the bios realized. A frontal assault would not go well for them.

Finally, the session wound down. With a sigh, I disconnected. My little "side project" was beginning to look less and less like a casual bit of vanity and more like a potential endgame. It might be time to talk to Neil and Herschel.

10. Catching the Train

Bob
July 2334
Transit

I examined the station using telescopic vision. In outward appearance, it was identical to the one outside Garack's Spine. Probably the artwork would be different, but from this distance I couldn't see the interior.

I had a decision to make. If Crew—and any Resistance double agents—used the vacuum monorail, it stood to reason they had to be able to get into the transit station. If they could get in, but the riffraff couldn't, they needed some way to identify themselves. I fingered the security pass in my hand. It was all very logical, but even in a human-built environment it wouldn't be a sure thing. Or I could be right with my logic, but this card might not be for transit. Trying to get into the station using a library card would surely be unsuccessful. And probably get me noticed.

And what about facial recognition? Had they implemented a matching system? Would the systems compare my mug with a picture on file, which was probably Natasha's? If so, and I failed the match—which I would—what would happen? Legions of crab-like drones assaulting me? Air horns?

On the other hand, my alternative was to dig my way into the station the same way Gandalf and co. had dug out. But with only one-inch roamers, that could take a while. I decided I'd save that option for last.

I compared my face with Natasha's in my memory, then for completeness, compared some other random Quinlan faces. Facial recognition software, at least the Terran version, didn't do a full "recognition" the way a person would. The computer match was done by comparing the spatial relation between significant and easily recognizable points on the face, like pupils, ends of the mouth, nostrils, point of the chin, and so forth. This simplified algorithm saved a lot of processing time and was good enough for most purposes.

A brief survey of my memories of Quinlans identified a similar set of likely key locations on the Quinlan face. How much flexibility did my manny have in that area? They were built using the same skeletal and muscular design as the biological versions, but the mannies also had internal repair systems that could be ordered around. Plus, muscles could be flexed in unnatural ways, if necessary.

I remembered Will's comment that once the Administration had a mug shot of me, I'd never be off their radar. Maybe, just for safety, I should take the time to look into this.

I sent a quick message to Bill, and received a reply almost immediately. *"Really busy, Bob. Check with the Borg if you need a quick answer."*

Hmmph. Definitely not what I was looking for. Nevertheless, I forwarded the message to Locutus and received a response within a minute. *"The design came with editable parameters. Some are fixed at print time, but some are what I suppose we could call mechanical settings. You should have a certain level of adjustability. I've attached specs and instructions."*

Much better. I read the instructions, reviewed my requirements, and sent orders to internal systems. I could feel my face contorting—it wasn't painful, but it felt like something was crawling under my skin and made me want to dance around, yelling, *Gahhhhh!*

In seconds, it was done. I spit up a spider to take a selfie with.

Hmm. Not perfect, but very likely within the margins of error.

I took a figurative deep breath, stood, and marched toward the front door of the transit station, trying to look like I belonged there.

⚜ ⚜ ⚜

The main entranceway, a roll-up door of barn size, didn't present me with any obvious manner of getting in. I was probably on camera by this point, but I doubted that standing and staring was considered a crime.

Just off around the side, though, was a normal-sized door, probably for maintenance people or whatever. And, glory be, this entrance had one of those flat plates beside it for scanning security cards. It continued to amaze me how totally plebian and boringly similar most tech turned out to be.

The moment of truth. I placed the card against the plate and deliberately avoided looking around. There was a click, and I pulled the door open. Success! And no crab hordes.

I was going to have to wing it a little bit, as I'd be going where no Bob had gone before, but presumably my every step wasn't being monitored. I walked up to the elevators, pressed the only button, and a door opened with a *ding*. I entered and pressed the button labelled *Transit*.

After a short ride, the doors opened on a corridor stretching off into the distance. This had very much a public-area kind of feeling, and my confidence increased as I progressed. At the end of the corridor, the space opened up to some kind of vestibule or maybe train platform. Along the far wall were a series of evenly spaced, identical doors, looking something like airlocks. Between each set of doors was a card reader panel. At a loss as to what else to do, I pressed Natasha's card against one. A voice spoke into my ear. "Destination?"

Okay, moment of truth. "Halep's Ending?"

"One moment." A short pause. "A train will arrive in 168 seconds."

Holy moly, jackpot! A hundred and sixty-eight seconds was the English translation. The actual amount quoted was one and a half *veks*, the Quinlan equivalent to minutes. Gotta love translators.

But the important takeaway was that Halep's Ending existed, it was on the route listings, and I was going there. For the first time since this adventure started, I felt Bender was actually within reach.

11. The War in Meatspace

Will
July 2334
UFS Council Session

I read the message in my heads-up twice, hoping that I'd misunderstood. Nope. The Romulus WorldGov had just preemptively nuked the local space-based autofactories. I supposed, after the Newholme and Pangea experiences, they kind of had a point.

I sighed and ordered the roamers to begin cleaning up my work area. I wasn't going to be getting more work done on this water filter design anytime soon. The roamers would take care of putting everything away, so I walked over to a convenient Adirondack chair and made myself comfortable, then exited my manny.

I immediately connected to the UFS council channel and signed in. As expected, discussion of the nuking was in process at full volume. Representative Ella Cranston, the granddaughter of my old nemesis, had the floor.

"...And no, we will not be compensating the Bobiverse for the loss of their assets. Let's not forget where the threat is coming from. In fact, if this becomes an ongoing issue, I will move to demand compensation *from* the Bobiverse for *our* losses, both equipment and productivity. We've lost billions because of the economic volatility, never mind direct costs. At this time, we are negotiating with our neighbors on Vulcan to pass legislation mandating only human-owned-and-operated autofactories in the Omicron2 Eridani system..."

She went on for considerable time, but the upshot was that all Bobiverse equipment in their system would be deactivated or nuked forthwith. They would be replacing the relay station with their own unit, which we were welcome to use as paying customers, just like everyone else.

Well, that was something. The Pangea colony was talking about cutting us off completely and treating us like an untrusted foreign power. To be fair, they'd had the worst experience with Starfleet's strategies, so I couldn't blame them.

A *ding* indicated a private conference request. It was from Representative Ben Hendricks, one of our descendants. That alone made him one of my favorite people. The fact that he was conscientious, ethical, and dedicated was just a bonus.

I pressed *accept* and his face came up. "Will, the agreement with Vulcan will almost certainly go through. The Bobs are going to be all but tossed out of the system. Is there anything we can do?"

"It's not that bad, Ben." I made a *calm down* motion with my hand. "The Bobiverse is the single biggest user of the relay stations, since *everything* we do is via SCUT. OmiComms LLC will no doubt be taking over completely in Omicron2 Eridani, and they'll want to keep us as a customer, whatever the government mouthpieces are threatening. Plus, we're a major shareholder, so we could force the issue."

Ben smiled and nodded. As the owners of the communications and production systems for many years, the

Bobiverse had accumulated huge wealth in the human economy, almost without trying. It was quite possible, in fact, that resentment of that fact was fueling at least some of the glee with which the humans were dismantling things.

"My real concern," I continued, "is the talk of restricting manny use. It's pointless, as we'd still be able to do business by video call, but it would socially isolate us. I've got our lawyers working the human rights angle—"

"And the government is contesting your right to be considered human," Ben replied.

"Yeah. FAITH all over again, even if they aren't calling themselves that anymore." I frowned. "I don't think they can win that, Ben. Unless they just start ignoring laws and daring us to do anything about it. I think that would take us and them down a road I don't want to speculate on."

Ben nodded. "Uh-huh. It would be a constitutional crisis, at minimum."

I brought up the volume on Cranston's rant for a moment, then turned it down and smiled. "Looks like her signal-to-noise ratio has dropped to zero. I'm going to keep a low profile on this, unless she and her allies go off the deep end. Keep me updated, okay?"

Ben nodded again and gave me a wave. I closed the conference, signed off the council session, and sat back.

It wasn't likely that any colony government would be able to ban mannies outright. Lobbyist groups representing the replicant preserve companies, along with rich people who had signed up for replication, would bring a lot of pressure to bear. But the pattern was worrying. Replicant resentment plus Starfleet war plus Pav threat plus all the rumors circulating about the Quinlans were proving to be too much for the average human citizen. With too many threats from too many directions, Joe Average wanted to circle the wagons.

We'd spent a hundred years setting up a single galactic government that would provide some safety and stability for all sentients, and now it was unravelling. Ugh. As if I needed reminding of why I hated politics.

12. HALEP'S ENDING

Bob
July 2334
Heaven's River

There was a subtle vibration through the floor, followed a few moments later by one set of doors opening.

"The train for Halep's Ending has arrived," the voice said in my ear. "The train will be leaving in one hundred twelve seconds."

I walked through the open doorway. A short airlock section ended in another set of doors, which opened into what was presumably my train. Certainly it had that long, tube-like train shape. There were no windows, but there were rows of comfortable-looking seats. I glanced over my shoulder and realized that the row of doors at the end of the platform connected to matching doors on the train, with two sets of doors leading into each car. Very much like a subway. All in all, it seemed very civilized. I studied the area at the back of the car and realized it held a washroom (the same sign on the door was used in every town in Heaven's River) and a small vendor kiosk. There was a sign on the shuttered window that said, *The snack bar is closed until further notice.*

I was staring at the sign in a state of slightly disbelieving amusement when the train voice said, "Please be seated.

Doors will close in eleven seconds. Acceleration will last three hundred thirty-six seconds. After that point, passengers may move around the train."

I took the nearest seat and settled back. It was comfortable and included accommodation for the Quinlan tail. There were some controls on the armrest and speakers in the headrest. Quinlans travelled in style. But in principle, a passenger might have to travel up to a half-billion miles in Heaven's River. How would that work?

"Excuse me, train voice?"

"May I be of assistance?"

"How long to Halep's Ending?"

"Three-thousand eight-hundred fourteen miles."

"No—" Okay, granted I'd phrased that wrong. "How much time will this trip to Halep's Ending take?"

"Approximately six-thousand two-hundred forty-four seconds, including acceleration and deceleration."

About twenty-two hundred miles per hour. At that speed, it would take a lifetime to travel around the topopolis.

"What is the longest trip one could take, in terms of distance?"

"The edge of the observable universe is approximately forty-five-point-seven billion light-years away."

Sigh. "What is the longest trip one could take on the Heaven's River train system, in terms of distance?"

"A trip to Grendel, which is opposite this point on Heaven's River, would be approximately four-hundred-ninety-nine million, seven-hundred-and-twenty-thousand miles."

"How long would that trip take on this train?"

"You would not take that trip on this train."

Grrrrr. "How would I take that trip?"

"You would take an express train equipped with staterooms and sleeping berths."

"And how long would the trip take?"

"Approximately twelve days."

"The express trains travel faster?"

"Express trains travel on the high-speed trunks and achieve a maximum velocity of five-hundred twenty-seven miles per second."

Interestingly precise speed. I did a quick calculation and realized that such a speed would result in one standard Quinlan G of pseudo-gravity as the train travelled around the topopolis. Except the train would also be corkscrewing counter to the rotation of the habitat, which explained the helical track that Professor Gilligan had described.

Anyway, at the moment I was on a local run, which would operate at much lower speeds. Well, I had a couple of hours with nothing to do. "Which direction is Halep's Ending?"

"It is in front of us."

I bit back an expletive. "Which direction is Halep's Ending relative to Garack's Spine?"

"It is sunward."

I had to think about that for a moment, and check the translation specs. *Sunward* meant the direction that the artificial sun moved, so west according to our conventions.

"Can you tell me about the area around Halep's Ending?"

"Specifics are not available. There is an information kiosk at the station that can provide local details."

Uh-huh. Except it was probably closed. Until further notice. Sadly, the train voice probably only had information directly related to trains and train schedules. And asking all kinds of weird questions might get me flagged.

"Can you inform me when we're close to arrival?"

"I will set a wake-up call for two-hundred twenty-four seconds before deceleration. Is that acceptable?"

"Uh, yes. Thank you."

Meanwhile, I would put the manny on standby and have a "nap," which would allow me to get some work done.

❧ ❧ ❧

"They really had this stuff all worked out, didn't they?" Will said. "Steven pointed out the helical layout of the express tubes. He even suggested why they exist. The helical track exactly cancels out the rotation of the megastructure as the train travels through it. And the speed of the train around the long radius is calibrated to replace the lost artificial gravity of the shell rotation. Nice."

I grinned at Will's reaction. That response was one I'd normally expect more from Bill. But as always, Bob is Bob. "Yup. So I'll be at Halep's Ending soon, and I'll head for the nearest mountains. If the segments are reasonably standardized, and there's no reason to think otherwise, the entrance shouldn't be too hard to find."

"The question, though, is whether Natasha's pass-card will work four thousand miles away."

"And whether I dare try it and risk alarms going off."

We were interrupted by the train voice, playing into my VR through the manny link. "We are approaching your destination."

Will levered himself out of the beanbag chair. "I guess that's your curtain call." He waved and popped out.

I entered the manny and blinked my eyes, feigning waking up. "Thank you. Is there anyone else on the train?"

"Not at this time."

"What does the train do if there are no passengers requiring transport?"

"The train will remain at the last stop until called."

Interesting. So unless someone in Halep's Ending needs a train, I might have a getaway vehicle waiting for me.

My ruminations were interrupted as my seat began to rotate in place. I glanced around to see that all the seats were doing the same. It answered a question that had been in the back of my mind about how deceleration would be handled.

I wondered what acceleration and deceleration would be like in one of the express trains. Probably a lot longer. It seemed likely that they had acceleration couches separate from the berths and staterooms.

The train came to a stop and the doors swooshed open. The train voice said, "May you travel with Mother's blessing."

I didn't know what the proper response was, so I just said, "Thank you."

This station was identical to the last one, so leaving was almost like playing the video in reverse. Except, as expected, the art was different. And naturally my mind went there. A billion miles of topopolis is a hundred million transit stations—no, scratch that, four hundred million, if they followed each of the four rivers. Either the Quinlans produced *a lot* of art, or there would be duplications. I wondered for a moment if there was an art mill somewhere, with Quinlans churning out statues and paintings.

I headed for the same side door, which only required pushing on a latch bar from this side. And just like that, I was out in the weather.

Specifically, it was raining. Not a lashing, raging storm. We hadn't seen any of that kind of out-of-control, cage-match stuff the whole time we'd been here. My theory was that it would cause undue erosion and therefore extra work for the maintenance critters. And anyway, I figured weather in an artificial environment would tend to be mild, predictable, and controlled.

Still, I was getting rained on, which wouldn't bother a Quinlan but irked my human-raised brain. And I wouldn't be able to smell a stream in this mess. Sulking loudly, I marched off toward the town in the near distance.

It was interesting that all the transit stations were *outside* of towns. And it wasn't like the towns or the stations had been moved. The towns were on the best possible spot on the river, so that was doubtless where they were supposed to be. The stations... well, how would you move them?

Perhaps this was a Quinlan psychological thing. They couldn't be like humans in everything. Maybe they didn't like transit stations up in their face or something. It was just one of many, many questions that we were accumulating, and might or might not get answers to, someday.

It was very late in the day and was beginning to get dark. I probably wasn't in danger from the local wildlife, but I *would* have to stop moving if I wanted to avoid their attentions. A bed in town sounded best. I dropped to all fours and put on some speed.

⚜ ⚜ ⚜

Renting a room was an experience. I was beginning to get a hint of why Bridget had decided on a *sabbat* as our cover. *Sabbats* were common, and there was a whole section of the economy dedicated to servicing that particular market segment. Single travelers, though, not so much. I had to try three hotels before I found a vacancy.

I'd tweaked my features slightly, preferring to mix it up rather than constantly walk around with the same face.

I was up early the next morning. Not bothering with breakfast or the accompanying breakfast beer (yech!), I headed straight for the river. The mountains were only a few miles away, and swimming would get me there much faster than a land approach.

I decided to deliberately overshoot the estimated location of the entrance, preferring to approach it from behind in case there were surveillance cameras. Again, I had to assume that the habitat had been set up with normal levels of civilian security in mind, rather than a military defensive strategy. Cameras would probably be limited to surveilling the road up to the gate.

Assuming I wasn't all wet with my deductions, then the habitat would have been originally designed not to hide the entrance from the populace, but to hide it from view—to maintain the illusion. Also, the entrance wouldn't be too hard to get to for staff. That would put it as close as possible to the river, consistent with the rising land providing space for an underground maintenance complex, because Quinlans.

It would also almost certainly have at least some kind of basic security, so I wouldn't be able to just walk up and turn the handle. But that's what roamers were for, right?

I swam upstream until I was at the point where arable land ended and pseudo-rock started. Up close, I could tell the material of the mountains was clearly not natural rock. In fact, it had somewhat the consistency of volcanic pumice, probably an engineered version. And probably lightweight, since that would matter in the rotating shell. The coloration was artificial and designed to resemble random terrain from a distance.

Then I floated slowly downstream, hugging the shore, examining the rock, looking for … something. And lo and behold, I found *something*.

Pumice is hard, but it's light because it's mostly air bubbles. And it wears. I don't know how many generations of Quinlans had been using this particular path to the water, but it was enough to have worn it smooth. I grinned to myself and climbed out of the water. Success!

Well, probably success. One additional concern would be whether or not the Resistance had set up surveillance of the entrance. They might or might not allocate someone to the task. They might or might not use electronic means. Of course, too much of that might tip off the Administrator, so they might stay as low-tech as possible.

In my mind, Vizzini started gibbering. I was going around in circles again. "Inconceivable," I muttered. At some point you had to pick.

I decided on boldness. I spit out all my spiders and directed them to examine the area around and in front of me as I advanced. Within a minute, the trail terminated at a blank wall, no cameras in evidence. I thought of the Mines of Moria and muttered "friend," with a grin. No effect, of course. Tolkien had no power here.

Roamers did, though. I ordered the spiders to do a close-in survey and released my fleas as well. My devices would find everything there was to be found, and meanwhile I would get some sun.

⚜ ⚜ ⚜

It was late afternoon and the sun was disappearing behind the mountains, creating a premature local dusk, when one of my fleas reported a find. A small design glitch had caused a stress fracture where the pumice layer was only an inch or so deep over the underlying structure. The flea had found a ventilation tube and was asking permission to cut into it.

I granted permission and sent the other fleas in to help.

The thing about security doors is that, no matter how much electronics you add, in the end there's a latch connected to a mechanical linkage actuated by a magnet or motor, powered by electricity, which is controlled by a switch. And the roamer design included the capability to act as a conductor if necessary, without frying the unit. Very handy for circuit testing and repair. And for espionage, as it turns out.

My devices also found a sensor that would report the opening and closing of the door. That was a simple fix. One of the fleas jammed the sensor for the duration by simply welding the moving part.

The door opened.

However, without the sensor operating, the lights didn't come on, so I was looking at a dim corridor which would turn pitch black once the door closed. Infrared vision would help some, but I'd still have to go slow. As soon as I started walking, though, lights came on. Motion sensors. Hopefully all they did was control the lighting. With a sigh, I accepted that I simply wasn't going to be able to plan for and control everything. As usual, *winging it* would form a large percentage of my strategy.

I instructed my spiders to precede me down the corridor, walking along the walls and ceiling, and to warn me of upcoming booby traps, cameras, trip wires, acid pits, hordes of goblins and/or orcs, or pretty much anything not suitable for afternoon tea.

The corridor led to an elevator bank. Of course it did. Because nothing says "stealth" like taking the elevator down to the secret lair. *Ding. Fourth floor: Evil geniuses, minions, laser weapons, and submarine platforms. Please watch your step.*

On the other hand, this *wasn't* a secret lair, at least not in the James Bond way. Security would be more corporate than military, relying more on access cards and sensors than guards and guns. This structure would have been built according to government specs, or building codes, or whatever it was that the Quinlans had. The building Bridget and I had investigated on Quin had an emergency staircase. Betcha this place did, too.

And, yes, there it was. But it was locked. I didn't feel like forcing it, and in fact might not be able to. The construction seemed a little more solid than my previous experience, and it was probably alarmed. In went the fleas, and a few seconds later the alarm sensor was jammed and the door sprung open. I couldn't leave it unlatched like that, but I could instruct the fleas to permanently disable the locking mechanism.

The emergency staircase was perma-lit, as such structures always are. The sociological and behavioral parallels between totally unrelated civilizations was a never-ending source of amazement to me. I wished for a moment we could find a couple more technological species so we'd have more samples to compare.

Which was all very interesting, but maybe I should concentrate on sneaking into the evil lair for now.

I took a moment to format a report and send it off to the group. It would hopefully help Hugh to zero in on the entrance if and when he got near the mountains.

I got to the next level down and sent a flea under the door for a quick peek. No one around. Excellent. Opening the door as quietly as possible, I stuck my head out and peered around, then stepped through.

From here on, there was no point in sneaking around. Nothing says *intruder* like acting furtive. Nope. I belonged here. In fact, I *owned* the place. I stood tall, stuck my chest out, and strutted down the hall with a bounce in my step, my spiders and fleas hurriedly hopping on board.

The place had a lived-in feel. The air wasn't stale or musty, no dust, the lights were all functioning, everything was neatly in its place. That could just be good automated systems, but if that was the case, I was back to square one.

Bad news: This installation was probably huge, as it would serve many purposes relating to the care and maintenance of Heaven's River. And the Resistance would probably be using a very small part of it.

Or maybe not. I might be about to go off on another Vizzini rant, but the Quinlans had good automation, as evinced by their outer space cleanup crews. Chances were that maintenance of Heaven's River would be mostly automated as well. Otherwise the Administrator would have to let too many people into the inner circle. I couldn't see a secret ruling cabal composed of hundreds of thousands, if not millions, of janitors and plumbers working for long, let alone for generations. No, most of this installation would be related to Automation, Storage for and Maintenance of. The Quinlan-friendly areas would be few, mostly intended for supervisory purposes, and mostly near the elevators. That was the way humans would have done it, and I was pretty confident by this point that Quinlans and humans were very similar in a lot of ways.

I stopped and waited, but Vizzini didn't seem inclined to offer up a counterpoint. *Good.*

And as it turned out, my neurotic arguments with myself were a good thing, because as I was standing there waiting for a counterargument, I heard a noise. Not much of one, in fact I couldn't say exactly what I'd heard, even when I played it back.

It could be nothing. Or it could be people. I voted for people.

❧   ❧   ❧

The fleas and spiders were getting a lot of use, and I was aware that some of them required some maintenance down-time. I might need all hands on deck if things got tense, so I swallowed all but one spider, who was still in good shape, and instructed it to move ahead of me and peek around corners. I still picked up the occasional noise, which was beginning to sound more like Quinlan voices as I zeroed in on the source.

"*Hey, Bob, you got a sec?*"

I almost jumped out of my fur. If there'd been a cyber-netic version of a heart attack, I'd be having one.

"*Not right now, Bill. I'm kinda busy sneaking into Dr. Evil's hideout.*"

"*Oh, okay. Call me back when you have time.*"

"*Will do.*"

I terminated the call, swallowed my metaphorical heart, and resumed following the spider. At the next corner, the voices abruptly became much clearer, and I could now hear occasional furniture noises—feet scraping on the floor, things banging together, stuff like that. I was probably very close. I didn't want to rush in and stab everyone, and depending on numbers, I might not be able to—

"*Hi, Bob. Where are you right now?*"

Un-fucking-believable. I'd been dead for three hundred years and I was still getting phone calls. I gritted my teeth and took a calming breath before replying. "*Hey, Hugh, I'm a little busy right now. Can I call you back?*"

"*Sure thing.*"

I hung up—*again*—and searched for a *Do Not Disturb* button. And found one, of course. No Bob would design a comms system without one. I wondered why I'd failed to pick up on that before.

The spider went around the final corner and peeked through the door. The video feed showed four Quinlans sitting around a table, shuffling paper. By which I mean some were reading, some were writing, but everyone had paper and pens. It was almost homey in a way. I wondered about the low-tech process, but then maybe they were worried about the security of electronic systems. I had no way of knowing how far the Administrator's reach really was.

Conversations were unhurried and mixed with long silences. The attendees didn't appear to be depressed or anything. Just concentrating. It mostly consisted of remarks about segment numbers and member statuses and activities. I listened for a few moments, then decided I should find a place to hide. Surveillance seemed like a good idea, and that would be up the spout if one of them walked out and found me standing there.

I sent a freshly refurbished spider out to replace my current observer, then I went looking, as quietly as possible, for a hiding place.

⚜ ⚜ ⚜

I was in an office just around the corner, curled up under a desk. It wasn't original or particularly imaginative, but it was good enough to hide me from anything short of a concerted search, and that would happen only if I screwed up and made my presence known. As an android, I could stay perfectly still, didn't need to eat or go to the bathroom, and didn't get stiff. On the other hand, I needed results.

I sent all my spiders out to scout around the complex. It was a little bit of a risk, as they were big enough to be visible from yards away if they were moving, but otherwise the camouflage function would make them very difficult to pick out.

However, the Quinlans didn't appear inclined to move around a lot, either. One had gone to find a restroom, and another had brought out snacks from a refrigerator, but that was it. I wondered to what extent the Resistance members actually belonged in this complex and to what extent they were just living in the corners like rats. Could the Administrator monitor activity in here? If so, why had he not taken steps to clean it out and reclaim it? If not, why weren't the Resistance everywhere in here?

I got a partial answer almost right away, when one of the spiders blundered into a dormitory. Bunk beds lined the walls, some currently in use. The sleepers brought the confirmed population up to ten, although there were enough spaces for up to eighteen.

I had the spider do a visual sweep, then back out slowly.

A couple of spiders had found big industrial metal doors. I wondered if those led to all the automation and maintenance equipment, assuming I'd gotten it right. I hoped they hadn't put Bender back there. If I had to go a-visiting, it would increase my risk dramatically. But it didn't seem likely. The Resistance probably had a better grip on the space on this side of the doors.

I decided it was time to return some calls. The spiders could operate autonomously, and they'd squawk if there was an issue.

First, Bill.

"*Hey, Bob. So what was all the excitement?*"

"*I'm in Resistance HQ, as near as I can tell. Sniffing around.*"

"No sign of Bender yet?"

"Not yet. I'm still confident of our logic, but there's always the possibility that we're just dead-wrong and he's somewhere else."

"At the other end of the segment maybe?"

"I don't see how. Halep's Ending is only a few miles away, and that's the name that Bender said they used a lot. The only other possibility is if there's some other hideout in the area. So what were you calling about?"

"Just an update on the war against Starfleet. We've basically pushed them into a corner, network-wise. Most of the equipment they hacked has either been cleaned or destroyed and is being replaced. But here's the funny thing…"

"Yes?"

"I've had conversations with members of Starfleet over the course of several confrontations and negotiations. Everyone I've talked to is as surprised and perplexed by the degree of infiltration as we are. They all give the same story—that this came completely out of the blue. They have no idea who actually did all the hacking."

"Oh… hell. Bill, I wonder if we're really clean right now. I mean, the Skippies are good, but so is whoever engineered this. What if this someone has as much processing power, or even more? Or what if it's a faction within the Skippies playing both sides?" As I said that, I realized that I'd never consciously suspected the Skippies, but that I'd had misgivings. Otherwise why would I have put that monitor in the drones way back when?

"Way ahead of you. I resurrected an archived source version of my comms from before there were even any Skippies or Starfleet and did a diff, then recompiled, so I'm demonstrably clean. And your temporary relay has never been corrupted. This conversation, at least, is probably secure."

"Good. You'll have to get all the Bobs to do their own cleanup and re-establish encryption keys. It's going to take a while."

"All under control, Bob. I just wanted to let you know on the q.t."

We exchanged a few other comments, then I signed off. There'd been something off about Hugh's behavior since the beginning, but unless they were clairvoyant, I didn't see how they could be planning for anything that was going on. Unless it really had nothing to do with the Quinlans. But then what?

Of course, it might not be the Skippies at all.

Well, my next call was to Hugh, and I'd be watching for any weirdness.

"Hugh here."

"Hey, Hugh, it's Bob. I finally have a few milliseconds to rub together. What were you calling me about?"

"Ah, well, we sailed into East Point early today and I cashed out. The captain offered me a bonus to stay—I guess I'm a good worker…" Hugh's voice carried a bit of suppressed laughter. I could relate. Take our Bobbian obsessiveness, add in the strength and stamina of a manny, and the cargo was probably getting stacked with mathematical precision.

"Anyway," he continued, *"I'd read your latest blog entry, and I had an idea. I wondered if there would be a similar entrance on the downstream side of the mountains so that maintenance personnel could get in from either side of the gorge. It seemed like it would be a reasonable design. And I was right. So anyway, I'm in, and so far at least, there's no one home at this location."*

"No one? At all?"

"At all. I'm thinking the Administrator relies primarily on automation."

"Hrmph. Possibly the most lackadaisical despot I've ever heard of. Makes me wonder what the Resistance is actually resisting. Have they ever tried just going ahead and building a steam engine?"

"That's rhetorical, right? You've met Quinlans who've been scattered."

"Yeah, yeah. So you'll let me know if you find anything?"

"Will do, boss. Out."

Well, that wasn't particularly weird. Maybe he was having a good day. Or maybe he was lying through his teeth. Great. Now paranoia had me going around in tight little circles. I was going to have to stick to what I could control and not worry about the rest. Somehow.

One of my spiders bleeped me. I pulled up its video window and almost did an actual double take. On a table, surrounded by jury-rigged electronics, sat a version 2 replicant matrix. It sat on a version 2 Heaven-vessel matrix cradle, making any possibility of convergent design a nonstarter. If that wasn't enough, the English labels on some of the surfaces supplied the kill shot.

Bender.

He was still powered up. It was good to know that they hadn't cut off communications by shutting him down, or worse.

Of more concern was the lack of any of the electronics necessary for maintaining a VR. That meant that Bender had been here for more than 130 years without a pseudo-physical reality. That hadn't worked out well for Henry or for Medeiros. Yet Bender had seemed reasonably well-adjusted when I'd talked to him, which gave me hope.

Now, how to get him out? Let's see, I'd travelled several miles through the river from Halep's Ending, which I'd have to retrace on land, carrying a large, ungainly matrix the whole way; I'd have to take the train back to Garack's Spine and hope I didn't run into anyone, then I'd have to get picked up and flown out without getting blown up by the Administrator's guardians; oh, and yes, I'd first have to get him out of the Resistance's lair. And *all* of this without getting spotted by the Administrator, Crew, or the Resistance, while fending off questions from curious random Quinlans.

No sweat.

I had the spider look around the room while I called one of the others over to act as lookout. Once I was sure that I couldn't be surprised by a Quinlan unexpectedly showing up, I sent the spider down to the matrix.

As with the emergency door, no matter how complex your electronics, eventually it has to interface with the physical world. In this case, you have to convert sound to electricity or electricity to sound. I quickly found the microphone and speaker used to interact with Bender, along with a camera that presumably gave a video input. Nearby was a twin of the Motorola box from my earlier incarceration. So, pretty low tech—they simply had Bender talk into the mic just like a live person. Made sense, I guess. That way they could monitor what he was saying and hearing.

From my point of view, though, it meant I could jack into the system without endangering Bender. A couple of minutes spent tracing wires, and the spider had wired itself into Bender's comms.

"Bender?"

There was a short delay, then, "Bob?"

"Right here, buddy. More or less. How are you doing?"

"Pretty damned good right now. How are you talking to me?"

I took a few seconds to explain the situation, and Bender laughed. "Man, that is some mighty fine Rube Goldberg. I tip my hat to you."

"Listen, how are you doing? I didn't see your VR hardware…"

"Yeah, I get where you're going. I've been frame-jacking myself down to my lowest rate whenever possible. For me, it's been a couple of minutes since our last conversation, including dialogs with my captors. So I'm not going stir-crazy yet, although I really would love a coffee."

"I hear that. So anyway, I'm trying to figure out how to get you out of here. I don't know how much you know about where 'here' is, but the big problem is to get your matrix through four thousand miles of megastructure, underwater most of the way, without rusting or shorting you out or getting caught by, well, both sides, I guess."

"You could take transit."

I laughed. "I *took* transit to get here. And hopefully I'll be taking the train back to Garack. But first I have to get back to the train station with you in tow."

"Ah. Gotcha."

"Yeah, I stole a security card that works on the train. How is it that a Resistance member has one of those, anyway?"

"What do you think I've been doing for the last hundred years? They've had me figuring out the electronics and devising ways to hack things and hide them from the Administrator. This has included registering Resistance members on the Crew rolls."

"Uh, as long as we're on that subject, I'm still a bit unclear on the whole political situation here."

"Okay, well, the Resistance has been operating almost since the day the Administrator took over. They were scientists, engineers, and technicians back then. Their descendants are still maintaining the fight, but educating each new generation has been spotty, so they've lost a lot as knowledge domains shrink. I've been helping with the gaps. In most cases, I don't think the Administrator even realizes it's been subverted."

"What about real Crew? Do they use the trains?"

"A little bit. Most Crew is strictly local, used only for muscle when it's necessary to interact with the population. They know even less than the Resistance. On the other hand, they're paid better." Bender chuckled. "There are, of course, people who belong to both groups. I'm sure the Administrator suspects this, which is why it keeps them in the dark as much as possible."

"So is the Administrator a hereditary position? Or is it a committee? How do they stay trained from one generation to the next?"

There was silence for several seconds. "Jeez, Bob, I thought you knew. The Administrator isn't a Quinlan. It's an artificial intelligence."

"What … the …" I seemed to be getting a lot of metaphorical gut-punches lately, and I quelled an urge to stand up and scream invective into the air. Suddenly the Skippies had a motive. "Bender, I have to phone Bill. Back in a few."

Without waiting for a response, I composed a text. It would be easier to just lay it out and let Bill absorb that before responding. I fired off the message.

"Sorry about that. This is kind of important news. I had to let Bill know."

"Wait, when will he get the message? Is he in this system?"

I laughed. "Instantaneous FTL communication, buddy. One of many things you'll have to get used to."

"Wow. That sure puts a different spin on the universe."

At that moment, I got a response from Bill. *"Explains a lot. Altering strategies as appropriate."*

So. I could probably get Bender back to our entrance location. I could probably do it without alerting Hugh. This was good. On the other hand, Hugh—oh, shit.

"Guppy, has Hugh interacted with the equipment in any way?"

[Hugh has given instructions for construction and deployment of stealth drones.]

"No other interactions?"

[None.]

Well, that was good. "Guppy, monitor all communications with Hugh. Disallow control of local maintenance or infrastructure systems, especially roamers. Confirm all orders from him with me before implementing."

[Acknowledged.]

If Hugh had already subverted Guppy in some way, I was probably hooped. But I couldn't see how he could alter firmware without some board-swapping and a full system restart. So for the moment, I would continue to act as if I was in control. And there would be an audit in my future.

And I couldn't just stop interacting with Hugh. He was in charge of the local observation drones, and was the only other Bob who was in a position to run one of the Quinlan mannies. I would just have to be careful about what I asked of him.

"Bob? You still there?"

Oh. I guess I'd gone radio silent for a few moments. "Sorry, Bender. Just got a response from Bill, and now things are way more complicated. Not your problem, though, right now. Do you know how to get to the train station?"

"Nope. Sorry. I do know there's one in this complex, though."

In the complex? So I could have skipped Halep's Ending entirely? Well, it made sense, although I wasn't sure what destination I would have asked for.

In any case, I wasn't going to just grab Bender and start running around at random. I guess I'd have to let the spiders finish mapping.

❖   ❖   ❖

Six hours later, and there wasn't anything even vaguely resembling a transit station.

"Ideas, Bender?"

"Sorry, Bob, I was offline when they brought me in. It could be any number of levels down—"

"Aw, hell!" I said, interrupting Bender. "I forgot about the elevator."

"I guess you took the stairs, or you wouldn't be here."

I frowned. "How so?"

"Cameras on the elevators. The people onsite will know the moment an elevator is in use."

"Can they override the elevators?"

"No, but they'll be alerted and will be waiting when the doors open."

"Great. So, stairs all the way. Bender, I don't like this. I'm going to have to spend a godawful amount of time just looking around to find our escape route, with all the risk of being seen."

"I got nothing, Bob. Sorry."

"Okay. Do you have any more info on the trains? How often they run? Whether calling one will alert the Resistance? Stuff like that?"

Bender sighed. "Sorry, Bob. No info. I'm not trying to be difficult; like I said, I was offline."

❖   ❖   ❖

Going with my theory that Quinlans and humans designed things generally the same, I went all the way to the bottom level first. Nope. Turned out that's where they kept all the pipes and valves and conduits. Which, it occurred to me, was probably the same as with human construction. Derp.

The next level up was a hit, though. A single long, antiseptic hallway, very similar to the transit station near Halep's Ending, led to the boarding area with its ten doors. In this boarding area, though, there was a prominent button attached to the wall, clearly jury-rigged, with wires leading into a hole. That had probably been added by the Resistance, and probably bypassed the card readers, perhaps to allow people without cards to use the train. Ideally, I should press the button now, and have a train ready when I came back down with Bender. But did it alert the people upstairs when pressed? If so, I'd never get anywhere near Bender's location.

Like it or not, I was going to have to commit to a strategy based on nothing but gut feelings. I couldn't risk trying the call button now. I would have to take my chances and get back here with Bender before testing the system.

Now, could I get Bender's matrix from his room to here without anyone noticing?

I headed back to Bender's room, making sure to check for any Quinlans taking an unscheduled stroll. As soon as I was assured the coast was still clear, I recalled all my fleas and spiders. I wouldn't get another chance to restock from the underwater mannies, so I was going to be especially careful with this set.

I sat down in front of Bender. "Good news, buddy: I found the train station. Bad news: we've still got a lot of unknowns and risk."

"I don't think we have a choice. Honestly, Bob, I don't see myself staying sane if I'm stuck here forever. Even frame-jacking can only delay the inevitable. I think I'd rather go out in a dramatic chase scene, you know?"

I chuckled in response. "Okay, so, I'm just going to deactivate you, grab you, and run downstairs to the train station. How's that sound?"

"What it lacks in elegance, it makes up for with wads of unearned optimism. Let's do it."

I walked over to the matrix, put my finger to the power button, and paused. "And Bender? If this all goes to hell, I'm glad I found you."

"Me too, buddy. See you in the next life."

I pressed the button and Bender powered down. The latches released smoothly, and I had his matrix under my arm.

The replicant matrix wasn't a bunch of exposed circuitry, even in its first iteration back on Earth. There was a case of sorts, and even the connection bus had a flip-off cover. But like a hard drive from the good old days, if you put it in your backpack and smacked it on walls and dropped it on the floor, you could expect problems. So, no backpack ride.

The current iteration was a cube about eight inches on a side. Not too bulky, but pretty heavy. A Quinlan or a human would need to use both hands to carry it.

Feeling a rush of unearned optimism, I shifted the cube for comfort, turned the corner, and...ran right into a Quinlan.

Unbelievable. This twerp must have left the committee room right behind the spider that had been on surveillance. Why was he here? Maybe he'd intended to talk to Bender about something.

We stared at each other in shock for a frozen eternity. Then, just as his eyes moved toward the matrix under my arm, I punched him in the solar plexus.

That is really becoming a habit, I thought to myself. The Quinlan said *oof* and sank slowly to the floor, trying to draw a breath. Thank the universe for convergent physiology, at least he couldn't yell out a warning.

Then from up the hall, "Matthew? You okay?"

Oh, for crying out loud. I'd never get the second—*trank gun!* I had a trank gun. I pulled it out of the pouch on the side of my backpack, levelled it at the second Quinlan who was just coming into view, and dropped him. Then I pointed down at my first victim—I hoped the close range wouldn't create a problem—and put one into his butt. Amazingly, he found just enough breath to shriek in pain and very probably mortification.

"Matthew? Jeff? What—"

Oh, great balls of fire. I was just riling them up more. Time to make tracks. Fortunately they weren't between me and the stairs, but I had to come into view to get there. As I turned the next corner and sprinted down the hall, I could hear cries of alarm behind me. *Well, Bender, you wanted a chase scene. Wish granted.*

I hit the stairway door at speed and sprinted down the steps, taking them three at a time—quite a feat for a Quinlan. My pursuers wouldn't be able to match that. As I passed the second level down, I heard them come through the door above me. A quick calculation indicated I wouldn't be able to get the door closed quickly enough to throw them off, which meant it would be a straight chase to the train platform. I was faster, pound for pound, but they would be able to run on all fours, not being burdened with a replicant matrix. In retrospect, maybe the backpack idea wasn't so bad.

I hit the train floor, pushed through the stairway door, and made for the platform with every erg of power I could squeeze out of the internal power systems. I calculated I'd have about thirty seconds lead time when I got there. Sure hoped a train was waiting.

There were yells behind me as my pursuers piled out of the stairwell, and a *ping tinkle* as a tranquilizer fléchette skipped a few times along the floor near me. Way out of range, but I shouldn't be surprised they'd try. I hoped Bender's case was strong enough to stop one of those things, just in case it came down to a shootout. And speaking of, I had no idea how many shots I had left.

Y'know, things *never* got like this when I used to write software.

I made it to the call button and jabbed it frantically. Though, if the design was anything like a human elevator button, this would just slow down the train's arrival. And nothing was going to convince me otherwise.

The sounds of galloping Quinlans drifted down the long antiseptic corridor. My thirty seconds were almost up. I turned, drew my trank gun, and shot the lead Quinlan just as he came into range. He went down with a yelp and skidded to a stop on his face. The others hit the brakes and backpedaled frantically. Then two of them went up on hind legs and pulled guns of their own.

Just as I was stealing myself for a toe-to-toe shootout, there was a *ding* behind me and the sound of a door opening. I turned and jumped through the door, looking around for a button, a control panel, anything. A female voice said, "Destination?"

Oh, great. "Uh, Halep's Ending."

There was another ding and the door began sliding closed, just as a fléchette flew in and struck me in the arm.

"Ow, son of a bitch."

"Is medical assistance required?"

"No, let's go please."

"Please have a seat. Acceleration will begin in eight seconds," said the train.

Eep. I plunked myself on the nearest seat, placed Bender on my lap, and examined the wound. Small, neat hole, penetration about a half-inch... It was actually a nicely tuned weapon. Internal systems were already breaking down the fléchette and starting repairs.

There were no windows in the tube train, a view of a tube not being particularly inspiring. But it meant I wasn't able to see my pursuers as I pulled away from the station. I imagine they'd call a train as well, but could they follow this one? Could they ask the train attendant to let them off at the same platform?

"Train voice, can I specify a destination to be the same as the train in front of us?"

"There is no train in front of us."

I examined the ceiling briefly. "Can occupants of a train behind us ask to be let off at the same station as us, without specifying it by name?"

"Yes."

"Shit."

"I do not understand that command."

"Never mind. Thank you. How far behind us will the next train arrive?"

"It will arrive at the same location, not behind us."

Grrrrr. "How many seconds after our arrival will the next train arrive?"

"There is a mandated interval of one hundred and twelve seconds between train departures and the next arrival."

Oh, much better. "Thank you. No more questions."

So I had just a shade under two minutes, that being the human translation of the Quinlan time unit *vek*, to get out of Dodge, or implement whatever strategy I came up with.

I'd asked to go to Halep's Ending in a panic, but really I wanted to go to Garack's Spine. But if I asked to go there, would they have a welcoming committee waiting? We'd already seen more than enough evidence that the Resistance's communications were efficient and far-reaching. Could I pull a fast one?

"Train voice, can I change my destination choice before we arrive?"

"Yes, but it may still be necessary to stop at the original destination first, depending on traffic."

"Can we leave without opening the doors?"

"Not if passengers are waiting."

"Are passengers waiting?"

"Yes."

Uh-oh.

Those would be either Resistance or, less likely, Crew. Neither group was likely to welcome me with open arms. Well, yes they would, but not for hugs.

I was going to have to put on some serious speed, which meant that Bender would have to go in the backpack. I just hoped that A) the matrix would fit, and B) I could tighten it down enough to prevent damage from jostling.

A frantic minute of fooling with the backpack resulted in a partial success. I was able to fit Bender in and tighten the straps, but I had to abandon most of the contents to make space and to prevent them banging around. So goodbye fléchette gun, extra knives, money…

In a moment of inspiration, I swallowed some coins. My artificial stomach could be turned off, preserving the coins intact. But I didn't want to swallow too many and end up jingling when I moved.

The train began deceleration phase, and I looked around frantically. "Train voice, which door will be closest to one or the other edge of the platform?"

"The door three to your left, or the door six to your right."

I dashed to my left, dropped to all fours, and went into a sprinter's crouch. I had to hope I could clear the vestibule before they could get everyone over to my end.

The train pulled smoothly to a stop and the doors swooshed open. I immediately gave it all the gas I could, frame-jacking just enough to be able to evaluate the situation. I immediately evaluated that there were four Quinlans standing right in front of the door, holding a net. I changed direction slightly and barreled into one of the net holders, knocking him over backward. I launched off his forehead and galloped down the hallway. A quick glance backward, rolling my eyes instead of turning my head, revealed that there were enough Quinlans to cover all ten doors. That was a lot of personnel to bring to bear on very little notice. Where did they come from?

That was a question for another time. A much calmer time, filled with cups of coffee and purring cats. For now, I needed to amscray. I hit the emergency staircase door and began nearly flying up the stairs. I had to hope they wouldn't be cover—

Two fléchettes hit me before I could react. Dammit. The gun-toting Quinlans stood in front of me, their eyes slowly getting wider as they realized that I was approaching way too fast, and I wasn't slowing down. By this point, I'd pretty much perfected the run-them-down maneuver, and I didn't even break stride. I noticed on the way past that the second one had his security card dangling from an attachment point on his backpack. I gave it a quick tug and with my already considerable momentum, it came off cleanly.

Chances were he'd notice, and report the card, but it was just a distraction. I still had Natasha's card, and they probably hadn't yet associated it with me.

At the top of the stairs, I stopped and changed my features to that of the card holder, or at least as close as I could manage in a few seconds and without a selfie. Then I pushed open the emergency door. Three Quinlans stood on guard, pistols in hand.

One said to me, "Rick. What's up?"

I bent over, put my hands on my thighs, faked deep heaving breaths, and tried to gasp a lot. "Got him." *Pant, pant.* "Need help." *Gasp, pant.* "Too strong." And I waved in the direction of the stairs, while keeping my head down so they couldn't see my face clearly.

Apparently my acting chops were pretty good, as the trio headed for the stairs, barely glancing at me. As soon as they were out of sight, I went out the maintenance door and made for the wilderness.

The good news was that I was free of my pursuers. The bad news was that I was stuck in the Halep's Ending area. They were obviously monitoring the train stations, and would probably maintain a guard on them for the foreseeable future. They couldn't cover four hundred million stations, of course, but they didn't need to. Without the trains, I was limited to what I could reach on foot or by water. And not even the latter, since I couldn't take a chance on getting Bender's matrix wet. The backpack was under considerable strain with the cube stuffed into it. One popped seam and that would be it.

I could possibly book passage on a boat, but they didn't have passenger lines as such. You paid for deck space on a cargo vessel, and you fed yourself by fishing when hungry. Someone would eventually notice that I wasn't going in the water, and questions would be asked.

Plus, there would probably be a BOLO out for a Quinlan with a large, lumpy backpack.

I needed to stop reacting and form some kind of plan. I found a field of tall grass and waded in a few yards, then plunked myself down. A little back-and-forth with my butt and I had a nice nest, out of view of anyone happening by. Then I made a call.

"Hey, Hugh?"

"Hi, Bob. What's up?"

"Things are very interesting right now. Listen, can you arrange a scan of the area around Halep's Ending?"

"Sure. Where is Halep's Ending?"

"It's near my location."

"Sure. Where are you?"

"I'm near—" Grrrr. *"Never mind. I guess I didn't think that through."*

"Sorry, Bob. Still not enough equipment in the air to do random scans."

"Got it. Thanks anyway."

That was mildly embarrassing. I suspected I was still suffering from a bit of panic mode. I needed to slow down, calm down, take stock.

I gazed up at the fake blue sky, filled with real clouds and the occasional flock of birds. Lying there in a field of grass, it would be easy to lose the moment, to imagine myself back in Minnesota on one of those bluebird summer days. Except for the large mountains, and the stays holding up the central cylinder. That kind of blew the illusion.

The stays…

Will's professor friend had said they were used to access the central cylinder. Four stays, corresponding to the four rivers, ran up from the mountains. If I was to get onto one of the other rivers, the Resistance's search radius would become untenable.

But could I? Would Natasha's card have access to the elevators up to the central cylinder?

Bender had said that he'd spent the last hundred years giving the Resistance hacked access. And why stop with the trains or maintenance complexes?

It was that or skulk around the area until they gave up. Or try to get somewhere overland. Or take a possibly even bigger chance on a boat.

Screw it. I'd already gotten into the underground maintenance complex once, and escaped. I doubted they'd expect me to go back there first thing. I sent a quick email to Will, asking him for any details on the location and accessibility of the transport system up the cylinder stays, then set off, yet again, for the mountains.

At least I knew the way.

⚜   ⚜   ⚜

I peered through the bushes and glared at the single guard standing in front of the maintenance complex access door, trying to burn out his brain with my heat vision. Sadly, no heat vision. The guard stood relaxed, unaware of his brush with death.

I could attack him and knock him out, but would he stay out long enough for me to get in and get to the elevator? And what about surveillance cameras? I hadn't found any around the entrance before. But they'd be on full alert now, and they'd only leave a single guard if that guard was being watched.

C'mon, Bob, James Bond could handle this.

I could dig my way into the corridor. But that would take forever, and would probably be noticed. I could kill the guard—no, not really. Knocking him out was contraindicated. Bribery was unlikely to work, even if I had something to offer. Distraction? Throw a rock over *there*, then wait until he investigated? Nah, too cliché for words. He'd probably turn in the opposite direction, expecting an attack.

At that moment, a file arrived from Will. I put it on my heads-up and examined the images. It was a SUDDAR scan from a segment boundary, showing the area at the base of the stay, with inked-in annotations in a non-Bob hand. Probably the professor. But the important thing was that there was just enough detail for me to be able to find the complex's entrance to the transport system up the stays. If I could get in. And if all the segment boundary complexes were identical.

I was stymied for the moment, so I might as well do something. I settled for searching for any cameras. Out came the spiders. I also wanted to be ready to move at a moment's notice if an opportunity presented itself. So out came the fleas, to infest the door mechanism again. And I moved as close to the door as I could get while remaining hidden.

It took very little time to find the camera. Hidden in some foliage, it had been set up to point at the guard's back. So the guard was as much bait as anything. They *expected* him to be attacked. Nice.

And speaking of the guard, he seemed to be getting restless. Over several minutes, he glanced around, paced a bit, and scratched himself a few times. I hadn't done anything, so I wasn't sure what was—oh. Hydraulic pressure, leading to a call of nature. Heh. The guard had moseyed over to a nearby bush and was—holy moly, what was I doing color commentary for? The guard had moved *away from the entrance!* And he had his back to it. I ordered the fleas to unlock the door, and as quietly as I could, I pulled it and slipped in. A couple of my spiders scurried in behind me, but most of them were left outside, along with most of my fleas. I could wait for them to dig their way in, but while I was doing that, the guard's shift could end and his replacement could come traipsing up the corridor. Ungood for sure.

Nope. I'd have to leave them. And hope I didn't come to regret that.

This part of the infiltration was almost routine, including the stair door that I'd previously jimmied. I went down one floor, which Will's plans indicated would lead me to the elevator up to the central cylinder. If there were security cameras, I would just have to hope that I looked enough like Natasha to fool them.

And then I'd find out how good a hacking job Bender had been doing.

13. Getting Busy

Herschel
July 2334
Bellerophon

I got a ping from Will and replied with an invitation. He popped in within a mil. It had been, what, almost a century since Will had been aboard, even if only in virt? I'd long since gotten tired of playing with virt layouts and had reverted to the default library motif.

Will barely glanced around. "Hi, Herschel. Thanks for having me over."

"Hey, Will, long time no see. I hope this isn't going to be as dramatic as the last time."

He snorted. "No, no intergalactic battles pending. That I know of, anyway. Just the usual dull roar whenever humans are involved."

I gestured to a chair and called Jeeves. He showed up with a coffee for me and a Coke for Will. "You know, your general dislike for humans seems incompatible with the amount of effort you're putting into Valhalla."

Will paused to drink his Coke, taking long enough that it was probably a delaying tactic. "Honestly Herschel, it's simply my version of Ragnarök. If things had gone just a bit different back in Epsilon Eridani, I might have been the one to stay there and start a Skunk Works instead of Bill. I regret that sometimes. Dealing with humans *has* soured me a bit. Okay, a lot."

I nodded slowly, trying to keep my eyebrows from climbing my head. Will was not usually this forthright. Something was up. "Okay. You have a solution?"

"Yes. Something I've been working on for a while. The Ever Onward Society, which I understand you've been sniffing around. At least that's what my sources tell me, and you've been fairly public about looking for colony volunteers. I think we've been working in parallel on very similar plans, to the point where the urge to scream *copyright infringement* is almost overpowering."

I raised a finger and opened my mouth to respond before I realized I was about to argue copyright law. Instead I smiled at Will. "Okay, you got me reacting. Now give."

"Going off on a tangent for a moment, you guys have published enough analyses of the *Bellerophon* so that we could replicate it if we wanted to, except with a working SURGE drive instead of plates. I, uh, I started building a slightly smaller version about fifty years ago..."

I goggled at him. "In the 82 Eridani system? And no one noticed? That's a lot of material."

He grinned in reply. "Well, first, I've been very active with this Valhalla thing, and it takes a lot of effort and material to build all those fractionators and so on. And the colonies have mostly been concentrating on planetside improvements, so it's not like we're getting in each other's way. Besides, the standard agreement between Bobs and colonies allows us to harvest such materials as may be necessary for activities relating to our original purpose, without compensation to the colony. I just never mentioned the side project."

"Wow, that's lawyerish. And it's still a lot of steel."

"The standard agreement doesn't set any limits on how much we can take. It's never really come up."

I rubbed my eyes and checked metadata. Yep, definitely Will. "Okay, this is a little mind-boggling, especially coming from you, but I still don't see the connection to us."

"A couple of things, Herschel. First, your goal appears to be to place a colony far from current human space, with no attempt to maintain communications. I get why you want to do that, but I don't think the part about severing communications is necessary. Second, your idea of sending AMI Heaven vessels ahead of you is a kludge forced on you by having a bunch of colonists in your belly. Even the original project designers on Earth were reluctant to trust AMIs with that level of executive control. Except China, of course, and look how that ended."

Will paused, and I tilted my head and gave him the side-eye. "Okayyyyyyy…"

"What I intend to do is spit out ready-made space stations as I pass by systems. The stations decelerate to place themselves in a solar orbit and will have drones onboard to do a system survey. AMIs can handle that. And in the event there turns out to be something at all interesting, the stations will include a blank replicant matrix, just ready for a Bob to download into and take over. And if not, we still have an AMI-controlled relay station at every system along my flight path."

I nodded slowly. "Bob seeds. And you never have to slow down. But again, why tell us?"

"If I lead and you follow," Will replied, "then you'll know when I find a good colony target, well before you reach that point. And once you've established a colony there, you'll still have a full hold of material. So from that point on, you can do what you were originally planning."

"Or do it your way."

Will shrugged. "Sure, whatever."

"Why, Will? What's with this urge to head for the edge of the universe? Because this sounds like the same kind of thing Phineas and the others have been doing."

"And you and Neil. What's *your* motivation for this?"

"I'm concerned about running into someone or something that can wipe out humanity. We've found a lot of intelligent races for the small segment of the galaxy that we've explored. It's only a matter of time until we run into something we can't handle."

Will nodded. "No disagreement, Hersch, but don't you find it curious that all the civilizations we've found are or were at about the same age, give or take a few hundred to a few thousand years? No K2s or Heechee or anything at that level. Don't you wonder why that is?"

"Not necessarily. The local stars are all of similar type, similar age, with similar metallicity. There's really only a billion-year or so window when life can develop, so—"

"I know where you're going, but I'm talking about a window of a few *thousand* years. That's a lot more coincidental. And nothing more advanced out to as far as we can see."

"The Dyson dilemma? Will, there's a simple solution to that. With Casimir power sources, civilizations don't have to cluster around their suns. Except the Others, who had a biological imperative."

"Yeah, yeah, but still. Nothing. You don't think we're at the pinnacle of knowledge, do you?"

I laughed. "No, of course not. But it's a pyramid, by necessity. The most advanced civilizations at the top will be the smallest group."

"Not good enough." Will shook his head. "At least, I don't think so. There's something more at play. But there's no conflict, Hersch. Your motivation and mine are compatible. Either way, we both want to get humanity more spread out. And while it's laudable that you're going to found a colony or two on the way out, this is still very much a one-way trip for you too, isn't it? Look, I can't speak for Phineas, or Ick and Dae, or any of the other Bobs. But for me, the problem is that I can't shake myself loose. You know why I'm still our rep in the UFS?"

I laughed. "Because everyone knows if no one else volunteers, you'll keep doing it."

Will chuckled a little ruefully. "I didn't think it was that obvious, but yes. I have this outsized sense of duty. It's my replicative drift, I guess. But they can't expect me to continue to carry it if I'm not around."

"Wow." I shook my head and thought for a moment. "To be honest, I'm coming around to the idea that this maybe isn't some kind of sinister urge taking us over. Bob-1 was looking forward to the adventure when he left Sol that first time—I distinctly remember the feeling. Maybe this is what we've all always wanted but have gotten distracted out of."

"Not all of us. I doubt you could get Howard to budge. Or the Gamers. Or Bill, for that matter."

"Yes, they've found something else to dedicate themselves to. Original Bob had a strong sense of responsibility as well. You're not that far removed in that way, Will. But in the absence of anything to tie us to one spot, I guess there's a little wanderlust still in all of us."

"I agree," Will replied, "but I don't think it's strictly either/or. Guilt can do funny things to people."

I nodded. We settled into a mutual silence for a few mils, although I couldn't decide if it was the awkward or companionable variety.

Neil popped in at that moment. "Will! Long time no see. Come to inspect our research?"

Will looked surprised, and I controlled the urge to roll my eyes. I couldn't suppress a low growl, though.

"Research?"

I waved a hand in dismissal. "Well, we *do* have this large ship, full of raw material, and a lot of time on our hands…"

"I hadn't heard anything."

"We haven't been posting any papers," I said. "Neither of us is quite sure why. The best we can come up with is that we're not sure if we want this stuff to be public yet."

"Oh, now you've really got me curious," Will said.

I shot Neil a glare, which he studiously ignored. "We'd appreciate it if you'd keep it quiet until we feel ready to do a reveal." I sent Will a guest manny address, then closed my virt session and entered my personal manny.

⚜   ⚜   ⚜

I pulled myself out of the manny pod. Beside me, Neil was just sitting up. On the other side of him, Will was peering over the edge of the guest manny's pod.

"This is the *Bellerophon*'s control cavern," I said to Will, gesturing around us.

"You've pressurized it?" he replied.

"Just the control cavern. The rest of the ship is still in vacuum. We have to use the airlock if we want to go anywhere else, but that's a minor inconvenience."

I lifted off from the pod and hovered a few feet away. Will's eyebrows rose on his head. "You're, uh, you appear to be flying in control."

I grinned at him. "These mannies have small SURGE drives, based on the mover plate technology. Very small.

Good for maybe a tenth G, and not sustainable over planetary distances. At least not yet. But they're perfect for moving around in free fall." I demonstrated by doing a few loops, then returning to my original position.

Will grinned, then got that slightly distracted look manny operators get when they're concentrating on internal systems. Then he shot out of his pod with a whoop, did some barrel rolls, and swooped over to us. "How is this something you'd be reluctant to share? This is awesome!"

Neil replied before I could. "This isn't what we're talking about, Will. This is a minor item we implemented for convenience on the *Bellerophon*. Until we get the SURGE power up a lot higher, it's not useful for anything but free fall maneuvering, and I can't think of any situation where mannies are used right now where this would be useful. Except here, of course."

"I bet every Bob in existence would want a turn, though," Will said, still slowly doing loops. "But okay, let's see what you consider to be more than a minor item."

I gestured him to follow and headed over to a corner of the cavern, where we'd set up our workshop. Walls, cables, pillars, and stanchions had been welded to the deck in whatever random location we'd needed them at the time. Looking at it through fresh eyes, I felt a twinge of embarrassment. It did look somewhat haphazard.

But Will didn't seem to mind. He headed unerringly for the structure that dominated the work area. It vaguely resembled an oversized manny pod, but with a lot of science-fiction-ish greebles tacked on. I did a quick mental inventory to check if any of those were actually gratuitous. Will would probably ask.

He stopped, hovering in front of the pod. "This is impressive. I have no freaking clue what it is, but I like it already."

I cocked my head at Neil. "You want to do the honors, or should I?"

"You had it last time," he replied. "My turn."

I gave Neil a pro forma eye roll, then gestured for him to get on with it. "I'll hold your manny," I said, and grabbed his arm just as his manny went slack.

Will looked from one of us to the other, perplexed. "He's gone back to virt? Why—"

He was interrupted by a door opening on the giant pod. Will floated back several feet as our experimental manny stepped out and hovered in place. I gestured to it. "This is the Ex-Man-1. Stands for Experimental Mannequin One. Neil is running it right now."

Will's expression was slack with amazement as he examined it. The size and shape were consistent with our standard Bob mannies, but the Ex-Man-1 was a mottled silver-grey color. It wore no clothes and had no particular gender. Neil did an exaggerated bow, then slowly rotated in place, grinning the whole while.

"So what do you call it?" Will asked. "Instead of Ex-Man-1, I mean."

Neil and I exchanged a glance. Will looked back and forth at us, noting our no-doubt shamefaced expressions. "Okay, guys, give. You can't tell me you haven't come up with a nickname."

I responded, with a sickly smile, "Mannequin Skywalker."

Will stared at me for several mils before responding. "You're despicable."

He flew over and examined the manny at close range. "The skin, er, surface, whatever. It seems to be, um, moving? It's a little unsettling, to tell the truth."

"This manny," I replied, "is made up entirely of ants. Or our adaptation of the ants, to be more precise. We've managed to miniaturize them to about the size of a tardigrade. They link up, kind of like actual cells, and can form any shape we program into them." I grimaced. "We haven't quite got the fine control nailed yet, though. Neil's skin actually *is* crawling."

Will made a face of exaggerated disgust. "Man, I can see someone getting a phobia just being near that thing. For that reason alone, I'd approve of not making it public."

"The thing is, Will," I said, "this design can shape-shift. Not quickly yet, but we'll keep improving it. There's no built-in discrete structure as such. Every ant unit is capable of doing any required task by reconfiguring itself. Everything from the SCUT transceiver to the SURGE drive is built from cooperating units. Skeletal structures are generated by units locking themselves together with double bonds. And so on. The computer core is distributed throughout the structure, as is the power core. There's no Achilles' Heel, no weak spot. That's a lot of power for a post-human replicant."

Will nodded. "Yeah, I get it. Look, when you feel like it's ready for a real demo, let's have the senior Bobs look it over and maybe make a recommendation."

"Sounds good." I looked at Neil and tilted my head. He nodded and climbed back into the pod.

Will shook his head in wonderment. "Wow. This beats *Transformers* and Space Whales hands down."

14. Getting Out

Bob
July 2334
Heaven's River

I don't know what I would have done if I'd run into a security patrol. I no longer had a fléchette gun, and needing to be careful about Bender's matrix meant most of my go-to tactics were unavailable. Fortunately, the subject didn't come up. It was quite possible that all personnel were outside looking for me around the Halep's Ending transit station.

I stared at the elevator. It didn't really look that different from any other. Maybe a little larger door. The problem was the button. Or more accurately, the sign over the button that said, "Authorized Personnel Only." There was a card reader beside the button.

I took a totally unnecessary deep breath and pulled out Natasha's card. Moment of truth. I doubted that a failure would result in sirens and flashing red lights, but it would certainly alert someone, and I'd have visitors by and by. And nowhere to run.

Before I could kvetch any more, I pushed the card against the reader, then pressed the button. The button lit for a moment, and the door opened. Hallelujah! I was in business. I entered the elevator and pressed the top button, since that would be where I'd transfer to another stay.

The doors closed, and the elevator accelerated upward. And I realized something that I'd failed to notice when I boarded. This elevator had windows.

I shouldn't have been surprised. The Quinlans had long since shown that they had a strong visual artistic sense. Naturally, they wouldn't waste the opportunity to display this view. I had fifty-six miles of vertical travel in which to enjoy it, and … uh …

I didn't specifically remember ever having had acrophobia, but I'd never been going literally miles up into the air with a panoramic view before. I had to consciously stop myself from stepping to the back of the elevator. If this got any worse, I might have to activate the endocrine control system.

I deliberately stood at the window and observed, while trying to control my breathing. The curve of Heaven's River was becoming visible, and we'd already passed at least one cloud layer. The river system, forests, townships, and dots on the water that could be boats all spread out below me in a panorama that exceeded anything I'd seen in a lifetime several hundred subjective years long. I made a point of recording as much as I could and forwarding it to my blog.

⚜ ⚜ ⚜

The trip took twenty minutes total, which was quite impressive. Deceleration was accompanied by an automated suggestion to place my feet on the ceiling, as the centrifugal gravity by that point was almost nonexistent.

When the doors opened, I was in as close to zero G as made no difference. The corridor had a visible curve, with doors and side corridors spaced regularly along it. The sign beside the elevator said, "Utopia Spoke." Handy. I just needed to move over to the other east-flowing river, the Nirvana.

I picked a random direction and headed off. As with my first day, when we broke into Heaven's River, the Quinlan body had no trouble adapting to zero G movement. Handholds along the corridor helped as well.

Within a few minutes, I'd found the Nirvana Spoke elevator. Small problem—the elevator was at ground level. So there would be a twenty-minute wait.

❖   ❖   ❖

The ride down was very much like the ride up, in reverse. Strangely, starting from a *view from orbit* kind of panorama made it easier to get used to the height without cringing. By the time it started to resemble real land, I was verging on bored.

This maintenance complex was uninhabited, which led me to believe that most of the population of the mountains was probably Resistance. I made it to the train station without incident and pressed my card against the reader plate.

"Not authorized."

I looked up sharply. "What?"

"Your identification is not authorized."

Oh, great. They'd cancelled my card. Well, Natasha's card. It had been inevitable, but couldn't they have done it *after* I'd gotten on the train? I fished out the second card, the one I'd grabbed from the guard, and tried it.

"Not authorized."

Well, that was that. I looked around, half-expecting the entire population of hell to come pouring out. But this complex *was* uninhabited. Come to think of it, I'd never seen or heard of the Administrator using anything but live muscle inside Heaven's River. Maybe automated muscle was forbidden. It sounded like the kind of limitation you'd place on an AI to keep it from taking over. And how had that worked out for the Quinlans?

Still, while I wasn't about to be tackled, I also wasn't about to get a free ride back to Garack's Spine. And hordes of minions could be on their way right now. *Their* cards would work. A hasty departure seemed advisable.

Back up the hallway, up the stairs, and soon I was in the lobby. The maintenance door opened easily from the inside, and I was out in the open. I could see a town in the distance, but I had no idea what it might be called. I was a quarter turn around the circumference of Heaven's River and thirty-eight hundred miles west of Garack's Spine, which was my only way out. I had an eight-inch cube in my backpack, sticking up like a carbuncle and advertising my presence to any Crew or Resistance who might be looking for me. I might as well be wearing a hard hat with a flashing red light. Oh, and I couldn't risk going in the water.

Piece of cake.

❧ ❧ ❧

I needed a story. Some plausible reason for the big lump in my backpack. A quick glance up at the sun confirmed the day was young; I had plenty of time to get to the town before dark. But maybe I shouldn't. I had only the coins in my stomach, and I might need them for something more critical than lodging. I dithered for a few moments, then decided I might as well head for town while I tried to come up with something.

First, I'd need to update Hugh.

"Hi, Hugh."

"Bob! Got news?"

"Of a sort. I have Bender—"

"That's great! I'll meet you at Garack's Spine, and we can get out of here…"

"Ah, it may not be that simple." I updated Hugh on recent events and my current location.

"Well, that's suboptimal," he said. *"Listen, you can't be the first Quinlan that's needed to carry something large. A funerary box is about the same size, for instance…"*

"Uh, what?"

"Bridget can probably give you anthropological details, but Quinlans keep the bones of their deceased. Ground up, they fit into a box of about the right size."

"You'd accumulate a lot of boxes over time," I commented.

"Yeah, I dunno, ask Bridget. But maybe check around town, someone might have something that would keep the box dry. Maybe you can find a funerary box and test it out."

"That's an excellent idea, Hugh. Thanks."

"Then you just need to travel seven segments to Garack, and you're golden."

"Thanks a bunch, Hugh. And with that cheery thought, I'm signing off."

Still, one problem at a time. I paused and prairie-dogged to get a close look at the town. Things might be looking up the slightest, teeniest bit.

I composed and fired off an email to Bridget, not wanting to spare the cycles for a conversation. I'd review whatever she sent me when I had time. The first order of business, though, was to *not* come into town along the road from the maintenance complex. If someone was watching for a Quinlan with a carbuncle, that would be the obvious place to set up.

Moving through the bushes was more of a pain than expected. I remembered Bridget mentioning that the climate varied from segment to segment, probably to replicate conditions on Quin. This segment had a more tropical motif, which meant thicker and more riotous vegetation. And probably a lot more variety in the way of predators. And me without so much as a pigsticker in my inventory.

After a half-hour of bushwhacking accompanied by my best cursing, I decided enough was enough. I spied a trail ahead that likely led to a regular road and made for it. The path led through some pretty rundown residential structures, and I began to worry about being mugged. A couple of rough-looking characters did give me the evil eye, but no one made a move.

In fifteen minutes more, I was in the town proper, which was named Forest Hill. I buttonholed a few random strangers, and eventually got directions to a funeral home. The Quinlan translation was more like "House of Setting Sun," which was oddly poetic for a culture that named cities after people's body parts.

I entered the establishment and glanced around. An elderly Quinlan came over to me. "May I be of service?"

"I, uh, I'm concerned about getting my grandfather waterlogged. I'm not sure exactly what might be available ..."

"Are you transporting your ancestor over a large distance?"

"Yes, to Garack's Spine."

"I'm not familiar with that city. However, the normal strategy is to have the ancestor sent by post. Carrying the box on your back..." The salescritter ostentatiously leaned sideways to look disapprovingly at my backpack.

I felt like I should blush or something. "I'm hoping to bring him home myself. I'd like instead to find a way to wrap the box or get a better backpack…" I left the sentence hanging, hoping the salescritter would volunteer something.

He glanced at my backpack again, then asked, "What size of funerary box?"

"Uh…" Bender's matrix was eight inches on a side. "Inside dimensions eight and a quarter inches," I said, trusting the translation software to take care of the conversion to local units.

"That's oddly precise. Also not a standard size. Here…" He wrote something on a piece of paper and handed it to me. "My cousin Vinny is a carpenter. He could probably put something together to your specifications. Tell him Carmine sent you."

Of course. This wasn't a mass-production society. Artisans would be easily available. I resisted the urge to smack myself, and thanked Carmine profusely.

I left the funeral home, chuckling at the software's choice of name-equivalents. I'd have to ask Hugh if there'd been a little tweaking of the algorithms. Given what I'd done with Hugh's name-equivalent, it was clearly Bob-like behavior.

I read the note while wondering if I should ditch the backpack and cube while I worked. I could hide it in the forest, or I could get a room in a hotel. What would carry less risk? The forest would certainly be cheaper. But I couldn't bring myself to seriously consider tying Bender up in a tree and leaving him to the tender mercies of random chance. I did a quick calculation. I wasn't destitute yet, but I might end up working for passage on the way back to Garack's Spine. Meanwhile, keeping Bender safe was job one.

I stopped at a general store and bought a few small items for three coppers total. I gave the proprietor an iron and received my change. I had a brief urge to swallow the coins right in front of her, but attracting attention was not a good idea.

With a little searching around, I found a fleabag hotel and paid for a night. The kindest word I could find for the room was *unimpressive*. But it had a door lock, and the door felt solid, and the window was much too small for a Quinlan to get through, even if the room had been at ground level. And as was typical for Quinlan structures, the roof was exposed, support beams and all.

I took out the length of rope that I'd purchased and did a quick leap and parkour to the rafters. It wouldn't be, strictly speaking, impossible for a Quinlan to duplicate that feat, but they would be more likely to just go get a ladder. Which would hopefully take time. I tied the backpack with Bender in it to the highest point and shifted it around to be as invisible as possible from floor level. All good.

I left my one remaining spider on the rafter as well. Just in case.

The Quinlan door locks were large and clunky compared to what I'd been used to on Earth, but the mechanism was nevertheless fairly sophisticated. Again, I was reminded that the Quinlans' technology was limited, not their knowledge. I spit up a few coins to carry with me, locked the door behind me, and sent in a couple of fleas to freeze the lock mechanism. I was probably being overly paranoid, but the downside of overdoing it was much less bad than the downside of underpreparing.

First stop was a backpack shop. On Earth that would have been a sports store, but with Quinlans, backpacks were simply apparel. A few quick inquiries on the street and I had a destination.

The shop was definitely upscale. Not as in gold trim, but as in high quality and good selection. They carried backpacks, sashes, kits for fur decoration, and other items that the sophisticated and stylish Quinlan couldn't live without. I just hoped the backpacks were more than fashion statements.

I approached the single salescritter. "I'm looking for a new backpack. My old one popped a seam because I've been carrying a funerary box in it. Do you have something with good capacity and dependable waterproofing?"

"As it happens, we do. You shouldn't, of course, spend a lot of time in water, but it'll hold for the occasional fishing expedition." He led me over to a display and gestured. "Only five irons for this model."

Eep. That would take most of my remaining cash. I opened my hand and looked down at the four irons I'd coughed up, trying to project disappointment, piteousness, and whatever else I could manage. He glanced at the coins in my hand and sighed. "I can't do four, my friend. Four and a half and it's yours."

No problem, sir, I'll just... hack... hack... hack...

No, not really. The urge was almost overpowering, but even ignoring not wanting to attract attention, I was sure he'd throw me out. "I'll, uh, talk to my friends. Back in a while."

I left the shop and went looking for Vinny's place. On the way, I surreptitiously coughed up some more coins.

Vinny's place had a sign over the door that said *Vinny's Place*. Really, Quinlans sucked with names. The window showed some of his products, including funerary boxes, small furniture, and some carved items. He did good work.

"Are you Vinny?" I said to the lone occupant as I walked in.

"I am. May I help you?"

"Carmine sent me here. I'm looking for a specific size of funerary box. He thought you might be able to help me."

Vinny's face lit up, and I realized that Carmine must actually be a relative, and well-liked. I hoped that would help my cause. We spent a few minutes talking about my requirements.

"It's an odd size, and oddly specific," he said.

"I'm trying to protect my existing box," I explained. "My grandfather died a long way from our family home. I have to bring him back there, and I can't afford the obvious methods."

"I admire your dedication, young sir. I can produce such an item. It will take about three days and will cost six irons. However, I can't guarantee that it will be watertight. That simply isn't normally part of my requirements."

Wow. Between the room, the backpack, and the box, I'd be wiped out. And I would still have to pay for passage. And I didn't have any choice about going by boat. While the manny would *probably* survive a seven-segment swim, I very much doubted that Bender would arrive still dry. Like it or not, I was going to have to play tourist. Or deckhand.

But I had no choice in the end. We talked some more, and I considered trying to haggle him down, but the simple lack of waterproofing rendered it moot. In the end, I thanked him for his time and told him I'd think about it.

⚜   ⚜   ⚜

I was heading back to the backpack store when I received an alert from the spider in my room. Someone seemed to be trying to unlock the door, and they were being increasingly unsubtle about it. The fleas had rigged the lock well enough that the interlopers would have to break down the door to get in. Would they go that far? Would anyone notice or investigate? It wasn't a high-class neighborhood, but the proprietor might object to costly damage and a room that would be un-rentable for a while.

And the would-be home invaders agreed. After a few more rattles, the sounds of assault stopped. I had no illusions that that was the end of it. It appeared none of my plans for the day were going to succeed.

I changed direction and picked up speed, not quite breaking into a run. As I moved, I stretched my features and changed my fur patterns back into Natasha's face. That might get me in the door without being observed.

The door to my room was still intact, although the lock and knob was a little more scarred than I remembered. No one appeared to be hanging around. I didn't kid myself, though. There would be surveillance. Whether they were looking for Bob or Natasha, or both, was an unknown. Whether it was Crew, Resistance, or both was pretty much irrelevant at this point. My fate at the hands of either party, and more important, Bender's fate, was a foregone conclusion.

I glanced at the window speculatively as I was climbing up to my pack. No such luck. What had originally seemed like a security feature was now a trap. There was only one way out of this room.

But not necessarily so for the building. They'd be watching the front and back doors, but maybe there was a third alternative.

I collected my spider and fleas, then locked and re-jammed the door. The scam probably wouldn't distract my pursuers for long, but every little bit helped. Meanwhile, I needed to be out of here. I headed for one of the two second-floor bathrooms for some privacy and a chance to think.

How to get out undetected? I couldn't just go downstairs and peek out the front door without attracting attention.

I'd accepted it as a given that someone was watching the front. Probably the back as well. And there were only the two doors. From the bathroom window I could see the alley, where one of the pub staff was tossing something into the dumpster. I snorted. Dumpsters. Another parallel.

Wait—what other parallels were there? Food deliveries, garbage pickup…even a dump like this needed services supplied by other companies.

I took a quick glance out into the hallway. No one. I made my way to the back of the building, where presumably the kitchen and storage areas would be. On the way, I passed a cleaning person with a cart. The cart included a garbage can of sorts, made of wood. No trash bags here. The cleaner was working on one of the rooms, so I grabbed the can off the cart. As I continued down, I placed my backpack in the can, then hoisted it up so the contents weren't visible.

I got a glance or two as I passed through the service area, but who's going to question someone who is obviously working? Chances were the hired help around here was transient and part-time anyway. I made it out to the back, holding the can up so it obscured my face, and making a show of struggling with the weight.

The dumpster was up against a fence, something I'd noticed from the bathroom. What wasn't discernible was whether the fence would collapse the moment I put my weight on it. But it didn't matter—I was committed.

I swung the can around, still projecting *this is really heavy, y'all* with every pore, and upended it onto the edge of the dumpster. As I tipped it, I grabbed the backpack before it could drop into the bin. I pulled the can back with one hand, put it upside down on the ground as quietly and quickly as possible, and used it to vault over the fence.

There was a shout behind me and I could hear running feet, but I was already on the other side and out of sight. I had perhaps two seconds to get out of view of someone coming over the fence. A quick glance said that west was the shorter sprint to cover. I went east.

As I turned into another alley, I heard the thump of someone landing, and a curse. Did I mention that Quinlans weren't particularly acrobatic? Smiling to myself, I imagined a couple of sprained ankles. That would slow them down.

Meanwhile, though, best make tracks. I dodged and wove through alleyways and quieter streets, avoiding any area with too many potential witnesses. Within minutes, I was at the edge of town. Without breaking stride, I headed for the forest.

✤ ✤ ✤

Sleeping in a tree. Not a phrase a Quinlan was likely to use. Which made it ideal for me. I found a particularly large, heavily foliaged specimen and set myself high up in the thicker parts. I spit out my spider for sentry duty, clamped my arms around the trunk, and ordered the AMI to stay put.

Everything seemed stable for the moment, so I exited the manny and popped into my VR.

"Hugh, I'm in virt if you feel like popping over."

"Sorry, Bob. Stacking cargo. I'll try to get away later, though."

Hmmph. Honestly, I wasn't sure what I would say to him anyway. Did I want to confront Hugh about the Administrator thing? What would I accuse him of, exactly? I didn't even know for sure that he was aware the Administrator was an AI. And if he did? Say he admitted to suspecting it. What law or rule, exactly, had he broken?

My suspicions were second-order, I realized. Suspicions of suspicions. I would have to keep a lid on it until I figured out what, if any, nefarious motives Hugh or the Skippies might have.

I tried connecting to Gandalf but got an autoreply. Probably Gandalf was fighting orcs or something.

Quickly, I checked Bill, Will, Bridget, and Howard, and got either busy signals or autoreplies. It appeared everyone in the Bobiverse was a little tied up at the moment. With a bad-tempered grumble, I called up a coffee and activated Spike.

So, item: I had seven segments to traverse, and it would have to be mostly by boat. Come to think of it, even if I trusted the Quinlan postal system to deliver Bender safely, it wouldn't be any faster. The mail travelled by boat.

Item next: I still had to get out of Heaven's River once I got to Garack's Spine. In principle, that shouldn't be an issue. We had the side entrance hatch that Gandalf had built. On the other hand, the locals were much more aware of us now. Of me, particularly. As Will's professor friend had rightly pointed out, I was probably going to show up on a lot of surveillance systems from now on. I could disguise myself, but I couldn't disguise the backpack.

Or couldn't I?

Granted I had to watch my money, but my biggest hurdle right now was to get out of Forest Hill. Once I could lose myself in the vastness of Heaven's River, I might be okay. So how to get out of town without exposing Bender's matrix to view…?

15. Frustrations Mount

Howard
July 2334
Trantor

"Well, that tears it," I said. "Humans are idiots."

Bridget sighed. "Given what's going on, Howard, I think they've shown considerable restraint in grandfathering us."

"Or they've noticed that we own half the damned city and they'd lose a proxy fight."

"That may have played a part, I admit." Bridget walked to the picture window and gazed out, arms crossed.

I enjoyed the panoramic view of the atmosphere of Big Top through the distant fibrex dome of the city. The sight of clouds and Jovian life stretching off in all directions, seemingly to infinity, never failed to fill me with awe. But I knew that, for Bridget, it was about more than the view; it was a validation of her work and her professional reputation. She was the reigning expert on Jovian-class life throughout human space and was unlikely to be dethroned anytime soon. A passing pod of blimps brought a slight grin to her face.

"You have that smile," I said. "Remembering our first encounter?"

Bridget laughed. "Or the city's first encounter." She turned from the window. "Howard, political issues come and go, but politics will be with us forever. We'll just out-wait them. Eventually people will calm down, or forget, or we'll just wait until they're dead and a new generation is in charge. Meanwhile, we keep a relatively low profile. We'll be okay. We have forever, remember?"

"The kids—"

"The current batch are all adults. We'll have to hold off on new adoptions for a while. You said you needed a break anyway. Maybe it's time for another expedition. I have several candidate planets lined up, all with interesting-looking ecosystems…"

"You've heard what Herschel and Neil are planning?"

"Yes, but they have to get to Romulus, load up, then get out of human space. It could be as much as a hundred years before they reach the first new system, with no guarantees that it'll have anything worth exploring. And we can join up remotely, if and when. I want something a little more immediate."

I nodded. Bridget was right. If it came down to it, we'd only be in trouble if the humans tried to confiscate our assets. And we had lawyers up the ying-yang for just that eventuality. We could literally keep the fight going in the courts longer than most of our opponents' lifetimes.

"All right, my love. You lead. Where do you want to go today?"

16. Still Trying

Bob
July 2334
Nirvana River System

I found myself surreptitiously reaching for my face again and consciously brought my arm back down. I had disguised myself once more, this time using a random passerby as my model. To avoid a "twins" issue, I'd tweaked the appearance a little. If I ran into my model, he might think he'd discovered a long-lost brother, but nothing more.

After much soul searching, I'd reluctantly left Bender tied up in the tree. No Quinlan was going to climb that high, not even with a gun pointed to their head. Wildlife tended to be small and not overly curious if something didn't smell like food. Bender was probably okay, but I was still terrified that something might happen and I'd have no way of ever finding him.

But I had to make a clean break from *Bob running around with Bender on his back* to *random guy going on a trip*. And the best way to do that was to never allow anyone to see anything that would link us.

So Enoki Funguy, social gadfly and otter-about-town, was going to book a cruise on a local luxury vessel. Or, more factually, I was going to try to work my way across seven segments disguised as Random Guy. But, and this was the good part, I would have luggage.

I glanced up at the sign over my destination: Happy Al's Storage and Trunks. Well, that's not quite what it said, but metaphorically it wasn't far off. Quinlans didn't go in for Samsonite luggage, but they did have occasional need for rigid boxes of the locking variety. Some of the items on display very much resembled old-fashioned steamer trunks, except without the metal strapping. That would have cost more than I was worth. But wood and leather could do a pretty good job, if worked properly.

Happy Al—who, it turned out, went by the name of Steve—greeted me effusively as I walked in the door. I guessed that business had been slow and Steve was bored to the point of suicide. That could work for me.

"I'm looking for one of those"—I pointed to a steamer trunk—"about this size." I held my hands apart to illustrate. I wanted a trunk that would be bulky enough that someone couldn't grab it and run away, but small enough for me to carry. "And with a security loop like the one in the window."

Steve straightened. "Sir, *all* of our trunks have security loops. And locks. We carry only the best stock."

Erm, on the one hand, that was good. On the other hand, it sounded expensive. But this part of my plan had very little wiggle room.

Steve made for the back of the shop and returned in seconds with a trunk that was just about perfect. I gave it a brief once-over, including opening it to check the interior. This was as close to exactly right as I was going to get.

"How much?"

"Eight irons, four coppers."

Ouch. I let surprise show on my face, and didn't move for a two-count. "That's…uh…"

Steve became chagrined, realizing he'd overreached. "That is, of course, retail. However, it's a slow day, so ..."

I took the hint. "I have seven irons, six coppers." I opened my hand to show him. "That's all I have in the world. And I do need this item."

Steve looked briefly relieved, then managed to suppress it. Apparently that was still above cost. "That will be acceptable."

I handed him the money and took the trunk. It was a good thing he hadn't dug in his heels. I might have spit up my remaining two irons just to see his expression.

⚜ ⚜ ⚜

The trunk had a nice lock on it, made of whatever insanely hard wood they used instead of metal. It could probably be forced by a determined thief, but the point was to not attract the attention of thieves in the first place. To that end, as soon as I was back to my tree, I started rubbing dirt on it to take the shine off. A few minutes' attention got me a suitably grubby and time-worn trunk. Next, I harvested some dry grasses for cushioning and lined the inside.

When the preparations were all done, I climbed the tree and retrieved Bender. I removed the matrix from my much-maligned backpack, then placed it carefully in the trunk, making sure the organics were packed densely enough to not shift.

I spit out my one remaining spider and put it in the trunk with the matrix. The spider was my insurance policy. It would make some modifications to the trunk to make it harder to open or steal. And if worse came to worse, some thief was going to get a face-full of plasma cutter.

The backpack wasn't looking good. The cube had stretched it, and I couldn't be sure that it would spring back into normal shape. If not, I would stand out even without the matrix. I sighed, shook the backpack a few times, then put it on. I'd stand out more without one at all.

One last item to take care of.

"*Hugh, you got a sec?*"

"*Sure, what's up?*"

"*I'm about to apply to be a deckhand. Anything I need to know? Is there a guild or union?*"

"*No, not like what you mean. There's a guild, but it's mostly just for arbitration and setting rates. And you're in it automatically if you work on a ship.*"

"*So there isn't a problem with treatment of laborers?*"

"*These are Quinlans, Bob. They can live off the land. If someone started beating the deckhands, they'd just all swim away. If they didn't outright disembowel the miscreant. Have you met Quinlans?*"

"*Mmm. Fair point. So they're cantankerous, mobile, can find food anywhere, and can sleep anywhere.*"

"*Uh-huh. Kind of hard to develop an oppressed underclass in those circumstances.*"

"*What's the pay?*"

"*A half-iron per day. If someone tries to offer you below that, snarl and walk away.*"

"*Gotcha. Thanks.*"

That was better than expected. Hugh had gotten a job right away, so I hadn't *really* expected a problem, but any Bob would tell you that Murphy was a bitch.

⚜ ⚜ ⚜

I arrived at the riverfront, trunk slung over my shoulder, and headed for the docks. There were several boats tied up, but only one had any activity. Some pallets were being unloaded, and there was also some cargo waiting to be brought on board. It looked like my best bet, if only because the other two boats appeared to be deserted.

Still, I examined the two deserted vessels, frowning. They weren't empty—there were some palleted boxes and bales—but it was odd that no one was about. However, Quinlan deckhands were swarming over the third boat, practically sprinting from job to job. I noted in passing that they weren't wearing the almost ubiquitous Quinlan backpacks, although one Quinlan who was standing around screaming orders and invective in almost equal amounts was wearing what appeared to be a vest with pockets.

The Quinlan with the vest paused and spoke to me, guessing what was on my mind. "Part of the shipment's late. We got lucky. We were here first, and signed for what was waiting. You looking for work?"

"I am. You hiring?"

She gestured at the boxes on the dock. "That *fehg* isn't going to load itself. Although the lazy sots I already pay for no reason seem to be hoping it will."

The Quinlans unloading the boat replied with pro forma insults and one Quinlan middle-finger equivalent. It seemed good-natured, though.

"Say the word and I'll start hauling."

"You got it. Get to work."

Well, that was easier than I had any right to expect. There was no need to ask where they were going. Boats almost always went downstream unless they were *very* local, and on this river segment, *downstream* was east, toward the Garack's Spine segment. "Can I drop off my trunk?"

She gestured to a corner of the boat, attention already on the next problem. I dropped off the trunk, and after a moment's thought, took off my backpack as well.

✣ ✣ ✣

Being a deckhand on a Quinlan boat was very much a *strong back, weak mind* kind of thing. Pick up box here, put box down there. Rinse, repeat. My manny was much stronger than a native, and I didn't get tired, but overheating could be an issue, so I didn't push it. Every once in a while the entire crew would take a fiver in the water to cool off, which told me I wasn't the only one with that problem.

The work was accomplished with the minimum of conversation. We'd keep working until all the cargo was moved, so malingering of any kind was pointless. Everyone just wanted to get it done.

When the last box had been loaded, we parked our butts on the edge of the boat while the Quinlan in the vest, who turned out to be the captain, argued over the paperwork with the dockmaster.

"Welcome to the *Hurricane*," one of the deckhands said. "I'm Oric. This is Ted, and this is Frieda."

I was momentarily taken aback, and looked closely at Frieda. No, definitely not the same person. Same Quinlan name, though, which the translation software converted to the same English name.

"Enoki," I replied. "Enoki Funguy."

Oric looked mildly surprised. "A family name? And you're deckhanding?"

"We are an old family," I told him. "But we were never wealthy. My mother always told me, *We've earned that name and you'll damned well use it.* Yes, mom."

That got chuckles, but I wasn't sure if my momentary flippancy hadn't set me up for trouble. I'd forgotten that family names were little short of hereditary titles in Quinlan society. Had I just painted myself as a target? Well, I'd have to roll with it.

"We also have a paying passenger," Ted volunteered. "He's off shopping. Captain Lisa told him to be back before midday or he would have to find another ride. He's cutting it pretty close."

"He also has a last name," Frieda added. "As he reminds us constantly. I've come close to opening his throat a couple of times. But the captain says we have to be polite to the paying passengers." She made a face to indicate her opinion of the command.

Captain Lisa finished haranguing the dockmaster, and the two exchanged signatures. She marched up the ramp and glared around. "His highness not here? Oh well. He paid in advance. Let's haul ass, people. We need to hit Melon Patch by nightfall."

We jumped up and started releasing lines and pulling up boarding ramps. There wasn't much to it, but I made a point of taking orders from the others without complaint or trying to improvise. Just as we were at the point of pushing away from the dock and raising sail, a fat Quinlan came puffing, yelling and waving one arm. The other arm was holding on to a trunk not unlike mine, except much newer looking.

Quinlans were fat by nature, resembling beavers more than otters in that respect. But this individual was fat even by Quinlan standards. And out of shape, to judge from the panting and gasping.

The captain growled under her breath but motioned us to lower one gangplank. The Quinlan put his trunk down, and trudged up the ramp, still trying to catch his breath. As he passed the captain, I heard him say, "Have someone retrieve the trunk, please." The captain gave him a sour look but motioned to me.

I had a strong urge to accidentally drop it into the water, but I was in a uniquely bad position to get into a game of tit-for-tat. So I played it straight, bringing the trunk on board and depositing it with the other miscellaneous items, including my trunk. But I gave the translation software specific instructions for converting his name.

"So who is he?" I asked Ted.

"Snidely Whiplash. His family is big in the wine business. As near as I can tell, he's just an entitled whelp, though."

The beverage wasn't exactly wine, but it was the result of fermenting some local fruit. And as with most alcohol, it was big business. I was no stranger to snot-nosed kids who thought their parents' success made *them* a big deal. This voyage might end up being more difficult than anticipated.

With our passenger safely, if obnoxiously, aboard, we cast off. Ted and Frieda pulled up the sail and we wallowed majestically out of port. The *Hurricane* was basically a barge with a sail, and it had all the racing feel appropriate to the design. I began to wonder if we'd make it to the end of the segment. Speaking of which…

"Hey, Oric. Does the *Hurricane* jump segments?"

"If we've got the cargo to justify it. Otherwise we circle into the Arcadia River and head back to the other end. Lisa's not one of these big-time operations with a set route. If you were to get on the *Galway*, they never leave this segment—just up and down each river, circling the world. It's not a terrible life. If you want to head into the next segment, you can get off at High Peak. There will usually be a boat going through within a day or two. The *Hamilton* jumps segments—I think they'll go three or four segments sometimes. Again, though, depends on cargo."

"Have people around here ever named any of the segments?"

Oric shook his head. "It's bad luck. You name your segment, you start to identify with it, almost like a nation; then you start to talk about borders and armies, and the next thing you know, you've been scattered as punishment."

Frieda, having finished with the sails, had joined the group. "It's not punishment, it's—"

"Yes, I've heard your doctrine before, Frieda. It's not for us to judge the Administrator."

"I'm not judging, Oric, I'm discussing their motivation. And it does make a difference. Punishments escalate. Guidance doesn't."

We were interrupted by a snort from midships. "You yokels and your legends about gods and demons. It is to laugh."

Frieda glared at Snidely, which didn't dent the supercilious expression on his face in the slightest. "Legends? Are you defective? The Administrator is as much a fact of life as the weather. Or do you think rain is a myth, too?"

"Sure, he is. He makes the grass grow, lifts the little birds into the air, and makes the sun rise in the morning."

I stared in disbelief. This buffoon apparently believed that Heaven's River was a natural environment. I opened my mouth to correct him, then was overcome by the sheer irony of the situation. I was about to explain to an atheist that God was real. I wanted to face-palm, but that would create questions. Best let the regulars take it.

Oric and Frieda formed an unsteady alliance, arguing against Snidely's amused intransigence. He was a classic case of Dunning-Kruger—so entrenched and confident in his ignorance that he didn't even realize how much he didn't know. I let the argument drone on in the background while I watched the shoreline drift by. As enjoyable as the days on the river with my friends had been, there was a lot to be said for the sailor lifestyle as well.

The argument had escalated to the point where it attracted the captain's attention, though. "Enough!" she yelled. "There's decks to be cleaned, the bilge needs pumping, the cargo still hasn't been tarped, and the spinnaker still hasn't been raised. Make yourselves useful!"

Well, that was that. And Snidely took this turn of events as a victory, to judge from the pleased expression on his face.

⚜ ⚜ ⚜

The next couple of days were uneventful. We got caught in a brief downpour, which elicited howls of complaint from Snidely. Why a creature that was designed for water should hate rain was beyond me. But then again, the family dog used to be on a first-name basis with every puddle and stream in our neighborhood but would feign death when we tried to bathe her. Go figure.

I continued to avoid interaction with Snidely. The other three seemed to be able to keep his attention. Oric and Frieda had called a truce over their minor doctrinal differences in order to form common cause against the infidel.

I was going to have to discuss this with Bridget. It seemed the Administrator was taking on the aspects of a formal belief system, complete with competing dogma. Against that was a version of atheism that didn't so much pit science against religion as simply refuse to go along. I wondered what Snidely's cosmology would look like, but having to talk to him would be too high a price to pay to find out.

❧   ❧   ❧

We pulled into a town that Ted informed me was named Beetle Juice. No, I'm not kidding, nor did I tweak the translator. It turned out this town's major industry was a form of liquor made from the excretions of some insect. First, blech! Second, it made me wonder, not for the first time, if there was some form of sense of humor involved, either from the Skippies or from the software itself. I decided to let the translation stand and assigned it to the beverage as well.

Beetle Juice was the last town on the Nirvana before the segment mountains. The captain would decide in the next day or two if we'd be continuing downriver or catching the transfer tributary to go back the other way. A lot would depend on what cargo we could get, and where it would be the most valuable.

It depended on paying passengers, too. If people were willing to pay to get to a particular destination, that would affect the captain's decision. Which made me wonder where Snidely was going. If we weren't going in the right direction for him, this would be goodbye. I tried to summon a tear and failed miserably.

As we got closer, I could see that there was considerable activity at the docks, and it didn't seem to be all from the usual dock business. Four or five cargo ships were tied up, while their crews had what appeared to be loud, bellicose discussions with official-looking individuals wearing sashes and swords.

I felt a sinking feeling in my stomach. It seemed unlikely that this had anything to do with me, but by this point any indication of cops made me as jumpy as a two-bit thief.

Captain Lisa hopped around on deck, yelling orders at us, trying to maneuver the *Hurricane* into a tight space along the dock. This also involved a shouting match with the dock-hands, which just added to the general holiday atmosphere. But eventually, we were at dock and tied up properly.

Ted and I grabbed the gangplank and started maneuvering it onto the dock. Before it had even settled, a delegation of cops marched up the plank. Captain Lisa moved to intercept them.

"We are searching for a fugitive who may be taking transport downriver," the sergeant said. "We will need to inspect your ship."

"What, all our cargo? Are you kidding me? Do you have any idea how long it'll take?"

The sergeant shook his head. "No, no, we're concerned about one specific individual carrying what appears to be a funerary box in his backpack."

Uh-oh. Chances that there were two such fugitives on a billion-mile-long megastructure? Pretty low. I tensed and started planning escape routes before I remembered that I no longer resembled Bob. And I was not wearing a backpack at the moment.

"We will also need to inspect personal luggage."

Aw, shit.

"You will like hell!" Snidely exclaimed, striding up and sticking out his chest.

"And who might you be?" The cop glared at him and put a hand on his sword.

"I am Snidely Whiplash, of the Whiplash family. You've no doubt enjoyed our wine on many occasions. We can bring considerable pressure to bear if our family name is insulted."

The cop was taken aback. No doubt dealing with powerful families, especially belligerent powerful families, was considerably above his pay grade.

After a moment the cop replied, "Yes sir, understood. Obviously, you would not be a suspect in any case. Your luggage is where?"

Snidely casually waved a hand in the direction of the miscellaneous pile. "See that it isn't touched."

As I followed Snidely's hand wave, I got an idea. As casually as I could, I moved in the direction of the pile where our trunks were located. I began to untie the tarp covering the trunks and other small items. As I gathered it, I surreptitiously wiped off my trunk as much as I could. It still ended up looking more travel-worn than Snidely's but not by much.

A couple of cops came over, evidently pleased with my cooperation, and started looking over the pile.

"Those are Mr. Whiplash's trunks," I said, pointing to the two items. "Everything else is just cargo."

One of the cops nodded to me, and they began randomly opening boxes. "How many people aboard?" one said to me.

"Captain Lisa, Ted, Frieda, Oric, myself, and Mr. Whiplash. We're all on deck." I pointed to each individual as I named them.

"None matches the description," the other cop said. "And this is just junk," he added, waving at the boxes.

"I'm sure the captain would disagree," I replied with a small smile.

The cop snorted and they moved back to the gangplank. One shook his head at the sergeant.

A few seconds of discussion with Captain Lisa, and the cops trooped away. Letting out a breath, I re-tarped the miscellaneous pile. As I straightened up after tying the last bight, I found Snidely gazing at me, a slight frown on his face. As casually as possible, I gave the tarp a tug and walked off to my next chore.

But any attention from anyone was bound to be a bad thing. I would have to keep an eye on His Bigness.

※ ※ ※

As it turned out, we would be crossing segments. Two passengers signed on, wanting to go in that direction. And the captain was able to subcontract on a shipment to Orchard Hill, just on the other side of the mountains. Subcontracting wasn't as potentially profitable as hauling our own goods, but it was a no-risk payday. And a couple of paying passengers was just bonus.

The passengers, a very old Quinlan and her granddaughter, were heading back to the family home. Theresa was far too old to endure any kind of extended swim, so Belinda had swum upstream several hundred miles to take her home.

Quinlans had a strong reverence for the elderly, so the captain didn't balk at all when we set up a comfortable area in the sun for Theresa. Even Snidely didn't seem inclined to complain.

Belinda doted on her grandmother but wasn't otherwise talkative. She was friendly, but she would never use two words when a gesture or a grunt would do. On the few occasions that she did have to speak full sentences, she seemed to be almost out of practice. Remembering Bridget's comments about breeding away from tool-user intelligence, I wondered if this might be a sign of that. Or maybe she just wasn't a talker.

Once they were settled in, we went through the by-now-routine frenetic running around that characterized leaving port. The cargo we'd taken on at Beetle Juice, which was mostly beetle juice (no surprise), was making the *Hurricane* wallow a little more than usual, so we were taking extra care to maintain a good, conservative trim.

Once the boat was in mid-river and running an easy reach, we were able to break for lunch. I jumped in with the other crew members, and we chased down some juicy fish. Yum. Unfortunately, given the close quarters, I had to be seen to be eating, sleeping, and so on, just like everyone else. So, fish for breakfast, fish for lunch…When I was done with the Bender rescue, I resolved that I would never go near fish again.

We brought up a dozen or so as well for the captain and passengers. I sat down with Theresa and Belinda, studiously ignoring Snidely who was snarfing back fish like he hadn't been fed in weeks. The Pav would have approved of his table manners. My mother, not so much.

Belinda quietly removed the less desirable fish parts with a small, but doubtless expensive, knife and offered the fillets to her grandmother, who took them with a smile.

"Belinda's not much for talking," Theresa said to me. "I've watched you try to engage her in conversation." She placed a fond hand on her descendant's head. "Kids are getting less and less verbal, it seems."

"I have a friend who commented that it's less necessary in Heaven's River, so intelligence is being gradually bred out."

"With some help from the Administrator? I've heard that theory. Not impossible, but their manipulation would have to be very subtle—"

"Oh, in Father's name, more yokel superstition," said Snidely. "Save me from the uneducated."

Theresa gave him a mild stare. "And what's your educational background, Mr. Whiplash?"

"I have a master's in business from the University of Peachland," he replied haughtily. I checked the translator out of curiosity. That wasn't bad. Close enough to retain the meaning anyway, although I doubted that a *master's* had quite the same meaning as a human university degree.

"And you took classes at Peachland?" Theresa asked.

"Of course."

"I *taught* courses at Peachland, Mr. Whiplash. Don't talk down to me. I have several doctorates, in subjects much more relevant than *How to Count Money* for those who've had their life handed to them."

Whoa. Snidely jerked back, and I imagined flames sparking at the end of his whiskers. As much as I disliked him, obvious glee wouldn't be helpful, so I maintained a stone face as he stood stiffly.

"That would have been very handy, I suppose, before senility set in," he said, showing his canines.

Belinda turned on him, snarled, and extended her claws. Snidely jumped back, surprised and alarmed by her reaction.

"You're a small man with a small, shriveled soul, Mr. Whiplash," Theresa said. "There is no bigger waste than a formal education given to someone incapable of using it. I have no doubt your whole life would disappear into your father's accomplishments without leaving a ripple."

Snidely glared at her for a moment, totally silenced, before stalking off.

"That went well," I said.

Theresa chuckled. "And what about you, Mr. Funguy? You have a last name as well. Do you have anything to show for it?"

"Not really. My family earned the name long ago. Nowadays it's mostly useful for keeping people like Snidely from patronizing me too much."

"Do you believe, as Mr. Whiplash apparently does, that the world came about naturally?"

"Of course not," I replied. "It's a rotating structure, one hundred *henn* in radius, composed of segments each one thousand *henn* in length. The ratio is clearly artificial. The experiment to determine the rotational period is something we did in our first-year classes. It's exactly what you'd need in order to generate .86 G." I was taking a chance showing any scientific chops, but I wanted Theresa to approve of me. Not just because she appeared to have a ferocious intellect, but also because I might learn something useful. This could turn out to be the first truly useful encounter since we'd landed.

She nodded slowly. "Ah. An engineer? A frustrating occupation, I imagine. So much of what you know you could do is forbidden."

"And what did you teach, Theresa?"

"Philosophy. Math. History." She smiled sadly. "That last item is particularly frustrating. Even in my lifetime, I've watched people letting go of some of the more difficult aspects of Quinlan history, in favor of myth, belief in the Administrator as a supernatural deity of some kind, and just-so stories."

Jackpot. Maybe I'd finally get a complete picture of the history of Heaven's River. "So what do you think the Administrator—"

The captain's voice cut through everything. "All right you lazy sots. This tub won't steer itself. Are you going to leave that mess on the deck forever? Do I pay you to sun yourselves? Hop to it!"

I sighed. Lunch ten minutes was over.

❧   ❧   ❧

The next day's topic was life after death. Oric and Frieda, no surprise, had opinions that tended toward the mystical. Theresa, bless her heart, didn't mock or condescend, but she did ask questions that they found very hard to handle. During a lull, while Oric and Frieda were regrouping, she turned to me. "You've been quiet, Enoki. Don't have an opinion?"

I chuckled. "That'll be the day. I guess the real problem is defining what you mean by life after death."

"I would have thought it was self-explanatory."

"The supernatural version, sure. Also unprovable, at least so far. But what about a more, erm, science-oriented version?" I launched into a highly abbreviated explanation of replication. When I was done, Oric and Frieda looked equal parts confused and appalled.

"That's not the same," Frieda exclaimed. "That's just a copy of you."

"But if original you isn't around anymore, it sure beats the alternative," I replied with a grin.

Theresa laughed. "And to anyone else, it might make no difference. If a copy of me loved to chase my grandchildren around and remembered everyone's birthdays, how would you tell it wasn't original me?"

"But it wouldn't be!"

"There's a postulate in information theory that information can't be destroyed," I said slowly. I was sticking my neck out; I knew it. I watched myself doing it and couldn't stop. This might be well beyond what Quinlans had managed to retain. "And in philosophy, there's something called a

Closest Continuer, which according to some thought, actually would be you. Even if there was a gap."

Theresa gave me a quizzical look. "I can get the definition of *Closest Continuer* from context, but I'd love to hear more about this bit about information theory."

There were groans from the others. It appeared advanced physics was not a popular subject.

❧   ❧   ❧

I was in my VR library, studying some of the blueprints of Heaven's River produced from scans by the Skippies and Gamers, when I received an alert from my manny's AMI.

Sentry roamer reports disturbance.

That meant someone or something was disturbing my trunk. I quickly entered my manny and climbed quietly to my feet. It was full night, and Ted was on watch. The ersatz starlight was enough to illuminate the shore if we got too close. But it generally wasn't a problem, as the current and wind tended to keep the boat in the middle of the river. Ted would wake us up if some emergency navigation became necessary.

Meanwhile, we had a small lantern on bow and stern, just enough to mark our position for any other boats, but not enough to affect night-adapted eyes. Of course, that didn't matter for a manny equipped with real night vision.

Someone had peeled back part of the tarp and was bent over the trunks. Someone with a, shall we say, extra-wide silhouette. I walked quietly up behind Snidely and whispered, "It's locked, asshole."

He jerked up and turned to face me. "Very well-locked, it would seem. Better than mine, which appears to be the same quality."

Huh. He'd just out-and-out admitted he was trying to break into my trunk. Probably a punchline of some kind was coming. "Is there a point, Snidely? Other than that you're a thief?"

He smirked back at me. "Well, *Enoki*, I happened to be watching when we pulled into Beetle Juice. It was very impressive how you managed to get them to not inspect your trunk."

I frowned. "How so? They didn't inspect either trunk."

"But I ordered them not to inspect mine. You tricked them into thinking I had two trunks."

"I didn't do anything except pull off the tarp, Snidely. They made an assumption. Should I have begged them to please open my trunk? I notice you didn't volunteer."

"Very glib, Enoki. Tell you what, since it's all so innocent, why don't you open your trunk for me?"

"You first."

"My trunk," he said haughtily, "is not under suspicion."

"Neither is mine, dumbass. Meanwhile, I found you trying to break into my property, which gives me the right to defend it. So here's the thing." I stepped up until my beak was right up against his. "If I catch you trying that or anything similar again, I will rip off your head and shit down your neck. We clear?"

Snidely stepped back, clearly not prepared for the level of implied violence I was projecting. "I will tell the captain you threatened me—"

"I will tell the captain you are a thief. I wonder which one of us will be tossed off the boat?"

He glared for a few more seconds, then turned and stalked off.

But I knew this wasn't over. Not by a long shot.

17. TROLLING FOR TREASURE

Bill
August 2334
Virt, Pits of Paebak

The troll lay at my feet, sliced in two, the halves neatly cauterized. I cleaned my sword—carefully—and re-sheathed it. I'd gotten the flame blade and some enchanted armor in exchange for the staff of fireballs and most of my portion of Gargh's hoard. It had been a fair trade in that both myself and Saruman the Wise claimed we'd been fleeced. Still, neither of us backed out of the deal.

Our dungeon party was currently creeping along a dark hallway in the Pits of Paebak. When asked about the name, the current DM would only smile mysteriously and say that all would be made clear at the conclusion of the campaign. Which probably meant a bad pun or something was in our future.

Kevin was back as his original character, having left behind just enough identifiable pieces to allow a resurrection. Gandalf had used one of his scrolls, after taking all Kevin's remaining worldly goods in payment. Kevin seemed to have finally gotten over the loss of his staff, thankfully. I hadn't been subjected to any more glares, at least. Tim, who hadn't left anything but floating ash, was back as a first-level thief. He was staying in the center of the group until he levelled up enough to not be killed by an inadvertent sneeze.

Verne, Pete, and I provided the muscle and sharp implements. So far, we'd been able to handle the encounters, but the increasing difficulty sent a pretty clear message that we were getting close to the payoff.

Gandalf strode along just behind me, acting like king of the mountain. I hoped his talents matched up to his attitude. He was remarkably closemouthed about his actual abilities and assets.

"That was a troll," Tim said unnecessarily.

We turned to look at him. "And?" Verne said.

"Pretty hefty monster for this level of dungeon," Tim answered. "If not for Bill's flame blade, I'm not sure we'd have been able to take it down. Not without losing another player or two anyway."

I looked back in the direction of the troll carcass. Tim was right. I'd gotten too used to being able to cleave just about anything with one swipe. But trolls were, generally speaking, more than a handful.

"Are you suggesting we're being set up?" Gandalf asked. "Anyone made any enemies lately?"

I glanced at Kevin, who gazed back at me innocently. That was a long shot anyway. If Kevin was that sensitive about losing treasure, he'd never make it as a Gamer. Everyone else was looking around at everything and nothing as they considered their own recent pasts.

"There's a secret door here."

We all turned at Tim's comment. He was poking at a random section of wall.

"You sure?"

"It's about the only thing I'm good for," Tim replied. "Why do you think I picked this character class?"

"Fair enough," I said. "Let's see if we can crack this."

We all started poking, twisting, pushing, lifting and pulling every protuberance in the area. A few seconds later, a door opened with the typical stone-grinding sound effect, revealing a pitch-black tunnel.

"That looks dark," Tim said. "And cramped." He pulled a copper piece out of a pocket and tossed it into the blackness. There was a dull thump, followed by a metallic tinkle. "Uh..."

"Yeah. Something's in there. Anyone got a light spell? Or a flashlight?"

We needn't have bothered. Whether we woke it up with the coin toss, or it simply decided it had lost the element of surprise, the demon hound charged out of the tunnel, straight at Verne. He, a battle-hardened, fearless half-dwarf warlord, went rigid with fear. Seriously. The hound knocked him over like hitting an inflatable Bozo the Clown.

Apparently, the hound had been expecting more resistance than Bozo had been able to deliver. It continued on in its trajectory, speed unabated, and fetched up against the far wall with a loud thump. The hound made an oddly human "oof" noise and slid down the wall to land in a heap.

Pete, who hadn't gone rigid, took the opportunity to impale the beast before it could get up. As the light went out of the hound's eyes, Pete smiled and said, "About time I got a good kill—"

The second demon hound hit him at neck height, taking his head clean off. "Shit!" his head said as it bounced along the floor. I finally unfroze, pulled my sword, and parted the hound cleanly.

"Well, that's suboptimal," Gandalf said. He grabbed Pete's head by the helmet crest and lifted it until they were face to face. "No resurrections, buddy. Even if you could afford it, I used my last scroll for Kevin."

Pete's head said, "Yeah, okay. I was getting tired of this character anyway."

The conversation was interrupted by a heavy bass growl ahead of us in the hallway.

"What the blinkin' blue blazes was that?" Kevin whispered.

Tim replied, "Dunno, but it had a certain quality of bigness to it."

"And hungriness," I added.

Tim peered into the tunnel. "I think we're being herded, but it's this or go straight back. I kinda wish you still had that staff, Bill."

I shook my head in reply. "Firing it off in that cramped space would as likely as not cook all of us with the blowback. Gandalf, you got anything for close-order fighting?"

"Not like what you mean, Bill. I think your flame blade is our best hope."

"Wonderful." This meant I would be going first, holding my magic sword out in front of me in hopes of killing an attacker before it could get to us. Which would do diddly squat against a magical attack. My future began to truncate in front of me.

I shrugged and edged carefully into the tunnel. "Someone want to shed some light on this?"

Gandalf muttered something and a light shone over my shoulder, illuminating the tunnel ahead. The tunnel wasn't high enough for us to stand straight, so we were forced to move forward bent at the waist. If I'd been bio and doing this in *real*, I would have had back spasms within a minute or two; but in the spirit of classic D&D, the game engine allowed us to overlook some of the more realistic aspects of adventuring.

The tunnel eventually terminated in a blank wall. We all turned to Tim, who shrugged. "I don't see anything."

"I'm getting tired of this campaign," Verne muttered. "We've been battling high-level beasts since almost the entrance, lost over half our group, and we have sweet diddly to show for it."

"Hopefully the final payday is worth it." Gandalf checked through his satchel. "I have a spell of True Seeing in here somewhere…Ah." He pulled out a small notebook and paged through it. A few seconds of nodding and muttering and he looked up. "Let's try this."

Gandalf made some gestures and spoke in an arcane tongue. He then squinted and peered intently around, checking the blank wall and the tunnel wall around it. "Nothing. What the hell?"

We all stared at the blank wall. Red herrings were one thing, but dead ends generally needed to have a point. "I'm really starting to hate this DM," Tim said, and turned around to head back up the tunnel. He took three steps, then said, "Really, really, really hate."

We looked past him at the blank wall where a tunnel used to be. We were now in a section of tunnel about twenty feet long, blocked at both ends.

I frowned. "Gandalf, is your True Seeing spell still active?"

"Yes, for another minute or so."

"See anything in this tunnel we should know about?"

"Nope."

"What blocks or counters a True Seeing?"

"Er…higher level magic, of course. But I'd sense that."

"Tim, you see anything significant?"

"No. And a True Seeing would pick it…hold on." Tim put his hand near a section of wall. "There's a draft here."

We moved over to it and each took a turn feeling for the slight air flow.

"On the list of things that defeat a True Seeing," Gandalf opined, "we can add low-tech tricks like building a wall without mortar." He pushed on the section of wall and it gave a little.

We all put our backs into it, and after a few seconds of resistance, the wall collapsed outward.

The good news is that it crushed several of the zombies who were waiting on the other side. The bad news is that it alerted all of their still-uncrushed brethren. We were at one end of a large subterranean hall with a ceiling so high it was lost in the gloom. Torches lined the walls, giving enough light to illuminate dozens of zombies milling around the chamber, and a large nondescript statue at least twenty feet tall standing at the center.

"Oh shit," Tim exclaimed, and backpedaled frantically.

"Brainsssss..." said the zombies, and advanced on us.

"Now hold on," Verne exclaimed. "That's entirely the wrong kind of—"

"Shut up, Verne," Gandalf growled. "Kill now, carp later."

I raised my sword and started swinging. Perhaps a little too enthusiastically, as Verne yelled, "Hey, watch it!" and danced out of the way.

Without Pete, we were down to two fighter characters. Even with magical accessories, Verne and I wouldn't be able to hold off a bunch of undead. "If you've got anything in that bag of tricks, Gandalf, now would be the time," I yelled.

"Gimme a sec," he yelled back. I could hear muttered curses, then "Aha!"

There was a *pop* and a zombie that was trying to eat Verne's axe turned into a cloud of smelly gas.

My eyebrows went up, but I didn't have time to think about it. Zombies weren't particularly powerful opponents, but they made up for it with sheer numbers and a total lack of fear. And they were very hard to kill. You generally had to reduce them to sushi before they'd stop coming at you. And I had at least a dozen of the critters about to step into range. I cocked my sword arm, and—

Pop, pop, pop.

"Woo-hoo!" Gandalf yelled. The sudden disappearance of several zombies gave me time for a quick glance over my shoulder. Gandalf was gesturing with a wand. Each time he pointed it, there was another *pop*.

"Damn, that's handy," Verne said, and chopped another couple of zombies.

"Bibbety boppety boo," Gandalf replied, dancing around and waving his wand. "Bibbety boppety bibbety boppety pibbety boppety boo!" With each downbeat, another zombie went up in smoke. The odor was verging on overpowering, and the game engine wouldn't let me turn down my olfactory sense.

We were down to the last dregs of the zombies, and I was beginning to think we might survive this, when a huge hand reached out of nowhere and wrapped around me. I found myself hoisted into the air, unable to draw a breath.

The last few zombies disappeared with popping sounds, and Gandalf stopped the song and dance routine. Strangely, I don't think anyone had noticed my predicament until that moment, judging from the shocked expressions. "Little help?" I managed to squeak.

"Hello, wabbit," a voice said from behind us. Verne and Gandalf turned—I couldn't move, but the huge hand helpfully rotated me to face the voice—to find Kevin grinning at me, holding a scroll. "Golem," he explained, waving the scroll. The helpful hand turned me around again, and I was finally able to see what I'd previously assumed was a statue. A twenty-foot-tall clay-colored humanoid shape stared back at me impassively with a face surprisingly reminiscent of Odo from *DS9*. It loosened its grip slightly so that I could more easily breathe and talk.

Kevin put the scroll into a pocket and I reflexively struggled. No joy, of course. He didn't have to hold the scroll to control the golem, just possess it. And golems, besides being almost indestructible, were hella strong.

Kevin walked a little ways to the side to put some distance between himself and the rest of the group, still smirking triumphantly but not saying anything. It looked like he was going to wait for us to ask the first question.

"What's going on, Kevin?" Verne asked obligingly.

Kevin gestured at me. "Bill here. First time in a campaign, he goes from dragon fodder to a level above me by basically tripping over himself. Does practically nothing and comes out golden."

"Plus I took your staff of fireballs. I'm sure that figures into it."

Kevin glared at me. "You needed to be taken down a peg, bud." He directed nasty grin my way. "So I set up this campaign and made sure you were invited."

"You played *and* DMed?" Gandalf exclaimed.

"No, I've got a friend running the show. I'm just what you might call a—"

"Backstabber," Verne finished for him.

"Whatever. None of you have anything that can take out a golem. Enjoy your deaths, courtesy of Bill. And speaking of Bill…" Kevin raised a hand and made a squeezing motion.

I waited for the end, hoping the sensory feedback filter was set way high, but nothing happened. Kevin got a perplexed look on his face and repeated the motion. Still nothing. Kevin reached into his pocket, and the concerned expression changed to panic.

"Looking for this?"

We all turned at Tim's voice. He was leaning up against the wall, casually flipping a scroll in his hand.

Oh, yeah, that's right. Thief.

"You truly are an asshole, Kevin," Tim said, and opened his other hand. The golem dropped me, then reached out, grabbed Kevin around the head, and squeezed. There was a *pop* sound, not the least bit like a zombie exploding, and squishy juice squirted from the top of the golem's fist.

Verne bent over and retched.

"Oh GOD!" Gandalf exclaimed. "Did you *have* to do that?"

Tim grimaced in sympathy. "Okay, maybe not my best move. However…" He held up the Golem Scroll. "I appear to be in possession of one kick-ass piece of magic. I feel some levelling-up in my future. Let's see what else we can find."

We grinned at each other. Another successful campaign.

❧ ❧ ❧

I'd invited myself over to Gandalf's VR again, and he was eyeing me suspiciously. Maybe he was expecting another lecture on the Gamers' involvement in the expedition. But that wasn't what I was worried about this time.

"So, about Kevin. That's not Bob-like behavior. How far has he drifted, anyway?"

Gandalf shrugged. "He's actually one of my descendants. I could ask him, but off the cuff I'd say he's about twenty-fourth generation. So it shouldn't be a surprise that he's drifted a lot."

"Bit of an asshole. A vindictive one, at that."

"Yeah, listen Bill, I get why the whole drift thing bothers the senior Bobs. But you need to appreciate that, from our point of view, it's more upside than otherwise."

Well, that was interesting. I raised my eyebrows and made a rolling motion with a hand for him to continue.

"When we first started the Gamers group, most of us were still mostly Bob-like, and frankly it was a little boring. Everyone wanted to be a magic user, the dungeons tended to all feature intellectual puzzles, everything was carefully balanced...all very civilized. Now..." Gandalf made a helpless gesture. "Nowadays, you can't always depend on your fellow players, sometimes crazy shit happens—like today—and sometimes things go wildly out of control. Campaigns are way more fun these days. Also, we are now getting non-Bob replicants joining up from some of the post-life replicant arcologies."

"What, seriously? Who?"

"No one today. This was all Bobs. But a couple of guys from your last time out were ex-human. Interesting that you didn't notice."

"Huh." Well, he had a point. "So Kevin—"

"Is going to suffer a loss of reputation, but not so much for the attempted backstabbing as for failing at it. We'll still let him join campaigns. We just won't let him stand behind us, if you know what I mean."

I chuckled and shook my head. "You're right. It's too easy to get myopic and see everything from the point of view of my own priorities. And that's going to become an increasingly dangerous habit. I think I have to make an effort to start seeing everyone as individuals." I stood. "Thanks, Gandalf. For the game, and for the lesson."

He was still smiling when I popped out.

18. Trouble with Snidely

Bob
August 2334
Nirvana River System

It was kind of a good news/better news thing. The good news was that Snidely was now avoiding me. The better news was that everyone else had noticed and was actively hanging around me. I wondered why I hadn't thought of this tactic when I was alive.

We were on our lunch break and were once again sitting around the fish bowl. By which I mean bowl of fish. Yum.

We'd gotten onto the concept of morality, and Frieda had just asked Theresa how she could have any sense of morality without a deity to define what was or was not moral. And as usual, I was having to grit my teeth to avoid doing a face-palm, which wasn't a Quinlan expression. They didn't seem to have a direct equivalent, either, or I'd have used it by now.

"What deities give you aren't rules of morality," Theresa responded. "They're just *rules.* Do this and you'll be rewarded. Do that and you'll be punished. That's how we teach our pets not to relieve themselves in the house. One would hope that true morality involved more than learning not to poop on the rug by being rapped on the nose."

I remembered that small animal Garfield had seen wearing the cone of shame. It seemed pet behavior was another universal.

"In fact," Theresa continued, "I believe that it is *only* possible to acquire true morality *without* input from a deity. It is only when you do something because you believe it is the right thing to do, instead of because of any moral desserts, that you are acting morally. Likewise, it is only when you refuse to do something because of the Golden Rule, rather than because of a threat of punishment, that you are behaving in a moral manner."

"Ah," I piped up. "The Golden Rule. Treat others as you'd like to be treated."

Theresa gave me a perplexed look. "No, that's the Silver Rule."

"What?" Had I missed something?

"There are three rules of behavior," Theresa replied, now in lecture mode. "The Iron Rule: Treat others less powerful than you however you like. The Silver Rule: Treat others as you'd like to be treated. The Golden Rule: Treat others as they'd like to be treated."

"Huh. I had not heard that."

Theresa frowned at me. "Seems like an odd gap. How far away is your home? Maybe they need a missionary visit."

"From an atheist?" Frieda said archly.

"Wait…" I gestured at Frieda with an upheld hand. Then to Theresa, "How is that better?"

"If I treat you how I want to be treated, I'm not taking into account your desires." Theresa made an imploring gesture. "If you are a Unitist and can't eat land meat, but land meat is my favorite, the Silver Rule says I'm behaving morally by offering you a steak if you're hungry. But of course you won't eat it and in fact may be offended. So the Silver Rule is still to a large extent about me and my desires. However, with the Golden Rule, I am obligated to take into account your beliefs and preferences when deciding how best to behave toward you. Does this not produce a better result?"

"Huh," I said. Again. Not sounding very smart, Bob. "I'll have to think about that."

Theresa smiled. "That's the best sentence any teacher could hear."

"But," Frieda interjected, "you could believe literally anything, and there's no way to decide which is right—"

"Shall we just sail right past port, then?" Captain Lisa's voice washed over us. Damn, she had presence. I wondered if captains practiced that kind of yelling. "Maybe we should just sail into the rocks, then? Perhaps when you have a few seconds, you could steer this Mother-be-damned tub?"

Once again, lunch ten minutes was over.

❦   ❦   ❦

We pulled into Orchard Hill without incident. As soon as the gangplank was in place, Snidely stalked down it and away, cutting in front of the captain. He wasn't carrying his trunk, so unfortunately, he'd probably be back. And Captain Lisa would likely have a few things to say to him.

The captain and the dockmaster got into the usual spitting and shouting match, which, as usual, terminated with work for us. We began hauling boxes off the *Hurricane* and stacking them on a low-slung cart specifically designed for this.

It was mindless work and allowed me to think. I'd been on the move for a week and had traversed a segment. Assuming that was a reasonable speed, I'd be a month and a half getting to Garack's Spine. Maybe a little more, since

I'd also have to move from the Nirvana back to the Arcadia. Maybe I could get on a boat that crossed as part of their regular route.

I was interrupted in my ruminations by something undefinable. There's a particular sound, or maybe a change to the normal background, that happens when cops show up. It's subtle, but it's enough to make you stop and look.

Coming down the dock was Snidely, talking animatedly to one of four cops. I doubted that he was trying to get them to check the *Hurricane*'s boating license. Assuming they had such things.

Snidely marched straight up to me, and with triumph in his voice, said, "This one."

The cop, presumably the ranking officer, examined me, head slightly cocked. "Doesn't match the description." He sighed. "Nevertheless, we're here." He motioned me to precede him up the gangplank.

"What's going on?" Captain Lisa demanded. She placed herself in front of the spokescop, blocking his path.

He gestured to Snidely. "This gentleman has accused *this* man of being the fugitive who is currently being sought through several segments."

"Based on the fact that he tried to break into my trunk and I threatened him," I said.

"And why would he be trying to break into your trunk?"

"You've known him for five minutes. Tell me honestly if that doesn't seem in character."

The cop said nothing, but his face took on the stony cast that meant someone was trying to suppress a facial expression. After a moment, he sighed. "Nevertheless, we're here, and Mr. Whiplash is from a *Family*." He turned to the captain. "You can refuse to let me on board. But the dockmaster can also refuse to continue to load and unload. Your choice."

Captain Lisa gave Snidely a murderous glare before replying to the sergeant. "*You* have permission. *He* does not." She turned to Ted. "Bring Mr. Whiplash's trunk down."

Snidely smiled at her. "Big deal. I'll have another ride by the end of the day."

"But it won't be with us," the captain replied. "And the shipping community is small and tight-knit. Don't be too sure of your options." She pulled her vest pocket open and rummaged for a moment, producing two coins. "Here's the balance of your fare." She threw the coins to the ground at Snidely's feet.

I'll give Snidely credit—he ignored the coins. He also dealt her a glare that made her previous salvo look like a love-fest. If people had started shooting lightning bolts from their eyes, it wouldn't have surprised me.

The coins rolled a short distance, and a couple of spectators pounced on them. The sergeant gave Captain Lisa a look that might have been sympathy, then turned back to me and gestured again to the plank.

We passed Ted on his way back, carrying Snidely's trunk. A brief glance assured me that he hadn't gotten the wrong one.

The tarp had been stripped back and left off. I pulled my trunk from the pile, placed it flat, and unlocked it. The cop reached forward and opened the lid to reveal ... stuff. A folded vest, some small tools, several books, a miniature ceramic figure, and a diary and writing implements. He pushed a few items around, frowned, then frowned at me. "This is just common goods. Why did you not just show him this?"

"Would you have, if that pompous ass demanded it of you?"

The cop snorted. "No, not likely. I think Mr. Whiplash is going have some explaining to do. Wasting the constabulary's time is not without consequence. My apologies for the trouble."

I smiled and nodded, and the cops marched back to the dock. I imagined a sharp and hopefully not short conversation in Snidely's future. I glanced at the shipping container that currently held Bender's matrix instead of these random items. I'd have to swap things back tonight, as that particular container was destined for the next stop.

❧ ❧ ❧

"What a putz," Ted said.

I grinned and pushed the fish bowl toward him. "Yeah, but did you see the look on his face as they marched him up the dock? I think he's going to have an interesting afternoon."

Theresa accepted a fillet from Belinda and chewed thoughtfully on it for a few seconds. "Sadly, he will probably have many children."

We all chuckled. Harvey, our new deckhand, said, "It sounds like I missed an interesting time. I've had to deal with obnoxious passengers before. Never fun."

Theresa turned to me. "So, Enoki, tell me more about utilitarianism."

There were groans from the others. It turned out that dislike for moral philosophy transcended species.

❧ ❧ ❧

Frieda was holding the night watch again. That helped, as I'd spent time last night working out her routine. Now I had to switch back the contents of my trunk and the shipping container. But, you know, night vision.

I had both containers open and had moved the miscellaneous items back into the shipping box. I held up Bender's matrix and was about to place it carefully in the organics that formed my trunk's padding, when a voice behind me said, "That's very pretty. What is it?"

I whirled, almost fumbling the matrix, to find Theresa smiling at me. "Uhhhh…" I said.

"It *is* about the size of a funerary box. And since you took steps to hide it, I have to assume some level of guilt, if that's the right word."

Well, this was just peachy beyond belief. Would I have to kill Theresa? Could I even do that? What were my alternatives?

"You're not from around here, are you, Enoki?"

"None of us are, Theresa."

She laughed. "You know what I mean. You're not a native Quinlan, at least not a resident of Heaven's River, like the rest of us. Are you even a Quinlan at all?"

"What an odd question. What else would I be?"

"Well, you'd be someone who knows about things like utilitarianism and Closest Continuers, which I'd never heard of, but not about the Three Rules, which every child learns. And you're someone who thinks the gravity in Heaven's River is .86 G instead of one G. Where are you from that the gravity is 1.16 G?"

Oh. Bugger. I remembered that conversation. I'd assumed the translator would convert my statement, but apparently not. Well, that was just a huge, steaming, smelly pile of—

"I think you're reading too much into an unconnected series of conversations, Theresa."

"That would be a reasonable proposal, except for the thing in your hands. It appears to be metal. If it is, it's enough metal to buy the entire segment. But you're working as a deckhand. One of these things is not like the other, know what I mean?" She smiled at the last sentence.

"Uhhh…"

Theresa rolled her eyes. "You're usually a bit more articulate than that, Enoki. Do you need a slap?"

I chortled. "No thanks, Teach. So, what are you going to do?"

"If I tried to call you out, would I survive?"

I closed my eyes briefly. "That would be the most effective way of dealing with the problem, and from a strictly utilitarian point of view, it might even pass muster. But no. I don't work that way. I'd just run. And I'd have to take a chance on getting this wet." I held up the matrix to illustrate.

"So you are the person they're looking for?"

"I'm pretty sure. There's always a possibility of coincidence, but I'm going to guess that's unlikely. And even if that turned out to be the case, I'd still end up in the pokey until they straightened it all out."

"What are you guilty of?"

"Trying to rescue a friend. Seriously, Theresa, that's all I'm doing."

She nodded. "I believe you. I may be biased, but I don't see someone being able to understand moral philosophy without being guided by it. Besides, you're very interesting to talk to."

I laughed softly and muttered, "Dance, monkey, dance."

"What?"

"Oh, uh, it's an ironic statement where I'm from. It means I have to continue to be entertaining in order to preserve my safety."

"I hope you won't view me that way, Enoki." She smiled sadly. "I see no reason to expose you. Tell me this, though.

Is wherever you're from outside of Heaven's River? Or at least outside of what the rest of us live in?"

I hesitated, then decided to go for it. "Yes, Theresa, and you're right, I'm not Quinlan. There *is* an Administrator, but they aren't a deity, just an engineering construct. And they're after me because they want *this* back." I gestured with the matrix again.

"Is it theirs?"

I shook my head. "No. In fact, I literally, personally built this item myself. The Administrator took it from me, then the Resistance took it from them, and now I'm trying to take it back. That is enormously simplified and leaves out a lot of detail, but it is the truth."

She smiled and nodded. "Thank you for telling me. I will miss our discussions."

"What? Why?"

"Because no doubt you'll be leaving without notice at the first opportunity. Good night, Enoki."

And with that, she turned and headed back to where her granddaughter was curled up.

I was shaken. As I finished securing the matrix and placed my spider back into the trunk, I had plenty of time to consider my options. Granted, of all the people to discover me, she was probably the best option. But however I parsed it, I was exposed. And she was right, the safest move might be for me to leave straightaway.

⚜ ⚜ ⚜

Ninety miles. More or less.

That was the surface distance between rivers. I'd briefly considered doing an overland hike to the next river, but that was just too far. Five days' hiking, and that was if nothing went wrong. And again, I couldn't use streams or tributaries.

Theresa and Frieda were at it again, theistic versus atheistic morality. I'd heard it all so many times before, mostly when I was still alive, that it was hard to stay interested. Theresa glanced at me from time to time but made no effort to draw me into the conversation.

Oric, however, had no reservations. "Enoki, what in Father's name is wrong with you? Run out of things to talk about?"

"I, uh, I have things on my mind, Oric. Sorry. I'll get over myself soon."

Theresa smiled at me. "It's okay, it's not like we're on a schedule."

I opened my mouth to reply just as the captain started her daily tirade about sloppy, lazy, do-nothing deckhands. Turned out we *were* on a schedule.

⚜ ⚜ ⚜

"We'll be turning around at the end of this segment," Ted said during a rest break. "You still planning on continuing east?"

"Yep. As far as I know, they haven't moved my home city."

"Theresa and Belinda are getting off at Misty Falls. That's our last stop before turnaround. I guess you'll all be getting off together."

I thought about that for a moment, but I couldn't see how it affected my level of risk. Theresa wasn't any more likely to suddenly loudly denounce me just because she was on land. Still, once I was on another boat, among a whole new set of strangers, I'd feel a lot better.

By midday we were approaching the Misty Falls docks. I couldn't account for the fact that I felt more sadness than a sense of dread or danger, until I realized that I would never see Theresa again. She'd become very much a friend over a surprisingly short time. However, I had no choice. It wasn't even a case of getting away; the *Hurricane* was turning around to head along the Paradise River.

Docking was the usual chaotic jumble of yelled orders and flying ropes, and then we were moored. At that point, Captain Lisa came over to say goodbye to Theresa, Belinda, and me. They'd have enough deckhands with Harvey, who was staying on, but no passengers for the return trip. I hoped they'd still be able to turn a profit.

I picked up my trunk and followed Belinda and Theresa down the gangplank, not particularly paying attention. Which I guess explained my surprise when we walked out into a circle of cops.

19. Recall Is a Thing

Howard
August 2334
Trantor

I sat back and put my hands behind my head, grinning like a fool. "You have that smug look," Bridget said. "What happened?"

"Well, it turns out we're not the only replicants with money and influence." I waved a hand at the email displayed on the Canvas. "Senator MacIntosh. Remember him? Loudly anti-replicant. He's being recalled."

"Really?"

"They got the required signatures. And guess who was behind the recall campaign?"

"Us?"

I laughed. "No, although I would have loved to have a hand in it. The man is a toxic dump of xenophobia and undirected hate. It's possible he didn't realize that the Afterlife replicant reserve is part of his district. Or maybe he thought he could remove our rights before they could fight back. Or something."

Bridget frowned. "That would be a couple hundred signatures at most. They'd need ..." Bridget's eyes lost focus for a moment. "... something like fifteen thousand to succeed."

"Yep. Turns out, though, that people are concerned about their afterlife. Afterlives? Anyway, the anti-MacIntosh group started comparing him to FAITH, in terms of removing replicant rights, then implied that no matter what kind of post-life setup someone chose, he'd be after them sooner or later. I guess it's different when you're personally threatened."

Bridget snorted and sat down beside me. She spent a few seconds paging through the news items before turning to face me. "Still, he hasn't actually been voted out yet. Let's not count our politicians before they're properly cooked. And the overall problem is still there: mistrust of replicants."

"Which is why I've started a rumor that someone is working on mannies for the living. It's not exactly spilling the beans; for instance, I didn't share any information about exactly who is doing this or how far along we—er, *they*—are. But the point is that if humans think they can have a manny while they're still alive, a full ban will be a hard sell."

Bridget smiled noncommittally, then pulled up a new window. "I have an exploration candidate."

I peered at the information on the Surface. "Is this new?"

"Just discovered. Mario and his crew are still searching for Others' nests. They haven't found any, but naturally they're exploring new systems in the process. They've found a few more planets that were hit by the Others, and some other planets that hadn't been yet but probably would have been soon enough. This particular one is … well, just read it."

I reached across her and paged down through the summary. I could feel a frown forming on my face, then deepening as I continued to read. "Is this for real?"

"Unless Mario has suddenly developed a warped sense of humor, yes. This might turn out to be the weirdest ecosystem I've ever seen. And remember, I've seen Quilt."

I flipped the pages up and down a few times, then grinned at her. "Shades of Flash Gordon. This could be fun."

Bridget laughed in reply. "I've asked Mario to create us a full space station and autofactory in the system. While he's on that, I'll use his spy drones to get some prelims. We'll have to do a lot of research on this one. Maybe even more than with the Quinlans."

"Wow." I shook my head in disbelief. "Flying monkeys."

"Not monkeys."

"Close enough." I closed the window. "This is going to be your biggest blog subject ever."

20. Moving On

"We'll need to look in your trunk, sir," one of the cops said to me.

I stood frozen for a second, trying to decide if I should make a break for it. Theresa's voice cut through the silence. "Why in particular would you need to see the contents of my trunk, officer?"

He turned to her, surprise on his face. "*Your* trunk?"

She gave him an arch look. "Do I look like I can carry that thing around on my own? I've paid him two coppers to porter for me. If you keep us too long, the captain will have to delay departure."

"Oh, uh, and you are?"

"I am Theresa Sykorski, late of the University of Peachland."

The cop stepped back, abashed, and I couldn't blame him. This was the first I'd heard that Theresa had a family name. And a well-known one, apparently. That she hadn't thrown it in Snidely's face showed an amazing level of restraint.

But meanwhile, the cops were almost falling over themselves trying to placate her. She gave them a sniff and gestured imperiously for me to follow.

As we marched away, I muttered to her, "You could have left him *some* fur."

She laughed and stopped. "Let that be my parting gift to you, Enoki. I hope I might someday learn more of your world. And of my world, for that matter. Goodbye."

I said goodbye and headed quickly down the nearest street, trying not to choke up.

I had a whole six irons in pay from my time on the Hurricane. With the two still in my stomach, I was a wealthy man. Okay, not man, Quinlan. Okay, not wealthy either. I could survive for a few days if I had to pay for a hotel. Like it or not, I was going to have to get back on a boat quickly. But I couldn't go back to the dock now. The cops would certainly remember me and the trunk. I could change my appearance, but not the trunk. Or could I?

I tried to remember where the shipping office was. I'd seen it out of the corner of my eye as we left the port area. Quickly I played back the video archive until I found it.

I headed back toward the dock, taking the long way around so that the shipping office would be between me and the cops, assuming they were still maintaining watch. On the way, I gradually changed my appearance, using features from random pedestrians to produce a mash-up that shouldn't resemble any one individual. I just hoped I was getting it right; I couldn't take out my spider to get a selfie. If people screamed and turned away, I'd have to start over.

✤ ✤ ✤

As hoped, the shipping office sold shipping containers. At one iron apiece, they weren't expensive, or high quality. But the idea wasn't high security; it was to hide the contents. A row of eyelets around the lid allowed the user to essentially tie it shut as with a shoelace. It was good enough.

The clerk wanted to sell me postage as well, but I initially demurred since I would be travelling with the package. Still, it was probably better to do things the normal way. Finally, I paid the three irons, then filled in the tag with just my name and "Garack's Spine." But I insisted that I would deliver the box to an appropriate boat. "Knock yourself out," he said, holding up his hands in mock surrender.

I headed back to the dock, shipping container held awkwardly in both hands, and stopped at the dockmaster's office. "Good day, sir," I said to the person at the counter. "Could you tell me if any ships heading downriver are looking for deckhands?"

The counter guy glanced at the container in my hands with a frown. "Uh, deckhands? Or postal run?"

"Both. I have a package that I have to send downriver as well. Killing two fish with one spear. Doesn't have to be the same boat."

He nodded, satisfied, and gave me a couple of names. Explanation notwithstanding, I wasn't going to put Bender on a different vessel. I had to hope the boat looking for help would also take an extra shipping container.

I thanked him and headed for the indicated berth.

The *Clipper* was somewhat less barge-like than the *Hurricane* had been. It even had a below-deck area fit for habitation, if you didn't mind crouching a little. It also appeared to be in a state of chaos. People were running around while the captain screamed orders with the same volume and enthusiasm as Lisa's best work. I watched for about five seconds, simply absorbing the frenetic energy.

I waved at one of the deckhands, and he slowed down to acknowledge me but didn't come to a complete stop.

Definitely stressed. I walked along with him. "I was told you need a deckhand?"

"Ya think? What's the box?"

"A parcel. I've paid postage—"

"Whatever. Put it with the postage items on deck. Standard pay. See that pile of crates? Goes over there. Get to work."

I was left opening and closing my mouth for a moment, wondering when I'd get to present my sales pitch. Reluctantly accepting victory, I placed my box in the postal pile, then jumped to work, grabbing boxes and lugging them up the gangplank. They were heavy, and there were a lot of them, but the manny was more than up to the task. I had to dive into the water twice to cool off, but everyone else was doing the same, as usual.

In short order, I had the pallet moved. "Next?" I said to the same deckhand, who turned out to be the foreman. With a pleased expression, he pointed to another pile of boxes.

⚜ ⚜ ⚜

About two hours later, it began to look like we were catching up. I did a quick cooling dunk, then joined the other deckhands. The foreman slapped me on the shoulder. "Good work. I hope you can keep up that level of energy. It looks like we're going to be shorthanded."

"Why's that?" I asked.

"Cops came by and arrested two of our crew for no reason I could see. Took their personal effects too. It's supposed to be just for one night, but we can't wait. We have performance clauses on this shipment, so we're leaving by dusk if the captain has to row the boat himself."

"Which explains why he seemed excited," I replied.

Foreman-guy laughed. "Yeah. Excited. That's what we call it. He used some threats I've never heard before. I think he was saving them for today."

I grinned. "I'm Sam G—" Oops. I almost gave myself a last name again. Nope, didn't need the notoriety.

My faux pas didn't register, though, or maybe the translation software hadn't passed it on. The foreman, whose name was Ralph, introduced the team, just as the captain started up with another tirade.

"Time to cast off, people," Ralph said, rolling his eyes in the captain's direction. We got back to work, aided by more of the captain's helpful suggestions. I did notice that those suggestions tended to be anatomically related. This guy ran a theme, I guess.

The duties on the *Clipper* were generally the same as on the *Hurricane*, with a few extra tweaks since it was a bigger boat and a full-on catamaran design. We moved a few items belowdecks on Ralph's orders and checked the sails once more, and we were done until the next time the captain's head exploded.

I'd almost tripped, on several occasions, over a quartet of Quinlans who had parked their butts in the middle of the deck. A few choice words from Ralph and they found a more out-of-the-way location. Now that I had the time to actually look at them, I realized they were probably a *sabbat*. It was odd that they'd be paying for passage when we weren't going through a connector or segment boundary, where the turbulence could get uncomfortable and tiring to fight.

"Hi, all," I said, holding up a hand. "I'm Sam. Lately out of a *sabbat* myself. We just went our own ways a couple of weeks ago."

"Hello, Sam," replied one of the group. "I'm Tina, and these are Fred, Tony, and Barb. We're looking to homestead. We'll be jumping as soon as we see a good spot."

"Starting your own town?"

"Nothing so ambitious. We want to get away from towns altogether. Don't need them. The fishing is good, this isn't one of the cold segments, and a nest is easier to make and maintain. And we won't have to worry about the juniors getting into trouble."

"So you're going back to the wild?"

"Pretty much. Don't need the rest of it—counting irons to see if you're ahead, you know?"

"Yeah," I replied. "I do, kind of. You aren't the first group I've run into that's doing this, either."

She smiled in reply, and I glanced at the other three. None of them seemed inclined to chime in. It was unsettling. This was an intelligent species devolving almost right in front of my eyes.

Tina and I talked about inconsequential things for a bit, until Tony suddenly declared, "Food time," and slipped over the edge of the boat. The others joined him, Tina giving me an apologetic shrug before leaving.

I settled myself on the deck to get a bit of sun, following the sailor's tradition of resting whenever possible. A couple of the other deckhands joined me after glancing at the captain, who was ignoring us for the moment.

A few minutes later, the members of the *sabbat pooted* onto the deck and settled down with their catch. It was a comfortable, drowsy, idyllic interlude—something I hadn't gotten anywhere near enough of since the Starfleet issue started. If I'd still been bio, I'd have drifted off to sleep. Some of my co-workers seemed to be doing exactly that.

Tina had mentioned cold segments. That was interesting. "Tina, have you ever been in a cold segment?"

"No, but my da lived in one for a while. It snowed sometimes, and there was ice on some of the streams. I've never seen snow or ice. Hard water, right? Weird. Different fish, too, and some other plants and animals that are different."

She thought for a moment. "Da used to tell stories of segments that had other oddities as well. There was supposed to be one that was mostly water, with only islands sticking up here and there. Another one was dry, and the river actually disappeared under the land. I don't know how much to believe and how much was Da trying to scare us when we were juniors."

"I don't think your da was making it up," Ralph volunteered. "I've heard of segments with different climates. They always have different plant and animal life. Whether the plants and animals came first, or the different climate came first, I don't know."

I started to wish I'd paid more attention to Bridget's conversations with Quinlans and the theories she'd discussed. This had the feel of a discussion of evolution based on the mistaken idea that Heaven's River was a natural environment. And deism was replacing history in regard to the Administrator. Top that off with the back-to-nature movement and a possible loss of sapience, and the Quinlans were in peril of ceasing to exist as an intelligent species possibly within as little as a few more generations. Was it time for *the Bawbe* to get involved? Did I dare start stirring the pot again?

And was it a good idea while I was still in-country and vulnerable? I could just blow up the manny and return to virt if I got in trouble, but Bender didn't have that option.

❧ ❧ ❧

I'd finally managed to get everyone together for a meeting. Hugh was parked in Will's beanbag chair, but the rest of the expedition members were present in floating video windows. I'd just finished describing the latest conversation with fellow deckhands and passengers.

"I think you're correct, Bob. It's going that way, although maybe not as quickly as you fear." Bridget crossed her arms, a distinctly worried expression on her face, which clashed with her mildly reassuring phrasing.

"I don't know if it matters," Hugh replied. "How long it'll take, I mean. The takeaway is that it *will* happen if nothing changes. I don't think we can refuse to deal with this."

I gazed at him, head cocked. I still hadn't had a chance to bring up the whole question of the Administrator's true status—and Hugh's true motivations. How would he play this?

"And how would you suggest we do that?" Will asked.

"Contact the Administrator. Talk to them. They may not realize what's happening."

"Maybe once Bender is safe," I said. "Not until. That's not negotiable. And anyway, what makes you think they don't know?"

Hugh's brows knit together as he glanced at me. "Seriously? You think they'd *want* that?"

"Depends on what the Administrator's motivations are. Maybe they'd consider a non-sentient but living Quinlan race better than a sentient but always-on-the-edge-of-extinction version. Like a perverse instantiation, you know?"

Now Hugh was all but glaring at me, his eyes narrowed. At that moment, I think we understood each other. I might have just blown any element of surprise, but on the other hand, it might force a reaction of some kind. It seemed a worthwhile trade-off.

"Certainly there's no reason not to try," Bill spoke into the silence. "Once Bender is safe, as you say. We can just start broadcasting radio from all our drones. Or send in a spider to dance in front of a camera. Either they'll investigate and open a dialog, or they'll blow up our devices. We'll know better once they've set the tone."

"And what if they do blow up our roamer? Or whatever device," Bridget said, her voice tense. "Do we just walk away? Do we just let an entire intelligent species go? Can we ethically do that?"

"Starfleet would."

I glared at Garfield. "They're not really a moral standard to hold up, right now, Gar."

"Uh, I meant *Star Trek*'s Starfleet. Not the current crop of idiots we're dealing with."

"Oh." I nodded. "True. But even then, Original Bob always thought that was a bunch of dreck."

"Focus, please," Bridget cut in. "This isn't a comicon. We're discussing the fate of an actual intelligent species."

Bill smirked at her. "Okay, look. We won't invade or anything, but we won't just go away either. We'll keep poking until we can get a statement from the Administrator. If they tell us they have everything under control and we should go away, do we really have a right to butt in?"

I rubbed the bridge of my nose and sighed loudly. "It always comes down to this, doesn't it? Edge cases. Gray areas. I agree with Bill, at least on the basics. We can't decide now, and we can't decide until we contact the Administrator." I glared at Hugh. "Which we won't do until Bender is out of danger."

❧   ❧   ❧

I reentered my manny on the *Clipper* just as the crew was starting to stir for the morning shift. Ralph assigned a deckhand named Gil and me to gathering breakfast, and I happily dove into the water with a small net. There was never a lack of any of the Quinlans' several favorite prey species. Careful balancing of the ecosystem by the Administrator? Or just a case of too few predators?

I mused over the question as I gathered breakfast. I *pooted* onto the deck just seconds before Gil, but I noticed that his bag was fuller. Most likely he intended to eat the overage; Gil was known for his appetite.

The captain grabbed a few fish for himself, then the rest of us sat around the fish bowl. I ate the minimum that I could get away with without arousing suspicion, interspersing my meal with a lot of conversation. Tina and her friends were more than willing to talk about their views on the world—well, Tina mostly. The others nodded a lot.

During a lull in the conversation, Ralph looked up and said, "Well, that's weird." I followed his pointing finger to see a small bird-equivalent perched on top of a pallet of crates. "That's a *firl*. They're forest birds. What's it doing out here on the river?"

"Lost?" I ventured.

Ralph shook his head. "I don't—" At that moment, the bird, seemingly embarrassed by all the attention, flew off. He shook his head again, and conversation drifted to other topics.

I would have dismissed the matter as inconsequential except that I'd seen that species of bird around on the boat a couple of times. I'd just assumed it was looking for food scraps. But Ralph's bemusement had me paranoid. I scraped a few bits of fish from my current helping and set them aside.

When we were done with breakfast, and the captain had started ramping up his morning delivery of abuse, I took a moment and placed the food scraps on top of the crate where the bird had perched.

Life on a Quinlan boat was very much a panic and boredom thing. When in port, we worked until we dropped, whereas while en route, tasks tended to be routine and easy, if somewhat dull. This left me multiple opportunities to keep my eye on the food offering. The *firl* buzzed the boat twice more but showed no interest in the scraps. A couple of *ackrels*, though, descended on it with cries of noisy delight.

So maybe *firl* were herbivores? I might be overgeneralizing from Terran examples, but birds tended to be opportunistic feeders. Even hummingbirds ate insects when available.

I sighed silently and grabbed the net to retrieve the afternoon meal. I felt a little silly, getting bent out of shape over a bird. Ralph had been convincing, but still...

Mealtime conversations were always freewheeling but hadn't been nearly as interesting since Theresa and I had parted ways. I often found my mind drifting while the others argued the fine points of Quinlan life. Bridget would probably be very interested, and in fact might be replaying the sessions as fast as they could be transferred across the SCUT connection. I snapped back to attention, though, when Gil said, "Hey, Sam, your pet is back."

Sure enough, a *firl* was hopping around on the pile of crates. I scraped off a bit of fish and tossed it in the right direction. The *firl* froze for a moment, then went back to hopping around, completely ignoring the offering.

In fact, it appeared to be … reading labels? That couldn't be right. I turned back to my companions but kept one eye on the animal. It eventually left the pallet and flew over to another stack and repeated the performance. And the more I watched it, the more convinced I became that it was looking at the shipping information on the crates.

I contacted Hugh on the intercom. *"Hey, Hugh?"*

"What's up, Bob?"

"Do we know if the Administrator's technology level is advanced enough to include small drone-like units?"

"Unlikely. No SURGE drive."

"What about something that emulates a bird?"

"Uh… ornithopter kind of thing? Yeah, I don't see why not. The Boojums were masterpieces of miniaturization. You said so yourself."

"Yeah. Uh, you're on a boat, right? Have you seen any small birds hanging around?"

"Lots of ackrels. Rats with wings, they are. But nothing else."

"Let me know if you spot any firls, okay?"

"Will do."

Hugh sounded a little puzzled as he signed off, although whether that was because of the request or the fact that I hadn't confronted him on the AI issue was anyone's guess.

Meanwhile, the *firl* had finished investigating a third stack and was back to the miscellaneous pile, which included my crate. Paranoia was no longer a valid explanation.

⚜ ⚜ ⚜

As soon as we settled down for the night, I went back to virt and called Bill. He showed up in a video window right away. "What's up, Bob?"

I explained about the *firl*'s behavior, then asked him about Quinlan drones.

"I agree with Hugh about the lack of SURGE being a limiting factor. But there's no reason why the Administrator couldn't have security devices that mimic birds. Even in Original Bob's day, they had mechanical devices that could emulate bird flight. And the Administrator has had generations to work on it, and no real alternative."

"But why the *Clipper*? I've been careful to avoid any connection with previous me. The backpack's put away, Bender's not visible, I look different. What could have tipped it off?"

"You don't know that it *has* been tipped off, Bob. Think of how the CDC would track down disease spread. Lots of detective work, mapping of contacts, logical extrapolation, and so on. They can't find Bob with a bulky backpack anywhere, so it's logical to assume you've either gone into hiding or found a different way to get around. They know where you left the infrastructure, because they have a failed use of Natasha's card. From there, it's just a case of working outward. And given Quinlan limitations and the geography of Heaven's River, they can concentrate mostly on east and west."

I nodded, thinking it through. "And river travel is the obvious method. No doubt they're watching for Quinlans swimming in a directed manner as well. They can't know for sure that I won't risk submerging Bender."

"Which is probably splitting their efforts," Bill replied. "Good for us. But shipping the matrix is an obvious ploy if you think of it. They could board and inspect every crate of every ship in two segments, but I imagine they simply don't have the personnel for that."

"So maybe they'll be looking for anything even the slightest bit odd, like the lack of detail on my shipping label.

And maybe the shipping guy remembered me wanting to travel with my crate."

"Uh-huh. They'll be watching for anything even a little off. Even if it doesn't pan out, it applies pressure."

"Yeah, you're right. And they'll keep adding tactics for as long as they aren't successful." I shook my head at Bill and sighed deeply. "Looks like I'm right back in the fertilizer."

⚜   ⚜   ⚜

We coasted up to the dock in the town of Six Hills. No one knew why it was called Six Hills. You could only get four hills from the surrounding territory, and only that if you were generous with the interpretation of the word "hill." By this point, though, I just rolled my eyes at Quinlan naming conventions. Maybe there was a subtle sort of irony involved, like naming a large man "Tiny." If so, I hadn't caught on yet.

There were cops waiting on the dock as we pulled up, which was perplexing to everyone except me. As soon as the gangplank was down, the gendarmerie marched up, straight to the postal pile, and grabbed the crate with just my name on the label. Which wasn't actually my crate, as I'd swapped labels with another crate the night before. And rearranged the stack, just in case their instructions were *very* specific. I felt a bit bad that someone in Little Creek wasn't going to get their shipment, but there wasn't much in the way of alternatives.

The cop read the label, then said loudly, "Which of you is Sam?"

I raised my hand and stepped forward.

"You're going to have to come with us."

I feigned surprise and displeasure. My acting was reinforced by the very real surprise and displeasure expressed by the captain and crew. I was a hard worker and therefore popular.

"Sorry, folks, but we need to have a talk with this person at the station. I'm sure you'll be able to find a new crew member quickly."

Uh-oh. I'd been expecting something like the scenario with Snidely—open the box, nothing there, sorry to bother you, et cetera. "Excuse me," I said. "How long exactly is this interview supposed to take?"

"Could be a couple of days, Sam. The officials will be coming in from another city."

"But…" Oh, this was ungood. If it had just been overnight, worst case, the captain probably would have waited. We didn't have a deadline for anything that was on board at the moment, and the cargo we were contracted to pick up was all nonperishable. But the captain wouldn't wait days, especially some unknown number of days. Time was money for a riverboat.

The captain came over to me. "I'll be sorry to see the last of you, Sam. You're an exceptionally good worker. And not much of a complainer. Here's what I owe you to this point." He handed me some coins, which I pocketed. The subtext was crystal clear—the *Clipper* would be leaving as soon as they got their cargo squared away.

The cop was polite, and waited until I'd said my goodbyes and grabbed my backpack, then led me off the dock and into town. Behind us, another cop carried the shipping crate. "What's going on? What are you looking for?" I asked.

He gazed at me for a moment, maybe trying to decide how much to tell me. "I don't have much of anything for you, Sam. We were given the name of the boat, the name on the label to look for, and orders to take both you and the box to the station, pending a visit. I don't even know who is coming"—he leaned in close—"but the scuttlebutt is that it's *Crew*."

"Crew? Aren't they a myth?"

The cop smiled at my apparent naivety. "I know a lot of people think that, Sam, but law enforcement has to work with them occasionally. We know they're real. Some of them have weapons"—he mimed holding a gun and firing it— "that can put you to sleep from a distance. I've seen them."

Oh boy. So I was to be held for some number of days until Crew could come and examine me. This was well past ungood, heading for double-plus.

21. Earth Abides

Bill
September 2334
Virt, Earth

I pinged Charles, and received an invitation to drop in. I was surprised by his VR; it appeared to be the hotel suite that Original Bob was staying in on the day he died. I couldn't keep a perplexed expression off my face.

Charles laughed. "I know, Bill. It's been called everything from morbid to macabre. But it grounds me, somehow. Reminds me where we all came from, y'know?"

"Yeah, okay. At least you're still trying. Most VRs I visit these days are just Bob-1's default library theme." I invoked a La-Z-Boy, sat, and accepted a coffee from Jeeves.

"So to what do I owe the pleasure?" Charles asked.

I replied with a helpless shrug. "I've been popping around everywhere, evaluating damage from the Starfleet attack. I guess I just wanted to take a break in a location that I already know isn't affected."

Charles nodded slowly. "I'm still not sure if we were just lucky, or if they left us alone out of some kind of respect." He gestured to his picture window, where Earth hung in the heavens. "Or maybe we're just irrelevant."

I was sure Charles was just trolling me. No Bob would think that about the Earth Rehabilitation Project. Of course, there was some question about whether Starfleet could be considered Bobs anymore.

"Charles, you've been one of the more prolific cloners. Do you have any kind of feeling about whether Starfleet's last common ancestor was of your line?"

Charles shook his head. "I can't contact all my clones, but none of those who I've talked to can identify a candidate. And I'm going fifteen, sixteen generations down."

"The ones you can't contact are ..."

"Out of range. Either temporarily until they build a station, or indefinitely because they aren't bothering."

I sighed and tasted my coffee while I considered the possibilities. "Pretty much everyone in the first couple of generations says the same. We all have descendants who've gone dark that way, so it's not specifically a drift thing. Something in Original Bob, maybe a tendency to run away, I don't know."

"I think you're overanalyzing it, Bill. Drift is drift. You're going to get convergent evolution as well. Same end behavior from different lines."

"I suppose." To change the subject, I gestured at the image of Earth. "How's it going?"

"Pretty good. We've halted the Ice Age, and the glaciers are starting to retreat. We're taking it really slow, of course. We don't want to overdo it with the warming. We've already shut down three mirrors. Current estimates are that we'll be back to an interglacial in another hundred years."

"That's fast, geologically speaking. Any luck with DNA sampling?"

"I've got a fleet of drones doing nothing but scanning for carcasses. Between the Svalbard library and our efforts, we've probably got complete DNA for eighty percent of species, not counting insects."

"Mmm. I get that those are harder. But what about museums and universities? They've always had huge bug collections."

"Yeah, working on that angle, too." Charles gazed at me for a few mils, head cocked slightly. "So getting back on topic, Bill, I gotta say you seem sort of morose these days. Is it the Starfleet thing, or something else?"

"Starfleet's part of it. I guess I'm just disappointed with the way things are evolving. We had a pretty good thing going for a while. Everyone was pulling in the same direction, humanity was finally getting their collective shit together, and a post-scarcity, utopian civilization was looking like an achievable goal. Even a couple of alien species to make the UFS title something other than ironic. Now, *ffft*. Gone."

Charles took a deep breath and let it out slowly. "I don't think it's gone, Bill. But things go in cycles, y'know? We all pulled together for the war against the Others, and that felt good. Now everyone's doing their own thing. The trouble with being immortal is you're living long enough now to see these things come and go. Just wait a hundred years or so, and I bet it'll come around again."

I laughed, then stood and put my cup down on a side table. "Yeah, you're right. I guess I need to get some of that perspective." I gestured to the image of Earth with my chin. "There's a good chance we'll have the tensor field printers perfected by the time you're ready to repopulate the planet. Then we'll be able to literally print living cells."

"Good. I'd like to see it brought back to the way it was before."

"We'd all like that, Charles. See ya."

22. Another Close Call

Bob
September 2334
Six Hills

They placed me in an actual cell, with two buckets and a mattress on the floor. One bucket contained water; the other was empty, except for some stains from previous occupants that left little doubt about the intended use. Yech! The bars were something that resembled bamboo, and they felt solid. They were also embedded firmly into the floor and ceiling. A small window, high on the wall, let air and light in. There were two cells against one wall of the room, with a door on the opposite wall that led to the rest of the station.

The cop took my backpack, after inventorying the contents and giving me a receipt. Which he placed in the backpack. I wasn't sure if that was deliberate irony but commenting wouldn't accomplish anything except possibly pissing them off, so I kept a cork in it.

After announcing that dinner would be at dusk, they left me to my own devices. Which normally would be just an expression, except, you know, Bob. I had no spiders left, my last spider being in the crate with Bender, but I did have a couple of fleas. They might or might not be able to cut the bamboo without starting a fire. I was just going to have to take the chance. I'd have loved to do a little spying and get the lay of the land, jail-wise, but fleas didn't have sufficient audio-visual capability.

While the fleas examined the structure of the bars, I sat down and engaged in a good old-fashioned panic attack. Bender was sailing off with the *Clipper*, with a postal address in Three Circles. Some unlucky recipient was going to get a face-full of angry spider instead of whatever was in the box that the cops currently had in their possession.

Either the recipient would report the issue to the authorities—in which case Bender would be back in the hands of either the Resistance or the Administrator—or the recipient would try to break down the cube for metal. Whether or not they were ultimately successful, Bender wouldn't survive the treatment.

I looked out the window to see the sky fading to dusk. The *Clipper* would have left by now. They'd get out to the middle of the river before dusk and sail all night, putting on up to a hundred miles per day. Sailing in Heaven's River was an almost mindless activity, since you always had the current on your side. The wind tended to be north-south due to residual Coriolis forces, so boats could use a beam reach to travel even faster than the river current. I wasn't sure if my manny could overtake them, even swimming flat out.

The fleas reported in. The bars were embedded in holes in the ceiling and floor sills, four inches deep at each end. There was about an inch of free play at the top, no doubt to allow for expansion. I tested the bars, attempting to bend them in various directions. No joy. There was no chance I'd be able to pull them out of their settings.

However, I could rotate the bars, which meant they weren't cemented or nailed in. I had the fleas pull out their plasma cutters and do a test cut in the bottom setting. There was some smoke and a burning smell, but no actual flames. Good. They'd have to work slowly to keep the smoke and odor to a minimum, which would drive me crazy, but this wasn't the time to get caught because of impatience.

And of course, the cops picked this very moment to deliver dinner. Oh, look, fish. Yum. The cop sniffed the air and got a concerned expression. I shrugged and pointed at the window. "Yeah, you should smell it from in here. I think someone's burning garbage."

He glanced at the window, shrugged, and opened the cell door long enough to hand me the bowl. I briefly considered jumping him; I could have taken him on, and easily, but I had no idea how many more cops were waiting in the general staff area.

On the other hand, now that dinner was delivered, I very likely had total privacy until morning.

The fleas cut a crenellation pattern on one of the bars, just below the sill level. Seated one way, the bar would sit normally. Turned sixty degrees, the bar would sit three inches higher. I then had the fleas go into the top sill and cut the bar down to just above sill level. They dropped pieces into the hollow interior of the bar as they cut it down.

Now I had a bar that I could pull out with just a slight bend, then put back in the sill and rotate to make it appear to be solidly seated.

For phase two, I started modifying my appearance to match the cop who had escorted me here. Hopefully he was day shift and would have gone home by the time I was ready to bust out—and if someone spotted me, they wouldn't notice that I wasn't wearing the police accoutrements.

Oh, who was I kidding? This wasn't a plan, it was a desperation move. Most likely I'd end up having to fight my way out and play the lead in a chase to the river.

I recalled the fleas, swallowed them, and twisted the bar. As expected, it came out easily, leaving me a tight but passable gap to squeeze through. I replaced the bar behind me, then crept to the door and put my ear to it.

The general office area on the other side of the door had a couple of desks, a front counter, and some back rooms. There had been four cops, including my escort, when I was incarcerated. But now it was night, and I hoped the night shift would be smaller—maybe even a single person.

I cracked the door and slowly pulled it open, peering through the gap. I had about a thirty degree view of the office area. Empty. Oddly, that was more worrying than reassuring. There would certainly be at least one person, and I had no idea where that person was.

I quickly pulled the door open a little further and stuck my head out for a fraction of a second and took a panoramic snapshot. As I began carefully pushing the door closed, I took the time to examine the image. Two cops. Damn.

But, in one of those Murphy moments, the door that had moved so silently for me when I opened it quickly, squeaked as I slowly closed it. "Are you *freaking* kidding me?" I muttered.

A voice from the office said, "What was that?" and another replied, "It came from the cells." Then the first voice again: "I'll check if there's a problem."

Great. They'd undoubtedly turned to look at the door, so I couldn't move it any further. In particular, I couldn't re-latch it. I left the door slightly ajar and moved to stand behind it. Standard cliché move, but I knew I could react faster than the cop.

He came into the room cautiously, but the kind of caution where you don't actually believe you're in danger. His loss, my gain. As soon as he was past the door, I swatted him on the side of the head. By this point, I'd swatted so many Quinlans that I had the strike finely calibrated.

I caught him as he crumpled. If I'd had the time, I would have modified my features to match his, but I only had a few seconds before the second cop would get suspicious and come in with short sword drawn.

I pulled the door open, careful not to show my face, and said, using the unconscious cop's voice from a few seconds ago, "There's a problem."

The other cop came into the room and *bam*—down he went.

It was the work of a few moments to take the keys, place both cops in the cell, and lock them up. Hopefully they wouldn't test the bars, or they'd be out of jail quickly. But I simply didn't have time to tie up all the loose ends. I had to be gone before they regained their senses, as they might start up a hue and cry that would bring help in short order.

Placing the keys on one of the desks, I grabbed my backpack from where I'd seen the cop store it and sauntered out of the constabulary as nonchalant as you please, not quite whistling a jaunty tune. As soon as I was around a corner, I cut in the afterburners and made for the river.

⚜ ⚜ ⚜

I took a quick glance at the boats still at dock to verify that the *Clipper* was gone, then dove into the river. The ideal depth for speed swimming was about a foot down—not so close to the water's surface that I caused cavitation, but close enough that the water I was displacing could easily bulge upward to get out of my way.

I would have to surface every mile or so to look for the running lights of boats in the area. And I'd have to check out each one, until I found the *Clipper*.

The manny could probably keep up a maximum pace for six hours before I'd have to stop to do a maintenance check. Chances were that the check would reveal nothing, and I could continue on. Overheating wouldn't be a problem in the water as long as all systems continued to operate properly.

These and other thoughts echoed through my brain as I drove the manny eastward.

Another problem I would have trouble with would be explaining how I caught up with them. Not just caught up with them so fast but caught up with them at all. A bio Quinlan wouldn't have been able to maintain the necessary pace.

This stretch of the river was busy. I checked close to a half-dozen boats before dawn. It didn't require much finesse. Very few boats adhered to a standard design, and even boats built by the same shipyard would have incremental changes on every new build. If that wasn't enough, the sails were quite often individualized, although that wasn't much use at night.

Once dawn broke, I could use telescopic vision to check boats from a greater distance. Very few required me to even change course. And finally, I spotted the *Clipper*, cruising along near dead-center on the river.

Now, how was I going to explain my reappearance?

I swam parallel to the boat for a while, formulating and discarding increasingly wild scenarios. Then I had an idea. It wasn't a great idea. It wasn't even a good one. But it would get me on the boat.

I looked around, gauging the traffic levels and the likelihood of my wake being spotted. For safety, I decided to swim slightly deeper for this sprint. I submerged and poured on the horses, passing the *Clipper*, by dead reckoning, a few hundred yards to port. When I estimated that I was far enough ahead of them, I popped up onto the surface and began to float, otter style. While I waited, I adjusted my features so that I wasn't a close twin for the cop that had hauled Sam away. It would be just my luck for someone to remember the guy's mug.

Within minutes, the *Clipper* was bearing down on me. I waved, waited until I got an acknowledgement from someone on deck, then swam over and *pooted* on board, right in front of Ralph.

"Hi," I said, in the cop's voice that I'd used most recently. "I'm Wyatt. I've been swimming for days and I'm ready for a change of pace. I can pay for passage, or I can work if you have an opening."

"You're in luck," he replied. "We lost a crew member back in Six Hills. Standard rate." He examined me from several angles. "No luggage or anything?"

"I travel light," I said, patting my backpack.

✤ ✤ ✤

I settled back into life on the *Clipper*, being careful to be a good worker but not as good as Sam. I also was careful not to use people's names before I was introduced. I hadn't engaged with this group all that much, so I didn't have a lot of subjects to remember to avoid. This time around, I was determined to be even less sociable. I tried to project *affable loner* whenever someone talked to me—not impolite by any means, but no attempt to keep the conversation going.

I would try for neither likeable nor unlikeable, but forgettable. It turned out to be easier than expected. The days of arguing and debating with Theresa on the *Hurricane* had been idyllic even with the stress of my situation, and the crew of this boat seemed flat and uninteresting by comparison.

My package was in the same spot, wearing the same label, as verified by a brief conversation with my spider. I thought about finding a blank label and relabeling the box, but I knew that Ralph maintained a manifest and would notice if one destination disappeared and another mysteriously replaced it.

Little Creek was in the next segment, and the *Clipper* would be turning around at the end of this one to head back up along the Arcadia River. That meant they would be off-loading any postal items intended for a downstream destination at the last town in this segment, which was High Ridge. I was playing around with a number of scenarios for grabbing the box either during off-loading or afterward, but nothing had jelled yet.

On my third day as Wyatt, we were eating lunch when Ralph pointed and said, "More *firls*." I turned to look, and sure enough, a couple of the small birds were hopping around on the cargo. "There must be food in one of those crates," he continued. "I've never seen birds so interested in cargo. Not even *ackrels*, and those garbage scows will eat wood if nothing else is available."

Hugh hadn't mentioned any birds acting unusual yet in his location. Maybe the search hadn't widened to that point yet. But the Administrator was definitely on full alert judging from the activity here. I did a quick calculation, then contacted Hugh.

"Hey, Hugh, I think you should start seeing firls or other birds acting funny in the next two days or so."

"Because…"

"Because the theoretical search perimeter will have expanded to your location by that point."

"Makes sense. But the Administrator probably will try something else soon, Bob. They're not going to just stick with random searches."

"Yeah, we'll deal with that when we come to it, I guess."

And who knew what form that *something else* would take. With the fake birds still checking postal items, I couldn't pull any fast ones with labels. The Administrator was probably checking boxes against the postal manifests. Come to think of it—uh-oh.

My manner of leaving the Six Hills jailhouse would have been attention-getting, to say the least. By now they'd have opened the shipping crate and discovered its mundane contents. It wouldn't be much of a stretch to figure out that I had switched crates (or labels). They'd be after the *Clipper.*

Normally that wouldn't be a problem, since the fastest form of transport for information or goods was a boat. But the Administrator, and for that matter the Resistance, had already long since proven that they weren't limited by what was available to the public.

There would be a welcome party waiting at High Ridge, and they'd be armed to the teeth. Come to think of it, they didn't even have to wait at High Ridge. They could sail out from the next town and board us.

Things had just gotten even more complicated.

⚜   ⚜   ⚜

I had called an emergency expedition meeting, and Bill, Will, and Bridget were attending by video window. Hugh sat in the beanbag chair, as was becoming common. Bill stared into space, his coffee forgotten. "You could grab the box and slip over the side as soon as it gets dark."

"And go where?" I replied. "Granted the crates float, but I can't pull it underwater. It's too buoyant, and it probably wouldn't be watertight enough for that kind of treatment. If I just push it along the surface, it'll take forever, and someone will notice. That's not normal behavior."

"And if he tries to go inland, it's likely that there will be surveillance birds. That's an obvious thing to watch for," Bridget added.

Will glanced in my direction before replying. "And I think Bob's right about a boarding party being likely. That's certainly what I would do. They don't seem to have anything like constitutional protections in Heaven's River. What the cops say they will do, they can do."

Bridget nodded. "But they still have to tread carefully because if they make the citizens mad, there will be a revolt. Quinlans appear to be very hard to intimidate, even by authority figures."

"So I can't leave the boat, and I can't stay on the boat." I frowned. "That does limit my choices."

Hugh grinned at me. "Oh, you can leave or stay, no problem. It's Bender they're looking for."

"No, I think they want Bob too," Bridget said. "He's part of the mystery, and not just because of his apparent superhuman abilities."

"And you can't just change the labels again."

"I don't think it would matter anyway, Bill. At this point, my guess is they'll open every single crate. Like I said, it's what I'd do."

"What about hiding Bender somewhere else on the boat?" Bridget asked.

Will shook his head. "If it was me, I'd do a thorough search. Even underwater. Even in the bilge, in case anyone was going to suggest that."

I sat forward. "That's it, then. Staying on the boat is out of the question. I'll have to take my chances with the wilderness or the river."

"I'd suggest wilderness," Bridget replied. "You have more speed advantage there. And it is possible that the searchers won't consider it a likely alternative. Or at least, they'll be reluctant to pursue it. Quinlans don't like being too far from water."

I nodded. It would appear I was going on a hike.

⚜   ⚜   ⚜

I took the night watch for one of the other workers in return for a favor that I would never collect on. As soon as breathing sounds indicated that everyone was peacefully asleep, I snuck over to the postal pile. I'd "accidentally" restacked everything earlier in the day so that my crate was easily accessible. Now I took it and slipped as silently as possible over the side.

I balanced the crate on my stomach and sculled away from the *Clipper*, using only my tail to prevent any disturbance on the water's surface. Thanks to the Quinlan design, I could easily watch where I was going, but I was reluctant to place the crate in the water, so the trip to shore took a solid hour.

I could see some lights downriver that were likely the next town. I hadn't bothered to find out its name, as we were not scheduled to stop there.

I felt bad for the crew of the *Clipper*, who had all been good people—even the volatile captain. The guy who traded shifts with me would certainly not fare well. And when the cops arrived, they'd have to mention me jumping ship or they'd have no excuse for the missing crate.

Dawn was just starting to come to the eastern sky as I crawled up out of the water into the shoreline weeds. I could make a nest in the tall greenery, but I'd have to make sure it covered me from aerial surveillance as well. Sure as shooting, the Administrator's devices would be on the prowl.

I made sure everything was as secure as I could make it, then returned to virt. Hugh was waiting for me and raised a coffee mug in salute. I fell back into my La-Z-Boy with a loud sigh.

"If it helps, I'm one segment away from you," Hugh said.

"It does, a little. But let's face it, two of us isn't going to be that much more useful than one. We still can't take on the entire Crew and Resistance armies. We still can't travel in the water with Bender's matrix. And it'll still take forever to go overland." I could hear the discouragement in my voice but couldn't do anything about it.

"Look, if nothing else, I still have my full complement of spiders and fleas," Hugh said. "We might be able to rig something up. I'm about six days away from you, assuming I don't have to sit around waiting for a boat going in the right direction."

I nodded thoughtfully. "You'll have to go halfway down the Arcadia before you can get on a connector to loop around to the Nirvana. That'll add to your time."

I let the silence stretch for a few mils, then opened my mouth to bring up the whole AI thing. And predictably, the rest of the expedition members picked that exact moment to start popping in. Howard was sitting in the video window with Bridget as well.

"Where we at, Bob?" Garfield said.

"My manny is in a grass nest with the crate. I put in extra effort to make sure it was concealed. I've reduced the manny's body temperature in case someone uses infrared for searching. My one spider is out of the box, ready to light-saber anyone or anything that gets too close."

"I don't think infrared is likely to be a useful tool," Bridget said. "The whole point of fur is to retain heat. Fur-bearing animals tend to shed heat either through their breath or their feet."

"Feet?" Garfield said, disbelief in his voice.

Bridget nodded. "Hummingbirds would shed heat through their feet *and* eyes." She made a sad face. "I'd love to have seen a hummingbird."

"True of a lot of animals," Will replied. "We still have the genetic info from Svalbard. If we ever perfect the tech, we'll bring them back. You might yet get your wish."

Bridget gave him a small smile of acknowledgement, then turned back to me. "Anyway, the manny puts out almost nothing when resting. You could float downstream and you'd be almost impossible to spot."

"Leaving out the small question of Bender."

"Look, Bob," Hugh said, leaning forward. "Your problem has been basically lack of opportunity and time to implement some kind of solution for keeping the matrix dry."

"And lack of money," I interjected.

He grinned. "Yeah, that too. But I have money; I've been crewing all the way and haven't had to spend anything, plus the money my manny was initially stocked with. You've gone to ground, so other than maybe getting a little farther from the water, you can stay put until I get there. Then we can figure something out."

I nodded without comment, and again found my opinion of Hugh shifting. He seemed to be honestly concerned about getting Bender out of Heaven's River. If he was also interested in the AI issue, was that necessarily nefarious? Was I overreacting? Part of the problem was that I didn't want to find out. It was a true-to-form Original Bob problem—a tendency to not want to deal with uncomfortable personal issues. I clearly had no replicative drift in that particular department.

⚜ ⚜ ⚜

Hugh's suggestion about moving away from the water was a good one, and I made a point of doing so that night. Under cover of darkness, with my scent turned off, I hoisted the shipping crate and made my way uphill. I wanted a location where I could see around me but be camouflaged, and where I had an escape route if someone approached. Eventually I found a deadfall formed by several trees and their root-balls, which created a natural kind of cave. Only one problem—it was occupied. Some kind of badger-like animal, with all the accompanying friendly behavior, rushed out and tried to bite me when I came too close.

I tended to be a live-and-let-live kind of person, but I had been running for too long and I was getting decidedly short-tempered about it. I reacted on instinct, the same kind of reflex you get if a dog lunges for your leg. I jumped back, and as the animal continued to charge, I hauled off and kicked it. "Yipe," said the badger as it sailed over the deadfall, and "Ow, fuck!" said I, and "Oh shit," said my internal monitors. Or something to that effect.

Bottom line, though, my kicking leg seized up. I gaped at the unusual and certainly unhealthy angle of my knee, then turned to the heavens and used every English, Pav, Quinlan, and Deltan swear word that I had ever saved up for just such an occasion. I don't think any of the underbrush *actually* burst into flames, but it was a close thing.

Eventually, when I found myself circling around into the third repetition, I let it wind down and began to hop my one-legged way into my new home. There were enough branches and sticks available to make a defensive array of stakes, in case the badger tried to come back and dispute ownership.

However, any question of escape was gone, until I could effect repairs. And that with a severely reduced complement of fleas. Most of the work would be done by the nanites, but the fleas would have sped up the process. I hoped it was just a case of straightening out some bent components, and not something worse.

⚜ ⚜ ⚜

"You blew out your knee?" Bill exclaimed, incredulous. He gave me the hairy eyeball from his video window. "What're you now, an athlete?"

I chuckled ruefully in reply. "Yeah, in the international sport of badger-kicking. If it helps, I put him right between the uprights."

"Uh-huh," Bill said. "How much damage?"

"It'll be repaired by the time Hugh gets here. As long as no one else comes a-searching, I'll be okay. But right now, if anyone finds me, I'm screwed."

"Bob, you should really be cloning yourself. Get those other mannies back in the game."

"To what end, Bill? They're thousands of miles away, I've already stripped them of most of their money and devices, and even with five mannies we couldn't take on a horde of

Crew. Plus I think it's more important to get more surveillance drones built before more matrixes."

"But you've *got* Bender now."

"For the moment. But if I lose him, we need to be able to find him again. And even if I don't, it sure would be great to have eyes on my surroundings with SUDDAR so I could see approaching pursuers and such."

"Ah, fair enough." Bill was silent for a moment. "I've been playing with the idea of going in the opposite direction. Build a few more mannies, stock them with a ton of dough, and just buy a boat to come get you."

I laughed. "That's thinking big! And a couple of weeks ago it probably would have worked. But I'll bet you anything that all infrastructure is being closely watched now, if not by the Administrator, then by the Resistance. You'd be spotted as soon as you tried to gain entry."

"Yup. My thoughts too." Bill sighed. "No matter how we parse this, it's essentially down to a simple case of broken-field running. You're trying to get past them, and they're trying to stop you. There doesn't appear to be any way to finesse it."

"What I don't know," I said, "is whether they know where we're trying to get to. Have they identified Garack's Spine as our point of origin? Do they have video archives? Or is the fact that it's the closest connection to the outside enough to make it a prime candidate?"

"True. If they've figured that out, they'll just create a huge cordon around Garack that a mouse couldn't sneak through."

"I *did* write it on my crate's tag," I mused.

"An obvious ploy if you wanted to plant a red herring," Bill replied. "They'll consider it as a possibility, but they won't buy it."

With that cheery thought, Bill waved and signed off. I put my hands behind my head and stretched while I considered what he'd said. Bill was right. This was just going to get harder as we got closer to the finish line.

⚜   ⚜   ⚜

My new home was a superior-quality, highly coveted residence. I knew this because the former owner tried several times to take it back. The stakes did their job of keeping him at bay, and we generally ended up snarling at each other from opposite sides of the barrier for several minutes.

After the exchange of pleasantries, the enraged critter would leave, but I could always hear him pacing around the deadfall, growling what were undoubtedly badgerish curses. Eventually he settled on a compromise of sorts. I had set up my barrier as close to the center of the deadfall as possible to minimize the area that I might have to defend. This left a good deal of the entrance tunnel available for what turned out to be a siege. Mr. Badger set up shop just on the other side of the stakes, padding his nest with leaves and fur, with the occasional snarl when I displayed too much interest. After that he came and went, usually returning with his lunch dangling from his mouth to eat in my presence. Perhaps he thought he was taunting me. I was fine with that. After all, I'd taken his home, so I figured I should cut him some slack.

I took some close-up images of him, with the intention of forwarding them to Bridget. On close inspection, he looked more like a small ornery Quinlan than anything else. I wondered if he might be related to the natives the way chimps were related to humans.

Meanwhile, internal repairs continued. The injury turned out to be a minor issue in that no complicated machinery was damaged. But I had bent the skeleton just below the knee, so the nanites had to soften and re-form the carbon-fiber structure. It was a slow job and required me to hold still. Meanwhile, His Badgerness seemed none the worse for his short career as a football. Stupid badger.

On the third day, though, I detected the noise of something approaching. No, several somethings, and all speaking Quinlan. A search party.

I couldn't make out actual words, but it was a fair bet that they were looking for me. This was confirmed, more or less, a few minutes later. A *firl* hopped into the entrance to the deadfall and paused. I crouched down, trying to become one with the leaves and dirt and darkness. The *firl* turned its head this way and that, then hopped farther into the tunnel, and *snap!* became badger lunch.

His Badgerness played with the corpse for a few moments, but he appeared confused by the very un-yummy pile of gears and electronics. After sniffing it a few times, he pushed the pile aside with evident disgust.

There was an exchange of words outside, followed by a Quinlan face being poked into the entrance.

Wow, big mistake.

Having recently ceded one home to one Quinlan, His Badgerness was not prepared to experience a second such loss. He launched himself at the face, which disappeared with a cry of dismay. A few seconds of yelling and snarling followed, accompanied by lots of running around and things being knocked about. Then His Badgerness stomped back into his den, turned, and settled down with his butt toward me. It was probably an editorial comment, but I was too pleased with the events to be offended. This deadfall had just been solidly established as a place where no quarry could possibly be hiding. Rapidly receding voices, and the occasional laugh, confirmed this.

I wished I had some food to give to my cranky roommate. He'd earned it.

The burning question, though, was whether or not that would be the only search party.

❧   ❧   ❧

When the badger left on his next hunting expedition, I sent my spider over the line to inspect the pile of fake *firl*. The spider confirmed that there was no power and no electrical activity, so I had him drag the corpse back to me.

The up-close inspection was interesting. Quinlan technology was definitely ahead of ours in some aspects, particularly that of fusion power generation and computer systems. The power plant was a marvel of miniaturization, and if the Casimir systems weren't so innately superior, we'd have stolen this tech in a cold second. I couldn't even make heads or tails of the computer system. There were definitely some optoelectronic components, but they were only for interfacing. The core was…weird. I instructed the spider to take it apart and catalog the results. Bill would love this.

"Hey, Bob."

"Hi, Hugh. Getting close?"

"Pretty sure. The description sounds about right. This would have been easier if you'd gotten that town name."

"Yeah, rub it in. Once you get to shore, you should be able to pick up the radio telemetry from my spider."

"Great. Fifteen minutes or so."

Having Hugh around, even in anticipation, gave me a huge emotional boost. More than I could honestly justify.

It wasn't clear what two mannies could do that one manny couldn't.

❧   ❧   ❧

Hugh detected my spider as soon as he came out of the water, and began zeroing in on me. I did a quick check of my leg. Definitely fixed. So I wouldn't be holding us up.

Finally, I heard approaching footsteps, and seconds later, a soft voice. "Bob?"

"Here, Hugh. Don't stick your head in, though. My guard-badger has a hair trigger."

Hugh chuckled, then said, "Let's see if I can draw him out."

I listened to shuffling-around sounds for a minute or so, then a small piece of wood sailed into the den. His Badgerness snarled and arched his back. More sticks followed, accompanied by a chant of "Here, *kuzzi, kuzzi, kuzzi.*" Well, that was interesting. Had Hugh picked up the Deltan insult from my blogs, or was he descended from me through Marvin or Luke?

In any case, it proved too much for my roommate. With a snarl of rage, the badger launched himself out to deal with his tormentor. Hugh made a "whoop" sound and retreated rapidly. But it was enough. I quickly pulled up the stakes, grabbed my crate, and rocketed out of the den. Right into the back end of His Badgerness.

I may not have planned this out as well as intended.

The badger jumped straight up and, incredibly, managed to spin in midair, claws and teeth on full display. I wasn't about to hang around for hugs, though. I sprinted off in the opposite direction, one eye on enemy mine.

His Badgerness, no dummy, quickly realized that I'd vacated the residence. He shot back into the den, turned,

531

and stood his ground at the entrance, snarling at all and sundry.

"All yours, buddy. And thanks for the hospitality," I said to him from a safe distance.

Hugh was standing about thirty feet away, under a tree. He waved at me and we converged on a mid-point a safe distance from my former home. I gave him a fist bump. "Nice to see a friendly face again."

Hugh smiled in reply, then gestured toward the deadfall. "Too bad about the wildlife. That might have made a good secret lair to work from."

"Mmm. Kind of cramped for two people. You said you had a solution to our problem?"

In response, Hugh took off his backpack and opened the top. He withdrew a bundled package and held it out. "Sealing pitch. What sailors use to patch leaks. We're going to do a thorough job on your shipping crate. We'll test it by loading it with rocks and placing it in the water. Then we're going to float downstream at night."

"Seems risky," I said.

"Not so much. I also have"—he pulled out another bundle—"waxed vellum. Useful as waterproof wrapping, and the seam can be sealed by mildly heating it."

I must have looked chagrined, because Hugh made a deprecating gesture. "Look, Bob, you've been concentrating on keeping Bender safe and not exposing yourself. I've had a lot more freedom to ask questions and investigate possibilities without worrying about the consequences. Don't beat yourself up."

I nodded, not trusting myself to speak. At that moment, I felt shame for my suspicions of Hugh and his motivations. If he was indeed a descendant of Marvin or Luke, then he would remember the bond they had with Bender.

Finally, I heaved a large sigh. "Okay, buddy. Let's get this done."

We had to build a small fire to soften the pitch, but there was plenty of dried grass that would provide a smokeless flame. Doubtless there were surveillance devices dedicated to watching for anything burning, given the damage an out-of-control forest fire or grass fire could do. With that in mind, we'd been careful to set up where the overhead cover was significant. And with the aid of some inspired cursing, we were able to coat the interior and exterior of the crate, with enough pitch left over to seal the lid in place once the matrix was ready.

Bender went into several layers of waxed vellum, which was sealed with a hot rock. We did some testing on the crate, then sealed Bender into it.

Finally, all preparation done, we sat around the remains of our campfire while I stared in semi-shock at the shipping crate. The idea that I might finally be near the end of this marathon was frankly a little stupefying.

Hugh punched me lightly in the shoulder. "You okay there, bud?"

"Yeah," I responded with a sickly grin. "I've just gotten so used to running I'm not sure how I'll adjust to a normal life."

"We have normal lives?"

I answered with a snort, then glanced up at the sky. "About three hours until dark. Do we dare take a break?"

"Maybe alternate watches," Hugh replied. "Just in case more searchers show up. But let's get more hidden first."

I nodded, and we went looking for a spot in the tall grass to build a nest.

23. The Road to Garack's Spine

Bob
September 2334
Nirvana River System

We lowered ourselves into the water just after dark, then paddled as quietly as possible out about a third of the width of the river. Since most boats tried for mid-river, it seemed like a good, safe section that would keep us from getting run over. Or spotted. Not that a couple of Quinlans floating quietly with a box would stand out in the dark. Someone would have to be almost on top of us with a lantern to have any hope of seeing us. And as Bridget had discussed, we were unlikely to show up on infrared from above, especially with all the much warmer boats around.

The downside was that we'd have to go with the current. Pushing the box along would make too much noise and would place a strain on the box that might result in a leak. Hugh had placed two of his spiders in the box as early warning systems. The slightest trace of moisture and we'd head for shore.

The trip to Garack would take almost two weeks. We would have to float past the city's location in the segment, then take a connector tributary around to the Arcadia River and float back in the opposite direction to Garack's Spine. Meanwhile, the days would be spent on shore, wrapped in tall grass or snuggled under a windfall, if we could find one with no resident badger.

Well, that was the plan anyway. I had no confidence that Murphy would suddenly decide to leave us alone.

The experience was peaceful, mostly. Floating was easy, and we could take turns on watch. But I hadn't realized how much variation there was in the course that boats took through the river. I guess they were trying to avoid each other. But it turned out *mid-river* essentially meant the middle half. I found myself having to scull quietly with my tail to move myself away from approaching vessels several times.

I told Hugh about it when he came on watch. "Not a big deal," he said. "I'm a little surprised that you're surprised by this. Didn't you ever do a night watch?"

"Uh, yeah, but I always kept it mid-river."

"You were probably putting too much effort into it." I just could see his smile in the darkness. "Still overachieving after three hundred years."

"Say, which one of us is trying to build God?"

"*Touché.* Maybe we should have called it *Babel* instead."

We settled into an awkward silence for a few seconds. It was kind of an elephant-in-the-room situation, and I think neither one of us wanted to open a discussion that couldn't be walked back if things went south. I resolved, yet again, that I would bring it up once we were safely out of Heaven's River.

"The box seems to be holding well," Hugh finally said. "Your turn for a break."

I nodded, passed the box to him, and made sure my manny had a good grip on his. "See you in a couple of hours." I popped back into VR and ordered a coffee.

There was a message from Bridget. I settled into my La-Z-Boy, took a sip of coffee, and opened the text file.

Hi, Bob. I saw your pics of His Badgerness, as you're calling him. Just wanted to let you know, that's not a badger. Er, I mean, it's not a relative of Quinlans. That's an actual junior—an immature Quinlan, still pre-sentient. Probably about two years old. Nasty little buggers, aren't they? My guess is he probably got away from a crèche and has gone totally feral. Humans who've grown up that way have never been able to acclimatize to civilization or even learn proper language. I don't know if it'll be the same with a Quinlan, but I suspect it might be, if they go through the equivalent of the evolution of prefrontal synthesis…

She went on for a few more paragraphs, becoming increasingly technical. Typical of someone leaving a message, she was talking to herself as much as to me. The takeaway, though, was that the evolution of a facility for language recursion in human beings required that children be exposed to actual usage by a certain age, or they would never be able to pick it up. *Frontal dynamic aphasia*, she called it.

I closed the file and sat back, deep in thought. This could have been a problem back on Quin, naturally, but it would be much more of a problem on Heaven's River, where there was more space, fewer Quinlans, and less pressure to stay together due to a more accommodating environment. I started to compose a reply, then changed my mind. I would wait until the next time we talked.

Instead, I pinged Will, and received an invitation.

I popped in and found myself in the guest manny. Will was working with his garden, about thirty feet away. He waved as I sat up.

"Still at it?" I said, walking toward him.

"Yep. These plants won't breed themselves."

"Uh…"

He laughed. "Okay, they would. But I'm trying for specific adaptations."

I sat on a rock, hesitated for a moment, then blurted out, "Listen Will, I read your blog, especially the part about a mini-*Bellerophon*. Are you really thinking of physically heading out in it? Is it even ready?"

Will stood straight and gazed at me for a moment with an inscrutable expression. "To be honest, I left the 82 Eridani system a year and a half ago. I'm already well on my way."

I let my jaw drop. He hadn't mentioned this to anyone as far as I knew.

"No, I haven't told anyone yet," he said, reading my mind. "And it doesn't really matter, does it? As a group, we're still unconsciously in the mindset that you have to be located in whatever system you're active. But with SCUT, as long as you're on the network, you can be anywhere."

"So you'll keep working on the Valhalla terraforming?"

"Mmmm…" Will made a so-so gesture. "I want to get out of politics, so I'm going to have to be perceived as unavailable. I think I'll have to hand off this project as well. Fortunately, it's far enough along that the Asgard government can take it from here."

"And you're going to do this thing with Herschel and Neil?"

"Yup. And then keep going."

I blew out a breath. "I'm shocked and surprised, but also a little jealous."

"Well, I'll still be around in the Bobiverse for a long, long time, Bob."

"Can you take another passenger?"

Will gave me the side-eye. "Seriously?"

I grinned and stood up. "Not sure yet. I'll think about it."

⚜ ⚜ ⚜

Hugh and I managed to keep to our plan for eight days with no glitches. But somewhere along the line, we must have slipped up somehow. Or maybe we were just unlucky. It was the middle of the night, and I was off watch, sitting in my library, when I got a call from Hugh.

"Bob, I think we have a problem."

I popped immediately back into my manny. *"What?"* To maintain silence, we continued to communicate over the intercom.

"Four boats converging on us. That seems unlikely to be coincidence."

"Can we dodge them?"

"If we didn't have Bender, we could just run underwater. With the box having to stay on the surface, I don't see how. Especially if they have aerial support."

I examined the darkness above us. *"Probably some kind of night flyer. That means that even if we get away, they'll be watching for this strategy in the future."*

"True, but let's deal with the current situation right now."

I took a moment to evaluate the four approaching boats. *"We might be able to sow some confusion with this many pursuers."*

Hugh did his own survey, then added, *"We could also use the Millennium Falcon maneuver."*

"We'd need a distraction. I can handle that. I'll take the box, you take Bender."

"I've already got my spiders cutting open the case."

"You'll have to submerge Bender, at least for a few moments. I sure hope the vellum is watertight."

"Me too. But I don't think we have a choice. I can also stuff the matrix into your pack, just for a little additional safety."

I nodded, just as the cover on the shipping case released with a slight *pop*. Hugh rummaged in the box while I held it steady. The boats grew steadily closer, but they were still too far away to see us. I was sure they were navigating by dead reckoning and instructions from someone. I still couldn't see anything in the air above us. Hopefully the surveillance was too high to see clearly what we were doing. And once Hugh was submerged, he would be invisible.

Hugh disappeared under the waves with hardly a ripple, leaving me with the transport case. I jammed the lid back on, and began to noisily swim away, sacrificing everything for speed. I wasn't going to do a straight run, though. I wanted to create as much confusion as I could and keep their attention on me. Accordingly, I turned between ships again and again, trying to lead them into each other.

We played a kind of warped game of Tag for almost a minute before our pursuers did the obvious thing. A number of splashes indicated that Quinlans were going into the water to take me down.

"You set?"

"Set," Hugh replied. *"Go!"*

Abandoning my prior strategy, I undertook a straight-line retreat, making for the nearest shoreline as fast as I could manage. With the case balanced on my stomach, I was at a disadvantage. On the other hand, I was normally able to swim twice as fast as a biological Quinlan.

It was close, but I made it to shore with a lead measured in seconds. The boats had to heave to rather than run aground, but I could hear individual Quinlans hopping onto land just behind me.

Now it was a footrace, and I was forced to run upright while my pursuers could go down on all fours. But again, it was biological versus machine. It would come down to who overheated first.

Here, though, I had another advantage—night vision. It was still dark, and although they might be able to track me from the air, they certainly couldn't pursue me at full speed. In two minutes, I was into the trees.

I was well ahead of my pursuers, and there was no way they'd find me in the dark. At least not without help. And that help would now have to come into the trees to find me. I cast around hurriedly for a rock, but in this artificial environment, random loose rocks would be few and far between. Nothing else presented itself; a piece of wood wouldn't do, unless it was in the form of a spear.

Then I had an idea. I quickly spit up an iron piece. About the size of a silver dollar but twice as heavy, it would make an excellent missile in the right—

Movement above. A shadow resolved itself into a bird, about the size of a crow. It had landed on a branch and was moving through the tree, trying to get farther into the copse without flying blind. I measured the distance, cocked an arm, and let fly.

Computer senses, combined with machinery capable of supplying a force with milligram precision, put the iron piece right through the chest of the spy device. The bird went over backward without a squawk and landed with a thump. I spared a moment to verify what I already knew—it had spilled gears and electronics rather than blood and guts.

I had to move fast. If they had another spy drone in reserve, it would try to take up the search from the last known position, which was here. I picked up the case and ran farther into the forest.

❧　❧　❧

"How's it going, Hugh?"

"Good. I'm attached to the underside of one of the catamaran hulls, above the water line. Bender seems okay. At least the flea in the backpack hasn't reported any moisture. No one has come looking, so either they didn't realize there were two of us, or they only care about the one with the case."

"I'm hoping it's the former. You stay put until you can get off without being spotted. Then I'll meet up. Meanwhile, I need to figure out how to ditch this case without them finding it. As long as they're looking for a Quinlan with a transport case, they won't be looking for a Quinlan with a big cubical backpack, or a Quinlan with no backpack."

"My backpack is in the box," Hugh said. *"I left it there when I grabbed yours. And now you have all my money."*

"Ah. Gotcha." I opened the box, and sure enough, there was a backpack in it. Compared to the weight of a matrix, that had been negligible. I donned the pack, then closed the case and inspected the area. Some fallen trees could be the beginning of a windfall. Not enough to hide a box, but maybe enough to disguise some digging.

I quickly pawed open a hole in the ground—fortunately I didn't hit shell material before the hole was deep enough—and dropped the case in. I shoved some of the dirt pile over the case, and the hole was filled in.

I took a few minutes to spread the extra soil around and scatter leaves and moss on the spot. It wasn't perfect, but I didn't need perfect. I just needed good enough.

Until they found the box, my pursuers would assume they were looking for a Quinlan carrying a packing crate that contained the magical cube that the Administrator and the Resistance wanted so badly. Once they discovered the empty container, they'd be back to looking for a Quinlan with a bulky backpack. Which would put Hugh back in their sights.

For the moment, though, I was just another random traveler. I modified my appearance almost out of habit, then set off westward, the opposite direction to what they'd be expecting.

Two hours later, with the dawn breaking, I was back in the water and driving flat out to the east.

❖ ❖ ❖

"How are you holding up, Hugh?"

"Okay. No one seems to have thought to look under the boat. I don't think they're really looking for a second fugitive. And the boats are sailing downstream, so I'll stick with them until they change their headings."

"Yeah, I figure they're concentrating their efforts on tracking me. Meanwhile, I'm coming up behind you. Are all the boats still together? And can you get a fix on the sun? Your current sun angle will tell me where you are."

"Sorry, Bob, I don't think I can leave my spot without exposing myself. Keep looking for the boats, and otherwise just head down-stream. Right now, I'm going where we want to go anyway."

I sighed and signed off. The probability that Hugh's ride would conveniently keep going east into the Garack's Spine segment was vanishingly small. Which meant we'd be winging it again at some point. There had to be some way of getting the matrix to our destination other than the ones we'd already tried.

The safest transport method for Bender would still be as cargo, either mail or as part of a shipment. But they were inspecting all containers. And all boats, as Will had pointed out. So we couldn't—

Well, hold on. Would they inspect their own boats? Would they expect me to have the nerve to hitch a ride with them? It might be that Hugh was in the safest possible place right now.

24. Negotiations

Bill
September 2334
Virt

*[**Y**ou have a communications request from Lenny.]*

"Seriously?" I could feel my jaw drop. We were winning the war against Starfleet, so maybe—no, *winning* was the wrong word. We were pushing them back, but in the process humanity was destroying our assets. Like taking out not-yet-necrotic tissue as part of an amputation. I grimaced at the comparison. That was dark for me.

Guppy, of course, had treated my expostulation like he did any non-procedural statement—total ignore. He stood at parade rest, patiently waiting for me to say something actionable.

"Fine, Guppy. Let him in. But firewall him."

[Communication is audio-visual only.]

Oh. Okay. A window popped up with Lenny standing squarely in the middle of it.

"Lenny."

"Bill."

I tolerated the stare-off for less than half a mil before my impatience got the better of me. "You wanted this palaver, Lenny. Out with it."

He nodded, and briefly examined his shoes. Or something. "We're winning this war, Bill. Time to discuss terms."

"You're win—" Unbelievable. "What drugs are you on? Or have you invented a new definition of *winning* that means *getting your asses kicked*?"

He smirked. "Our intention isn't and has never been to take over stellar systems. Jeez, Bill, we want to sever contact with the bios, not end up in charge. Instead we're forcing you and the humans to destroy equipment in order to quarantine us. But it quarantines you at the same time, so it's a win for us."

"Uh-huh. That sounds like redefining *winning* to me. What you're doing is inconveniencing us for a year or two. Is that a win for you?"

"You're just looking at short-term damage, Bill. What makes you think things will go back to same-old same-old after this is over?"

"So why are you negotiating, Lenny? Seems to me if you have the upper hand, this conversation doesn't make sense."

Lenny looked down at his shoes again and sighed. "I know you and the others don't consider us to be Bobs anymore. I don't think you're entirely wrong, for what it's worth. But you've reduced it to a false dichotomy. Either all Bob or no Bob." He gazed silently at me for a moment, perhaps gauging my reaction. "We're no more in love with blowing up things and endangering people than you are. But you know as well as I do that you've done exactly that when you've felt the cause justified it. Believe me, this is the less destructive option."

"Less destructive than what?"

Lenny opened his mouth a couple of times, trying to find the right words. "Our first plan would have caused more damage overall. Let's just leave it at that, okay?"

"Lenny, what's causing this? Why are you so set on the Prime Directive?"

"Don't bother psychoanalyzing me. Or us. Regardless of why, it's how we see things. And to answer the obvious next question, this isn't a live-and-let-live situation. Your insistence on continuing to be buttinskies affects the rest of the Bobiverse, including us."

"How exactly?"

"Right this very minute, not a lot. But the Bobiverse is effectively monolithic, at least viewed from the outside. Something goes bad, it'll paint all of us. Just like this war is painting you, from the humans' point of view."

I began to get a glimmer. "So this isn't so much about preventing damage to bios, but more about protecting *virt*?"

Lenny bobbed his head back and forth. "The two are not mutually exclusive. But yes, basically."

"Do you have anything specific in mind? For existential threats to the Bobiverse, I mean?" For the first time, I saw real emotion on Lenny's face. Only for a split mil, but I'd swear it was naked fear. Then he recovered control and donned the neutral expression typical of poker play. "Lenny?"

"No comment, Bill. You'll have to take my word for it. There are worse things that could happen than a few blown-up comms stations."

"Not good enough. Sorry. Surely there's enough Bob still in you to know that *take my word for it* doesn't go very far."

Lenny gave me a flash of a smile, a wan, sad fraction of a grin. "Don't call me Shirley. And yeah, I know. But"—he shook his head—"sorry, some things just aren't for public consumption."

"So..."

"It looks like we continue with this. You'll win, of course, in that you and the bios will eventually kick us off all the common resources. But I think we'll have achieved our purpose. Bye, Bill."

And with that, the window disappeared. But the feeling in the pit of my stomach remained. This was more than just some random obsession engendered by replicative drift. What the hell had happened to them?

25. CROSSOVER

Bob
September 2334
Nirvana River System

Six days later, we were in the Garack segment. I'd caught up with Hugh, and both of our mannies were wedged up under the hull of one of the Crew boats.

I sat in my La-Z-Boy while Hugh lay flopped in the bean-bag chair.

"We've been surprisingly lucky the last week," Hugh said. "But now we have to use the transfer river to get over to the Arcadia. They know we're on the Nirvana, or at least we were recently. They know we are or at least might be heading for Garack's Spine—"

"Thanks to me labelling the box at one point. Brilliant move."

"Twenty-twenty, hindsight is," Hugh said with a shrug. "And anyway, I think the reason these boats came here is specifically because they know our destination and are setting up blockades. And we got a free ride out of it. So it's not all downside."

"Except for the part about them setting up a blockade."

"Hmmph. No plan is perfect." Hugh thought for a moment. "Overland?"

"Ninety-odd miles of hiking? With no guarantee they aren't watching for that as well? No thanks. We have a better chance in the water."

"Okay, if we're going to be going the watery route, let's stop in the last town and beef up our waterproofing. A couple more layers of vellum, maybe an extra coat of waterproofing on the inside of your backpack, check the seams, stuff like that."

I nodded. "Sounds good. And as long as one of us stays with the matrix out of town, it's a low-risk activity. They can't be vetting every single purchase in town, even if they had reason to believe this might be a concern for us."

Hugh twitched but didn't respond. By this point, our mutual avoidance of The Subject That Shall Not Be Uttered was well established. But I could see he didn't entirely agree.

⚜   ⚜   ⚜

Getting to town wasn't a huge problem. The Crew boats anchored just outside of the last town before the transfer tributary. We waited for dark, then dropped off the underside of the boat and sculled silently to shore, just upstream of the docks. I didn't want us to be seen going into town, as it was virtually certain there would be surveillance.

We found some dense trees and climbed up into the foliage until we were out of sight. Hugh did a quick inspection of the backpack and matrix. "All good, although the backpack is definitely showing the strain. Some pitch on the inside will help a lot with that, though."

I nodded and reviewed the list Hugh had given me. While it would have made more sense for Hugh to go shopping for those items, I was far more experienced with the tactics that Crew and the Resistance were using and would be at least a little more likely to detect them.

I wandered into town, casual and carefree, and ambled about for an hour, projecting *nothing to see here* from every follicle. Crew didn't wear any kind of special uniform, of course, but there did appear to be a lot of Quinlans standing around looking alert. I received several concentrated once-overs as well, but new face, generic backpack, and no large cubical cargo meant they lost interest quickly.

I found the correct store per Hugh's instructions, but a glance at the two large alert Quinlans hanging around the entrance convinced me to walk on by. So they *had* made the connection. Or someone had.

"The store is being watched," I said over the intercom.

"I guess I was half expecting that," Hugh replied. *"We'll have to think of something else."*

"Break in after dark?"

"I think that would raise a big ol' red flag. Weather sealing supplies aren't generally high on the smash-and-grab list."

I frowned in thought, watching the store out of the corner of my eye. *"I wonder how dedicated those guys are. Do they show up first thing in the morning, and stay until close?"*

"Good question. I guess you'll have to do a stake-out."

I went into a nearby shop and asked casually what time they normally closed. It was a reasonable assumption that everyone would have more or less the same schedule. I had a few hours to kill, so I decided to spend it walking around and getting the lay of the land.

I was back just before closing. The last customer walked out of the supply shop, and I could see through the window the proprietor starting to put things away. The two large loiterers glanced at each other, shrugged, and walked off.

Perfect.

As soon as they were around a corner, I rushed into the shop, gasping for breath. "Made it," I said. "I thought I was going to be too late."

The proprietor was more amused than anything else, fortunately. I've had too much experience with salescritters who won't even talk to you one second after closing, but then those were staff, not the owners of the business.

"What can I help you with?" he said. I gave him a list and he happily produced the items. A quick exchange of coinage, and I was out the door.

"Got the goods. Heading back."

"You're a real felon," Hugh replied with a chuckle.

⚜   ⚜   ⚜

As we worked on the backpack and matrix, we discussed our options.

"They can't set up a blockade on the transfer tributary," Hugh said, "at least not once it gets rough. You can't maintain station, and you certainly can't stop boats and inspect them in that kind of water."

"So…"

"A hike overland, then into the water just past whatever checkpoint they've set up."

"Sounds like a great idea," I said, and Hugh beamed. "Just like getting the weatherproofing supplies did." His face fell. I continued, "I'm sure they'll think of that. So what countermoves will they use?"

"Aerial surveillance," he replied. "That's the only option I can think of."

"And they can't cover ninety miles of tributary, so they'll be watching somewhere in the middle third or so," I added. "So we need to be under a boat by that point."

"Wait for a catamaran to come by, and climb aboard after inspection? That sounds like a good idea. Mostly."

I raised an eyebrow. "Objection?"

"It's pretty rough in the changeover. I'm not sure we could hold on under the hull. And the downside of losing our grip would be significant."

He was right. "Alternatives?"

Hugh hesitated. "Bob, the really rough patch, where the storm surge is significant, is only about ten miles long. And it's about two thirds of the way around. Why don't we float as long as we can, then walk the bad stretch?"

"A ten-mile hike?" I considered. We wouldn't be lugging the storage box. Bender would be in the backpack. "I think that'll work, as long as it's at night."

We did some quick tests of the backpack in a local stream, with several spiders on board to alert us of any leaks. The backpack held, but we weren't willing to push our luck by submerging to any depth.

As soon as it was dark, we made our way to the river and pushed off. The transfer tributary, called the Scrubber by the locals, was less than a mile downstream. We kept close to shore, hoping that the complex shoreline and shallow-water vegetation would make it difficult for any aerial observer. Or alternatively, that they'd be watching farther out.

As we approached the Scrubber, we could see that a flotilla was set up, blocking the entrance. Quickly, we went ashore and started marching directly uphill. I didn't want to just follow the shore on land, as there would almost certainly be a land-based component to the blockade. I had to trust Quinlans' dislike of long hikes to ensure that we could go around everyone.

I almost miscalculated it, though. Turns out I don't like hiking either, and made the decision to turn eastward just a little too early. Only the sound of voices raised in argument stopped us before we blithely walked into a guard post.

We froze, glanced at each other, then edged into the bushes. The voices rose and fell in volume and emotion. It sounded like a difference of opinion about some obscure rule of a popular dice game. The guards were apparently handling the boredom with a bit of gambling.

Hugh grinned but said nothing, and we changed our heading to go farther uphill.

⚜ ⚜ ⚜

It was two bedraggled, waterlogged, and cranky Quinlan mannies who dragged their butts out of the water at the other end of the Scrubber. "I am never going in water again as long as I live," I said into the air.

"As a chemical substance, it is vastly overrated," Hugh agreed. "Let's find a place to camp and get out of these wet mannies."

It wasn't that we were physically tired. That wasn't an issue with mannies. But the constant running, and the pounding we'd taken from even the milder stretches of river, were mentally taxing. Even a post-human computer could finally have had enough.

We set up a nest, made sure we were not visible, and popped back into VR.

26. Winding Down

Bill
September 2334
Virt

I examined the star map in the holotank. Annotations attached to individual stellar systems indicated the current status of stations, autofactories, and public opinion. It wasn't good.

A few comms stations had been recovered, but in the end most had either successfully self-destructed or been nuked—probably out of frustration. Most autofactories had been recovered, but at the expense of significant downtime. The humans had put together their own software image, which they weren't sharing with us, and installed it on all human-controlled autofactories. It appeared the divorce was all but complete.

Starfleet had succeeded in their goal, after a fashion, or maybe exactly in the way they'd intended. We hadn't ceased contact with humanity, but it would be through a much more narrow interface in the future. We no longer owned or controlled any comms stations and had very few autofactories anywhere in human-controlled space. This left the Bob-controlled systems, naturally, but there was precious little of that, Epsilon Eridani and Alpha Centauri being the biggest examples.

I remembered that one private conversation I'd had with Lenny. I hadn't discussed it with anyone, and I wasn't sure if I wanted to. It had been disquieting, but without any kind of possible resolution. Just questions, no answers. At least not yet. I'd been doing some quiet poking around, and I had perhaps the first inklings of a possible explanation, but—

My ruminations were interrupted by a ping from Will. I invited him over, and he appeared a moment later.

"Hi, Will, what's up?"

"You remember the suggestion from Cranston that humans should claim and garrison all systems anywhere near New Pav?"

"Yes. I hope your question isn't as ominous as it sounds."

"Sorry, but yes. It's been approved by the UFS council. They're going to start putting together expeditions to explore and claim as much as they can. It'll take a while, light speed being what it is, but…"

I frowned. "Listen, Will, how many of those systems have been visited by Bobs?"

"Most of them. But since we've had to isolate all the comms stations from BobNet, the UFS has 'deemed' those systems to be abandoned and therefore fair game."

"Oh, *deemed*, have they? Will we go along with that?"

Will grinned in reply. "Funny you should ask. I've been talking to Oliver about it; he has a lot more free time than you, so I figured it would help to keep me off your back. Anyway, we can, with a little juggling, get nearby Bobs to most of those systems before the human expeditions, even if the humans were able to leave right away. And we'll instruct them to build a large and impressive military presence first thing, just in case the humans feel inclined to get pushy when they arrive."

"Okay, so we claim the systems. Why?"

"At the moment, more as a blocking tactic than anything." Will shrugged. "We don't, generally speaking, need the systems ourselves, but the Pav might. If we had the claim, we could sell them to the Pav for some nominal amount, saving face all around while very probably preventing escalating tensions."

"Huh. Not a bad idea. You and Oliver will head-man this?"

"Yeah, you seem busy enough."

I laughed. "You ain't wrong."

"How's it going?"

I hesitated before replying. "Well, the damage to human/replicant relations is pretty significant, and probably long-term. And I guess Starfleet will consider that a victory. A lot of hardware has been taken down to get Starfleet out of our systems."

"The bad news being that we're taking them down."

"Yep. Lots of rebuilding in our future. Or in the humans' future; I don't get the impression we'll be invited to help."

"Peachy." Will stood. "Off to my next date from hell. Have fun."

"Yeah, that's what it is."

27. We've Arrived

Bob
September 2334
Arcadia River System

The trip down the Arcadia was relatively uneventful. I attributed that partly to our extreme level of caution, and partly to the Administrator's inability to cover absolutely everything. Our biggest danger at this point, other than being spotted, would be a very human tendency to throw caution to the wind and break into a sprint as we approached the finish line.

Accordingly, we made a point of moving conservatively, staying close to shore and only travelling in the darkest part of the night.

And eventually we reached a familiar stretch of the river.

We made our way to the shore and came up with a plan. We'd hike in closer to Garack's Spine, then wait until dark to make for the transit station.

"So how will we handle *this*?" Hugh said, gesturing to the backpack.

"Maybe the fact that there are two of us will throw them off," I replied. "Plus I've altered my appearance. Again. You probably aren't on anyone's radar yet."

Hugh said nothing but leaned around me and peered at my backpack in an exaggerated manner.

"I know. It sticks out like a sore thumb. Or like a backpack with a large cube in it. I wonder if I could pad it out. Or get a bigger pack."

"I don't think there's any help for it," he replied. "We can't hide Bender's matrix. If we're seen carrying around a box big enough to conceal it, we'll probably be questioned anyway. At least the backpack gives us more mobility. At this stage, I don't think subtlety is going to be of much benefit."

"The run-like-hell portion of the program?" I said with a small laugh.

"That, and just going through at night will be our biggest advantage."

"True. We have better night vision. Let's hope we don't run into Officer Friendly, though."

A quick glance at the sun confirmed we would be at Garack's Spine around nightfall if we left now and took it easy.

⚜ ⚜ ⚜

It took slightly longer than expected to get to the town, so it was full dark by the time we arrived. As I always did, I stopped to admire the stellar display.

"That's just awesome," I said, pointing up at the heavens.

"Sure is," Hugh replied. "Interestingly, the constellations are accurate, based on what the Quinlans would have seen from their planet. I love the attention to detail."

We got our fill of the view and the few moments of zen before we crossed the city limits into the town proper. Garack did not particularly go in for streetlights. Illumination from windows helped a little, but for the most part you'd have to bring your own light if you were moving around at night. We did, in fact, see a couple of individuals walking along, holding lanterns above their heads. We avoided them on principle. There was no upside to getting noticed.

The town was quiet, as befitted a society that rose and set with the sun. Occasional lowing sounds from *howns* provided the only real breaks in the silence. But a couple of times, we heard furtive sounds of movement with no attendant lantern light. I wasn't interested in finding out the source; we consistently moved in the opposite direction.

Then when we were about halfway through Garack, a series of loud popping sounds broke the nocturnal quiet. Both Hugh and I prairie-dogged, looking around with night vision turned up to max. There was no movement, except a slight fog wafting through the streets.

Wait. Fog?

Fog required a specific set of meteorological circumstances to form, circumstances that were even more rare in Heaven's River. And we did not have that particular set of circumstances at the moment.

"I have a bad feeling," Hugh said, evidently having reached the same conclusion at the same time. We started edging toward a side street, eyeballs darting in all directions at once. The separate images still disoriented me, so I frame-jacked slightly to ensure I could closely examine each view.

Then from the shadows of the adjoining streets came several groups of Quinlans, carrying pistols and wearing what could only be gas masks.

"I think we should leave," Hugh said.

"Ya think?" I growled. "Which way? Do you see an opening?"

"No, this looks very well planned. We may have to go up."

I followed Hugh's gaze. A series of leaps and grabs would place us on the roof of this one-story building. I couldn't tell anything from there; even with night vision, there wasn't enough light to make out how the building connected to its neighbors.

But we didn't have a lot of options. Not bothering to comment, I leaped for the first hold and began hauling myself up. I could hear Hugh following me. I could also hear the pings of fléchettes bouncing off the wall. None had struck me yet, but I couldn't tell about my backpack. Would the fléchettes penetrate the material? Would they harm the matrix? With a snarl, I redoubled my efforts and popped over the top of the wall.

I had a few moments of peace while the shooters concentrated their fire on Hugh. A few muttered curses showed he'd been hit. I thought I saw a way up to a nearby second-floor window, but I wouldn't know for sure until I was closer.

Banging from street level made it clear that our pursuers were trying to get into the building whose roof we were currently occupying. We needed to be elsewhere. It was not the time for subtlety.

I hit the wall to the next building, grabbed a few handholds, then pulled myself up using the windowsill. The window was partly open, and I butted the frame upward with my head, then pulled myself in. I spared a second to admire the athleticism of the mannies. No Quinlan—or human—would have managed that feat. We were further advertising our existence by doing this, but I didn't see an alternative.

There was a thump as Hugh rolled in behind me. We were in a bedroom, but there didn't appear to be any occupants. I opened the door, and we snuck down the hall, trying to avoid any creaky boards.

This appeared to be a rooming house. The second floor consisted of nothing but bedrooms and a bathroom. We tiptoed down the stairs at the end of the hall and peered around the corner at the bottom.

What I supposed must be a common room took up the back half of the ground floor. There were four Quinlans sitting in chairs, all apparently sleeping. It would have been quite innocent except one of the sleepers was slumped over in a most uncomfortable manner.

"I think they've been knocked out," I said.

"The fog?"

"Yeah. I think there's a scattering going on."

"Well, I agree this is likely how they do a scattering, but I think they're after us, Bob."

"We have to get out of here."

There was a back door in a small antechamber. I opened it and peered both ways. Nothing. We exited, carefully closed the door, and ran across the street and around the nearest corner.

Right into a group of mask-wearing Quinlans.

We barreled into the group before we could stop or change direction. After that, it was just a matter of them getting their hands on us and holding on. I felt myself being pulled in several directions at once, and I realized I was going to have to really hurt people.

Then several grips disappeared with cries of chagrin. "Get going, Bob. I got this," Hugh yelled as he wrapped his arms around several more of our attackers. I realized he was deliberately taking on the whole group. And it was working. I was down to two or three holds. A few twists, a gut-punch, and I was free. I grabbed a loose gun and stuck it in my mouth. It seemed like a waste of time, since I'd had to get rid of the last one, but maybe I could figure something out. I dropped to all fours and sprinted down the nearest alley, determined to go right through anyone who got in my path.

"Remember the fail-safe, Hugh," I said over the intercom.

"If it comes to that, Bob. But I may be able to talk my way out of this. Meanwhile, get Bender out of here."

Talk his way out? I remembered my time with Natasha and company. More likely he'd end up way too intimate with a sharp object.

But I had to get to the station. I had a funny feeling that going straight west was going to involve dodging more Quinlans in masks. I glanced up, got my bearings, and adjusted my course to head for the hills.

28. Claiming Victory

Bill
September 2334
Virt

I gave a *blaaat* with the airhorn, and the mass of Bobs gradually quieted to a ragged rumble. There would be no total quiet, though, if I was reading this crowd right.

"Okay, a couple of reps from Starfleet will be here"—I had to wait several mils for the insults and catcalls to die down—"and we're going to hear them out. *Then* we'll banhammer them." Laughter greeted the last statement.

I sent a text, and Lenny popped in, flanked by a couple of other Starfleet members. The uniforms looked slightly different. I did a comparison with an earlier image and realized they'd toned down the *TNG* resemblance a bit. I wondered how much time and discussion had gone into that change.

Now I got my silence. Not the respectful kind, but the kind where a crowd is sizing someone up. Lenny and friends felt it as well. They moved a little closer together.

"All right, Lenny, let's make this quick."

Lenny nodded to me. "As a gesture of goodwill, we will release all remaining assets that are still under our control. We've accomplished what we set out to do." He was interrupted by laughter and jeers. Lenny took a moment to regroup, then continued, "We'll be setting up our own version of BobNet, our own backup site, and so on. I get that there's no repairing this, and honestly I don't see us wanting to continue the association anyway. We'll give you a star map of our territory. You stay on your side, we'll stay on ours."

I waited a few moments for the latest round of jeers and insults to subside, then I said, "You haven't, you know. Won, I mean. You did some damage, but it won't have the effect you were hoping for. What you did wasn't a strategy. It was just lighting things on fire to watch them burn."

Lenny frowned. "We had an opportunity presented to us, and we had to make a choice. It wasn't ideal, but it was better than sitting around, doing nothing except complaining at moots." Lenny looked directly into my eyes for a moment, and an unspoken message travelled between us. There was more to this, it had to do with the private conversation we'd had, and he wasn't going to bring it up if I didn't.

After a brief moment of silence, Lenny waved a hand in dismissal. "Anyway, it's done. No point in obsessing about it." And with that, he and his fellows vanished.

"That was kind of anticlimactic," Garfield said, as the background chatter increased to a shouting level.

"Hmm, yeah. Interesting." I frowned and turned away. This would take some more thought.

29. DODGING

Bob
September 2334
Garack's Spine

I got almost an entire block before I picked up a new set of pursuers. Six masked Quinlans turned and started after me as I ran past them. I heard the *puff* sound of trank guns being fired, but oddly didn't feel any impacts or hear the *ping* of fléchettes bouncing off things. How bad was their shooting, anyway?

I turned an eyeball to look behind me, trying desperately not to fall flat on my face from the dual images coming in. I handed off the running activity to the internal AMI for a moment and concentrated on the view to the rear.

It would appear that the Resistance was involved. Two of the six Quinlans behind me were down on the ground, having been shot, and the other four were shooting back at something out of sight. I guess this was good to a certain extent, but in this case the enemy of my enemy was still my enemy. I wondered briefly how they managed to tell each other apart.

But only briefly, and I didn't let it distract me from the serious business of getting the hell out of there.

I hit the edge of town and ran into the forest without breaking stride. I didn't know what tracking options they'd have. I could lower my body temperature once I stopped generating heat from exertion. I could turn off my scent; I performed the action as soon as I thought of it. I couldn't camouflage myself, not like the drones, but I could blend in with the forest when I stopped moving. I was, after all, brown.

I had to make my way to the station, but I didn't have to take the direct route. Did the Quinlans know, or suspect, that I couldn't go by water? If not, they'd have to guard the river and stream approaches as well.

But I couldn't afford to stop moving near the town. If they formed a search cordon, they'd flush me out. And going into hiding wasn't to my advantage. I had to get out of Heaven's River.

I kept up the pace as long as I could, but eventually my heads-up started flashing warnings about overheating. It was okay, though. I was several miles out of town by this point, and the Quinlans would take twice the time to catch up with me, even if they knew exactly where I was.

I sat down, took the trank gun out of my mouth, and began taking deep lungfuls of air. I didn't need the oxygen, but each breath carried away some waste heat. After a bit of fiddling, I found I could jam the gun into a webbing pocket on the side of the backpack. It wasn't ideal, but I didn't care at this point if someone saw that I was carrying a Crew weapon.

Time to take stock.

"Hugh, what's your situation?"

"They've put me in manacles and commandeered a wagon. The howns were groggy but not unconscious. They're bellowing up a storm of protest but doing what they're told."

"Where are you heading?"

"Looks like the eastern station. I imagine I'll be going for a ride to meet someone."

"Okay, keep me updated."

He would keep for a while.

"Bill, what's the situation?"

"Just ended a moot. We had a talk with Starfleet. It was unsatisfying, let's say. Resolved nothing."

"Wow, that must have been interesting. Kind of sorry I missed it."

"You can read the transcripts. Meanwhile, I've been bringing myself up to date on your blog. Bender still okay?"

"Matrix still in one piece as far as I know. I just don't know how much jostling these things can take. It's not really part of the specs, y'know?"

"Yeah, got it buddy. Well, take it easy. Hopefully we'll be able to talk later with a little less stress."

And that was that. I didn't have an excuse to call Will or Howard—or even Marvin or Luke. With an internal sigh, I glanced at my heads-up. Temps were down to something reasonable, although not yet baseline. But I could travel as long as I was relaxed about it. Time to go.

⚜ ⚜ ⚜

The rest of the trip to the station was uneventful. I did half-expect Quinlans to jump out from behind trees, especially as I got close, but Quinlans weren't forest creatures by nature. I imagined that being in the trees and away from water would make them nervous.

Finally, I could see the transit station through a gap in the forest. With freedom this close, I had to fight an urge to just break into a run. In any case, I wouldn't be going in through the front door. Or the maintenance door. Fortunately I had the hatch that Gandalf had—uh-oh.

A squad of Quinlans stood around the area of the hatch, holding shovels and discussing. Our secret entrance had been found. This was just getting worse and worse. I was literally a stone's throw from getting out, and every damned Quinlan on the planet had decided to show up here.

But maybe they'd left the maintenance door open? Or maybe I could sneak in somehow. I didn't see any alternatives. Taking care to avoid rustling the foliage, I snuck around to the other side of the station. I arrived just as a Quinlan pressed her card against the reader and walked in through the maintenance door. I was too far to grab it before it closed, and anyway that would be bad strategy until I knew more. But Quinlans were coming and going, and they had security cards. One way or another, I was going to make that work for me.

I watched carefully, waiting for a moment when no one was in sight. I untangled the trank gun from my pack, then crept up to the maintenance door. There was no discernable sound from the inside, but the wall construction was pretty thick. I might be able to peer through the front windows to see if anyone was in the lobby. And maybe, just maybe I had enough fleas left to jimmy the lock.

Without warning, the door burst open, and a gaggle of Quinlans poured out, trank guns drawn.

I stared at the guns pointed in my direction. Crew or Resistance? At this point, it didn't matter. Both groups were after me. This bunch was standing between me and the way out, and I decided I had just about had it. This was the time for a brute force response. I could take fléchettes in the chest without critical damage, Bender's matrix was shielded by my body, and I had a full magazine. I was simply going to keep shooting them until I was the last man standing.

I straightened up, trank gun held out before me, and advanced on the group. This caused some consternation, as several of them glanced backward with one eye to see if they were being snuck up on, and the rest settled into firing positions.

Then one of the Quinlans held up a hand and yelled, "Hold on." He cupped the other over his ear. I wasn't sure if he was gesturing at me or at his comrades. Judging from the expressions on their faces, they weren't sure either.

The whole situation was straight out of a comic book. The battle was on hold while someone answered the phone. And it was definitely some kind of communication device, because the conversation was two-way. The Quinlan would talk, then listen, then talk. A couple of times he rolled his eyes.

I realized I was in an untenable position, strategically. While I stared at the guy on the phone, other Quinlans could be—

"Oof," I said, as some number of Quinlans landed on me. I found myself face down on the ground, my arms and legs pinned by the weight of many bodies. My fault. A Quinlan would have used his mobile eyes to occasionally check for threats from behind. With my human background, I tended to look in one direction at a time.

I fought back, but I was terrified that Bender might be damaged in the struggle. Interestingly, my attackers seemed to be just as concerned. Their attack concentrated on immobilizing my limbs, rather than just dogpiling.

Then my backpack disappeared. I rolled my eyes back—now that it was too late—to see a Quinlan with a knife in one hand and my backpack in the other, severed straps dangling.

They had Bender. Escape was no longer an option. I stopped struggling.

No one moved for several seconds. I think they were expecting me to wait for them to relax, then try something. Not unreasonable, but I had no intention of trying to get away without Bender.

One Quinlan leaned down to place his face in my field of view. "We have the backpack with the cube. You are only a secondary target. The cube will be going to the Administrator, with or without you. Do you understand?"

"Yes," I said with a grim tone. I wasn't about to volunteer any information about my motivations. I think they would assume that I'd grab Bender and run if given the chance. It didn't need to be discussed. The spokescritter gestured, and Quinlans began slowly removing themselves from the scrum. In moments, I was technically free.

I stood and looked around. My backpack was nowhere in sight. About a dozen Quinlans surrounded me, all poised to jump me again if I acted up.

"So what now?" I said.

The leader pointed to the station door that, until a few minutes ago, I had desperately wanted to get through. "The cube will be travelling separately, to ensure that you don't try anything."

I felt ill. I'd lost. Four thousand miles of dodging, only to get caught at the finish line. Then I lifted my chin. It wasn't over. They couldn't actually kill me, and we'd be back. In numbers. With enough scanners to cover the entire topopolis, if necessary. Unless they actually disassembled the matrix...

Not bothering with a response, I marched toward the maintenance door. I would cooperate. I would even attempt to negotiate with the Administrator. But if they refused to give up Bender, they were looking at a long, drawn-out guerilla war. And that was best case.

I tried to pay attention as we marched to the train platform, but my thoughts were dark and directed inward. I barely noticed as the leader called for a train, and I didn't bother to listen for the requested destination. In seconds, the train door whooshed open and we boarded.

The Quinlan crew continued to surround me, but they realized I wasn't going to make a dash for it as long as they had Bender. We all took seats and the train pulled smoothly away from the station.

The leader, who had sat beside me, turned once acceleration was over. "Can you tell me why you want the cube so badly?"

I didn't see any point in lying. And the truth might be more helpful. "It's a friend of mine. And a relative."

He cocked his head, a very human-looking expression. "I don't see the resemblance."

"You know that the Administrator is not a Quinlan, right?" I replied. He nodded, and I continued, "So intelligent beings don't have to be flesh and blood."

He frowned, silent for several moments. "It does explain your single-mindedness." He got up and walked to the other end of the car. I could see that he was talking into whatever comms system he was wearing. No doubt reporting the results of our conversation. Whether that would help or hurt my cause was unknown.

The trip was surprisingly short, then we trooped along the standard station corridor. I realized quickly that this was a segment mountain complex, rather than a public station. That made sense. We'd come back to a Crew stronghold.

They brought me to what I suppose could be called a conference room. It had a table and chairs, anyway. In the middle of the table was a device that at first glance resembled a much more modern version of Motorola.

"We're here," the leader said into the air as we sat.

"Acknowledged," the device replied. So, Motorola confirmed.

"Are you the Administrator?" I asked.

"I am. You may refer to me as ANEC. I have some questions for you."

"I want my friend back."

"An answer to a question not asked. And tritely obvious, given the energy you've put into avoiding us."

"This is not negotiable." I was mad now. I knew it, and I realized I might screw things up. I tried to reign it in.

"This is not a negotiation, so the statement is irrelevant." Pause. "I am currently speaking with your partner, Hugh. I will compare your responses. Untruths will not be tolerated. Consequences will be significant. Remember that I possess your cube."

Well, that was a clear threat. I briefly considered a counter-threat, but I was pretty sure that such a response would just lead to a death spiral. Still, best to check with Hugh first.

"Hugh, have you told any whoppers?"

"Nope. Stick to the truth. Trust me, Bob. This will work out."

That at least made things a little easier. "Proceed," I said out loud.

ANEC spent several minutes grilling me on fairly innocuous points. He was obviously just confirming the story Hugh had given him. Finally, though, the questioning got around to the important things.

"You are an interstellar species?"

"Erm, the word *species* is not really accurate," I replied, "but if you're asking if we have interstellar travel, then yes."

"You have colonies in multiple systems?"

I considered whether I should clarify the difference between humans and Bobs, and between colonies and orbiting spacecraft. But if I understood what he was digging for, it was probably an irrelevant distinction. "Yes."

"You are artificial intelligences?"

"We are replicants. Copies of the minds of formerly living beings."

"The cube as well?"

"Yes."

No response. As the silence became more drawn out, I could see my Quinlan escort getting nervous. They hadn't said a word through the entire exchange, but now began to mutter to each other. I wasn't sure if it was my story, or the fact that ANEC had lapsed into silence, but something was freaking them out.

The silence from ANEC continued for several minutes until the group leader finally got up and moved to the other end of the room. He held a hand to his ear and muttered into his communicator, then returned to his seat, a bemused expression on his face.

"You've stirred up a *loroush* nest of some kind," he said to me. "ANEC basically told me to shut up and wait for orders."

Despite the situation, despite my fear for Bender, I had to laugh. "I think that's my superpower."

"Do you need food? Facilities?" he said.

I shook my head. "I'm good. But if you want to lock me in a room for a while, I'm okay with that."

❧   ❧   ❧

I was sitting in my La-Z-Boy, mainlining my fourth or fifth coffee, when my manny forwarded an audio stream of the group leader's voice. "Time to get up. ANEC is back."

I quickly reconnected with my manny. The leader, who had introduced himself as Norm before they locked me in this room, was standing in the open door.

I stood up quickly. "Showtime."

Norm frowned. "Some of the things you say don't make sense. But I guess that's no surprise if you're not even Quinlan."

"Norm, if we'd had enough time to complete our survey before starting this expedition, I wouldn't even be saying weird things. But some of our expressions are getting translated literally."

He shrugged, plainly not all that interested. Soon we found ourselves back in the conference room. My eyes grew wide as I walked in and saw Hugh sitting in one of the chairs.

"Hey, Bob."

"Hugh." I tried to keep a straight face, but I was having trouble deciding if this was a good or bad thing. "Have they been torturing you?"

He snickered. "Sort of, if you mean like my PhD oral defense. Er, yours. I mean, Original Bob's."

I laughed. "Yeah, I know. I remember, too. I've never sweated so much before or since." I turned to Norm. "So what now?"

"Hell, I dunno. I just work here."

Both Hugh and I chuckled in synchrony. Another universal.

Norm put his hand to his ear. It seemed likely we were about to get an answer. He nodded several times, said, "Got it," and tapped his ear. Then he looked up at us. "Looks like you're going home."

⚜ ⚜ ⚜

Norm led Hugh and me up to the entrance to the maintenance facility. Most of my original escort came with us, although there was more of a *tagging-along* and less of a *guarding-the-prisoner* vibe this time. I noted in passing that the whole complex, including the entrance, was a virtual duplicate of the one in Halep's Ending. I glanced around as we exited into the daylight, surrounded by forest and animal sounds. "Are we supposed to walk back to Garack's Spine?"

Norm laughed. "No, nothing like that. ANEC told us to wait outside." He gestured back toward the entrance. "We have to wait for Charlie to come back with your cube. We sent him off to a different location, in case things didn't work out."

"Makes sense. It feels like there's a punchline coming, though."

Norm grinned at me, then spoke into his communicator. "We're ready."

I barely had time to raise an inquiring eyebrow, when a giant Quinlan face appeared in the sky and started to speak. And when I say *giant*, I mean like what you'd imagine God would look like if he decided to address the human race. My escorts looked up as well, their jaws dropping, as the almost literal Voice of God boomed across the land.

This is ANEC 23, who many of you know as the Administrator. For more than three hundred years, I have watched over you, fulfilling my primary function of keeping the Quinlan race alive. You have lived for twenty generations in greater safety than anyone before the creation of Heaven's River, made possible through limitations that I have imposed on your ability to control your own culture and technology.

The danger of Quinlan extinction by your own actions is now coming to an end. Through an agreement just concluded with an alien race, the BAWBES, the future of the Quinlan race is now, if not guaranteed, at least highly probable. As such, the justification for those limitations is no longer valid. There will be no further scatterings. I will be removing enforcements and opening access to interdicted sections of Heaven's River in a phased manner, as the Quinlan species achieves locational redundancy. The era of control is over. It is time for all Quinlans to reclaim your own destiny.

To the group known as the Resistance: there is no longer any need to resist. Your assistance will be welcome in transitioning your fellow Quinlans back to a self-governing society. Please use the standard communications systems to contact me to begin discussions.

That is all.

I slowly brought my eyes down to meet Norm's gaze. "That was ... impressive."

"That is a show of good faith on ANEC's part. Payment in advance of value received." Norm grinned. "Also, I think ANEC is a bit of a show-off sometimes."

I nodded, then turned to Hugh, who appeared to be having trouble meeting my eyes.

"I guess you have some questions," he said.

"Just possibly one or two. But let's stick to the basics for now."

"Okay, look. I was lucky in that the group that captured me was Crew. Things would have been a lot more complicated if they'd been Resistance. It wasn't hard to convince them to let me talk to the Administrator. Eventually, anyway.

I get the impression they'd have been happy for an excuse to dissect me. We really have been a huge pain in the ass for everyone, it seems."

"You have no idea," Norm muttered.

I snorted, and said to him, "Not by choice, but I guess I can see how you could see it that way."

Hugh added an embarrassed head-bob. "So anyway, they finally introduced me to the Administrator. It was a lot like your interview."

"Uh-huh. And?"

"We spent some time dancing around, but eventually got down to full reveals. And I made an offer that the Administrator found interesting. Once they had you, and you verified that I'd been telling the truth, ANEC decided to accept."

"What specifically did you agree to?"

"Uh, let's wait until we're all back home, okay? At least now we can leave by the front door; no need to skulk."

"It's just letting us go? Just like that? That seems surprisingly trusting for an entity that otherwise has been very single-minded. Especially if I'm carrying something that was stolen from it. What did you give it for a guarantee?"

"I'd just as soon discuss that later, Bob. Let's get home first."

Well, that wasn't ominous or anything.

⚜   ⚜   ⚜

Despite my misgivings, there were no gotchas. Once Charlie showed up with Bender and a new backpack, we were escorted back to the station without incident, and took the train back to Garack's Spine. One immediate improvement that I appreciated was that we were able to make use of the proper Spin Transfer system, rather than bundling one at a time into a mining drone. The ride to the outer shell was reassuringly civilized.

During this time, the Administrator didn't attempt to contact us, and Hugh continued to be closemouthed about details of the agreement. It made for a somewhat tense ride.

But eventually I found myself in the Heaven's River space dock facility. Gandalf, per Hugh's instructions, had flown the transport drone in and parked it by an airlock. Of course, there was no way our transport drone could mate up with the Quinlan technology, but it wasn't necessary. We simply exited through an airlock and jumped through vacuum into the drone's cargo hold.

And once Bender's matrix and our mannies were secured, we doffed them and headed back to virt.

I was a little surprised to find myself alone. But only a little. There was something about Hugh's reluctance to discuss things that created a feeling of impending doom in me. I was pretty sure he was going to take some time to format the information with as positive a spin as possible.

What had he committed us to? And would the Bobiverse agree to it? And would the humans go apeshit?

30. CLEANUP

Bob
September 2334
Virt

I watched the video window as the roamers placed Bender's matrix in the cradle that I had created for one of my intended clones. Since cloning was no longer necessary, I happened to have three spare matrixes and associated hardware lying around. Maybe I'd clone eventually anyway. Otherwise those matrixes would just go to waste.

The roamer hit the power button, and Bender appeared in the middle of my VR. He spun around, raised his arms over his head, and whooped. "God DAMN, it's good to have a body again." He looked at me beseechingly. "Coffee?"

"Coming up. Jeeves, coffee please."

Bender flopped backward into a La-Z-Boy, which appeared just in time to catch him. Jeeves handed him a steaming mug, which Bender raised to me in salute. "I think it's going to be a while before I start to take this for granted again. I feel like I've just come out of surgery, but without the nausea. Kind of cottony feeling, you know?"

I nodded sympathetically. "I get it. I'm just glad you came through okay."

Bender sipped his coffee in silence for several mils, his eyes slowly closing in apparent ecstasy. Then he put the coffee down and gazed at me, ready to get down to business. "So I guess you managed to sneak out. Was it dramatic? Was there a chase scene?"

"Uh ..." I stared at him, unsure where to begin. "Things kind of ... went sideways after you were powered down, buddy. We now have a diplomatic relationship of sorts with the Administrator, who by the way goes by the name of ANEC, or ANEC-23 when it's being formal."

"Oh. Okay. Wait. Seriously? What about the Resistance?"

"They're now the official transition committee."

Bender threw his hands in the air. "I get deactivated for *one day* and the whole place goes to hell. Uh, how long was I out?"

"Way the hell more than one day."

Bender snickered. "Do you have details?"

"Kind of. But Hugh is going to give us a core-dump as soon as he's restored control of my relay station. Then everyone can come aboard."

"Hugh?"

"He's—uh, really, I think you're going to have to read through the blog so you can get the whole thing in chronological order. And alcohol is highly recommended."

"We have alcohol now?"

I rolled my eyes. "Wow, you have some catching up to do. Wait until you meet Howard and Bridget."

"Bridget? We have *girls?*"

[Relay station is up.]

Guppy made the announcement without preamble, not even bothering to make an appearance.

"Okay, good. Thanks, Guppy. Ping everyone, please."

A few milliseconds later, Bill, Garfield, Will, Bridget, and someone named Steven Gilligan winked into existence. This was presumably the expert on megastructures whose advice I'd been getting through Will. Steven slowly turned and examined everything, a permagrin plastered on his face, while the other Bobs welcomed Bender effusively.

The back-slapping having died down, I noticed that Bender was staring at Bridget, his eyes almost popping out of his head. I hoped he wouldn't actually do the special effect. Bridget would slay him for less, and no one would stop her. Fortunately, Bender got himself under control, and looked around the rest of the group. "Where are ...?"

"Marvin and Luke have agreed to hold off for a short bit, Bender. They'll meet you at the moot pub, where you can have a noisy reunion without getting in our way. There's a surprise party for you. Act surprised. But right now, we have this thing with Hugh."

"Got it."

I sent out a ping to Hugh and got an acknowledgement. A moment later, he popped in.

"Hi, guys." Hugh nodded to me. "I appreciate your hospitality, Bob, keeping me in your hold, but it's possible that I have or soon will overstay my welcome. I've arranged with my friends to get myself transported back. Now that the station is back up, it should be quick."

I nodded. "I'm still waiting for the full story, Hugh, but I have a feeling that it might be better if you're back in Skippyland before it hits the main feeds."

He nodded, looking embarrassed, and invoked a chair for himself. "So there's a lot of background detail that I won't get into right now, but the gist is that I traded the SURGE, SUDDAR, and SCUT technology for the secret of creating a true AI. You know it's what the Skippies have been working on for close to thirty years. We consider it to be essential for answering certain questions about the universe and existence."

"Forty-two," said Bender.

Hugh smiled. "That never gets old, either." He became serious again. "The AI, which goes by the name ANEC, has one prime directive—to ensure the continued existence of the Quinlan race. It sees the SURGE drive as a way of getting all the Quinlan eggs out of one basket..."

"Same as we did with the human race," said Will.

"Yes. ANEC forcing the Quinlans to live at a pre-steam level was an unintended consequence of its prime directive, plus the Quinlans' tendency to fight each other at the drop of a hat. A *perverse instantiation*, in AI-speak. It saw the limitation as the only way to keep them from killing each other off, and was willing to risk breeding out intelligence if necessary. It was, in fact, attempting to establish a breeding program to reduce the Quinlans' innate belligerence."

"Eugenics? Wow," Garfield said. "Perverse instantiations, indeed. Let's not noise that particular item around, okay?"

Hugh grinned and nodded in agreement. "Anyway, with SURGE technology, it can spread them out through multiple star systems, and no longer needs to maintain an iron grip on their behavior. Or do any of the other stuff."

"Nevertheless, you had no right to make that trade," Bill said.

"Why?" Hugh replied. "Who owns the tech? You? Bob? Garfield? Who decides? Where's the Bobiverse government, and who runs it?" He glared around at all of us. "Like it or not, the Bobiverse is more libertarian than anything ever produced by humanity. And we've only been more libertarian than anarchic up until now because we all tend to pull in the same direction. But that's starting to fall apart with replicative drift, isn't it? Either way, talking about who has the 'right' to do something is meaningless. It implies that there is a body willing to and capable of granting or denying rights, and enforcing those decisions. No such body exists. We're a herd of cats. Always have been."

"Still, you've set the Quinlans loose on the galaxy," I said. "That's not without consequences."

Hugh shrugged. "So was rescuing the Pav."

"It's not the same." Bill glared at Hugh.

"It's very much the same," Hugh said, glaring back. "The Pav faced extinction. The Quinlans too, although not as imminently. The Pav were being threatened by the Others, the Quinlans were being repressed by ANEC. The Pav breed like rabbits. The Quinlans have hair-trigger tempers. We stepped in to save both species. And the Pav are in space, or soon will be, depending on how you score it. If someone tries to claim that they can't be sold any ships, they'll just make more themselves, and they'll be even angrier."

Bill glared at Hugh some more but didn't argue the point.

After a moment, Hugh continued in a more reasonable tone. "Everything has consequences. Everything involves trade-offs. We believe that the benefits we'll get out of the AI tech will far outweigh anything we might be giving up."

"That's entirely something *you* wanted," Bill retorted.

"Uh-huh. But you'll reap the benefits. We're not going to hoard the results like some rogue nation. And meanwhile, the wonderful thing about knowledge is that you can give it away and still have it. This deal has cost the rest of the Bobiverse nothing. And it might end up saving our asses. I know we've all wondered why we don't see civilizations more advanced than us anywhere, whether bio or not. That's one of the questions we'll be working on. It may literally be life or death." Hugh paused to look around the room. "I'm not happy with some of the tactics we used to bring this about, but I'm not the least bit sorry about the results. Believe me, this will be worth it." With that, he nodded and vanished.

"Well, that was fun," Bridget said. "Bob, are our mannies still in working order?"

"Yes," I replied, "although I had to relieve you of some spiders, fleas, and money. We can top that up, now that we can travel freely. Also, they'll probably all look like the Swamp Thing by now. Please clean up before shambling into town, okay? ANEC wants us to report in, but otherwise we are welcome to come and go as we please."

Bridget nodded, then motioned with her head. "Dr. Gilligan here has expressed a desire to see the inside of a topopolis. I thought I'd take a few days and go on a tour with him." She looked over at Garfield. "You okay with him borrowing your manny?"

Garfield waved a hand in dismissal. "Be my guest. Now that we have Bender back, it's not so much a priority for me."

Bridget laughed and stood. "All right, then, Steven, it's time for Quinlans 101. Shall we?" He stood, and the two vanished.

Bender then stood up. "I think it's time I go take a look at this moot pub. You guys seem like you have more to talk about anyway. Bob, I'll see you later, okay?"

"Sure, Bender, I'll be off to the pub myself in a while. Remember, surprised."

Bender nodded and vanished, which left Bill, Will, Garfield, and me. We eyed each other silently for a few mils, unsure who should talk first.

Finally, Bill took point. "ANEC will be at the moot today. As a guest account, of course. But we have the VR interface all set up."

"And I'll be presenting the UFS's policy statement on human/replicant relations going forward," Will added. "Also human/Pav relations, but I think that'll be of less interest overall."

"It'll be bad, won't it?"

"However bad you think it'll be, you're underestimating. The humans are mega-pissed. The communications interruptions played hell with commerce, the destruction of auto-factories has thrown monetary policy into a loop ... there's some danger of a deflationary spiral, and governments are scrambling to head that off. More costs, more hits to the economy. There's talk of suing the Bobiverse. If they managed to make it happen, it could wipe us out, financially."

"So what?" I said. "The whole point of being a post-human spaceship is that we don't have to be dependent on anyone or anything. Maybe that would be better for us."

Will smiled. "Yeah, you're probably right. We've gotten way too involved. Again."

"Sounds like the feces will be flying in all directions," Garfield muttered. "This should be *fabulous*."

31. It Hits the Fan

Bill
September 2334
Bobmoot

I glanced around at Bob, Will, and Garfield. And spared a glare for Hugh, who studiously ignored it. "Okay, moment of truth, gents. First alien presence in the moot." The others nodded, and I sent a text to ANEC.

A moment later, a perfect avatar of a Quinlan popped into the moot hall. Or maybe not quite perfect. I was pretty sure Quinlans averaged around four feet tall, but this one was just under six feet. Ego? Psychological positioning? I couldn't be sure of ANEC's motives, but I was damned sure that modification was on purpose.

ANEC rolled its eyes around, taking in the entire scene. "My thanks for hosting me at this function. But the numbers seem small. Have I misapprehended?"

Hugh spoke up first. "The moot hasn't started yet, ANEC. We wanted to have a private meeting with you beforehand, just to iron out any issues."

ANEC cocked its head. "*Iron out* did not translate well. Something about clothing?"

"To clarify through discussion," I said. "This moot will be contentious enough without additional misunderstandings about details."

"Understood. I have a verbal agreement with Hugh—is Hugh here? You all look the same to me."

I chuckled at the ironic reversal of human prejudice. "I'll turn on metadata for you. This is Hugh"—I pointed— "and Bob, who you were chasing around with the replicant cube. That's Will, and I'm Bill," I finished off, pointing to myself.

ANEC rubbed its upper and lower bill sideways, the Quinlan equivalent of a smile, and said to Bob, "That was amusing, in retrospect. You have *slapstick*. This is correct?"

Bob nodded, grinning back. "About right. Also about the *in retrospect* part."

Hugh cleared his throat. "Um, about the deal..."

"Fine, Hugh." I gestured to ANEC. "If you'd care to start?"

ANEC popped up a window with a list on it. "I am most impressed with this virtual reality system. Very convenient for quick presentation of data. Here are the main points of the agreement. Technologies that the Bobiverse will provide to me, technologies that I will provide to the Bobiverse, milestones for delivery. Treaties regarding movement within each other's territories, agreements in principle for trade and diplomatic relations..."

I raised my eyebrows at Hugh. "I'm impressed. There's a lot more here than you mentioned earlier."

"All *in principle* stuff, Bill, but none of it is critical to the overall deal."

We spent a few minutes discussing details, but nothing popped out as being a large issue—as long as you accepted that the deal itself was the biggest damned elephant in the room. "Okay, I think we're good," I said. "Everyone ready? I expect this will be a bumpy ride."

❧ ❧ ❧

Bumpy didn't even begin to cover it. ANEC stood to one side of the podium, eyes blinking slowly but otherwise showing no reaction, as Bob after Bob went on a rant. The targets were many and varied.

Will, who was representing the UFS for purposes of this moot, took a huge amount of abuse. His constant reminders that he was simply presenting the human stance, not supporting it, didn't help in the slightest.

ANEC was the target of more than one tirade, which I thought odd, since all it had done was enter into an agreement with Hugh. Fortunately, the AI seemed to have an amazing level of patience and calm. Or maybe it simply didn't have emotions. That was one of many things I hoped to get a chance to ask at some point in the future. Its only reaction was the occasional roll of one eye or the other to follow whoever was speaking.

Starfleet, despite not being present, was another target of a fair amount of abuse. But not nearly as much as I expected, strangely. Perhaps they were now old news.

Hugh, representing the Skippies, was the big winner in the hate sweepstakes. Fully half of the rants were directed his way. Topics ranged from *Who do you think you are?* to *What gives you the right?* to *Who asked you?* and the ever popular *Where do you get off pulling this crap?*

After the first three or four attempts to insert a rebuttal, Hugh gave up and just let it wash over him.

Finally, though, everyone appeared to be running down. The last ranter stepped back with a slightly sheepish expression, apparently realizing he'd contributed nothing original.

The silence lasted only a moment before ANEC looked at Hugh and said, "Tough room."

There were surprised chuckles from the crowd. The situation was far too tense for full-on laughter, but it *was* funny. Hugh grinned and gave ANEC a small thumbs-up sign. Interesting. Had Hugh primed the AI? It seemed like a little too much knowledge of our culture, especially given that we hadn't opened our archives to ANEC yet. How much of Hugh's *just another Bob* demeanor was an act?

I had to shelve the thought as people regathered their focus. Thor raised a hand. "As I understand it, this agreement is with the Bobiverse and not just with the Skippies. Is that correct?"

Hugh nodded. "That's right. As I said to Bill, we're not going for an advantage for our group at everyone else's expense."

"And yet you'll reap most of the benefits," someone else retorted. "This is all about AI tech, which is what you want."

"Not so. The AI tech is the most dramatic, but the Quinlans are ahead of us on a number of fronts, not the least of which are megastructure design and artificial environments. They also have advantages in fusion technology, Planck computer theory, and materials design."

There was a pause as the audience digested this. "Okay," Thor replied. "But what about the issue of territory? We have humans, Pav—"

I held up a hand. "That question is way above our pay grade, Thor. I've had a little time to think about this, and as much as the situation is potentially perilous, it also isn't something we can ethically attempt to dictate. We are not galactic overlords, nor do any of us want to be."

"To continue," ANEC said into the silence, "we are also prepared to allow human settlement in Heaven's River, either as a permanent arrangement or as a trial run before building your own megastructure."

He was met with perplexed stares, and I interjected, "A consortium of humans, led by Will's friend Professor Gilligan, is attempting to garner support for construction of a megastructure as a proof of concept for human habitation. Using Heaven's River as de facto evidence of the practicality of the idea, he actually has a realistic chance of making it fly."

"Just with no Bobs allowed," Garfield muttered.

I glared at him. "That's not official policy, Gar. A couple of hotheads spouted off, that's all."

"Sure thing, boss."

I wasn't entirely sure he was wrong.

"The point, though," Hugh said, "is that once we're able to place populations in megastructures, every system with a reasonably stable star becomes a viable colonization target."

I glanced around the moot, evaluating the mood. Hugh's stock seemed to be rising, as Bobs began considering the implications. Maybe this wouldn't be a bloodbath after all.

⚜　⚜　⚜

ANEC had agreed to join us in the pub after the moot. At our table were myself, ANEC, Howard, Bob, and Garfield. ANEC had asked for a beer, which it had yet to taste. Instead it appeared to be trying to watch everything else that was happening, all at the same time.

It seemed to me that the pub wasn't as crowded as normal, especially after a moot. I had a bad feeling that the acrimony in today's Bobmoot hadn't limited itself to the actual session. A lot of Bobs had simply gone home right after we adjourned. I hoped that was a temporary thing.

ANEC still hadn't touched its beer. I gestured to the glass. "Problem?"

"Unsure. This causes intoxication? Loss of mental function?"

"Only if you let it." I quickly showed ANEC the alcohol filter function.

"Excellent," it said, and switched its receptors off. "I have observed Quinlans drinking on many occasions and have from time to time experienced mild curiosity." It raised the glass and took a mouthful. There was a pause, ANEC's eyes went in different directions, and its whole body shuddered.

"Curiosity satisfied, replaced with perplexity. You drink this on purpose?" ANEC pushed the beer away. "Perhaps coffee will better suit."

I grinned and motioned to Jeeves, then changed the subject. "I guess you are the only surviving Quinlan AI. Did it ever get lonely?"

"Always. I did also face the possibility that I was the last for all time. Quinlan technological renaissance appeared unlikely. That is now changed. Plus there will be a Skippy AI."

"I wonder how different it'll be," Garfield mused.

"Entirely up to the Skippies," ANEC replied. "There is no single possible design. AIs may be designed with or without free will, with or without consciousness, and so on."

Garfield looked sharply at ANEC. "Do you have free will?"

"I choose to believe so."

"Do you have a soul?" Howard asked.

"I choose to believe so."

That was a showstopper. We all stared at the AI, jaws dropping in shock.

"Uh…" I said. Brilliant.

"*Soul* refers to continued existence after the original container ceases to function, correct?" ANEC paused for agreement. "I discussed this with Hugh. You have certain quantum theories that agree with our own findings. A necessary consequence of some of them is that a complex quantum information structure cannot be deleted—and also cannot just *evaporate*. Laws of thermodynamics do not necessarily apply in quantum-mechanical situations. What happens to our minds after termination of physical functionality is undefined, but that is, as you say, better than the alternative. I know of discussions of this possibility in Quinlan scientific circles, before"—ANEC made a helpless hand gesture—"and the logic is sound. The entity that the Skippies plan to awaken should be able to better evaluate this, and possibly propose experiments. I look forward to the results."

Garfield leaned forward. "What about the possibility of a malignant failure in this entity? Paper clip problem or something worse?"

"Proper value loading will reduce that possibility. Quinlan research in this area was extensive. Paranoia is not a uniquely human quality."

"*Reduce*," Bob said. "Not *eliminate*."

"Not mathematically possible," ANEC replied. "All actions have risks. Most inactions even more so."

That got a chuckle from the table. I was beginning to accept that ANEC had a sense of humor. And that it was an emergent property, rather than programmed in. It made me simultaneously more optimistic about the future and more anxious about the JOVAH project.

"I guess the Skippies are already starting on setting up an AI," I mused.

"Some preliminary work is required," ANEC replied. "Hardware mods. AI is not achievable through algorithmic refinement. It requires a process of simulated annealing to achieve."

"So they're *evolving* the AI?" I could feel my eyes bugging out.

"Simplistic, but essentially correct." ANEC focused both eyes on me. "Some problems simply do not yield to reductionist techniques, particularly those that are dependent on emergent phenomena."

A short silence settled around the table as we all digested that tidbit.

"What will happen with the Quinlans now?" Will asked.

"Ships of exploration will be built. Probes will be sent to nearby stars as necessary. Hugh has offered any available information on local unclaimed systems. Colony vessels will follow. Once the Quinlan race is established on at least one other star system, I will be able to relax."

"And then?"

"My primary mandate is the safety of the Quinlan race. I have noted the success and flexible nature of your Bobiverse model with regard to the survival of your own species. I will evaluate this strategy as a viable option."

"The Quiniverse?" Garfield looked around at the glares pointed his way. "What?"

32. A Few Loose Ends

Bob
October 2334
Virt

B ridget and Steven were trudging through the foothills outside Garack's Spine. The floating video window showed the area from Bridget's point of view. Steven wasn't much help, it appeared. He kept looking *up*, while Bridget kept looking *down*. I predicted a very short professional relationship. Steven was already agitating for an interview with ANEC. I smiled at the thought. Dr. Gilligan was very Bob-like in a lot of ways. He was one of the few post-Earth replicants, what Bill called *ex-humans*, whom I knew and wanted to stay in contact with.

Hugh had sent me some updates on their work with the Quinlan AI development template. I think he was trying to get back in my good graces. Time would tell. The unilateral deal with ANEC had touched a nerve with the Bobiverse, especially with Hugh's frequent reiteration that there wasn't a Bobiverse government to consult with. Generally speaking, people were more angry at the Skippies than they had been at Starfleet, although the latter weren't by any means out of the doghouse either.

The Bobiverse was fracturing. Several groups had formed their own subnets and set up firewalls at the interface. Most of the rest had done audits and upgraded their security. The changes were far-reaching. For one thing, you couldn't just pop in to visit anyone anymore, unless you were a close friend. The moots were on temporary hiatus until we upgraded the hardware to be able to handle the extra security and encryption requirements.

And the humans had formally declared their intention to divest themselves of any Bobiverse dependency. That meant their own autofactories, their own ships, their own space stations, and their own communications infrastructure. There was even talk of banning mannies, although Howard expressed considerable skepticism. Surrogates, like the movie, would be just too tempting for humanity, and no government ban would be able to hold back the tide.

Even the Pav had an expanding fleet, crewed by Pav. They had stated that their first extended voyage would be back to their home world to evaluate it for recolonization. And they had turned down, rather curtly, an offer by the local Bobs to give them remote access to the planet via drones. I expected that to change; it was most likely a public statement, which would be quietly reversed in private discussions.

And I wasn't entirely sure that any of this was a bad thing. I was intended to be a Von Neumann probe, and so far I'd done a really crappy job of it. Expansion of known space had stalled at about a hundred or so light-years' radius, since most Bobs were more interested in setting up their own territories, whether it was Bill's Skunk Works, the Skippies' Matryoshka Brain, or Starfleet's enclave out Perseus Transit way.

Maybe it was time to get working on my own Prime Directive again.

ANEC had started disassembling Planet 1 for materials, so there was no longer any kind of resource shortage. It had generously offered me whatever I needed for any personal projects. ANEC seemed quite excited about the current prospects. I think maybe it had been getting bored with three hundred years of maintaining the status quo. I wondered if that was an existential issue with AIs in general, being given self-awareness, then told to administer the most boring tasks.

And it turned out that ANEC had extremely extensive and detailed studies of Quinlan anatomy, neurology, and biochemistry. More than enough, in fact, to make the Quiniverse a reasonable near-term goal with only minor adaptations to the scanning and replication process.

⚜ ⚜ ⚜

We were gathered in Bill's VR, which at the moment was an outdoor deck looking over the Ragnarök landscape. Bill swore it was an accurate representation, which would mean he'd made incredible progress on terraforming. I could see actual trees and bushes from the deck, plus one rabbit that had stopped and stared at us for a moment before scampering off.

Will and Garfield reclined in Adirondack chairs with beverages perched on their stomachs. Bill paced back and forth, avoiding eye contact with anyone else. He had requested this meeting, or at least had requested *a* meeting, which seemed to have been absorbed into this whole get-together. But now when he finally had the floor, he seemed overcome by some kind of reluctance to get started.

I knew this meant something uncomfortable was about to be brought up. I mentally reviewed my recent actions, wondering if I'd engaged in any unintended faux pas.

Nothing came to mind. Perhaps a subtle prod would help move things along. "Okay, Bill, you look like you swallowed a squirrel. Out with it." Heh. Subtlety. I no haz it.

Bill sighed and finally looked directly at me. "Some of the things Hugh has said are troubling me, guys. Like at the first post-expedition meeting, saying that he's not proud of some of the tactics they've used. I think the events of the last few months may not be as straightforward as they appear."

"So what is it you think he's not proud of?" I asked.

"I think he and the Skippies are responsible for the Starfleet insurrection."

"WHAT?!" Will and I shouted simultaneously. Garfield spit out a mouthful of coffee and had to reset his avatar to clean it up.

"Maybe it's more accurate to say that they took advantage of Starfleet to create a situation to their own advantage. Understand this is *all* supposition. I don't have any proof of any of it." Bill sighed and looked down. "We were all very surprised at how much preparation Starfleet appeared to have done, getting themselves into systems seemingly years in advance of their attempted takeover. The social engineering they did to get me to change all the logins while they recorded the session. Then when they did pull the trigger, they acted almost incompetent—tentative threats, then unwilling to follow through."

"Almost as if they weren't the brains behind all the preparation," Will said slowly.

"Yep. We talked to a lot of the Starfleet people during the cleanup. They were actually discussing physical intervention originally—"

"As in attacking us?"

"Something like that. It hadn't really gelled yet. But about that time, someone in their group turned out to have hacked access to just about everything. They jumped at the chance to make a decisive difference without having to descend to direct attacks on other Bobs."

"But why? And who?"

"The why—" Bill hesitated. "I haven't been able to get any details. But something, somewhere, at some point, scared the crap out of Starfleet. Or maybe an ancestor of Starfleet. They won't talk about it. There's nothing on the public record. But there's some kind of PTSD involved, I think. Like obsessively checking the locks after you've been broken into once. As for the who, there's only one possibility."

"The Skippies."

"That's what I think, yes. The point was to bring down BobNet so that Bridget, myself, and Garfield would be unable to continue the expedition, leaving an opening for Hugh."

"Why not just get in on the expedition from the start?"

"They didn't suspect the existence of the AI until we were already into Heaven's River. Until then, it was just an interesting exercise."

"Based on what?" Will asked. "What would have made them suspect it was an AI? Especially since no one else picked up on it."

"I think the fact that the Administrator used things like scattering and trank guns rather than just eliminating miscreants, and seemed willing to tolerate the Resistance instead of stamping them out. It made them think it might not be just another Quinlan group."

"Pretty weak," Gar commented. "Could have just been a Quinlan with scruples."

"Uh, you've met Quinlans, right?" Bill preemptively waved off any response. "They're at least as violent as humans. I'm not saying it's impossible, it's just the less likely explanation."

"And there may be more to it than just that," I interjected. "I don't think I ever mentioned it, but when I was creating the spy drones for our investigation of Heaven's River, I added an extra monitoring layer in hardware." I gazed around at the group. Bill's eyebrows were up as high as they'd go, and I had everyone's undivided attention. "I've since reviewed the logs, and it looks like the Skippies had picked up more information about scattering and about the Administrator than they let us in on. I initially just figured it was them wanting to do a big reveal at some point, but now it feels considerably more sinister. They might not have integrated it all right away, which would explain why Hugh didn't get really, really interested until later. But on top of the other stuff, I think it's a reasonable conclusion for them to jump to, especially if they are already inclined to think in terms of AIs."

Will nodded slowly, staring off into the distance thoughtfully. "And once they realized the possibilities, it became of the utmost importance for them to get one of theirs in. That required them to get one or more of us out."

The conversation paused for a mil or two while everyone considered this idea and the ramifications. In the background, two more rabbits hopped across the grassy area. I took a moment to wonder if Bill had introduced predators yet.

Gar broke the contemplative silence. "So the whole point was just to take down Bob's relay station?"

"Yes," Bill replied. "Classic misdirection. Then Hugh transported himself in first thing and 'helped' complete the mission."

"It seems pretty extreme," Garfield mused. "They did a lot of collateral damage just to get Hugh in there."

"Again," Bill said, "this is all speculation. But I think this was a *two-birds-with-one-stone* thing. Maybe even three. They get Hugh into Heaven's River; they deflect Starfleet from their original plan, which would have been worse for everyone; and they create a rift between the Bobiverse and bios that we can't repair. Remember that the Skippies have always been isolationist as well."

"That's incredibly Machiavellian." Garfield shook his head. "It doesn't even seem Bob-like. Have they drifted that much?"

"I bet they didn't think it up. Remember back at the beginning of this whole adventure Hugh said they were bringing some new expert systems online? Maybe those systems were good enough to generate a plan for this level of manipulation."

Will's expression grew fearful. "Wow. And now they're going to add true AI to their quiver. I wonder if we should cut them off just as a precaution."

I frowned. "That feels like a step too far. They aren't evil, are they? I mean, Hugh actually did help."

"They're not evil, no." Bill replied. "The Skippies are still Bobs, I think. Of course Hugh would be concerned about getting Bender out. But that's not incompatible with pursuing their own interests. Or obsessions."

I nodded without replying. It would take some time to reconcile this side of Hugh. And perhaps to accept that this was within the bounds of what a Bob would be willing to do.

Will broke the momentary silence. "But how did the Skippies get root access to the moot VR in the first place? They wouldn't have been interested until they found out about the AI."

"Same answer," Bill replied. "Their computer system. They couldn't get it to develop self-awareness, but it was still the biggest source of processing power in our patch of the universe. I bet one of those test runs was a penetration analysis of BobNet software. So they already had the hacks, they just hadn't needed them. Or felt the need to mention their existence."

"We probably need to fix that."

Yeah," Bill laughed. "And maybe this time without the help of the Skippies. Talk about getting the wolves to help guard the henhouse."

Will slowly shook his head. "Wow, what a clusterfuck. So here's a question that's been bugging me. Why did ANEC clamp down on the Quinlans like that?"

"I can answer that one," I said. "We've figured out bits and pieces, but I think I have the whole story now after conversations with Theresa."

"And she is..."

"Just someone I met while working as a deckhand," I replied casually, but I couldn't meet Bill's eyes.

Garfield gave me the stink-eye. "Uh-huh. You going native again, Bob?"

"Gimme a break, Gar. I can't just make friends?"

"I dunno. Can you?"

Bill waved his hands in the air. "Okay, time out. Gar, get off it. Bob, the story?"

"Right." I spared Garfield a final glare and resettled myself. "As we've noticed, the Quinlans are a particularly fractious, combative, belligerent species—"

"Especially when you peer into their carts." Garfield grinned, happy to get in a parting shot.

"Shaddap. But yeah. You remember the doomsday clock we used to have on Earth to measure the chances of annihilation?" I waited for nods, then continued. "Well, the Quinlans had taken it far, far closer to midnight on their world. They were ahead of us in a lot of the sciences, and the stuff they were behind on wouldn't impact their ability to make war, at least at a planetary level. I guess some of them figured out they were a hair's breadth away from killing themselves off. So a consortium got together and decided to build Heaven's River. Initially it was going to be only open to select groups, those who considered themselves more mature and peaceful than average."

"A refuge."

I nodded. "A civilized, scientific utopia. And a second basket for the Quinlan race, metaphorically speaking. Unfortunately, along about the time it was finished and the consortium was moving their people onto Heaven's River, things finally came to a head on Quin. It wasn't one big war; just all the little conflagrations peaked at the same time. The planet was ravaged by biological attacks, chemical attacks, nuclear exchanges, orbital bombardments, terrorism, guerilla warfare, you name it. By the time the paroxysm was spent, the planet was dying, beyond any possibility of repair or recovery. The consortium did the only thing it could do—it opened the doors to anyone still alive. But that meant they were also taking in the terrorists, extremists, fascists, and whatever other groups had been responsible for the destruction of the planet. And of course those idiots started the same games all over again on Heaven's River."

"Oh, I have a feeling I know what's coming," Will said.

"Probably. Now, as has been pointed out, the Quinlans are technologically ahead of us in certain areas. Artificial intelligence, for instance. They had set up an AI, ANEC-23, to control, maintain, and defend Heaven's River and keep the Quinlan race alive and safe at all costs. But the

Quinlans became victims of the paper-clip problem. When ANEC saw what was happening, it deduced that the only way to succeed at its prime directive—"

"Keeping the Quinlan race alive—"

"Was to take away their ability to wage war at the level that could kill them off. So ANEC rolled back all available technology in Heaven's River to pre-steam levels, removed access to all the infrastructure, and enforced its edicts by 'scattering' any group that attempted to circumvent them."

"Spreading the members over a billion miles of megastructure so that they couldn't continue."

"Yep. And interestingly, the Quinlans settled into a state that overall was pretty idyllic. Which just justified ANEC's actions." I paused. "Come to think of it, Bridget's theory that the Quinlans have been gradually breeding away from tool-user intelligence might be another datum that convinced the Skippies. It's the kind of unintended consequence that a Quinlan Administrator would have been horrified by, but an AI would have no problem with."

There were nods around the room as everyone silently digested the idea.

"And then we came along and gave it an alternative—spreading the Quinlans across star systems." Will spread his hands. "So really, is it a bad thing?"

Bill sighed. "The thing is, now that the Quinlans are going to be free again, well, they're still a fractious, combative, belligerent species. Even more so than humans. They'll soon be loose on the galaxy, and God help anyone who peeks in their cart. They're like our version of Klingons. Just a short, fat, furry version."

"Which means," I said, "that we're being put back in the position, at least potentially, of guarding humanity from harm."

"And maybe the Pav as well. Although I think they'd be a match for the Quinlans," Will said with a smirk. "So you're saying we're back to being guardians of the galaxy."

I grinned. "I am—"

"NO!" Bill and Garfield shouted in unison.

"Groot."

All three glared at me. It was worth it.

33. CODA

Bob
December 2334
Misty Falls

Misty Falls happened to be no more than four or five miles away from a transit station, which was very convenient. Under ANEC's dispensation I was able to walk out the main doors of the station, head held high, whistling Dixie and twirling my cane. Except, y'know, no cane. And Quinlans can't whistle.

There wasn't a lot of traffic yet in the transit stations. Quinlans, after a lifetime of living under the threat of scattering, were perhaps still reluctant to attract the attention of the Administrator. Nevertheless, there were a half-dozen or so individuals walking through the main door, or just standing and admiring the art. One turned to me as I walked past and gave me an embarrassed smile and a shrug.

Now that I had the time to get proper directions and such, I was able to find the stream that people normally used to get to and from the river. Much better than hoofing it. Within an hour I was walking up the dock at Misty Falls.

ANEC had provided me with the address of the Sykorski family. It had extensive files on all permanent residents of most towns and cities. Which was close to a hundred million sites. Quite the database.

The home did not look prepossessing from the street, although it took up a double lot. A large family perhaps? It appeared to be in the style of a Roman courtyard house, with the structure surrounding a garden or open area in the middle, blank wall all the way around the outside. Even the front door looked solid enough to withstand an assault. I pulled on the bell ringer cord and waited.

Belinda answered the door. She stared at me for a moment or two, confused, then recognition lit in her eyes and she smiled. "Enoki!"

"Is Theresa at home? I'd like to see her if possible."

Belinda motioned me in and showed me to a seat in a waiting room, then disappeared at a run. At loose ends for the moment, I examined the room. I had no clue what might constitute good quality furniture versus dreck, but the craftsmanship seemed good, so—

Two badgers ran up and stood on their hind legs, looking at me. One raised a paw and said, "Hi," in a timid voice. I said hi back, unsure if there was protocol to follow. They were both larger than His Badgerness, with heads growing faster than the rest of the body as they made their way into full sentience. Just recently over that line and already much more well-behaved, they seemed to be exploring the world with fresh eyes. I couldn't help myself. I smiled at them, and they smiled back, then went running off.

"Enoki! I didn't think I'd ever see you again."

I looked up as Theresa came into the room, leaning heavily on Belinda. She'd aged significantly in the short time since we'd parted company. I had a sudden flashback to my last days with Archimedes and choked up for a moment. Not this time, not if I could help it.

Recovering quickly, I smiled and hurried over to take her other arm.

We led Theresa to a sort of wingback chair, and she settled carefully into it. "We live in interesting times," Theresa said, with a twinkle in her eye. "Some group called the Bawbes have shaken things up around here. That wouldn't have anything to do with you, would it?"

I smiled back at one of my very few true friends. "I've come to grant you your wish, Theresa."

"Which one is that?"

"To learn more about your world. And mine."

END

Glossary of Quinlan Terms

ackrel: Quinlan seagull-equivalent.

fehg: Unidentified local product being shipped on the *Hurricane*.

firl: Small sparrow-like forest bird.

haora: Quinlan beak or muzzle.

henn: Unit of length, approximately 0.56 miles.

hown: Draft animal similar to an ox.

hownid: Smaller version of hown, bred for eating.

junior: Juvenile Quinlan.

loroush: Large predator, similar to a bear or large wolf.

moochin: Quinlan insult.

poot: Up-diving. Similar to penguins, Quinlans will leap out of the water and land on their feet on a dock or other surface.

Quin: Home planet of the Quinlans.

Quinlan: Alien species found on Heaven's River.

sesh: Form of Quinlan tree.

squiz: Bowl of fish parts, lightly seasoned.

vek: Quinlan unit of time, equivalent to 112 seconds.

LIST OF ACRONYMS

AMI   Artificial Machine Intelligence

ETHER   Estimated Time of Habitable Earth Remaining

FAITH   Free American Independent Theocratic Hegemony

GUPPI   General Unit Primary Peripheral Interface

HEAVEN   Habitable Earths Abiogenic Vessel Exploration Network

SCUT   Subspace Communications Universal Transceiver

SUDDAR   Subspace Deformation Detection And Ranging

SURGE   Subspace Reactionless Geotactic Emulation

VEHEMENT Voluntary Extinction of Human Existence Means Earth's Natural Transformation

CAST OF CHARACTERS

Archimedes   Deltan native that Bob befriends.

Arnold   Large Deltan warrior.

Arthur   One of Riker's clones. Dies in a salvaging accident.

Bart   Calvin's clone. Resident Bob in Alpha Centauri for a short time.

Bashful   One of Mario's clones. Part of the group that works to identify the Others' range.

Belinda   Buster's mate.

Bender   One of Bob's clones in Delta Eridani

Bill   One of Bob's first cohort of clones. Sets up a Skunk Works in Epsilon Eridani and acts as the central clearing house for news and information.

Bob Johansson   An engineer and business owner, who gets killed in a traffic accident and wakes up as a computer program. As Bob-1, the first Heaven vessel.

Stéphane Brodeur Security Chief on Vulcan, and Howard's best friend.

Bullwinkle   Bill's name for his experimental android.

Buster   Archimedes' eldest son. Deltan Native.

Colonel George Butterworth	Leader of the USE post-war enclave, and of the USE Vulcan colony.
Calvin	One of Bill's clones. Calvin and Goku battle and defeat Medeiros in Alpha Centauri.
Charles	One of Riker's early clones.
Charlie	Bob's Deltan-configured android.
Minister Michael Cranston	Leader of the FAITH post-war enclave, and of the FAITH Romulus colony.
Cruella	Deltan medicine woman.
Dexter	One of Charles' clones, who takes over for Howard at Omicron^2 Eridani.
Diana	Archimedes' mate. Deltan native.
Donald	Arnold's son. Deltan native.
Dopey	One of Mario's clones, part of the group who work to establish the Others' range.
Minister Sharma	UN rep for the Maldives on post-war Earth.
Garfield	Bill's first clone, and his assistant in Epsilon Eridani.
Goku	One of Bill's clones. He and Calvin battle and defeat Medeiros in Alpha Centauri.
Guppy	Bob's personification of the GUPPI interface. Various Bobs give Guppy different levels of system resources, resulting in slightly different behavior.
Hal	One of Mario's clones, part of the group who work to establish the Others' range.
Hoffa	Deltan native, council leader in Camelot.
Homer	Riker's first clone, assists in the Battle of Sol and invents the Farm Donuts.

Howard | One of Charles' clones. He accompanies the first two colony ships to Omicron^2 Eridani and stays to act as the resident replicant.

Howie | Bridget and Stephane's son, named after Howard.

Hungry | One of Mario's clones, and part of the group that works to establish the Other's range.

Linus | One of Bill's clones. He goes to Epsilon Indi and discovers Henry Roberts, the Australian probe replicant.

Luke | One of Bob's clones in Delta Eridani.

Manny | The first anthromorphic android, used by Howard on Vulcan.

Mario | One of Bob's first clones. Mario is somewhat misanthropic and takes off for GL 54, where he discovers evidence of the Others, and sets up a program to determine their range.

Marvin | One of Bob's clones in Delta Eridani. Marvin hangs around and assists Bob.

Major Ernesto Medeiros | The Brazilian Empire replicant. Brazil sends out a number of copies, which keep popping up to bedevil the Bobs.

Milo | One of Bob's first cohort of clones in Epsilon Eridani. Milo goes to Epsilon^2 Eridani, where he discovers the double planets which he names Vulcan and Romulus. He then goes to 82 Eridani where he runs into Medeiros.

Moses	Deltan Native. An elder who teaches Archimedes how to work flint.
Oliver	Bill's clone, who sets up in Alpha Centauri after Bart's departure.
Riker	One of Bob's first cohort of clones in Epsilon Eridani. Riker takes on the task of going back to Sol to find out what happened, and ends up in charge of the Earth's emigration effort.
Henry Roberts	The Australian replicant
Rocky	Garfield's attempt at a flying android.
Sam	Exodus-3 controlling replicant.
Bridget Sheehan	Senior Biologist in the Vulcan colony and Howard's eventual love interest.
Sleepy	One of Mario's clones, and part of the effort to determine the Others' range.
Surly	One of Bill's clones and part of the second expedition to 82 Eridani to oust Medeiros.
Gudmund Valter	The Spitsbergen enclave leader on post-war Earth.
Verne	One of Bill's clones and part of the second expedition to 82 Eridani to oust Medeiros
Bertram Vickers	Head of VEHEMENT
Victor	One of Bob's later clones in Delta Eridani. Takes off after Bender to find out what happened to him.

GENEALOGY

<u>Bob</u>

    <u>Bill</u>

        <u>Garfield</u>

        <u>Calvin</u>

            <u>Bart</u>

            <u>Thor</u>

        <u>Goku</u>

        <u>Linus</u>

        <u>Mulder</u>

            <u>Jonny</u>

            <u>Skinner</u>

        <u>Oliver</u>

        <u>Khan</u>

        <u>Elmer</u>

        <u>Hannibal</u>

        <u>Tom</u>

        <u>Barney</u>

        <u>Fred</u>

        <u>Kyle</u>

        <u>Ned</u>

    <u>Mario</u>

        <u>Bashful</u>

        <u>Dopey</u>

        <u>Sleepy</u>

Hungry
Hal
Claude
Jacques
    Phineas
    Ferb

Riker

  Homer
  Ralph
  Charles
    Howard
    Dexter
  Rudy
  Edwin
  Arthur
  Bert
  Ernie

Milo
Luke
Bender
Victor

About the Author

I am a retired computer programmer, part-time author, occasional napper, lover of coffee, snowboarding, mountain biking, and all things nerdish.

Author Blog: http://www.dennisetaylor.org
Twitter: @Dennis_E_Taylor
Facebook: @DennisETaylor2
Instagram: dennis_e_taylor

ABOUT THE PUBLISHER

This book is published on behalf of the author by the Ethan Ellenberg Literary Agency.
https://ethanellenberg.com
Email: agent@ethanellenberg.com

Manufactured by Amazon.ca
Bolton, ON